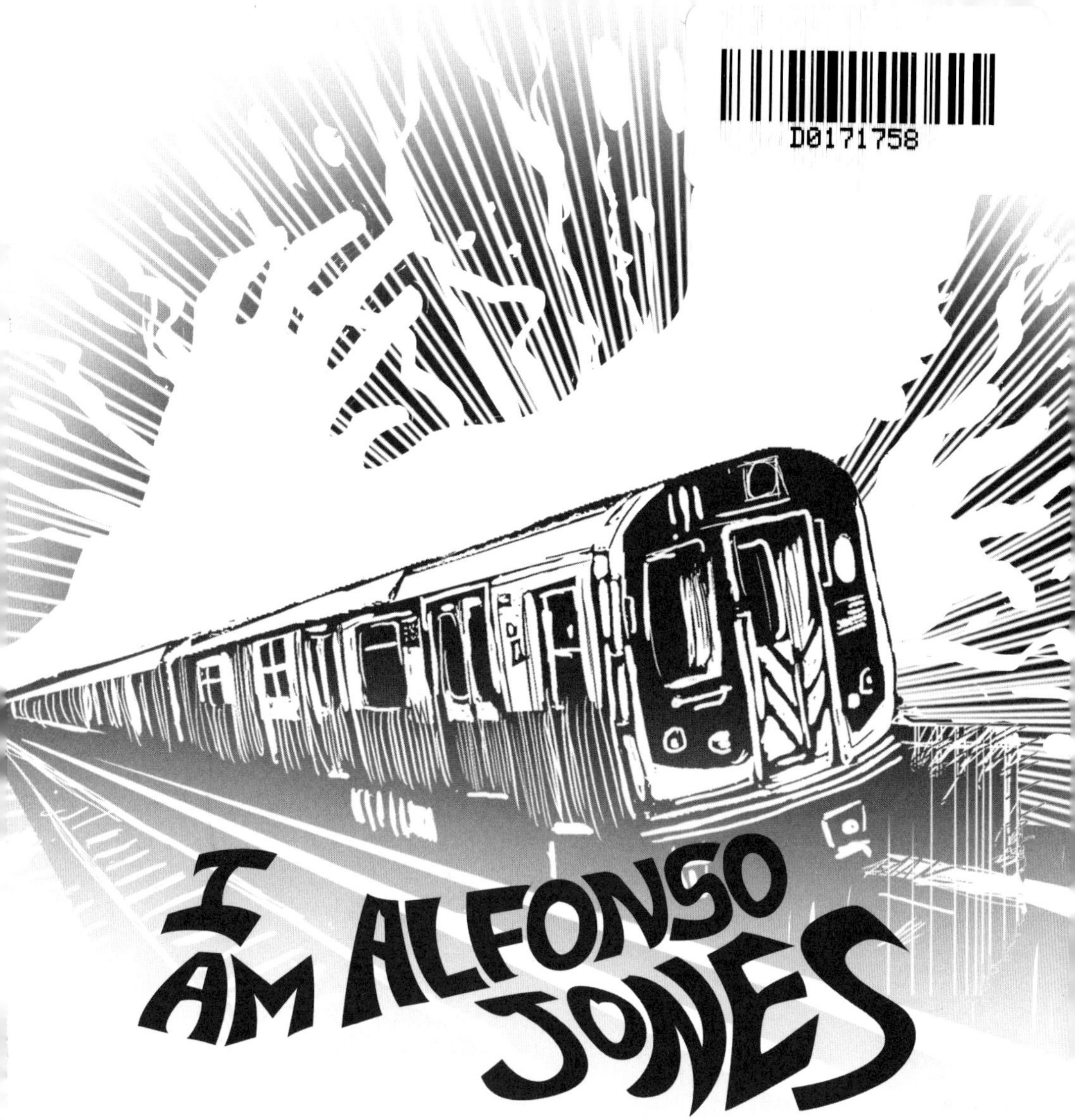

I AM ALFONSO JONES

written by Tony Medina

illustrated by Stacey Robinson and John Jennings

foreword by Bryan Stevenson

Tu Books
An imprint of LEE & LOW BOOKS Inc.
New York

TU BOOKS, an imprint of LEE & LOW BOOKS Inc., 95 Madison Avenue, New York, NY 10016
leeandlow.com

Manufactured in the United States of America by Worzalla Publishing Company, Jan 2018

Book design by Stacey Robinson
Lettering and logo design by Damian Duffy
Additional inking by Anthony Moncada, Arie Monroe, Jeremy Marshall,
Mike Harrington, and Nick Meccia
Book production by The Kids at Our House
The text is set in MeanStreets and SuperStrong
The illustrations are rendered in ink

10 9 8 7 6 5 4 3 2
First Edition

MIX
Paper from responsible sources
FSC® C002589

Library of Congress Cataloging-in-Publication Data
Names: Medina, Tony, author. | Robinson, Stacey, 1972- illustrator. |
Jennings, John, 1970- illustrator.
Title: I am Alfonso Jones / Tony Medina ; [illustrated by Stacey Robinson & John Jennings].
Description: First Edition. | New York : Tu Books, an imprint of Lee & Low Books Inc. [2017] | Summary: The ghost of fifteen-year-old Alfonso Jones travels in a New York subway car full of the living and the dead, watching his family and friends fight for justice after he is killed by an off-duty police officer while buying a suit in a Midtown department store.
Identifiers: LCCN 2017014950 (print) | LCCN 2017047529 (ebook) |
ISBN 9781620145913 (epub) | ISBN 9781620148228 (mobi) |
ISBN 9781620142639 (paperback)
Subjects: LCSH: Graphic novels. | CYAC: Graphic novels. | Police shootings—Fiction. | Death—Fiction. | Ghosts—Fiction. | Justice—Fiction. | Black lives matter movement—Fiction. | African Americans—Fiction. | New York (N.Y.)—Fiction.
Classification: LCC PZ7.7.M446 (ebook) | LCC PZ7.7.M446 Iam 2017 (print) |
DDC 741.5/973—dc23
LC record available at https://lccn.loc.gov/2017014950

Foreword

We provide no guides, manuals, tutorials, courses, or training to help children of color survive the presumption of guilt and dangerousness with which they are born. Black and brown young people bear an unfair burden in America. They are required to understand a history that is not clearly taught in school, develop survival skills that few teachers impart, and navigate unfounded suspicions no one should confront. Many young people of color must find hope even when they are surrounded by tragedy, trauma, and experiences that constantly reinforce the fact that survival will be hard, success even harder.

The narrative of racial difference in the United States has created a smog that pollutes many communities and marginalizes people of color. It began when white settlers came to this continent and killed millions of Native people, forced them off their land, and declared them to be "savages." That same narrative of racial difference sustained two centuries of human enslavement where African people were abducted, kidnapped, beaten, abused, sexually exploited, and denied human dignity. The Thirteenth Amendment prohibited involuntary servitude and forced labor, but said nothing about the ideology of white supremacy and the narrative of racial difference that was slavery's true evil. Slavery didn't end in 1865; it evolved. For another hundred years our nation witnessed racial terror lynchings, widespread mistreatment and economic exploitation of people of color, segregation, Jim Crow laws, bans on interracial romance, and unaddressed racial bigotry. A heroic civil rights struggle helped move things forward, but the narrative of racial difference endured.

Today, we have mass incarceration and a criminal justice system that treats you better if you're rich and guilty than if you're poor and innocent. The Bureau of Justice predicts that one in three black male babies born in this country will spend time in jail or prison; this was not true throughout most of the twentieth century. An epidemic of police violence claims the lives of people of color, who are frequently menaced, targeted, and harassed. In schools, on streets, and frequently in media and popular culture, black children are presumed criminal and must do exceptional things to enjoy the opportunities other people are freely given. We are Alfonso Jones.

There is hope. Black and brown people in the United States have created a remarkable history of survival, achievement, and progress even in the face of extraordinary obstacles. We shall overcome.

It is tragic that we need a book like *I Am Alfonso Jones* today, but we do need it. For many, this is required reading. Like the gifted creators of this amazing book, we need to tell the truth about our history. We need the wisdom of generations before us who have endured the pain of racial inequality. We need the hope of our courageous ancestors to overcome the injustice that defines too many communities.

Hopelessness is the enemy of justice. Silence, fear, and anger are the elements that sustain inequality. *I Am Alfonso Jones* makes an important statement about ending the silence, confronting the fear and anger, and ultimately building a new way forward. This is a powerful story, with a powerful message that we all need to learn: Justice is a constant struggle. Join the struggle.

Bryan Stevenson
Executive Director of the Equal Justice Initiative
Author of *Just Mercy*

Dedicated to the memory of my cousin,
Lorenzo José Tolbert (July 20, 1992–July 20, 2016),
whose twenty-three years on the planet, full of such possibility and promise, were
horrifyingly too brief, and whose untimely passing left unbearable confusion and pain
in its wake, denying the world such beauty, intelligence, and talent.
May your spirit-force soar free!—T.M.

Dedicated to my son Solomon and my daughter Nyla-Simone. I'm honored to be your father
and proud of the people you are becoming.—S.R.

For my nephew Alex, and all the promise and hope that you embody.—J.J.

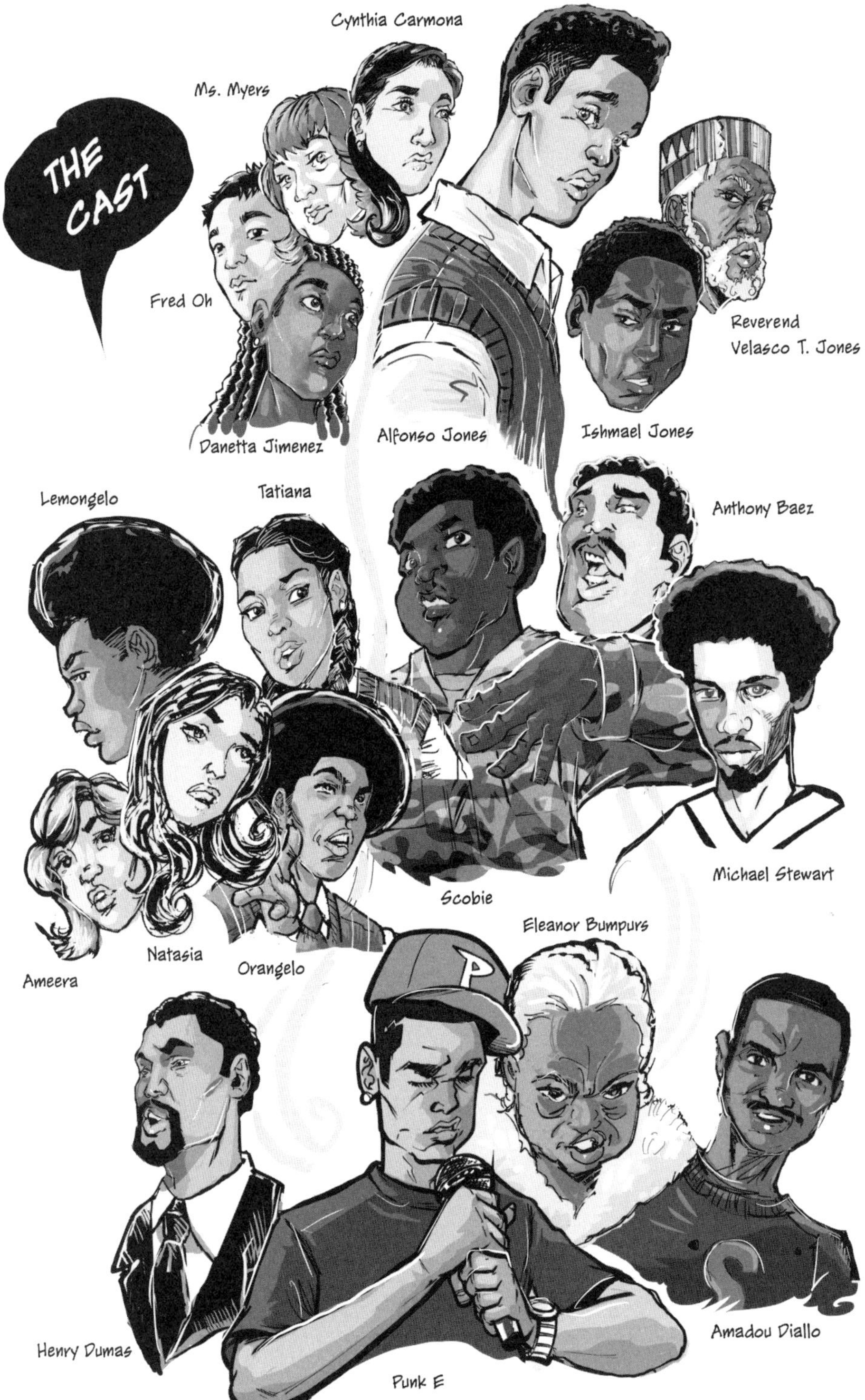
THE CAST
Cynthia Carmona
Ms. Myers
Fred Oh
Reverend
Velasco T. Jones
Danetta Jimenez
Alfonso Jones
Ishmael Jones
Lemongelo
Tatiana
Anthony Baez
Michael Stewart
Scobie
Eleanor Bumpurs
Ameera
Natasia
Orangelo
Henry Dumas
Punk E
Amadou Diallo

For murder, though it have no tongue, will speak.

—Hamlet by William Shakespeare

Chapter One—Prelude to a Diss

Bullet

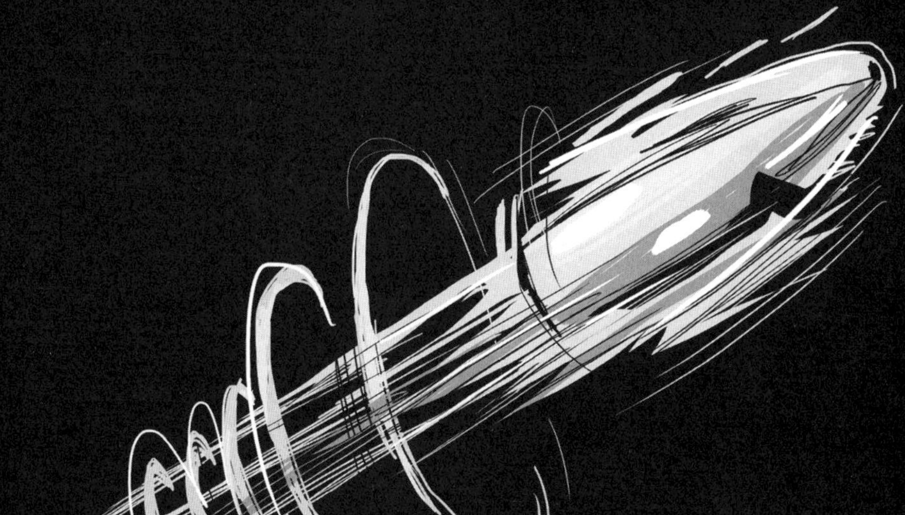

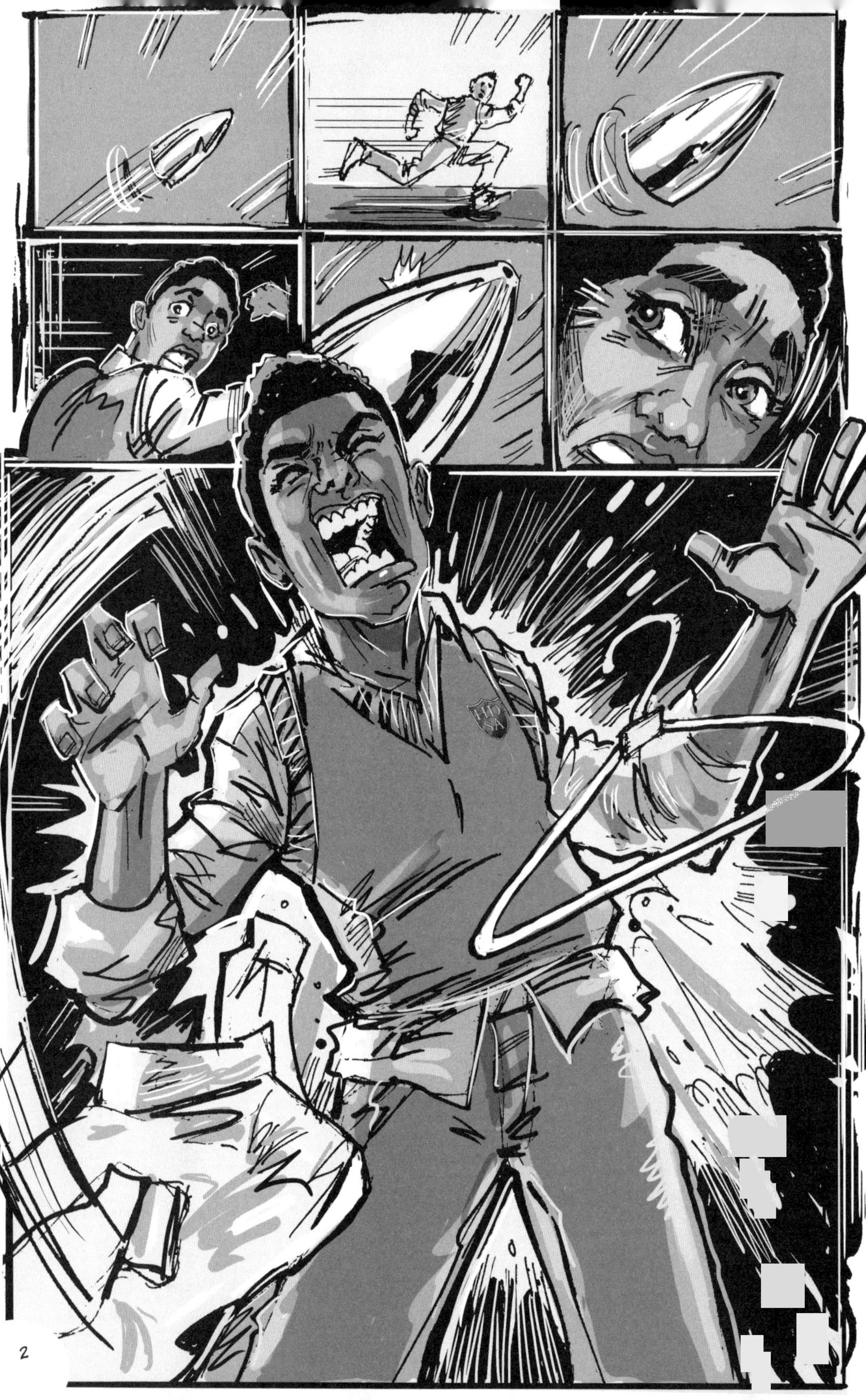
HD SA

Chapter Two
Messenger

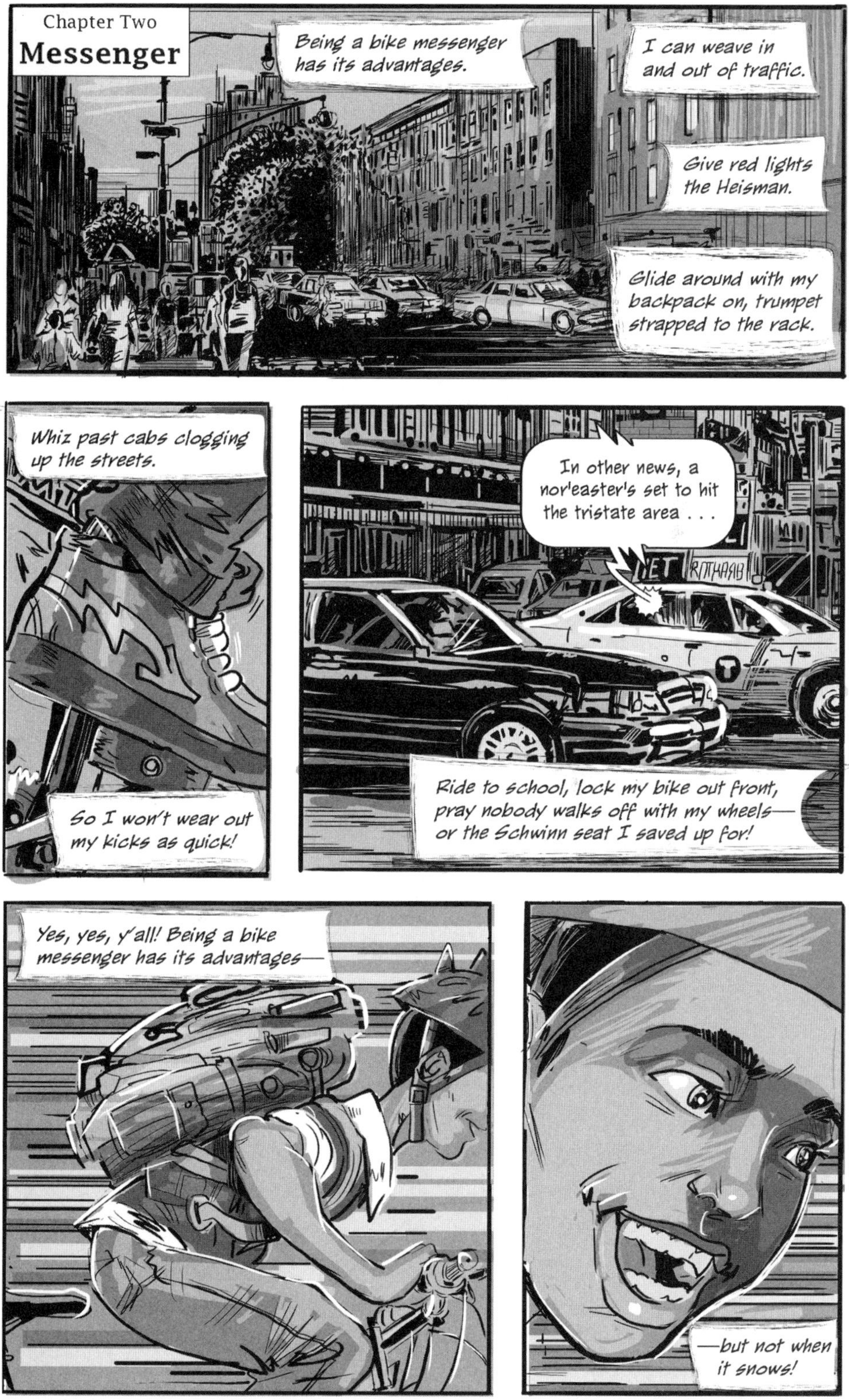
Being a bike messenger has its advantages.
I can weave in and out of traffic.
Give red lights the Heisman.
Glide around with my backpack on, trumpet strapped to the rack.
Whiz past cabs clogging up the streets.
So I won't wear out my kicks as quick!
In other news, a nor'easter's set to hit the tristate area . . .
Ride to school, lock my bike out front, pray nobody walks off with my wheels—or the Schwinn seat I saved up for!
Yes, yes, y'all! Being a bike messenger has its advantages—
—but not when it snows!

Chapter Three

Huffing Through Harlem

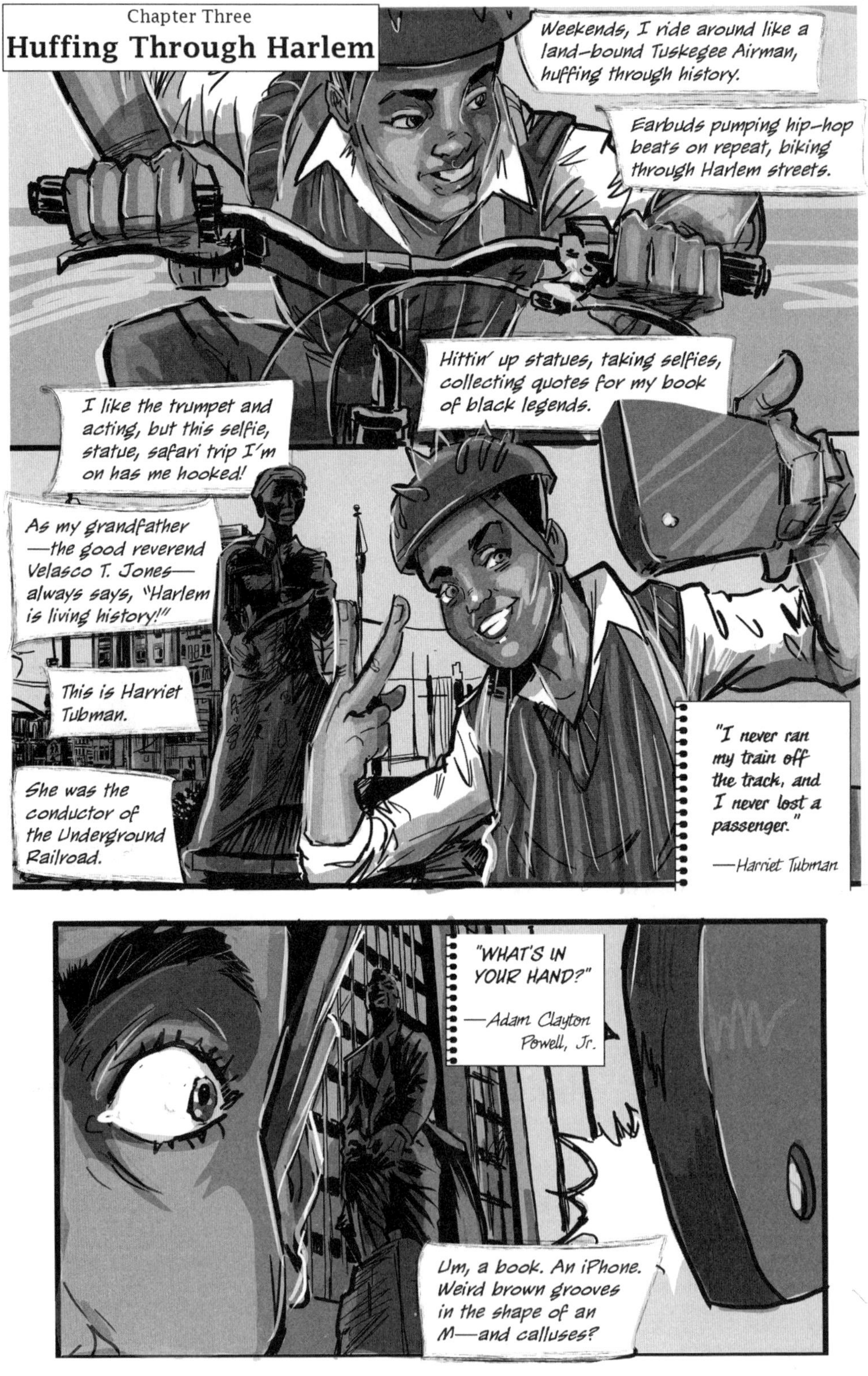

Weekends, I ride around like a land-bound Tuskegee Airman, huffing through history.
Earbuds pumping hip-hop beats on repeat, biking through Harlem streets.
Hittin' up statues, taking selfies, collecting quotes for my book of black legends.
I like the trumpet and acting, but this selfie, statue, safari trip I'm on has me hooked!
As my grandfather—the good reverend Velasco T. Jones—always says, "Harlem is living history!"
This is Harriet Tubman.
She was the conductor of the Underground Railroad.
"I never ran my train off the track, and I never lost a passenger."
—Harriet Tubman
"WHAT'S IN YOUR HAND?"
—Adam Clayton Powell, Jr.
Um, a book. An iPhone. Weird brown grooves in the shape of an M—and calluses?

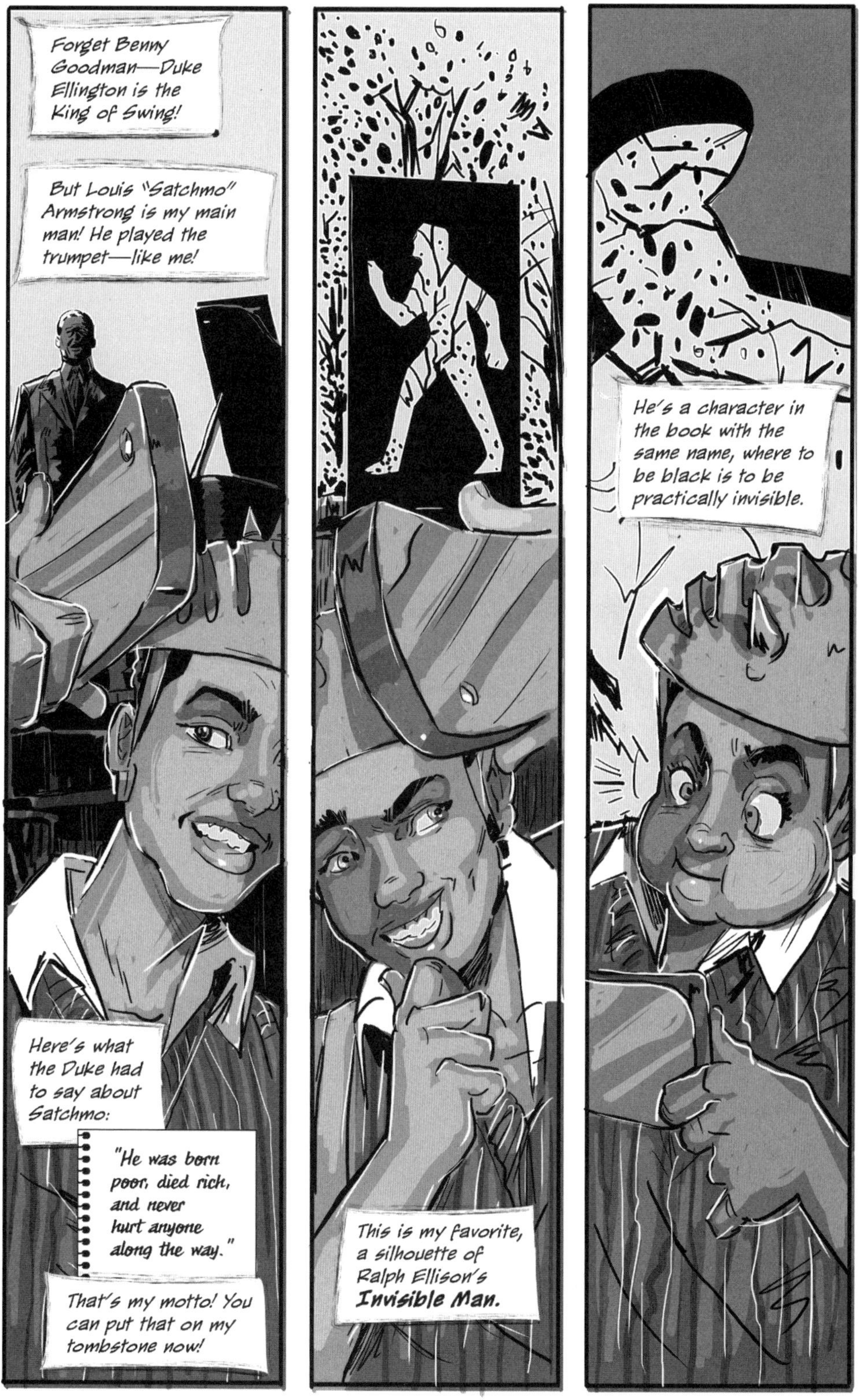

Forget Benny Goodman—Duke Ellington is the King of Swing!
But Louis "Satchmo" Armstrong is my main man! He played the trumpet—like me!
Here's what the Duke had to say about Satchmo:
"He was born poor, died rich, and never hurt anyone along the way."
That's my motto! You can put that on my tombstone now!
This is my favorite, a silhouette of Ralph Ellison's **Invisible Man.**
He's a character in the book with the same name, where to be black is to be practically invisible.

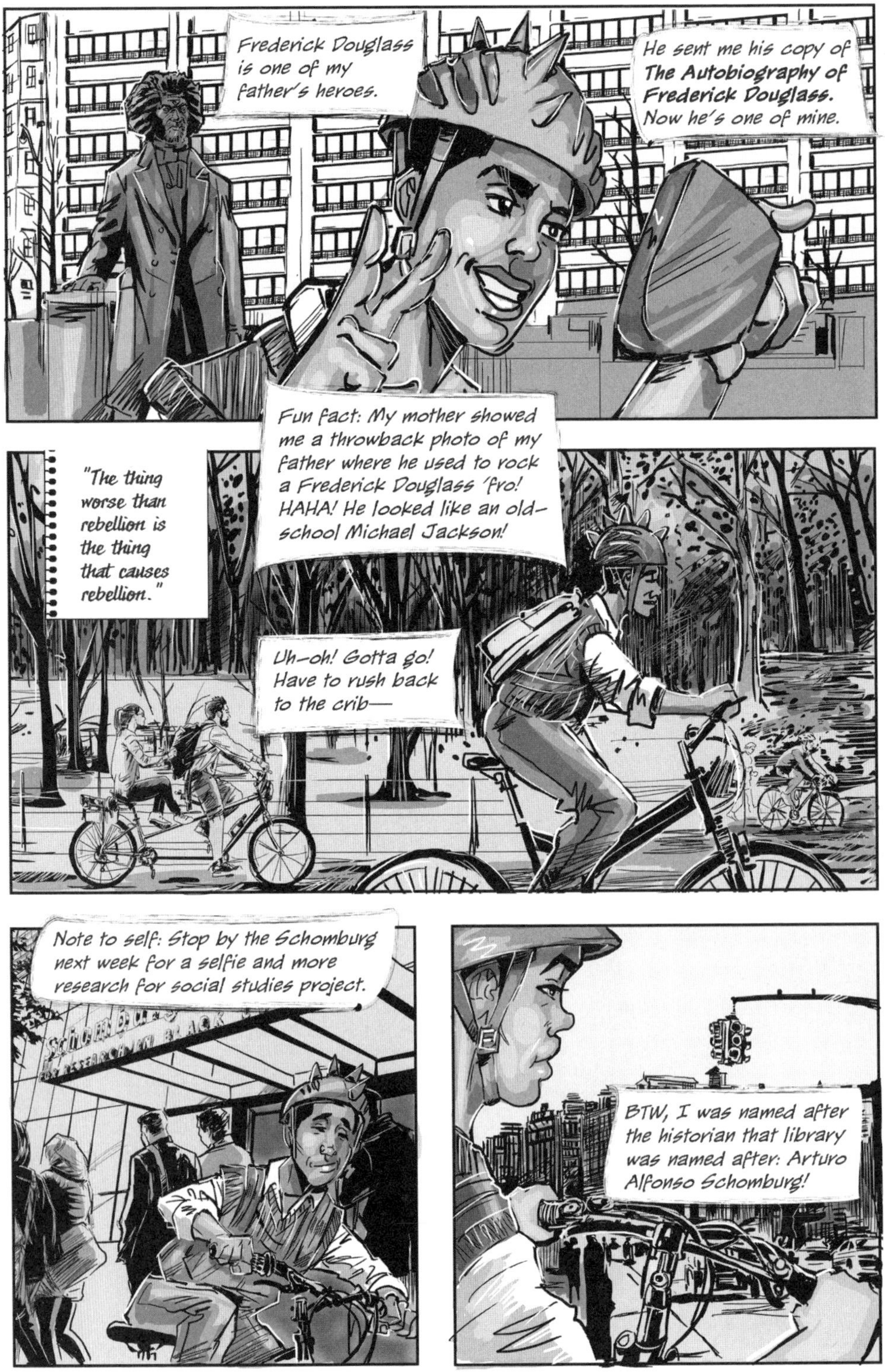
Frederick Douglass is one of my father's heroes.
He sent me his copy of **The Autobiography of Frederick Douglass.** Now he's one of mine.
Fun fact: My mother showed me a throwback photo of my father where he used to rock a Frederick Douglass 'fro! HAHA! He looked like an old-school Michael Jackson!
"The thing worse than rebellion is the thing that causes rebellion."
Uh-oh! Gotta go! Have to rush back to the crib—
Note to self: Stop by the Schomburg next week for a selfie and more research for social studies project.
BTW, I was named after the historian that library was named after: Arturo Alfonso Schomburg!

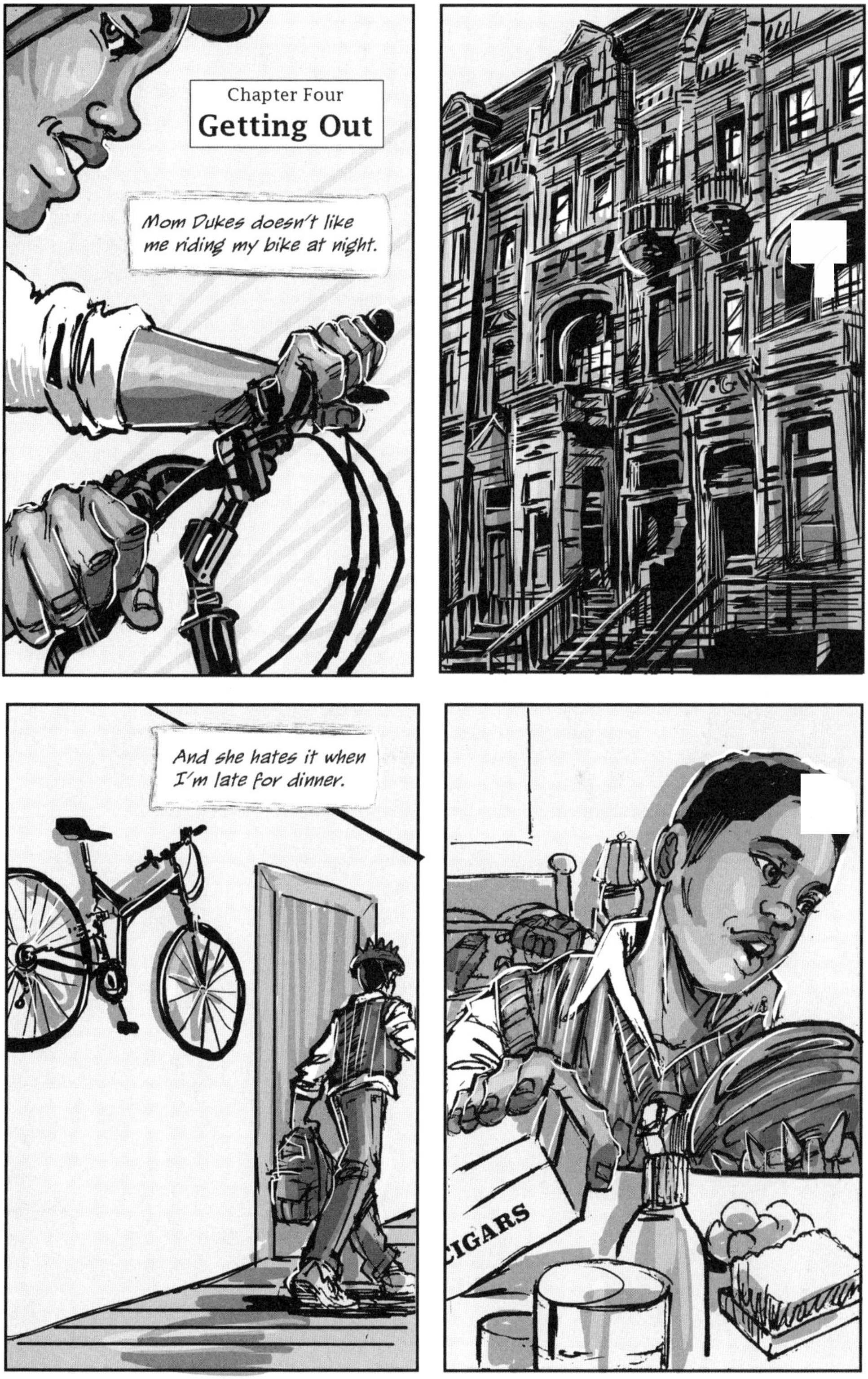
Chapter Four
Getting Out
Mom Dukes doesn't like me riding my bike at night.
And she hates it when I'm late for dinner.
CIGARS

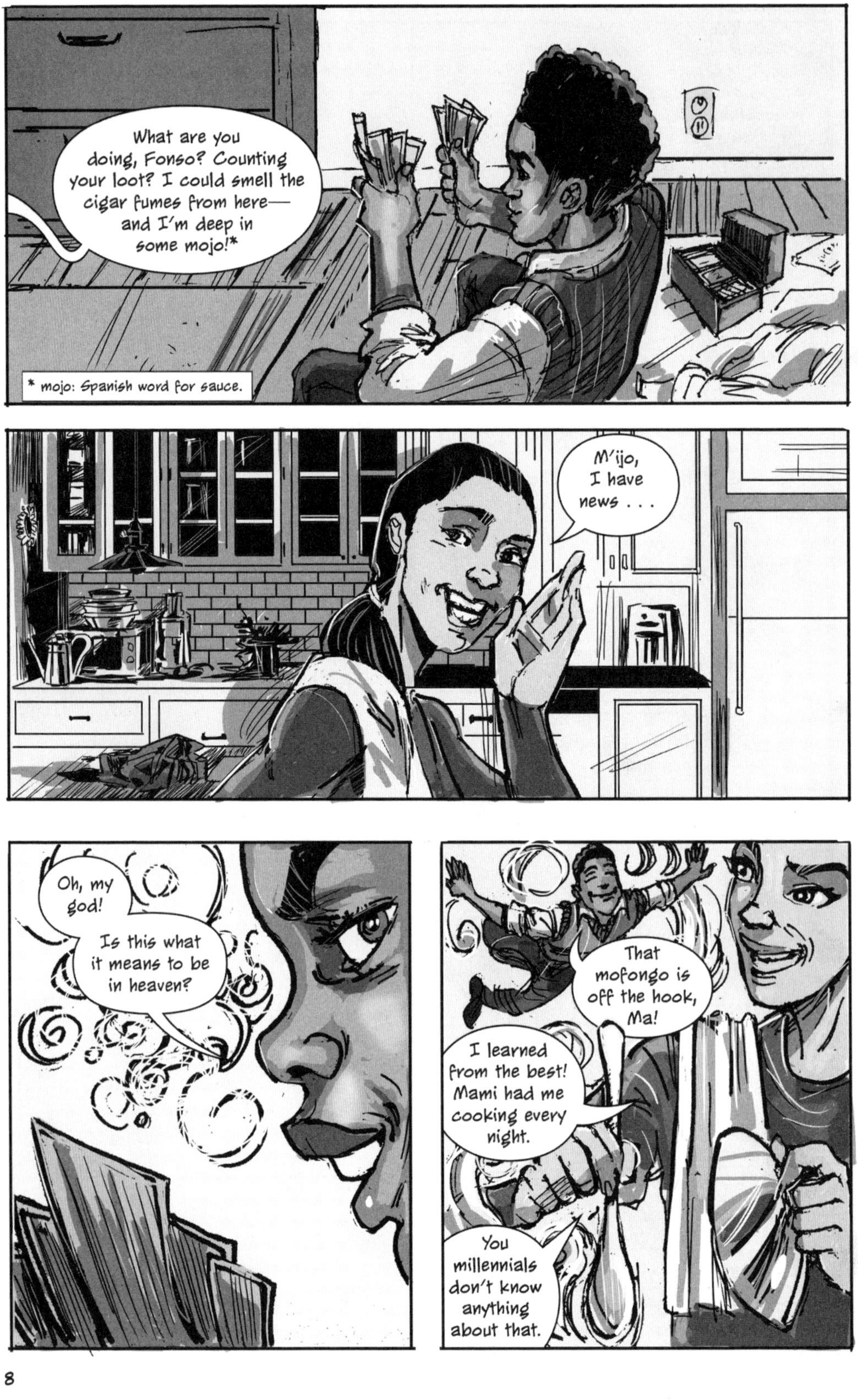
What are you doing, Fonso? Counting your loot? I could smell the cigar fumes from here—and I'm deep in some mojo!*
* mojo: Spanish word for sauce.
M'ijo, I have news . . .
Oh, my god!
Is this what it means to be in heaven?
That mofongo is off the hook, Ma!
I learned from the best! Mami had me cooking every night.
You millennials don't know anything about that.

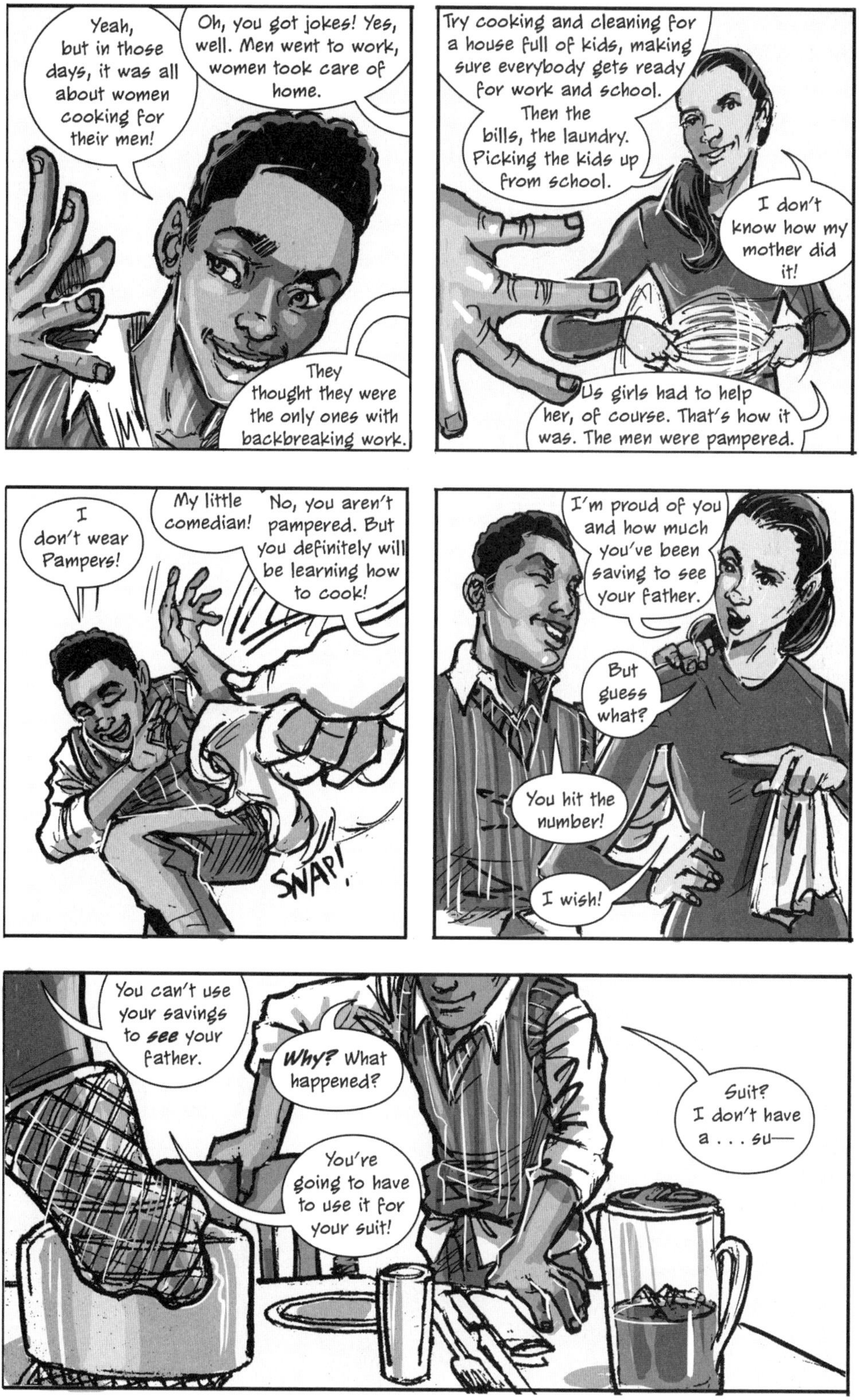
Yeah, but in those days, it was all about women cooking for their men!
Oh, you got jokes! Yes, well. Men went to work, women took care of home.
They thought they were the only ones with backbreaking work.
Try cooking and cleaning for a house full of kids, making sure everybody gets ready for work and school.
Then the bills, the laundry. Picking the kids up from school.
I don't know how my mother did it!
Us girls had to help her, of course. That's how it was. The men were pampered.
I don't wear Pampers!
My little comedian!
No, you aren't pampered. But you definitely will be learning how to cook!
SNAP!
I'm proud of you and how much you've been saving to see your father.
But guess what?
You hit the number!
I wish!
You can't use your savings to see your father.
Why? What happened?
You're going to have to use it for your suit!
Suit? I don't have a . . . su—

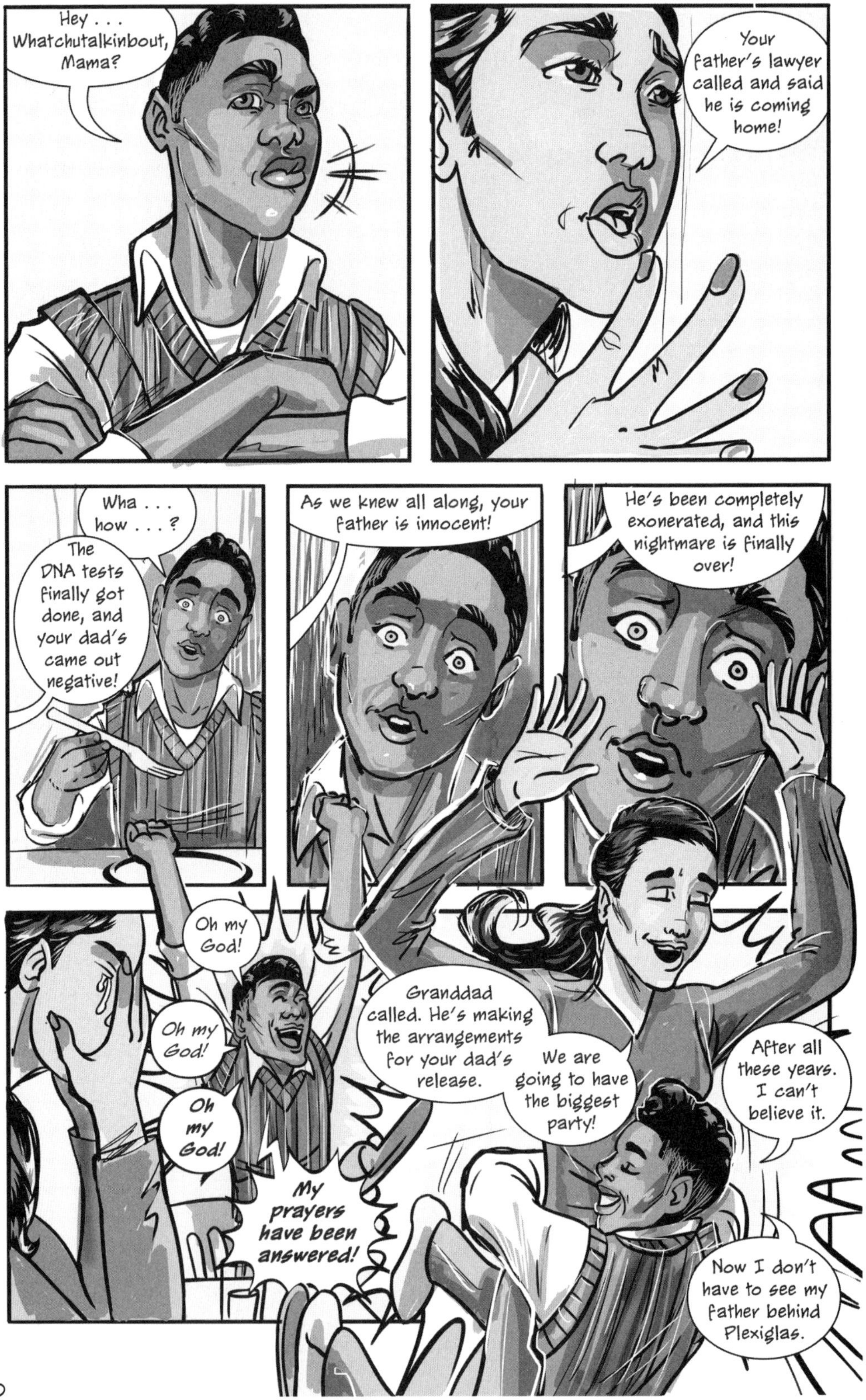
Hey . . . Whatchutalkinbout, Mama?
Your father's lawyer called and said he is coming home!
Wha . . . how . . . ?
The DNA tests finally got done, and your dad's came out negative!
As we knew all along, your father is innocent!
He's been completely exonerated, and this nightmare is finally over!
Oh my God!
Oh my God!
Oh my God!
My prayers have been answered!
Granddad called. He's making the arrangements for your dad's release.
We are going to have the biggest party!
After all these years. I can't believe it.
Now I don't have to see my father behind Plexiglas.

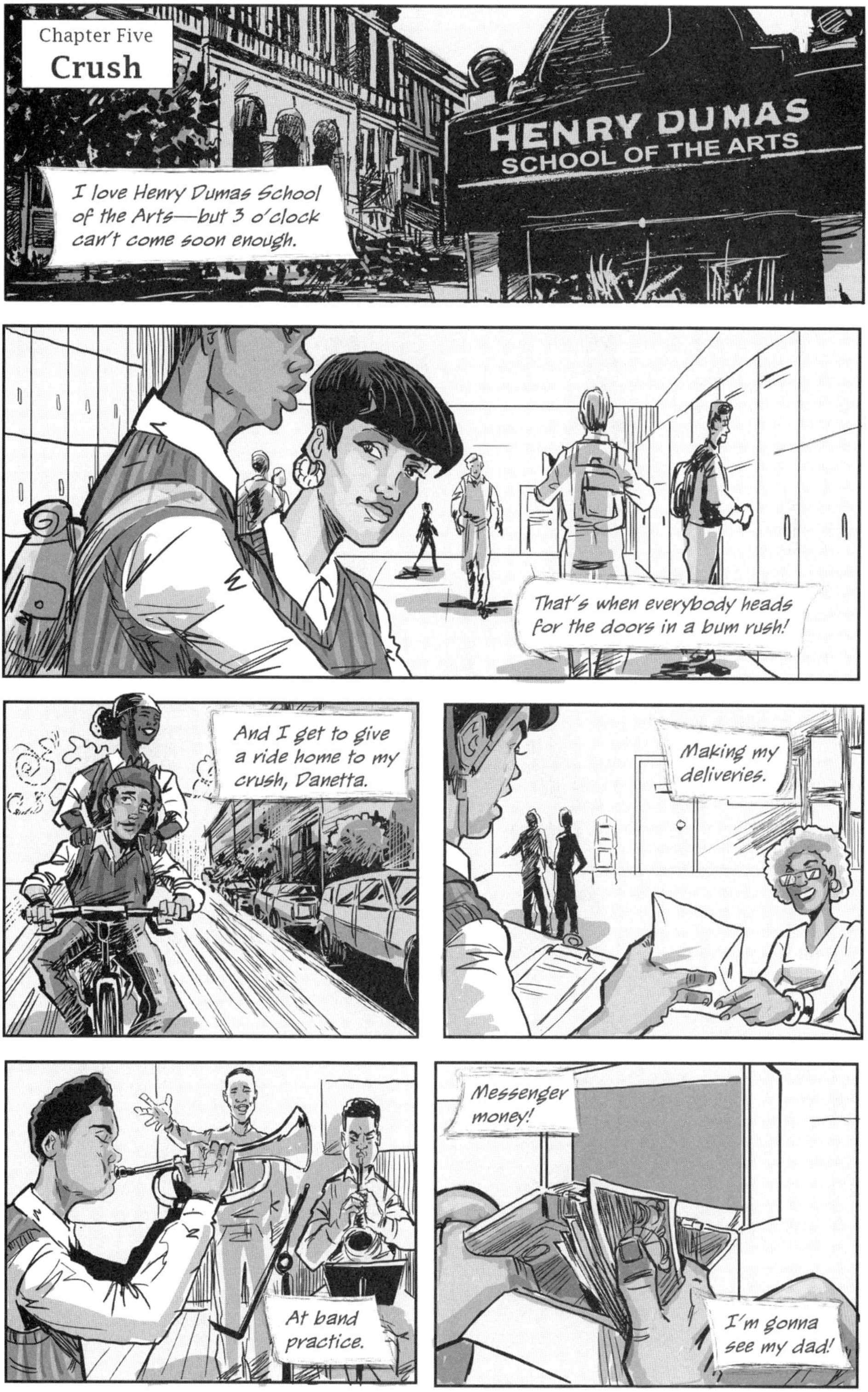
Chapter Five
Crush
HENRY DUMAS
SCHOOL OF THE ARTS
I love Henry Dumas School of the Arts—but 3 o'clock can't come soon enough.
That's when everybody heads for the doors in a bum rush!
And I get to give a ride home to my crush, Danetta.
Making my deliveries.
At band practice.
Messenger money!
I'm gonna see my dad!

Chapter Six
Ghost

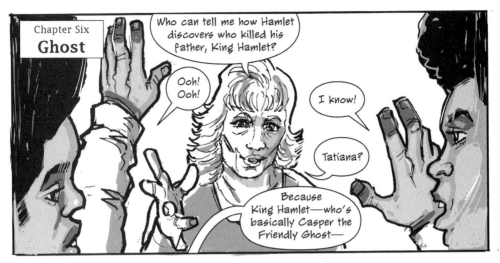

Who can tell me how Hamlet discovers who killed his father, King Hamlet?

Ooh! Ooh!

I know!

Tatiana?

Because King Hamlet—who's basically Casper the Friendly Ghost—

—pops up and tells him!

Shoot! I would've crapped my pants and ran out of there like the Road Runner.

You would've been ghost!

Ha! Cor—ny!

Eww! Gross!

If you would've crapped your pants—I would've been ghost!

White people are *cray*. You wouldn't find me sticking around talking to no ghost.

That's what you know.

My family is all about the spirits.

Yeah, fool. It's part of African culture—talking to spirits and deities and stuff.

You Puerto Rican—not African!

Security!

HA HA HA HA HA HA HA

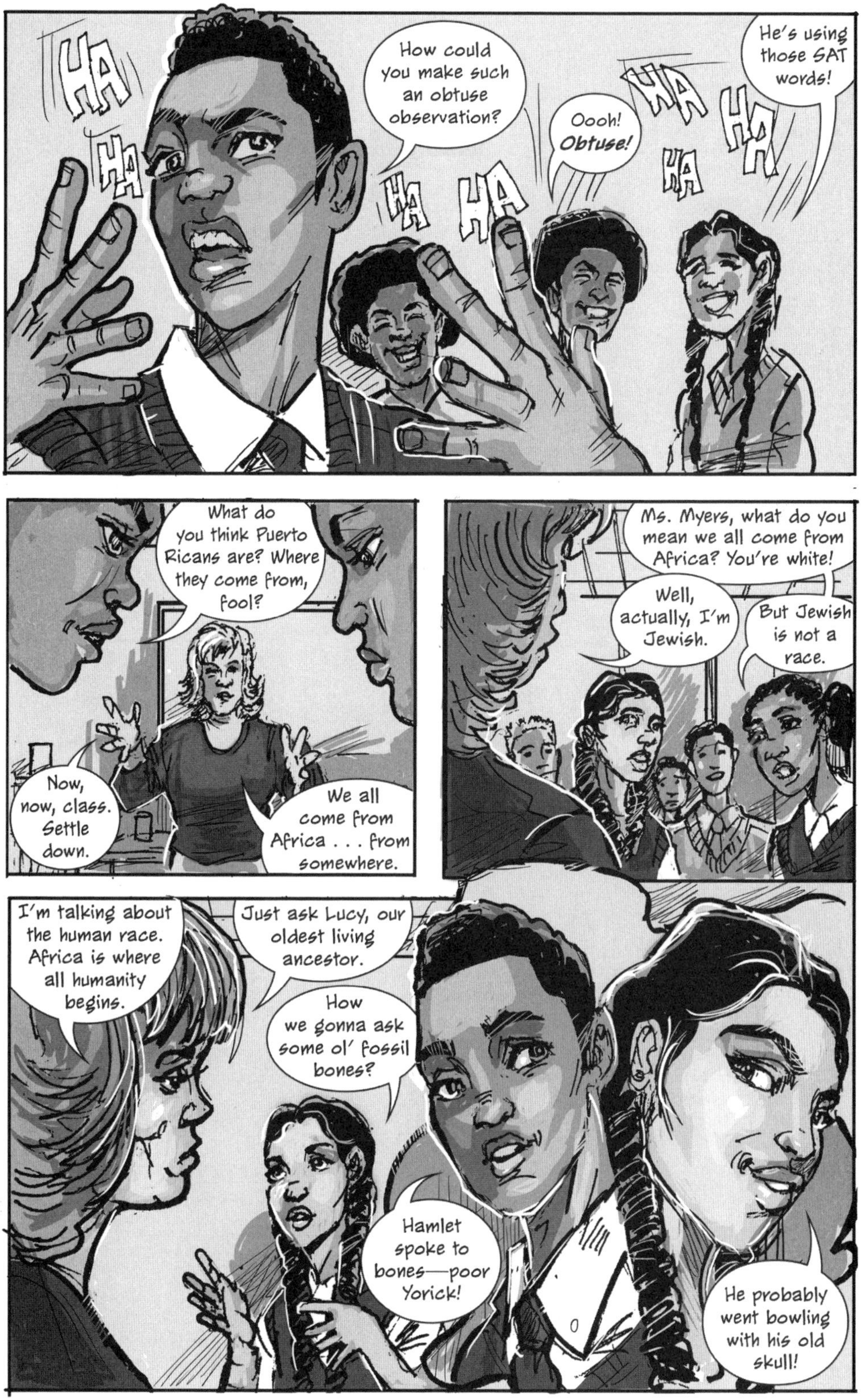
HA
HA
How could you make such an obtuse observation?
HA
HA
Oooh! **Obtuse!**
HA
HA
HA
HA
He's using those SAT words!
What do you think Puerto Ricans are? Where they come from, fool?
Now, now, class. Settle down.
We all come from Africa . . . from somewhere.
Ms. Myers, what do you mean we all come from Africa? You're white!
Well, actually, I'm Jewish.
But Jewish is not a race.
I'm talking about the human race. Africa is where all humanity begins.
Just ask Lucy, our oldest living ancestor.
How we gonna ask some ol' fossil bones?
Hamlet spoke to bones—poor Yorick!
He probably went bowling with his old skull!

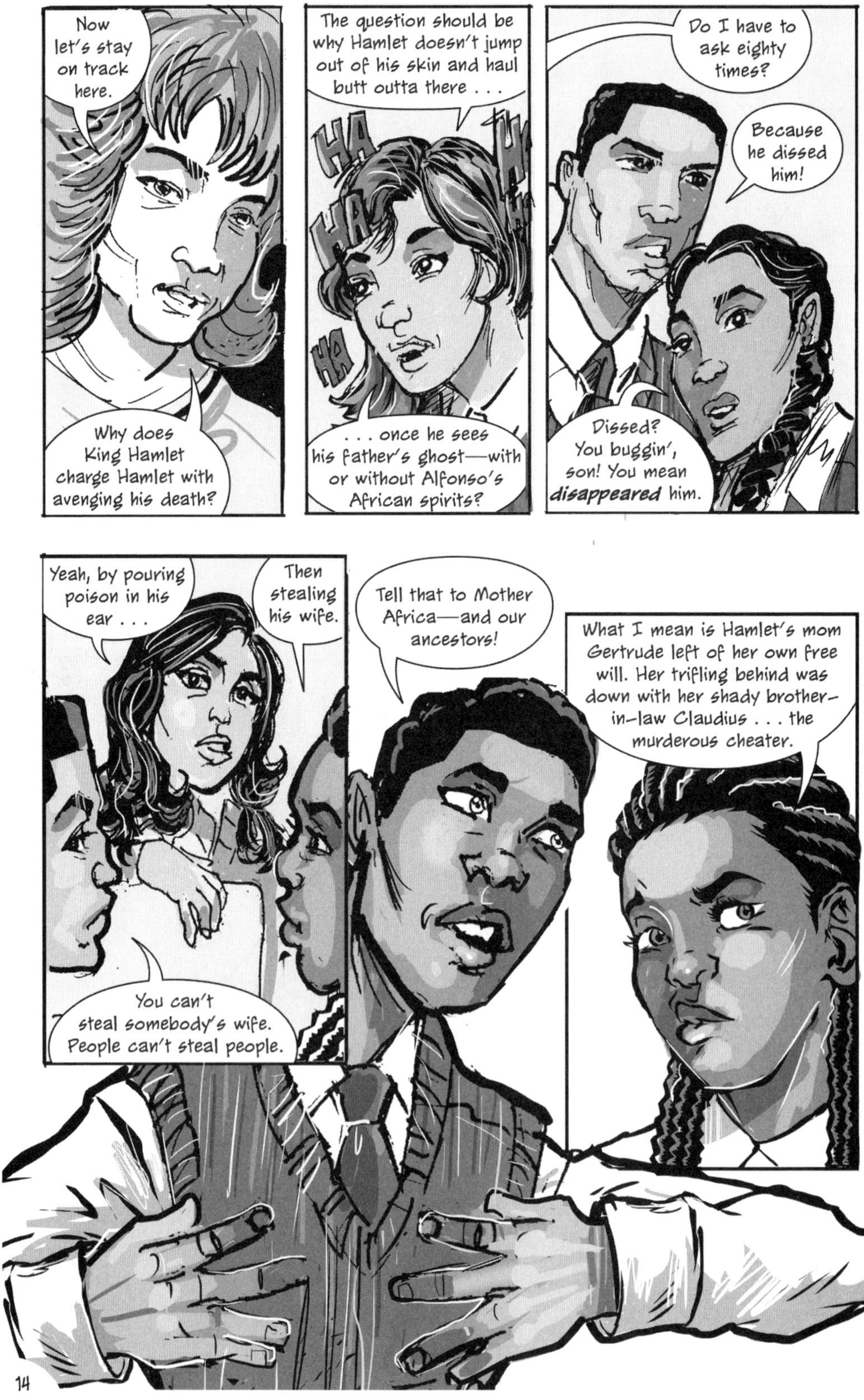
Now let's stay on track here.
Why does King Hamlet charge Hamlet with avenging his death?
The question should be why Hamlet doesn't jump out of his skin and haul butt outta there . . .
HA HA HA HA
. . . once he sees his father's ghost—with or without Alfonso's African spirits?
Do I have to ask eighty times?
Because he dissed him!
Dissed? You buggin', son! You mean ***disappeared*** him.
Yeah, by pouring poison in his ear . . .
Then stealing his wife.
You can't steal somebody's wife. People can't steal people.
Tell that to Mother Africa—and our ancestors!
What I mean is Hamlet's mom Gertrude left of her own free will. Her trifling behind was down with her shady brother-in-law Claudius . . . the murderous cheater.

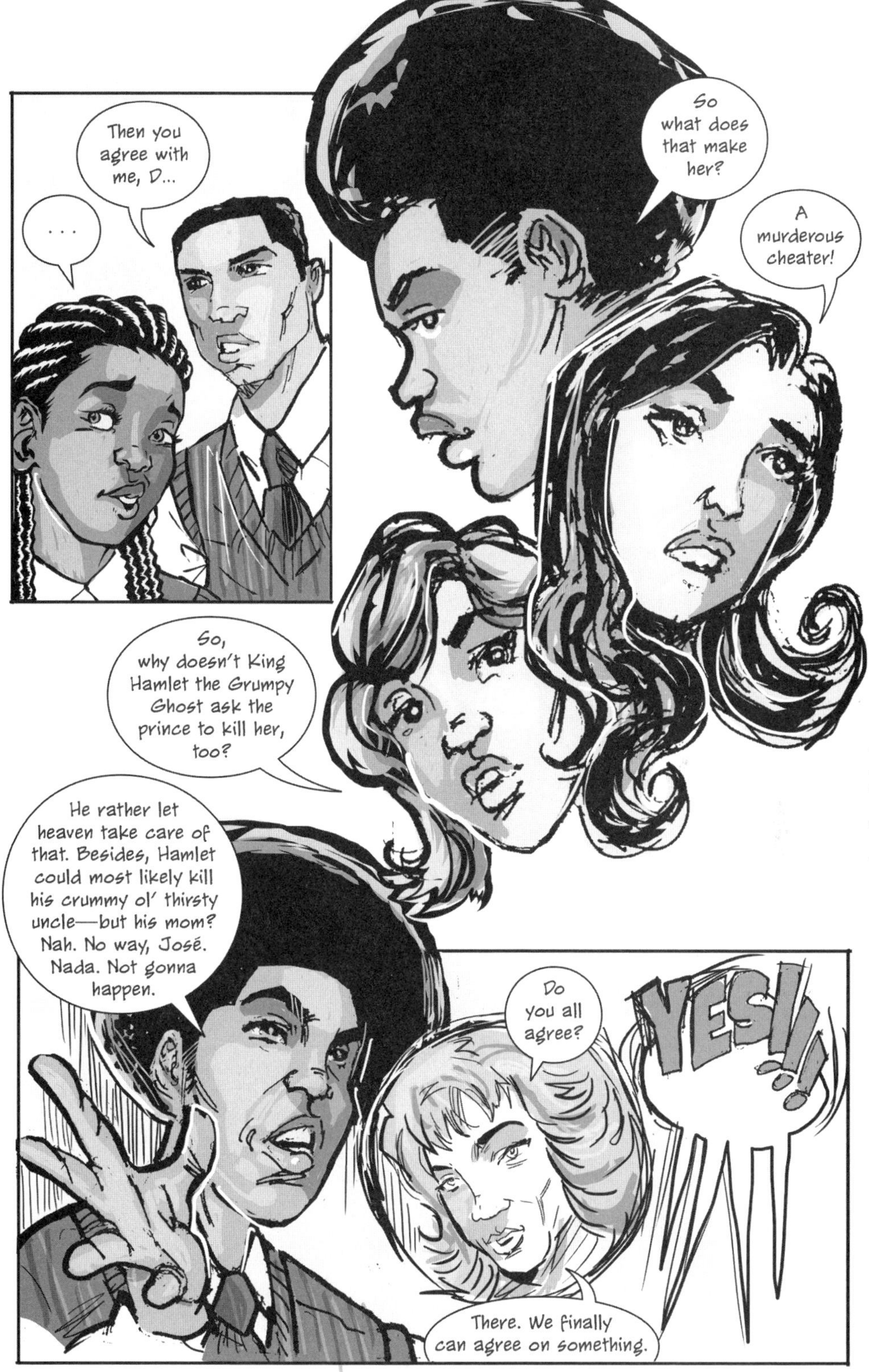
. . .
Then you agree with me, D...
So what does that make her?
A murderous cheater!
So, why doesn't King Hamlet the Grumpy Ghost ask the prince to kill her, too?
He rather let heaven take care of that. Besides, Hamlet could most likely kill his crummy ol' thirsty uncle—but his mom? Nah. No way, José. Nada. Not gonna happen.
Do you all agree?
YES!!!
There. We finally can agree on something.

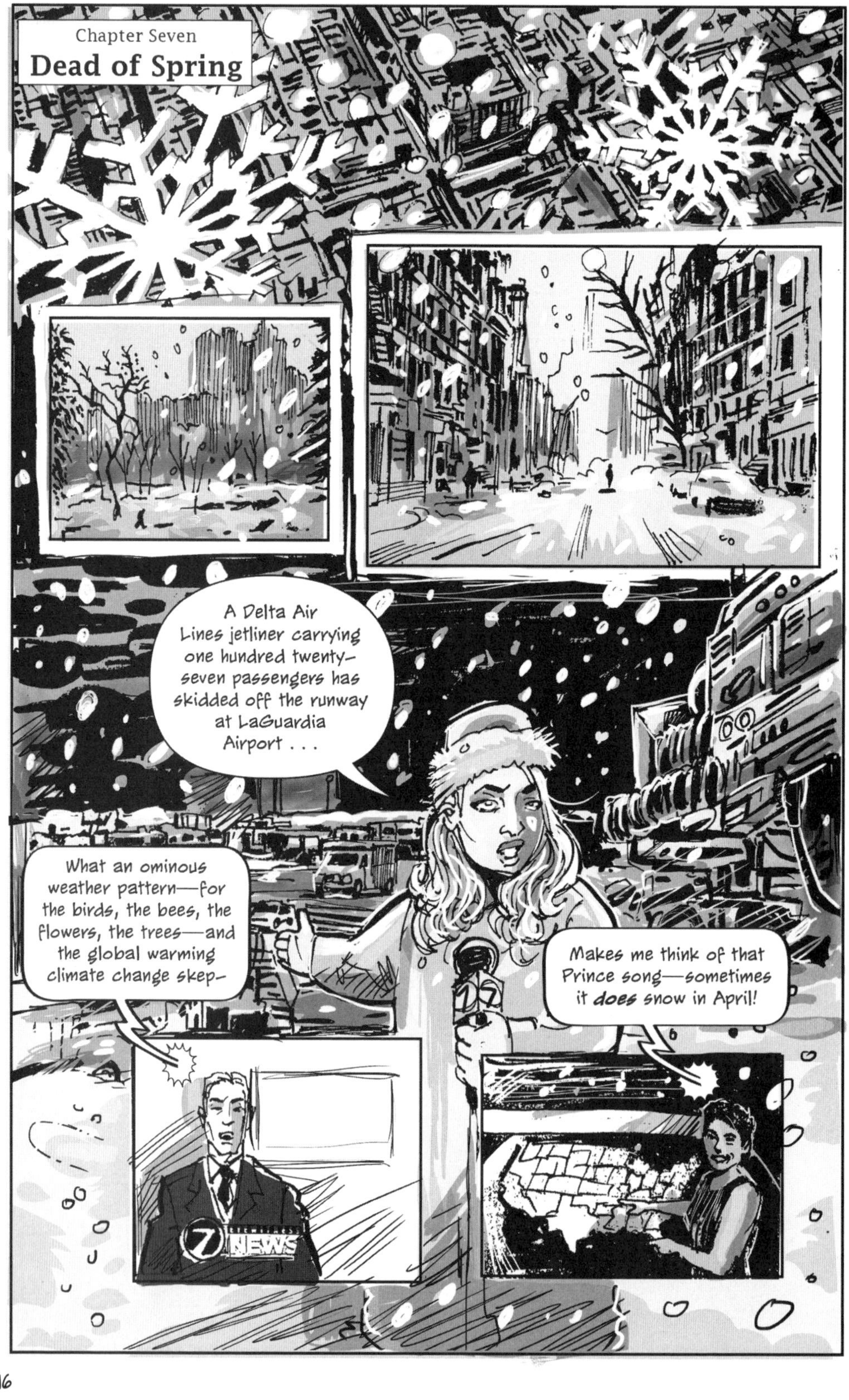
Chapter Seven
Dead of Spring
A Delta Air Lines jetliner carrying one hundred twenty-seven passengers has skidded off the runway at LaGuardia Airport . . .
What an ominous weather pattern—for the birds, the bees, the flowers, the trees—and the global warming climate change skep-
Makes me think of that Prince song—sometimes it *does* snow in April!
NEWS

Chapter Eight

The Morning After

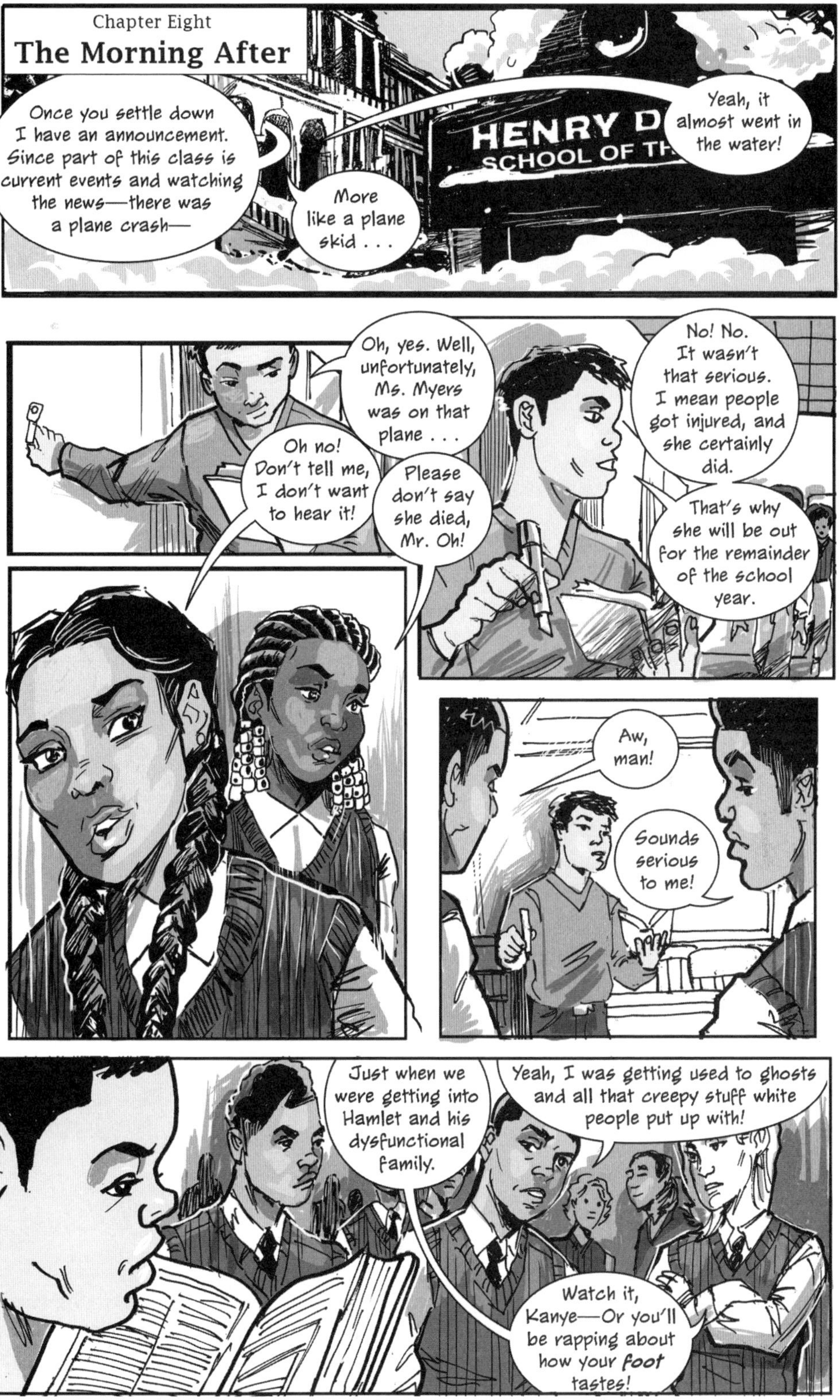

Once you settle down I have an announcement. Since part of this class is current events and watching the news—there was a plane crash—
More like a plane skid . . .
Yeah, it almost went in the water!
HENRY D
SCHOOL OF TH
Oh, yes. Well, unfortunately, Ms. Myers was on that plane . . .
Oh no! Don't tell me, I don't want to hear it!
Please don't say she died, Mr. Oh!
No! No. It wasn't that serious. I mean people got injured, and she certainly did.
That's why she will be out for the remainder of the school year.
Aw, man!
Sounds serious to me!
Just when we were getting into Hamlet and his dysfunctional family.
Yeah, I was getting used to ghosts and all that creepy stuff white people put up with!
Watch it, Kanye—Or you'll be rapping about how your *foot* tastes!

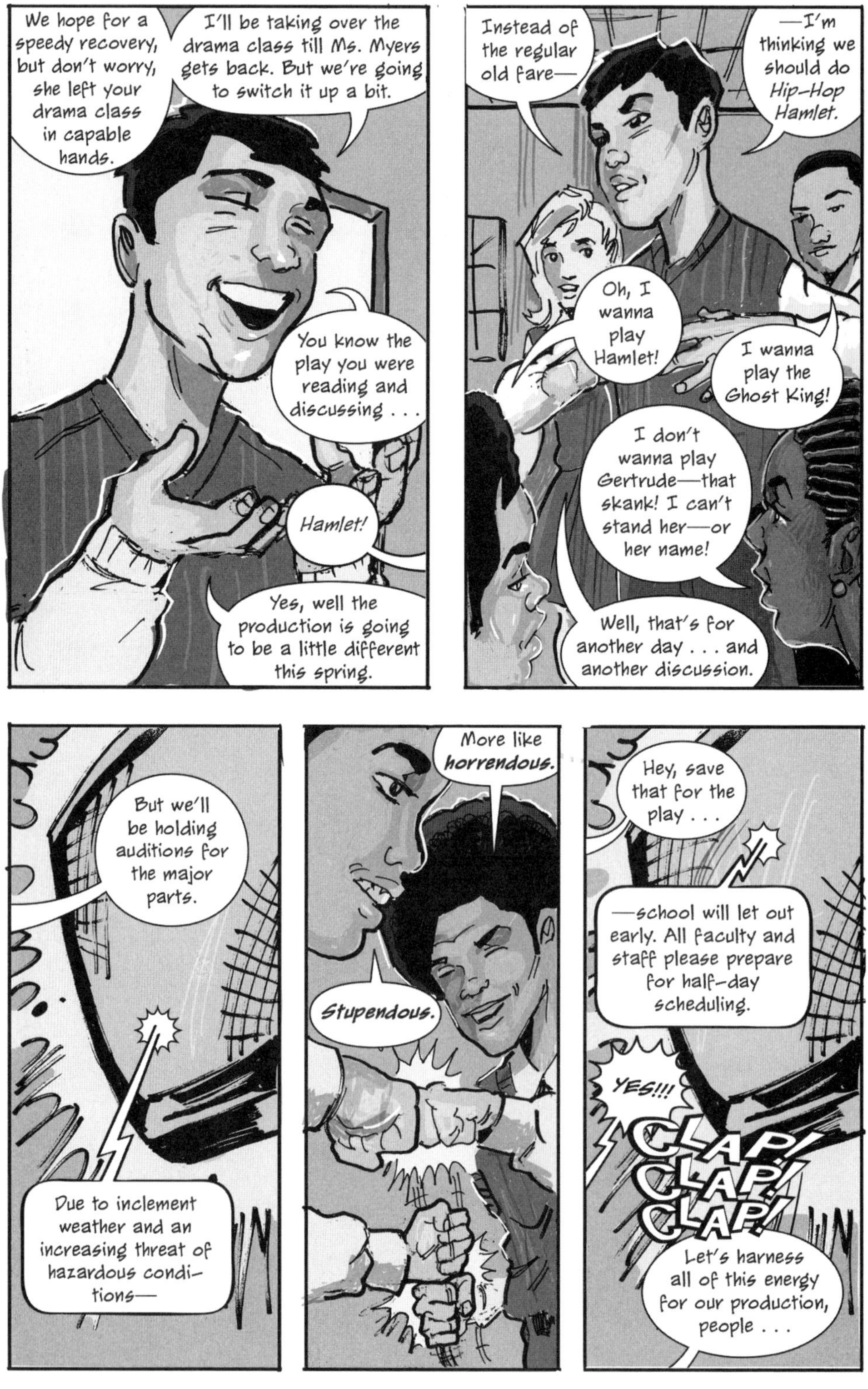
We hope for a speedy recovery, but don't worry, she left your drama class in capable hands.
I'll be taking over the drama class till Ms. Myers gets back. But we're going to switch it up a bit.
You know the play you were reading and discussing . . .
Hamlet!
Yes, well the production is going to be a little different this spring.
Instead of the regular old fare—
—I'm thinking we should do Hip-Hop Hamlet.
Oh, I wanna play Hamlet!
I wanna play the Ghost King!
I don't wanna play Gertrude—that skank! I can't stand her—or her name!
Well, that's for another day . . . and another discussion.
But we'll be holding auditions for the major parts.
Due to inclement weather and an increasing threat of hazardous conditions—
More like horrendous.
Stupendous.
Hey, save that for the play . . .
—school will let out early. All faculty and staff please prepare for half-day scheduling.
YES!!!
CLAP! CLAP! CLAP!
Let's harness all of this energy for our production, people . . .

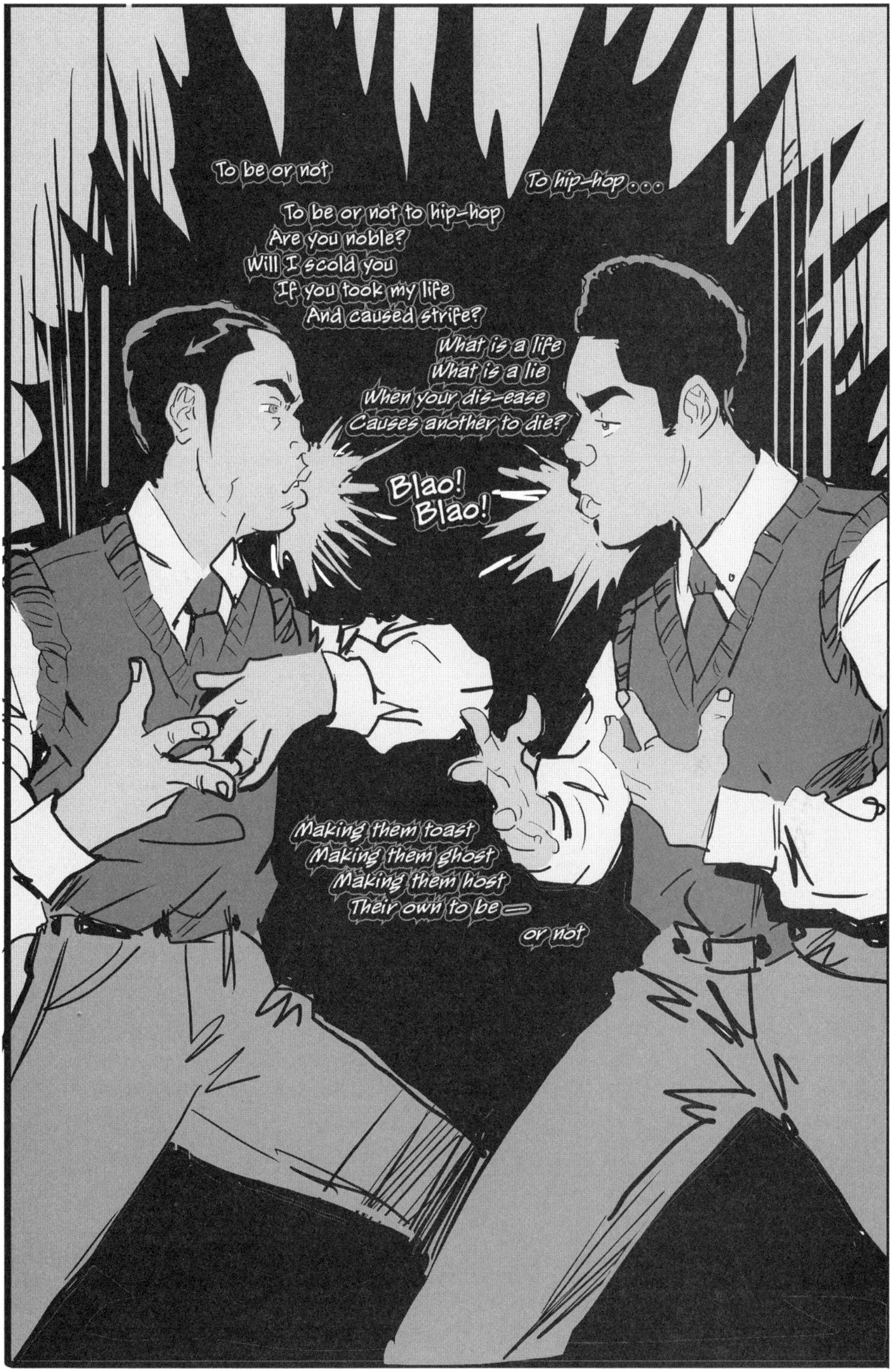
To be or not
To hip-hop . . .
To be or not to hip-hop
Are you noble?
Will I scold you
If you took my life
And caused strife?
What is a life
What is a lie
When your dis-ease
Causes another to die?
Blao!
Blao!
Making them toast
Making them ghost
Making them host
Their own to be —
or not

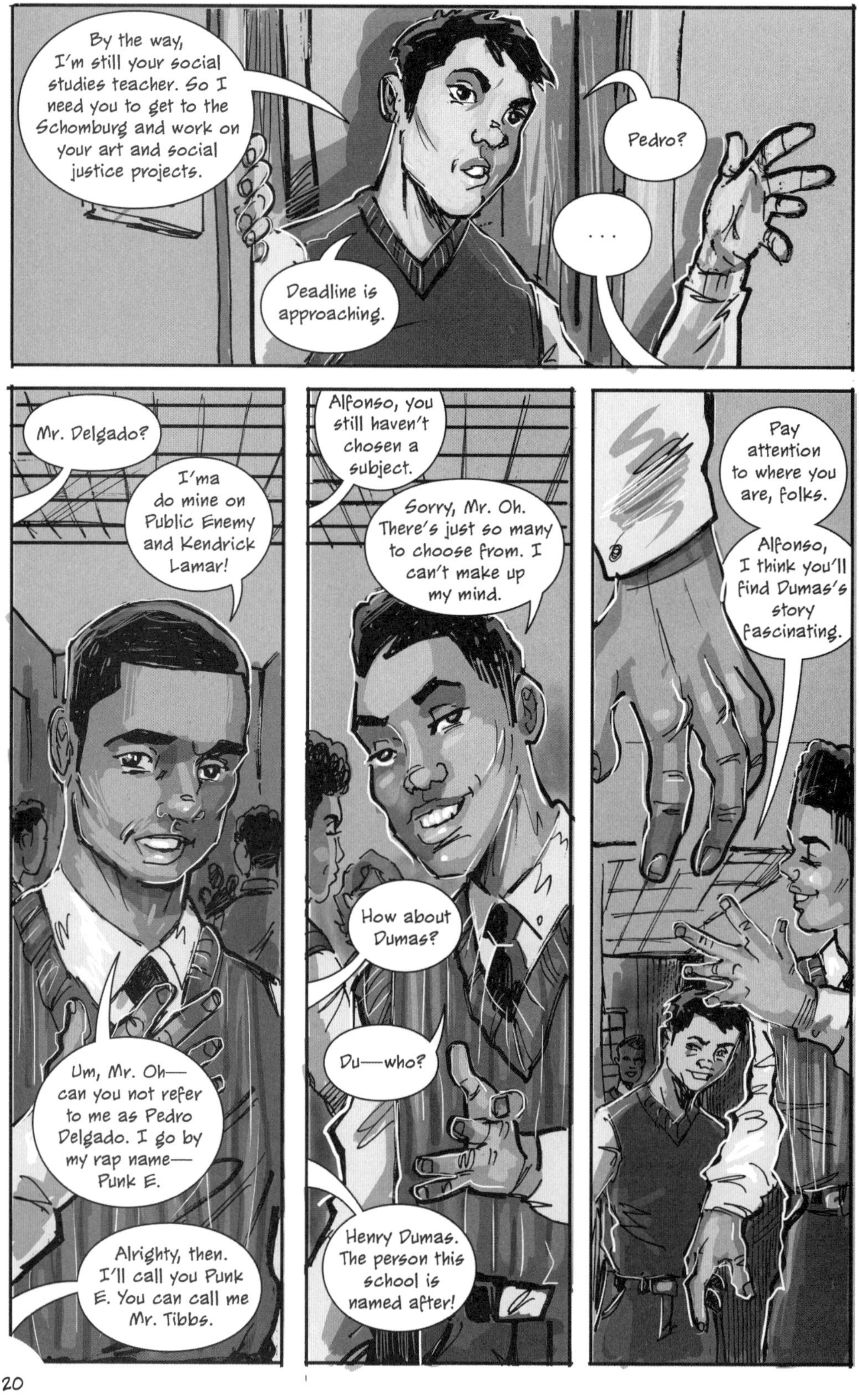
By the way, I'm still your social studies teacher. So I need you to get to the Schomburg and work on your art and social justice projects.
Deadline is approaching.
Pedro?
. . .
Mr. Delgado?
I'ma do mine on Public Enemy and Kendrick Lamar!
Um, Mr. Oh— can you not refer to me as Pedro Delgado. I go by my rap name— Punk E.
Alrighty, then. I'll call you Punk E. You can call me Mr. Tibbs.
Alfonso, you still haven't chosen a subject.
Sorry, Mr. Oh. There's just so many to choose from. I can't make up my mind.
How about Dumas?
Du—who?
Henry Dumas. The person this school is named after!
Pay attention to where you are, folks.
Alfonso, I think you'll find Dumas's story fascinating.

Chapter Nine
First Suit

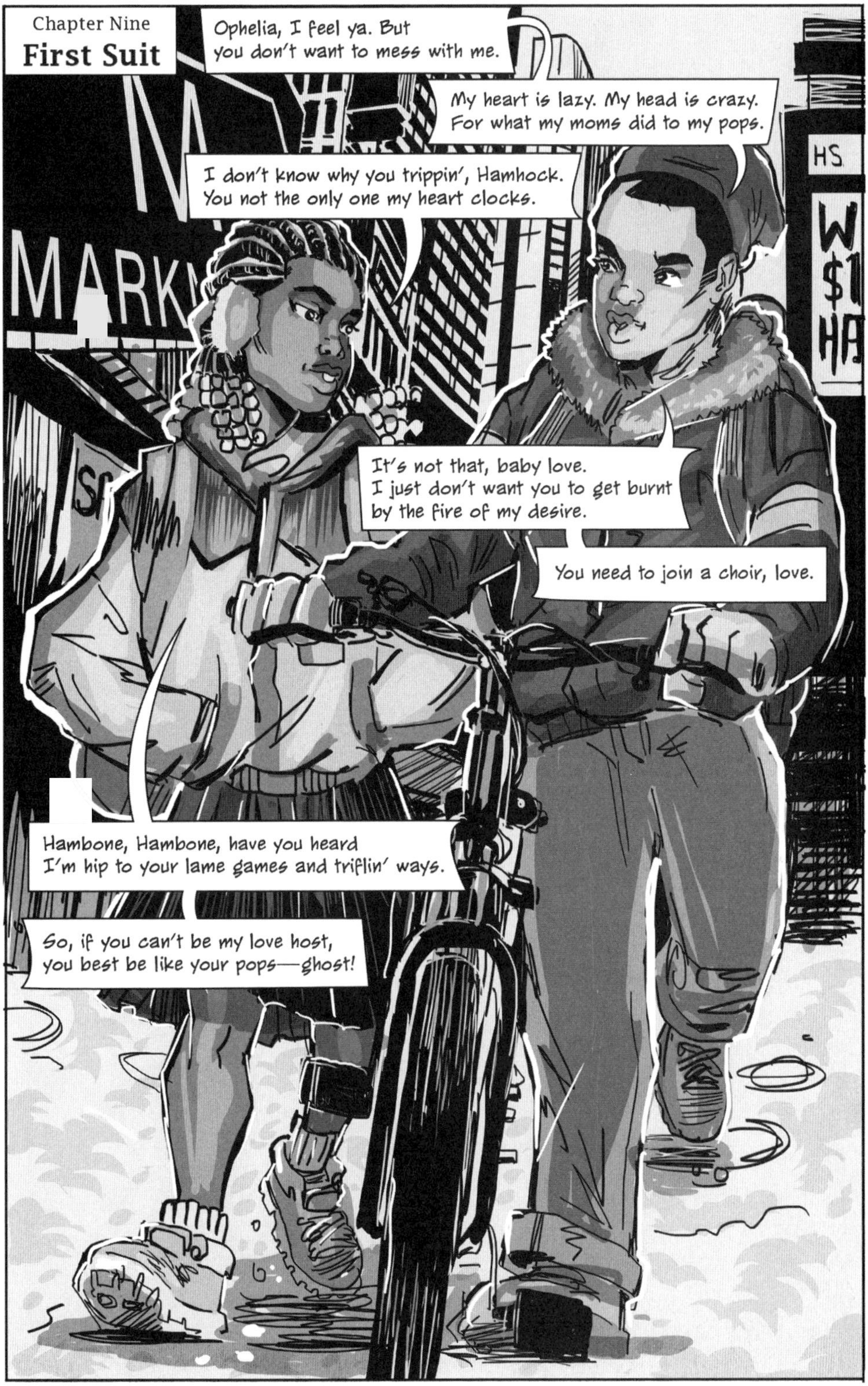
Ophelia, I feel ya. But you don't want to mess with me.
My heart is lazy. My head is crazy. For what my moms did to my pops.
I don't know why you trippin', Hamhock. You not the only one my heart clocks.
It's not that, baby love. I just don't want you to get burnt by the fire of my desire.
You need to join a choir, love.
Hambone, Hambone, have you heard
I'm hip to your lame games and triflin' ways.
So, if you can't be my love host, you best be like your pops—ghost!

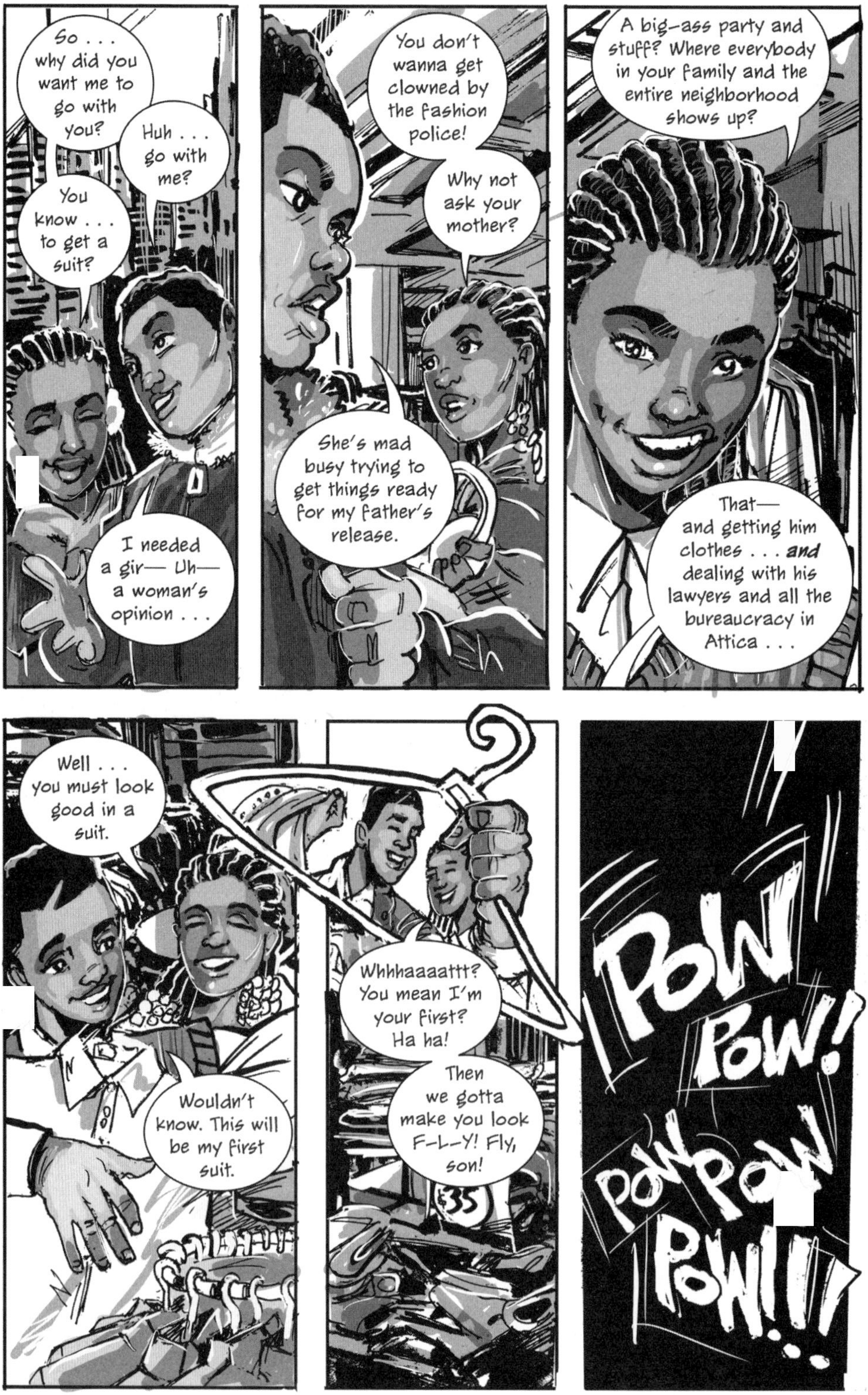
So . . . why did you want me to go with you?
Huh . . . go with me?
You know . . . to get a suit?
I needed a gir— Uh— a woman's opinion . . .
You don't wanna get clowned by the fashion police!
Why not ask your mother?
She's mad busy trying to get things ready for my father's release.
A big-ass party and stuff? Where everybody in your family and the entire neighborhood shows up?
That— and getting him clothes . . . **and** dealing with his lawyers and all the bureaucracy in Attica . . .
Well . . . you must look good in a suit.
Wouldn't know. This will be my first suit.
Whhhaaaatttt? You mean I'm your first? Ha ha!
Then we gotta make you look F-L-Y! Fly, son!
$35
POW POW!
POW POW POW!!!

Chapter Ten
Ghost Train

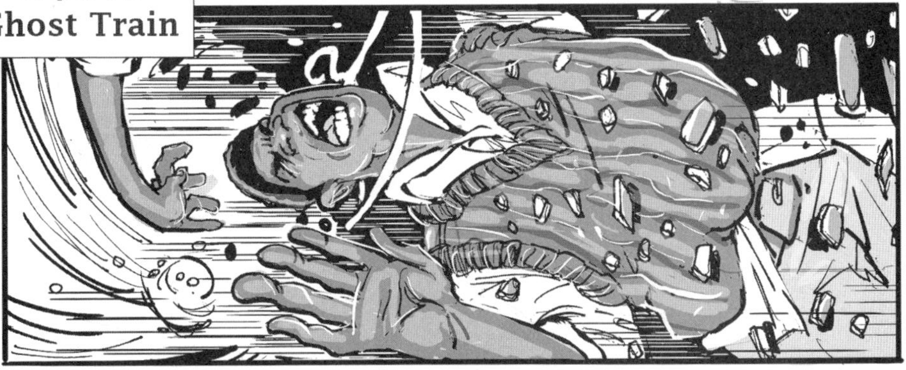

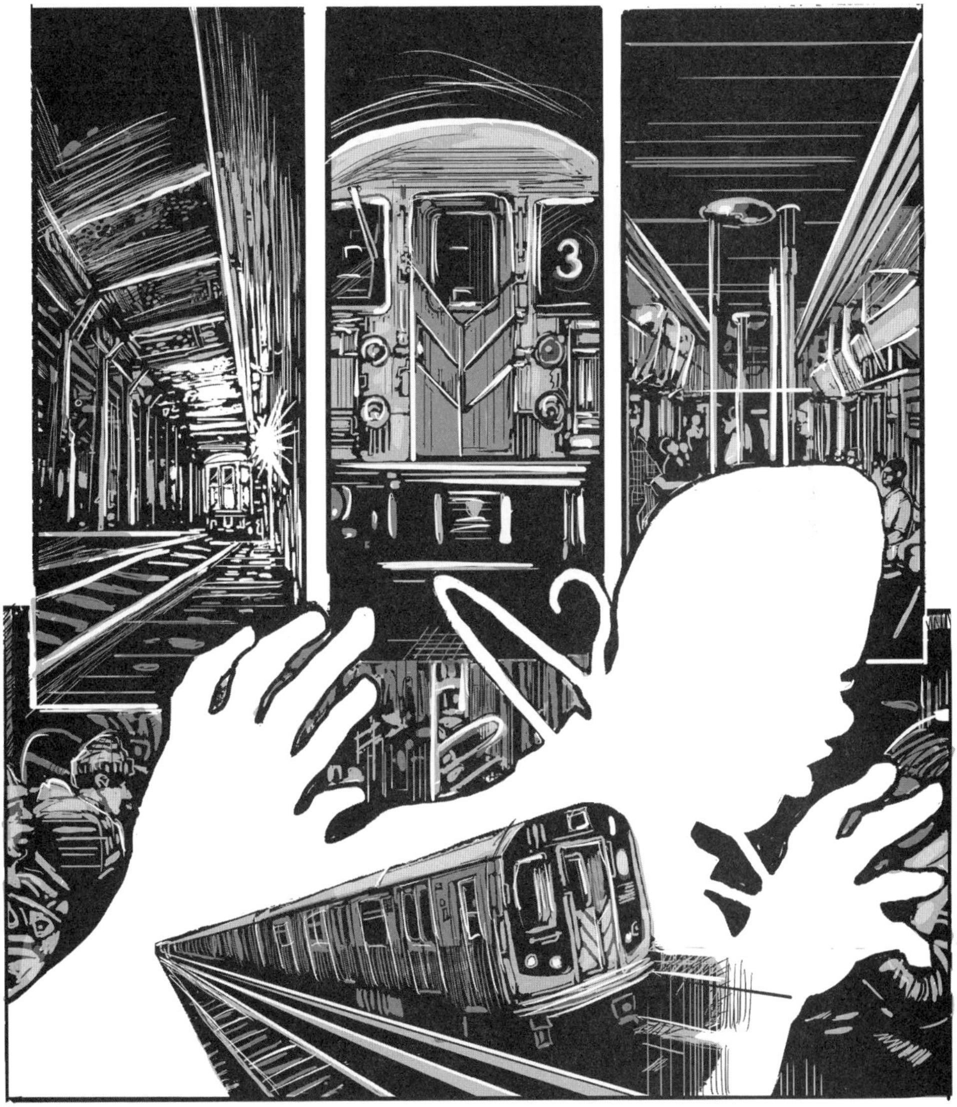
3

Chapter Eleven

Where the Ghosts Know Your Name

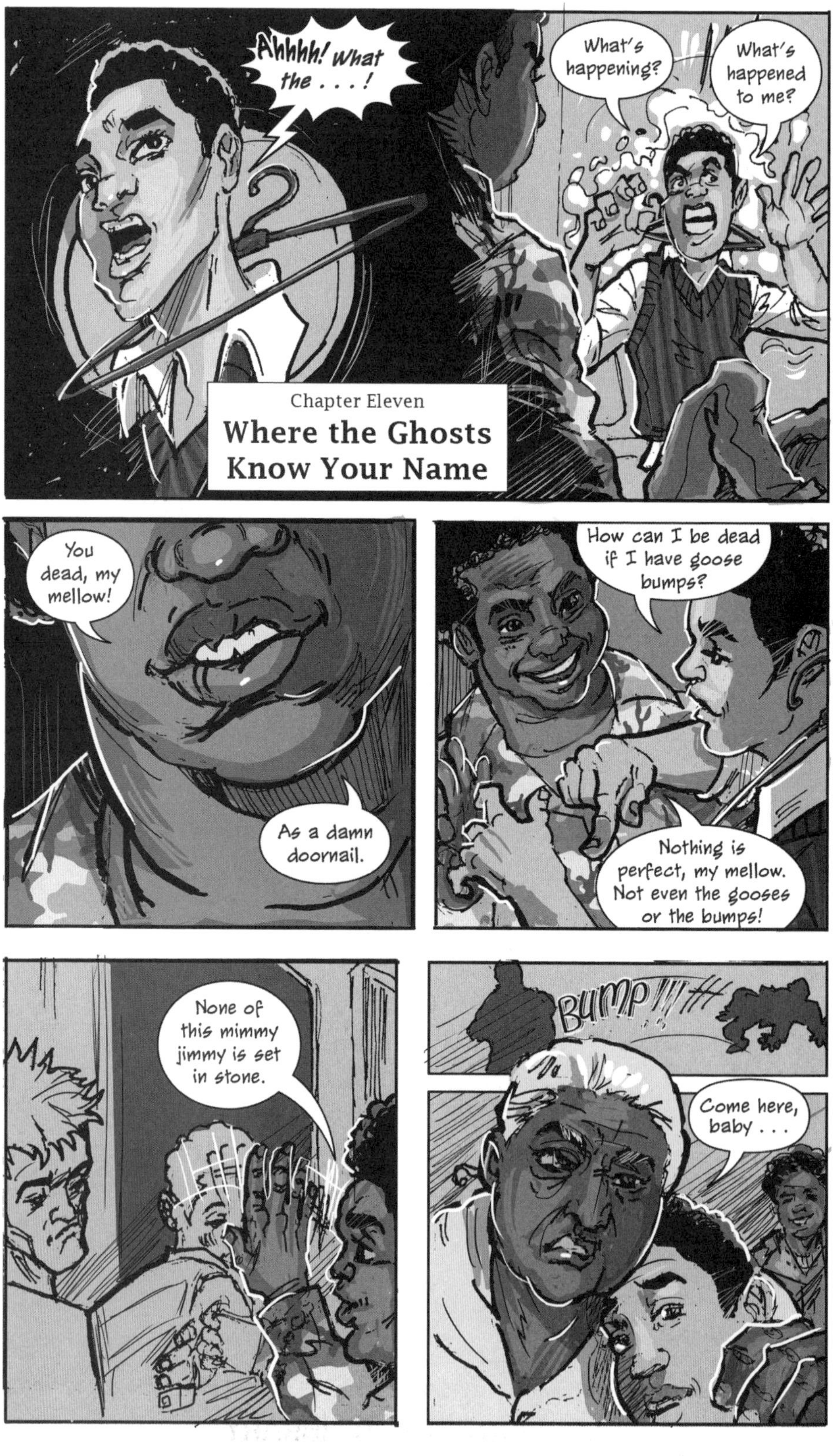
Ahhhh! What the . . . !
What's happening?
What's happened to me?
You dead, my mellow!
As a damn doornail.
How can I be dead if I have goose bumps?
Nothing is perfect, my mellow. Not even the gooses or the bumps!
None of this mimmy jimmy is set in stone.
BUMP!!!
Come here, baby . . .

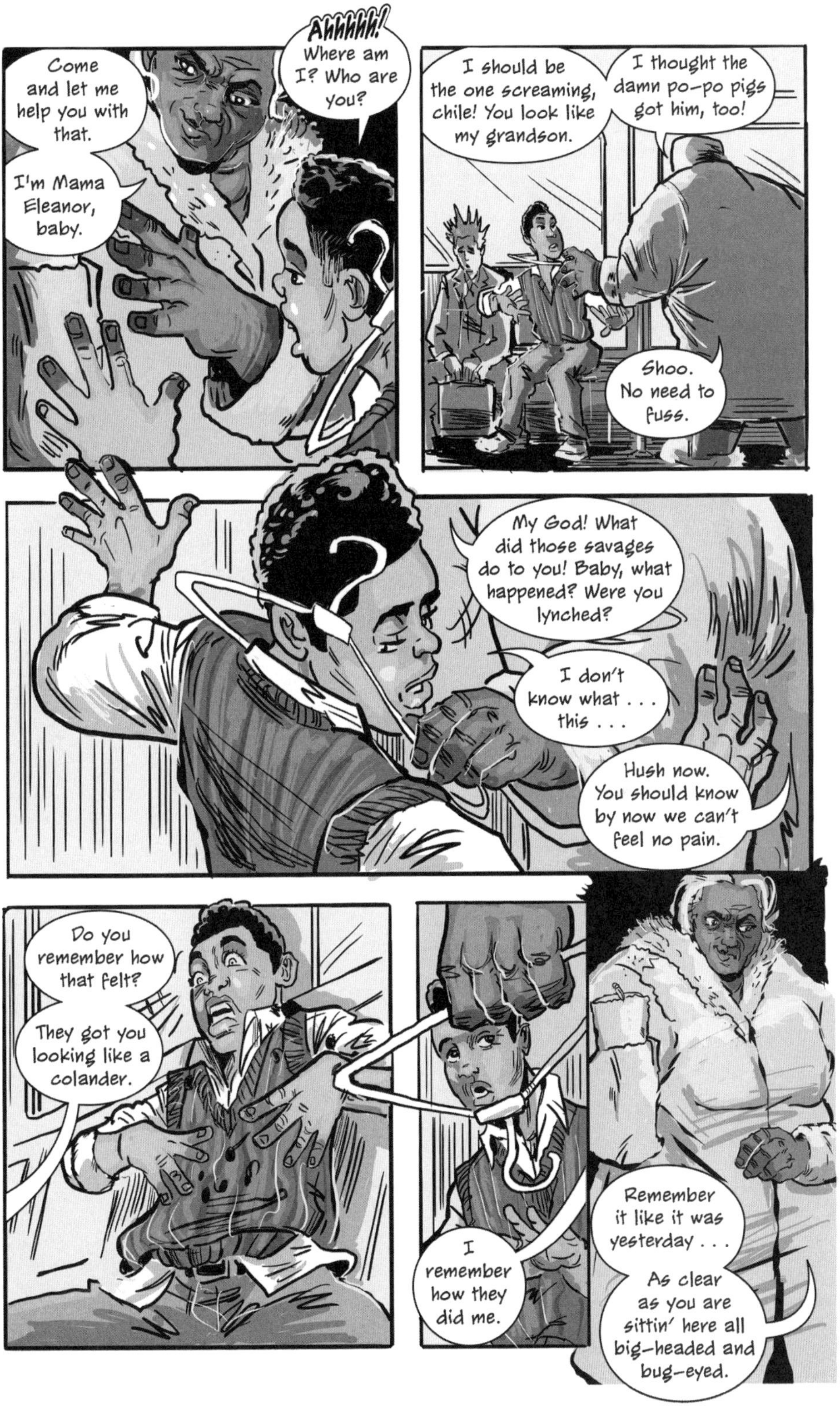

Come and let me help you with that.
I'm Mama Eleanor, baby.
Ahhhhh!
Where am I? Who are you?
I should be the one screaming, chile! You look like my grandson.
I thought the damn po-po pigs got him, too!
Shoo. No need to fuss.
My God! What did those savages do to you! Baby, what happened? Were you lynched?
I don't know what . . . this . . .
Hush now. You should know by now we can't feel no pain.
Do you remember how that felt?
They got you looking like a colander.
I remember how they did me.
Remember it like it was yesterday . . .
As clear as you are sittin' here all big-headed and bug-eyed.

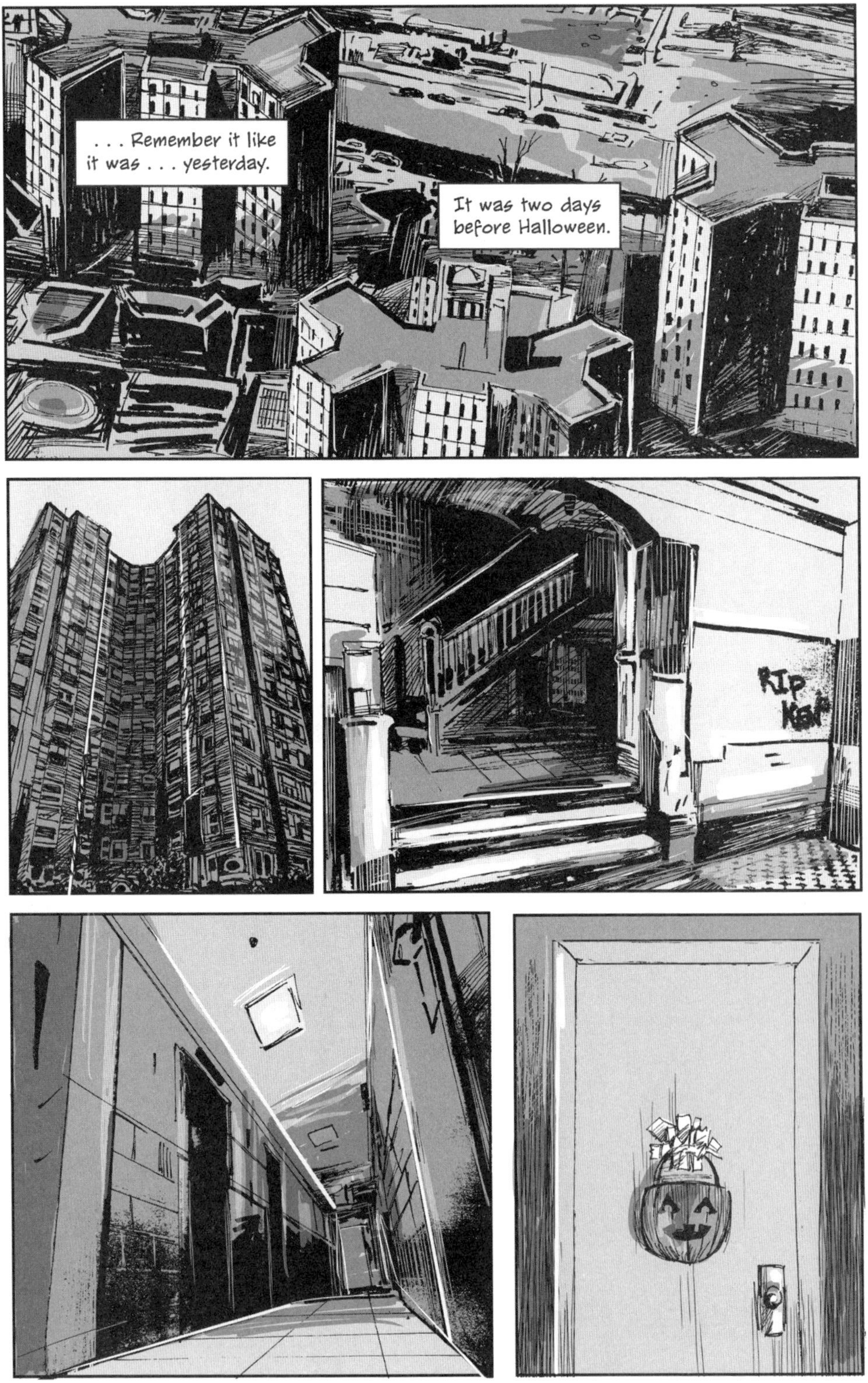
. . . Remember it like it was . . . yesterday.
It was two days before Halloween.

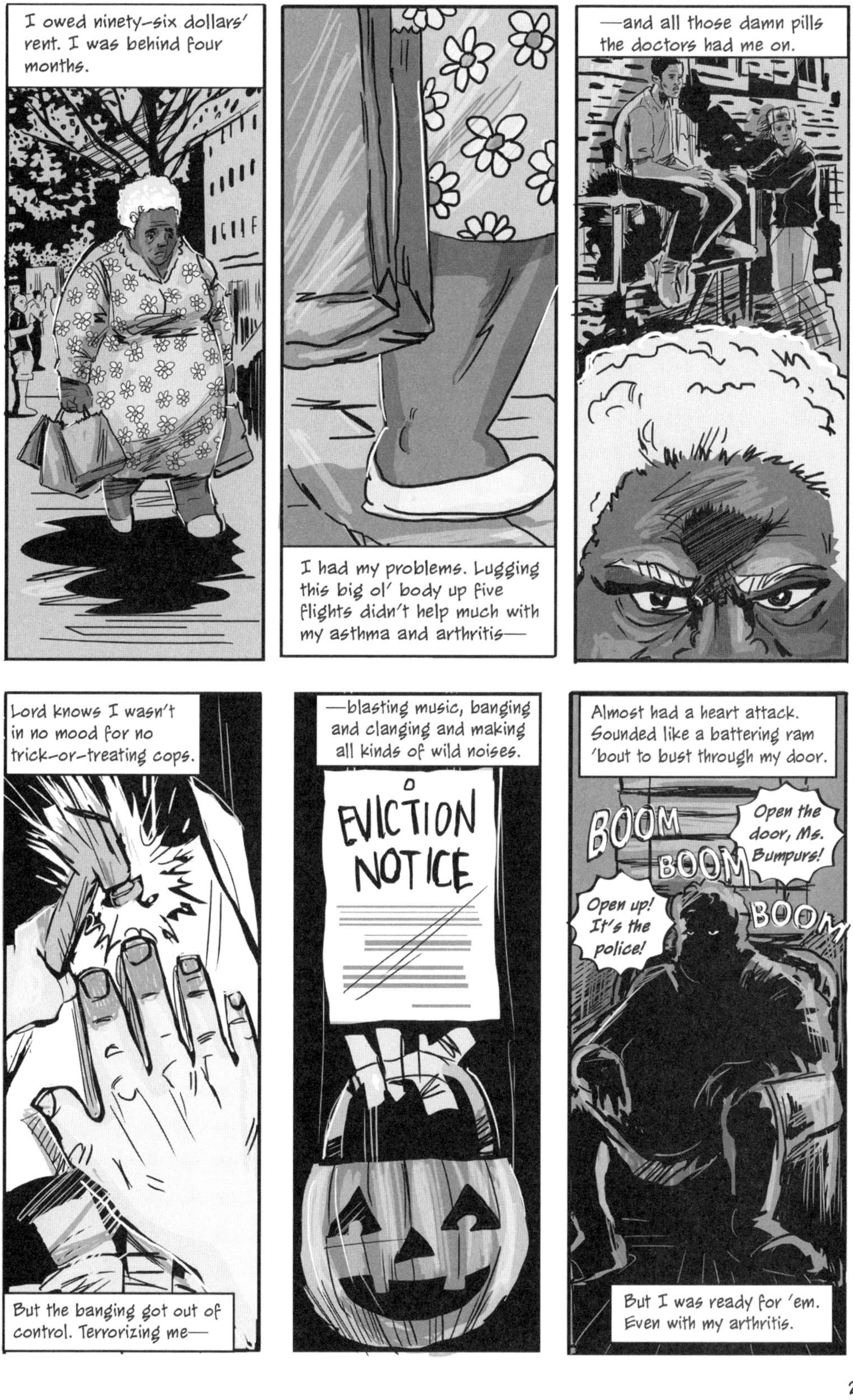
I owed ninety-six dollars' rent. I was behind four months.
I had my problems. Lugging this big ol' body up five flights didn't help much with my asthma and arthritis—
—and all those damn pills the doctors had me on.
Lord knows I wasn't in no mood for no trick-or-treating cops.
But the banging got out of control. Terrorizing me—
—blasting music, banging and clanging and making all kinds of wild noises.
EVICTION NOTICE
Almost had a heart attack. Sounded like a battering ram 'bout to bust through my door.
BOOM
BOOM
Open the door, Ms. Bumpurs!
Open up! It's the police!
BOOM
But I was ready for 'em. Even with my arthritis.

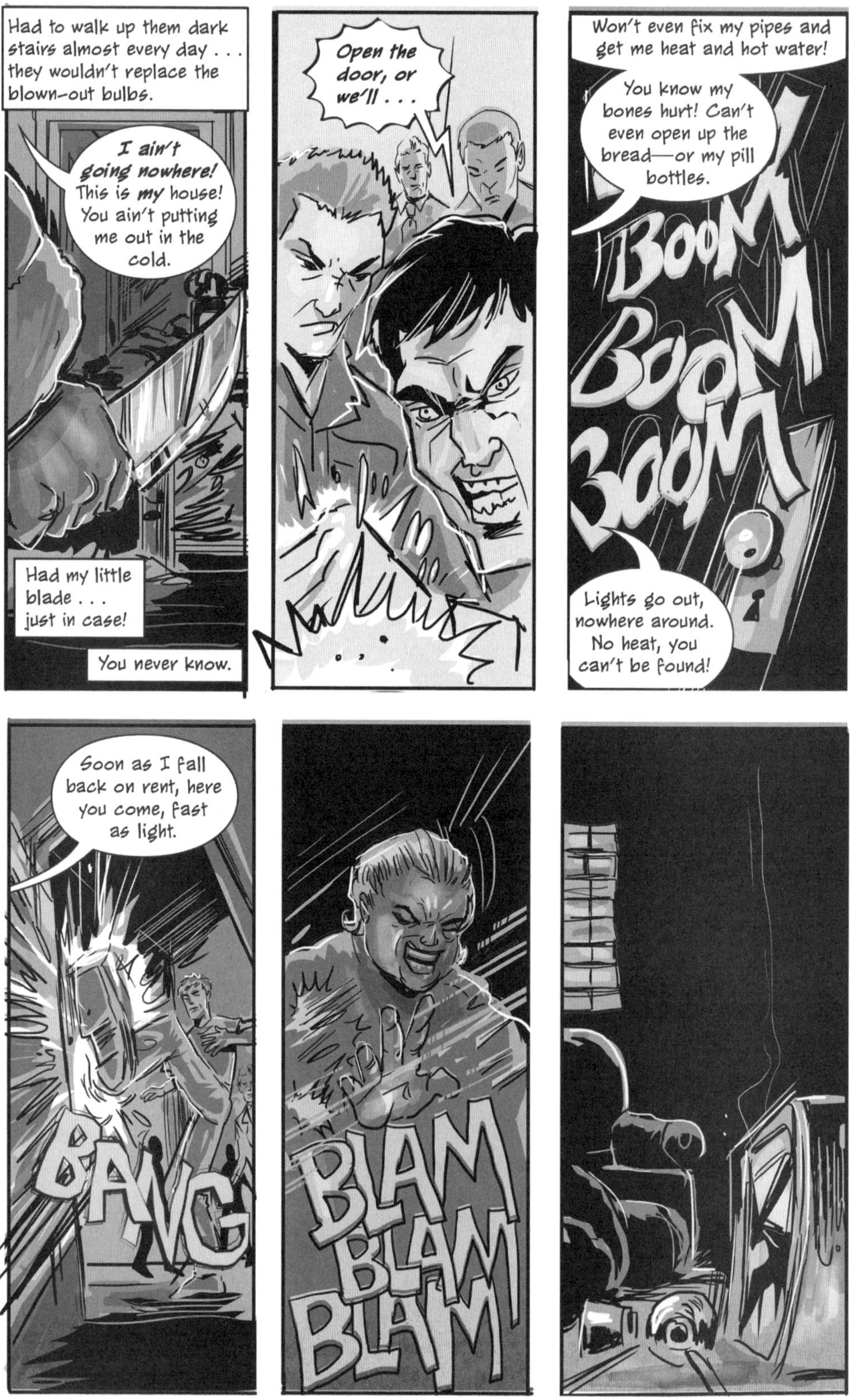
Had to walk up them dark stairs almost every day . . . they wouldn't replace the blown-out bulbs.
I ain't going nowhere! This is my house! You ain't putting me out in the cold.
Had my little blade . . . just in case!
You never know.
Open the door, or we'll . . .
. . .
Won't even fix my pipes and get me heat and hot water!
You know my bones hurt! Can't even open up the bread—or my pill bottles.
BOOM BOOM BOOM
Lights go out, nowhere around. No heat, you can't be found!
Soon as I fall back on rent, here you come, fast as light.
BANG
BLAM BLAM BLAM

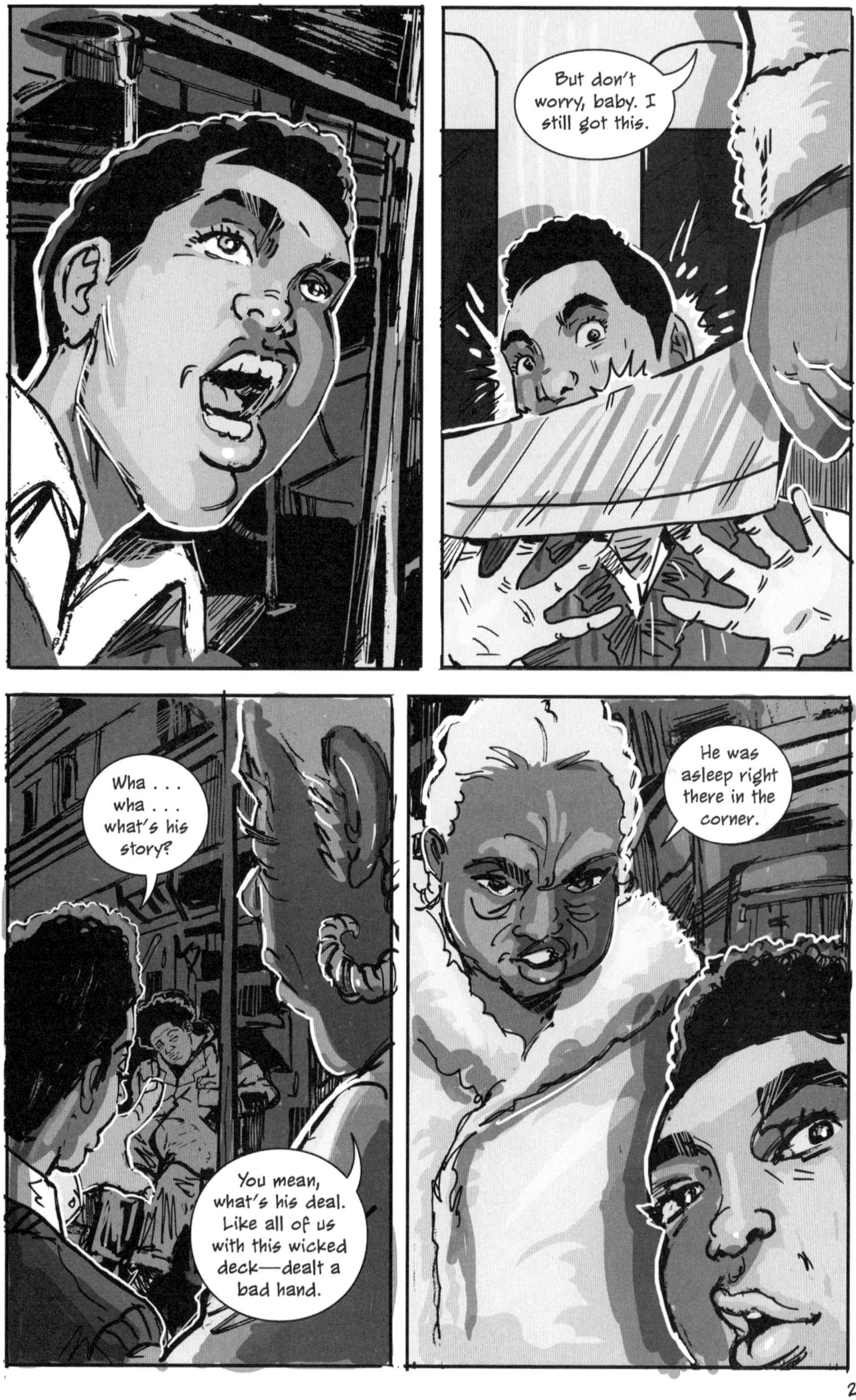
But don't worry, baby. I still got this.
Wha . . . wha . . . what's his story?
You mean, what's his deal. Like all of us with this wicked deck—dealt a bad hand.
He was asleep right there in the corner.

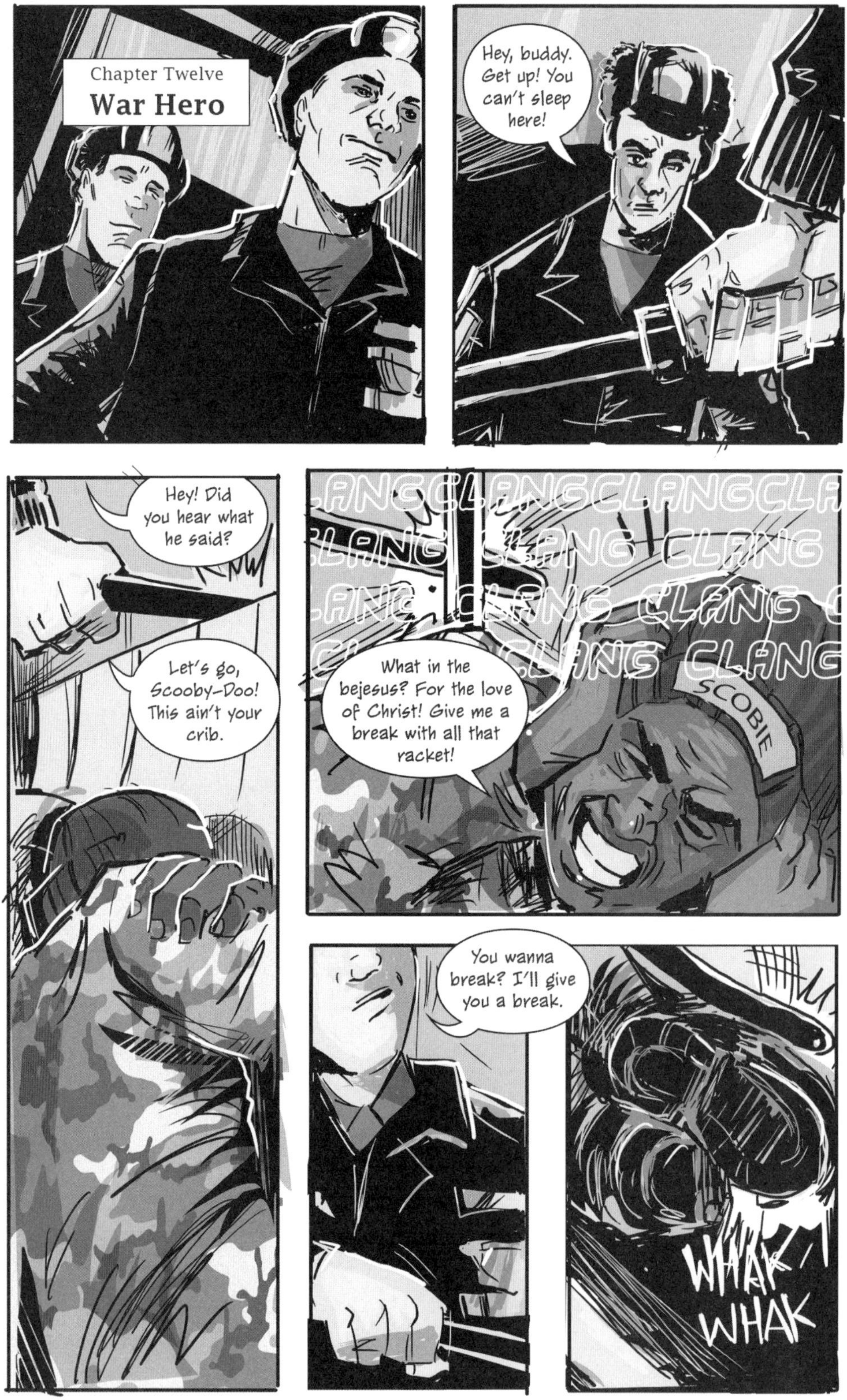

Chapter Twelve
War Hero
Hey, buddy. Get up! You can't sleep here!
Hey! Did you hear what he said?
Let's go, Scooby-Doo! This ain't your crib.
CLANG CLANG CLANG CLANG CLANG CLANG CLANG CLANG CLANG
SCOBIE
What in the bejesus? For the love of Christ! Give me a break with all that racket!
You wanna break? I'll give you a break.
WHAK WHAK

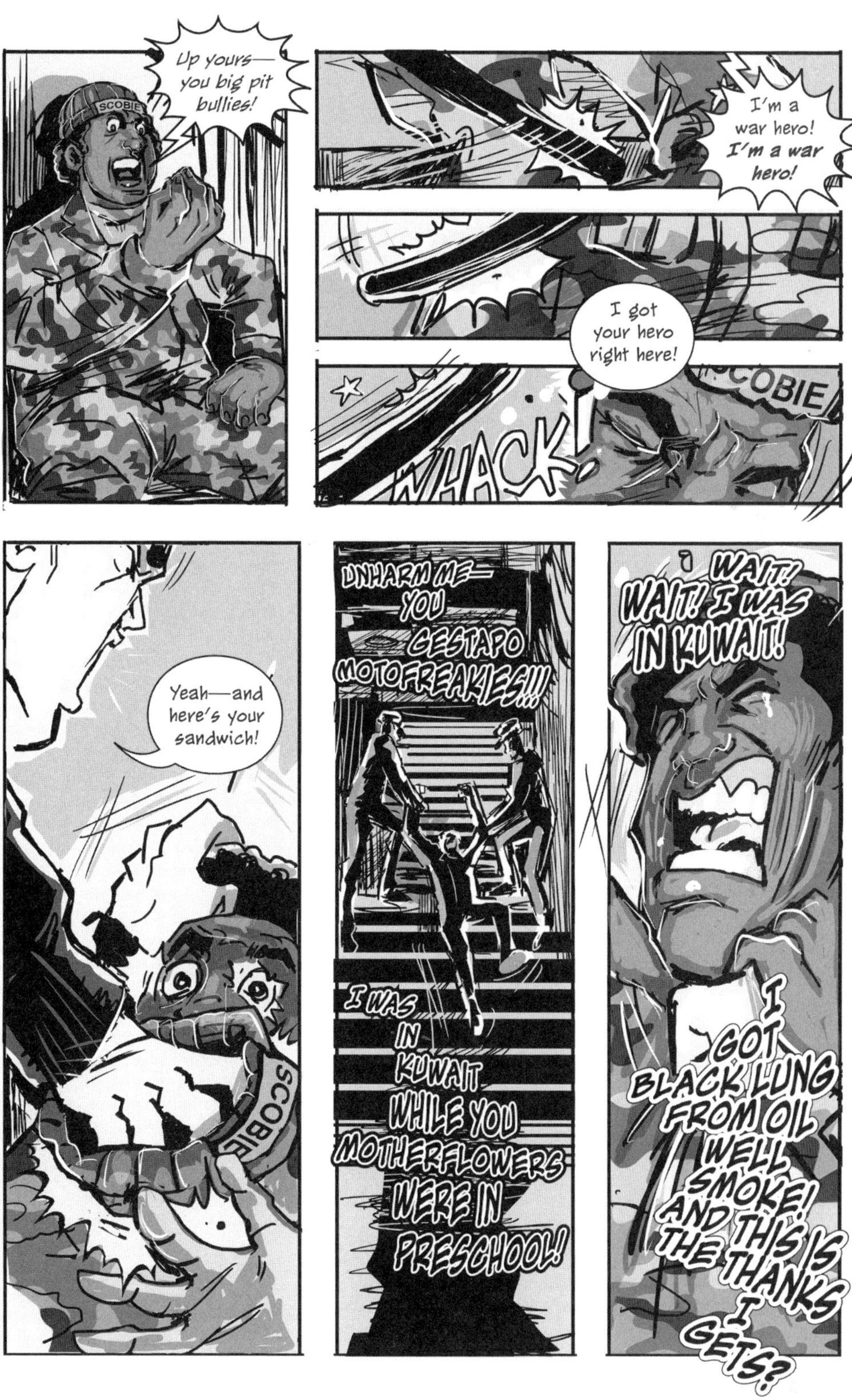

Up yours—you big pit bullies!
SCOBIE
I'm a war hero! I'm a war hero!
I got your hero right here!
SCOBIE
WHACK!
Yeah—and here's your sandwich!
SCOBIE
UNHARM ME—YOU GESTAPO MOTOFREAKIES!!!
I WAS IN KUWAIT WHILE YOU MOTHERFLOWERS WERE IN PRESCHOOL!
WAIT! WAIT! I WAS IN KUWAIT!
I GOT BLACK LUNG FROM OIL WELL SMOKE! AND THIS IS THE THANKS I GETS?

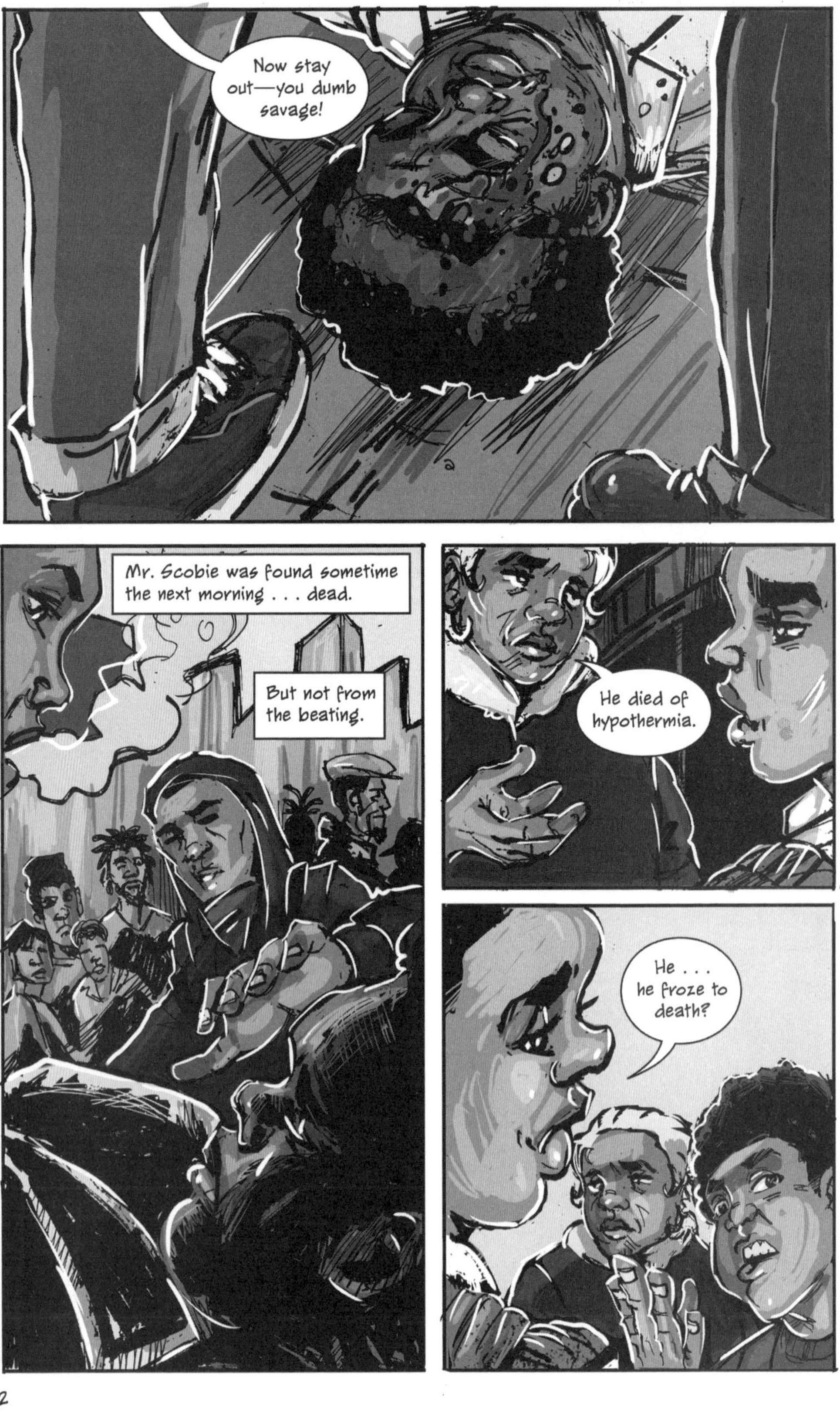
Now stay out—you dumb savage!
Mr. Scobie was found sometime the next morning . . . dead.
But not from the beating.
He died of hypothermia.
He . . . he froze to death?

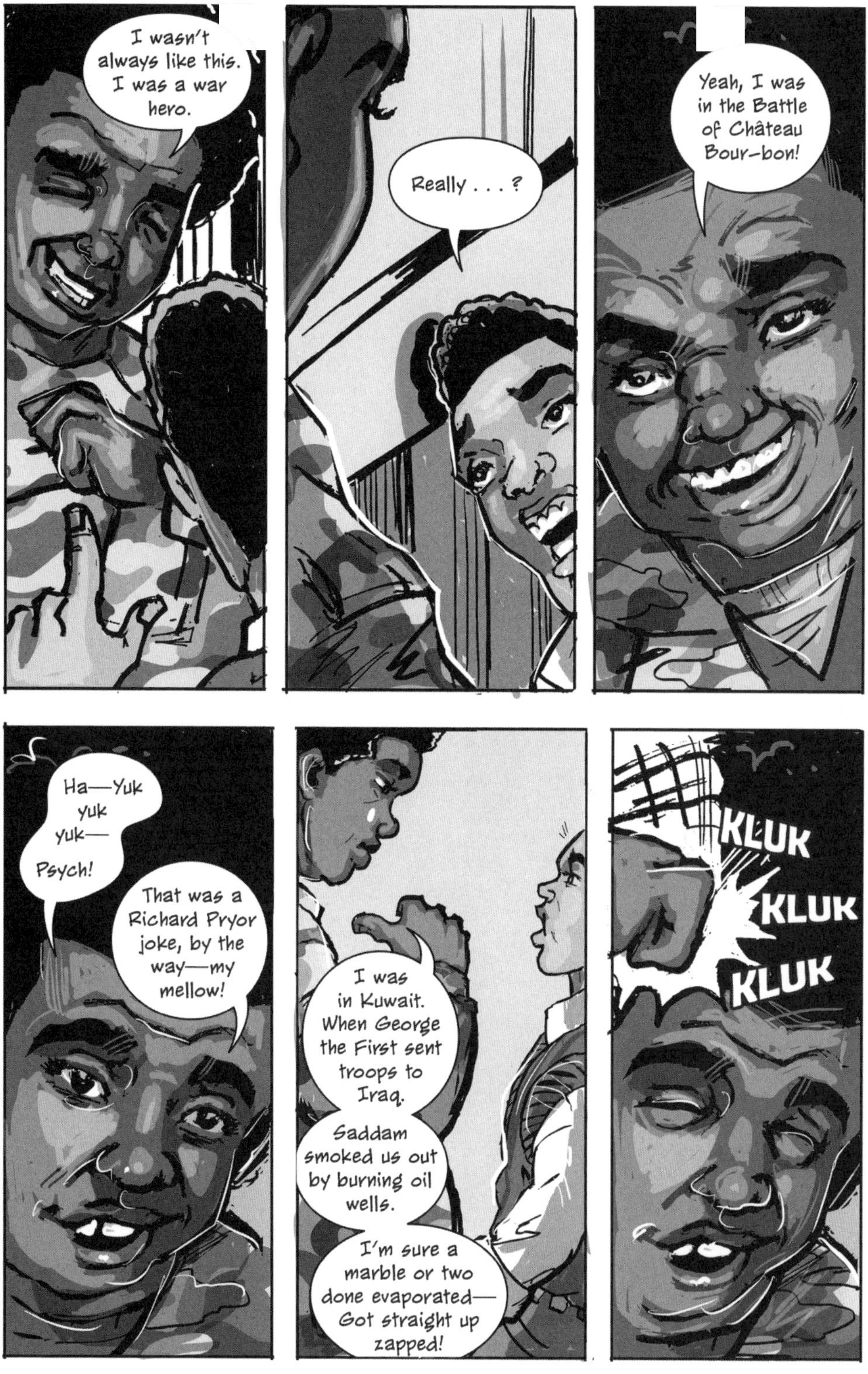
I wasn't always like this. I was a war hero.
Really . . . ?
Yeah, I was in the Battle of Château Bour-bon!
Ha—Yuk yuk yuk—
Psych!
That was a Richard Pryor joke, by the way—my mellow!
I was in Kuwait. When George the First sent troops to Iraq.
Saddam smoked us out by burning oil wells.
I'm sure a marble or two done evaporated— Got straight up zapped!
KLUK
KLUK
KLUK

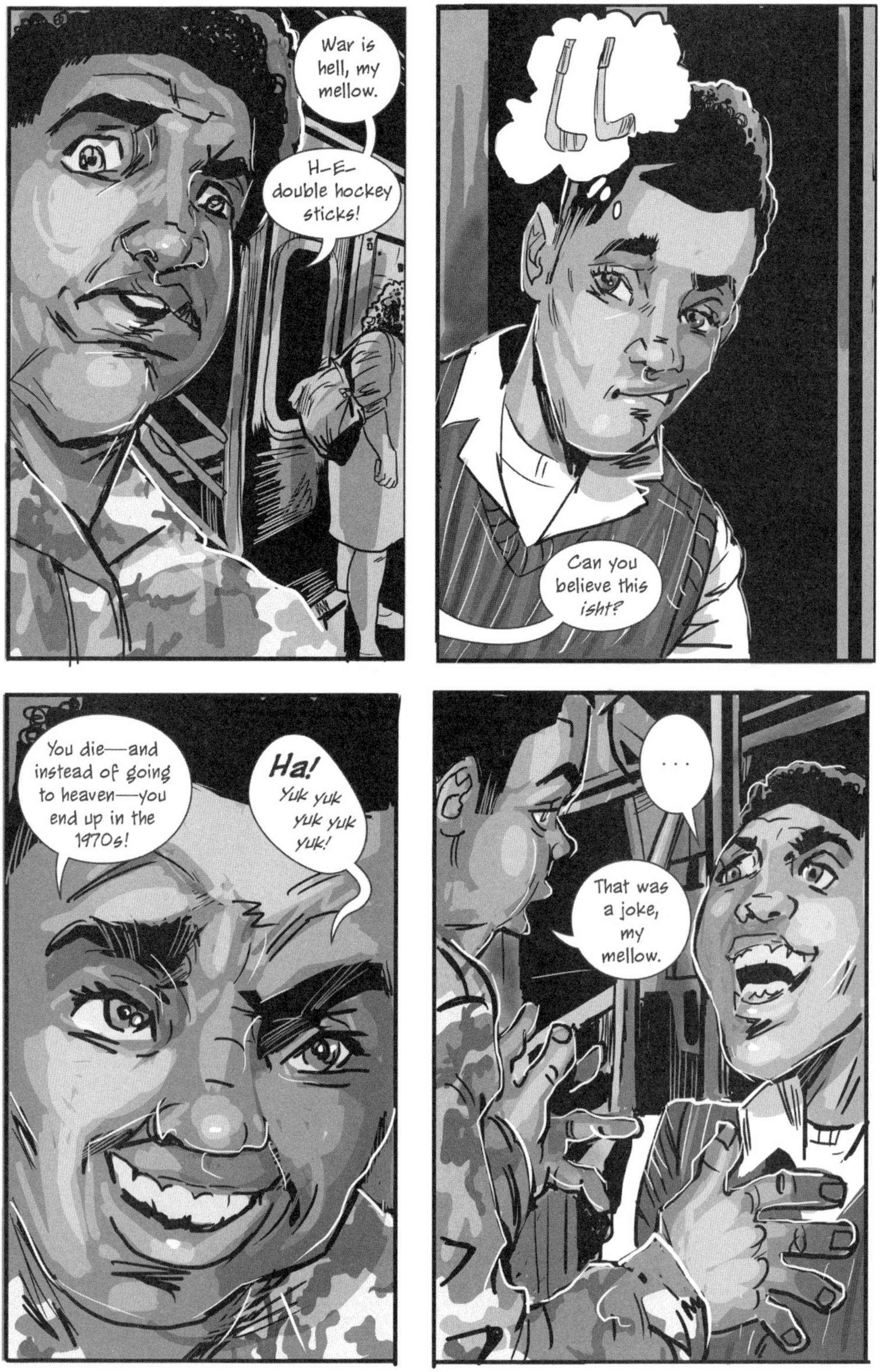
War is hell, my mellow.
H-E- double hockey sticks!
Can you believe this isht?
You die—and instead of going to heaven—you end up in the 1970s!
Ha! Yuk yuk yuk yuk yuk!
. . .
That was a joke, my mellow.

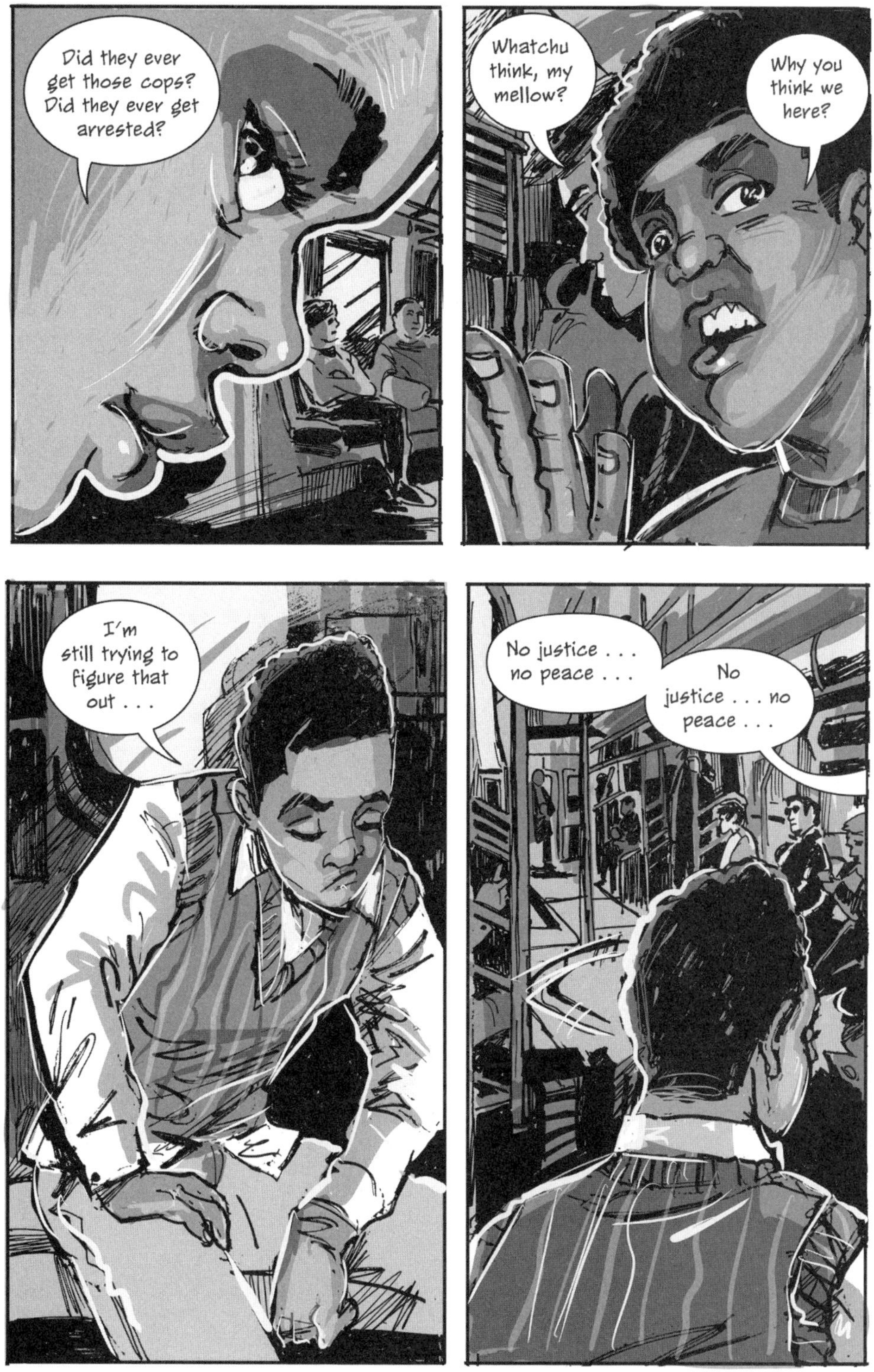
Did they ever get those cops? Did they ever get arrested?
Whatchu think, my mellow?
Why you think we here?
I'm still trying to figure that out . . .
No justice . . . no peace . . .
No justice . . . no peace . . .

Chapter Thirteen
Angel/Ancestor

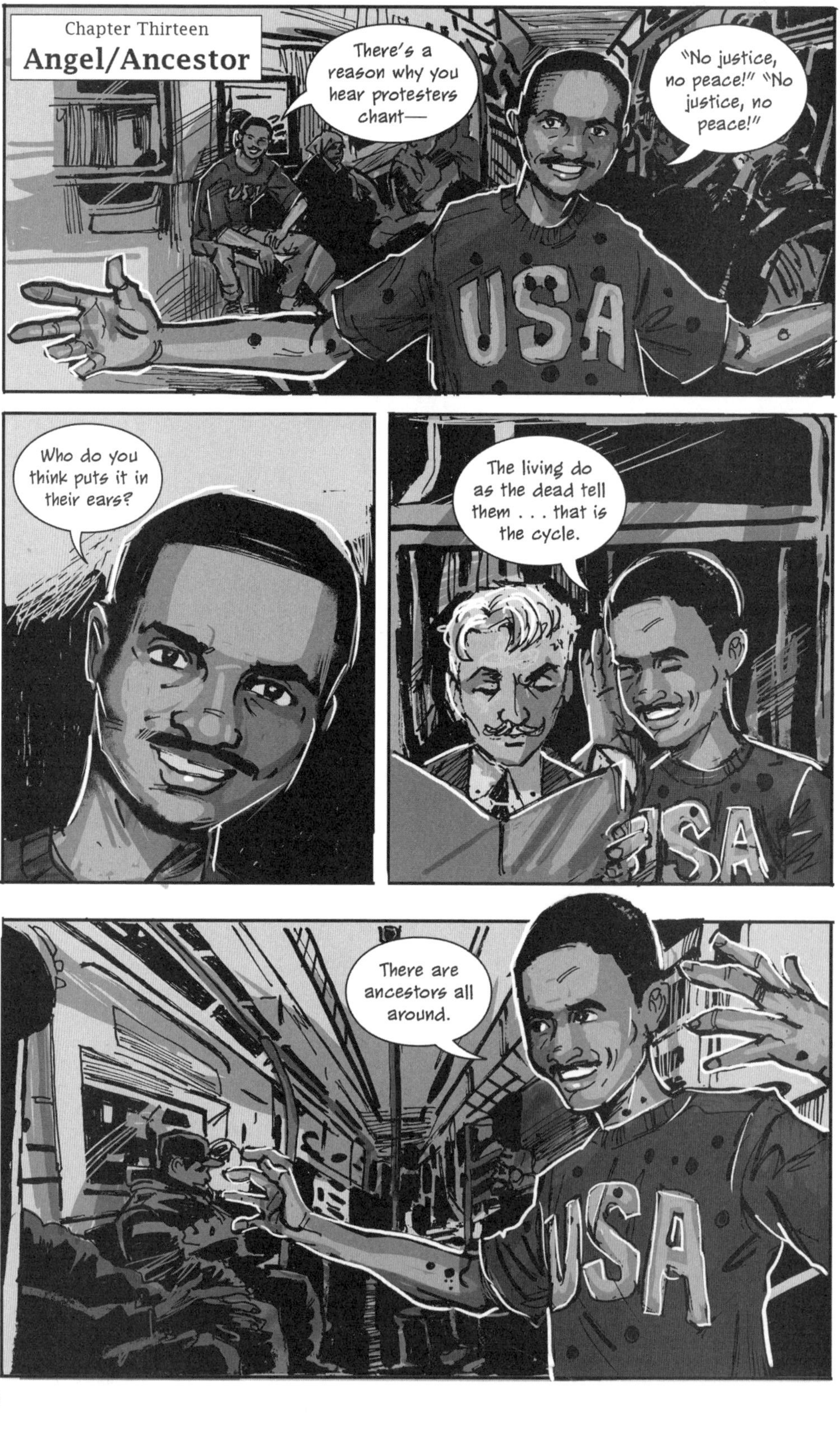
There's a reason why you hear protesters chant—
"No justice, no peace!" "No justice, no peace!"
Who do you think puts it in their ears?
The living do as the dead tell them . . . that is the cycle.
There are ancestors all around.

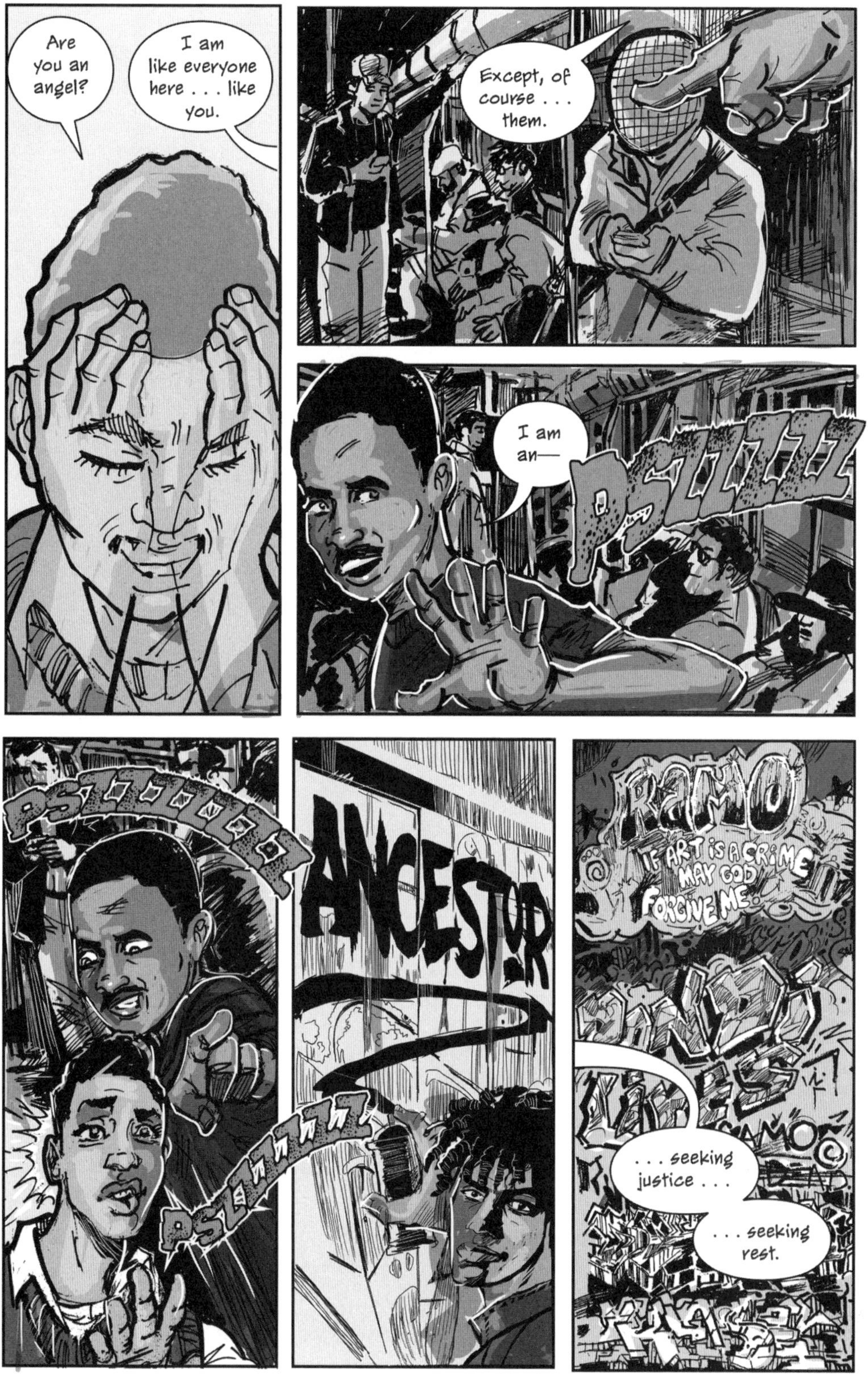
Are you an angel?
I am like everyone here . . . like you.
Except, of course . . . them.
I am an—
PSZZZZZ
ANCESTOR
RAMO
IF ART IS A CRIME MAY GOD FORGIVE ME.
. . . seeking justice . . .
. . . seeking rest.

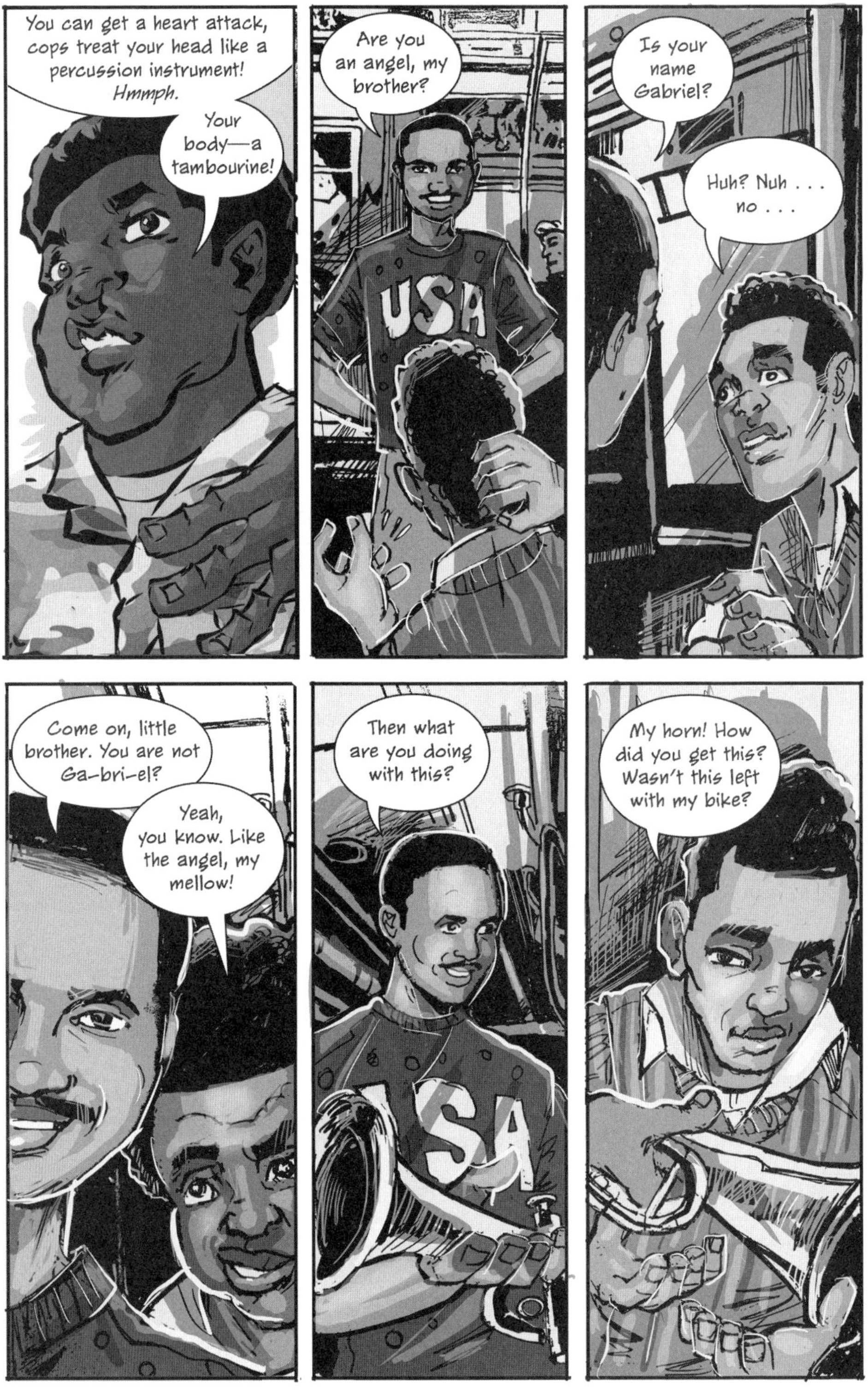
You can get a heart attack, cops treat your head like a percussion instrument! *Hmmph.*
Your body—a tambourine!
Are you an angel, my brother?
Is your name Gabriel?
Huh? Nuh . . . no . . .
Come on, little brother. You are not Ga-bri-el?
Yeah, you know. Like the angel, my mellow!
USA
Then what are you doing with this?
SA
My horn! How did you get this? Wasn't this left with my bike?

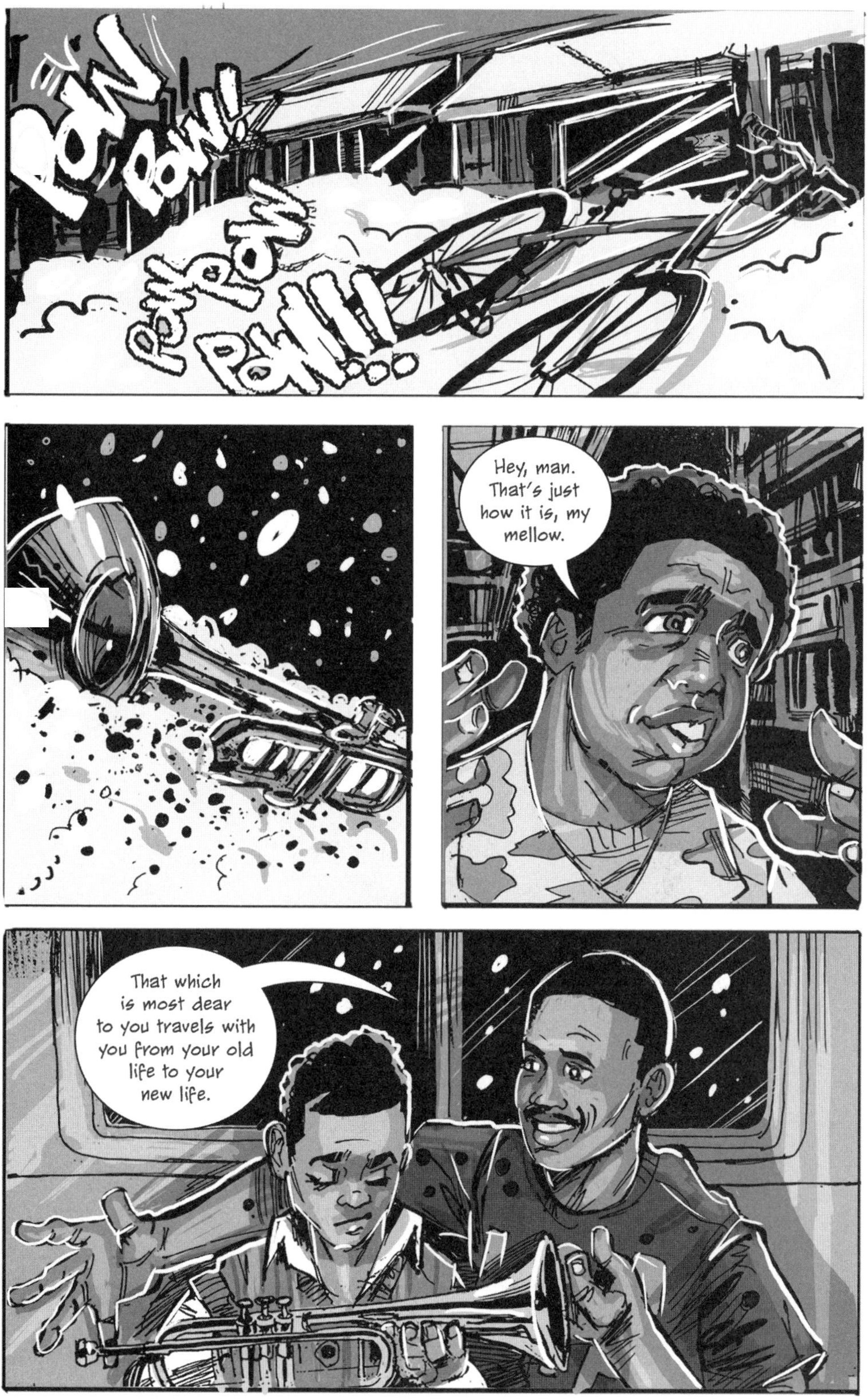
POW POW!
POW POW POW
POW!!!...
Hey, man. That's just how it is, my mellow.
That which is most dear to you travels with you from your old life to your new life.

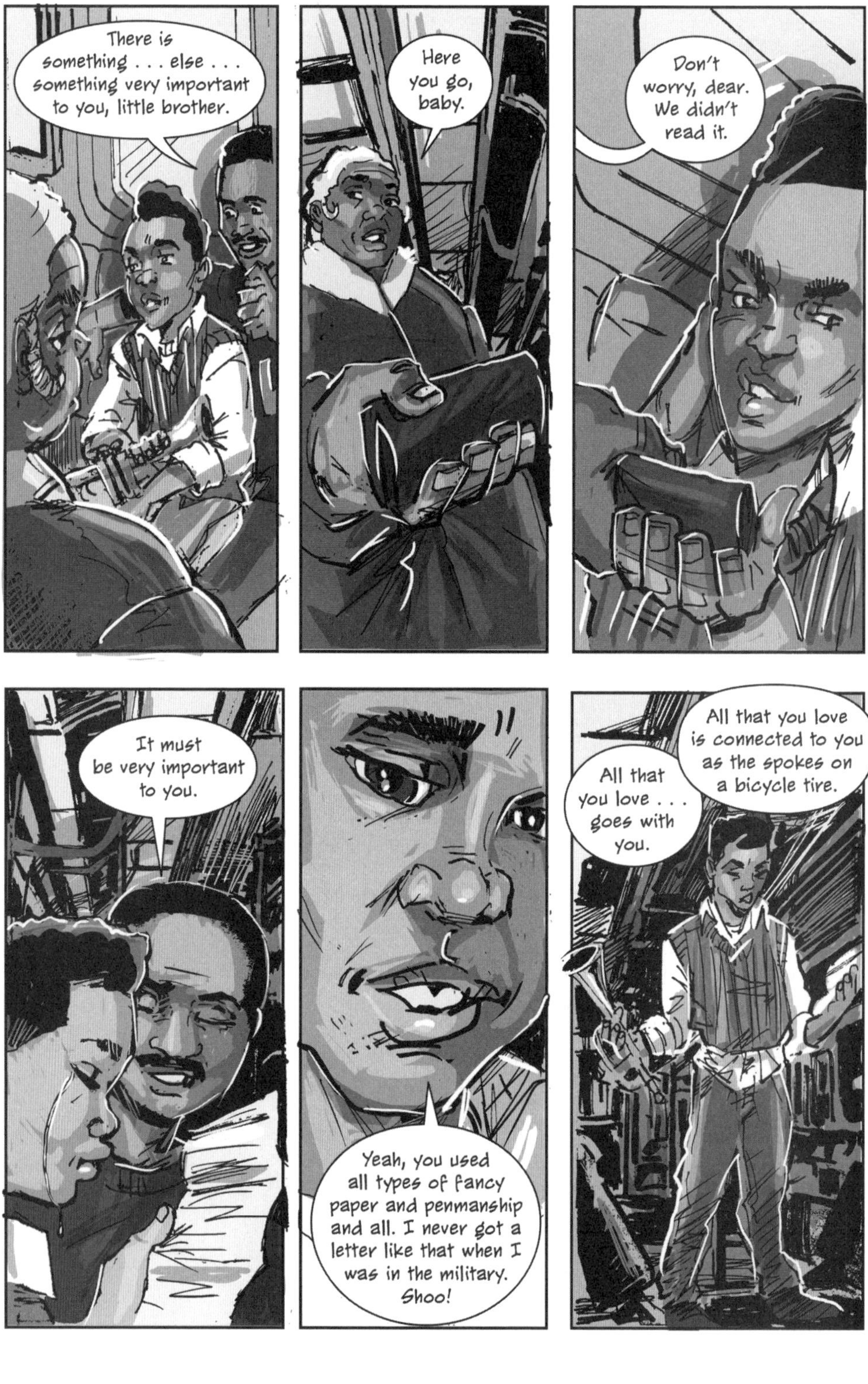
There is something . . . else . . . something very important to you, little brother.
Here you go, baby.
Don't worry, dear. We didn't read it.
It must be very important to you.
Yeah, you used all types of fancy paper and penmanship and all. I never got a letter like that when I was in the military. Shoo!
All that you love . . . goes with you.
All that you love is connected to you as the spokes on a bicycle tire.

Chapter Fourteen
Breaking News

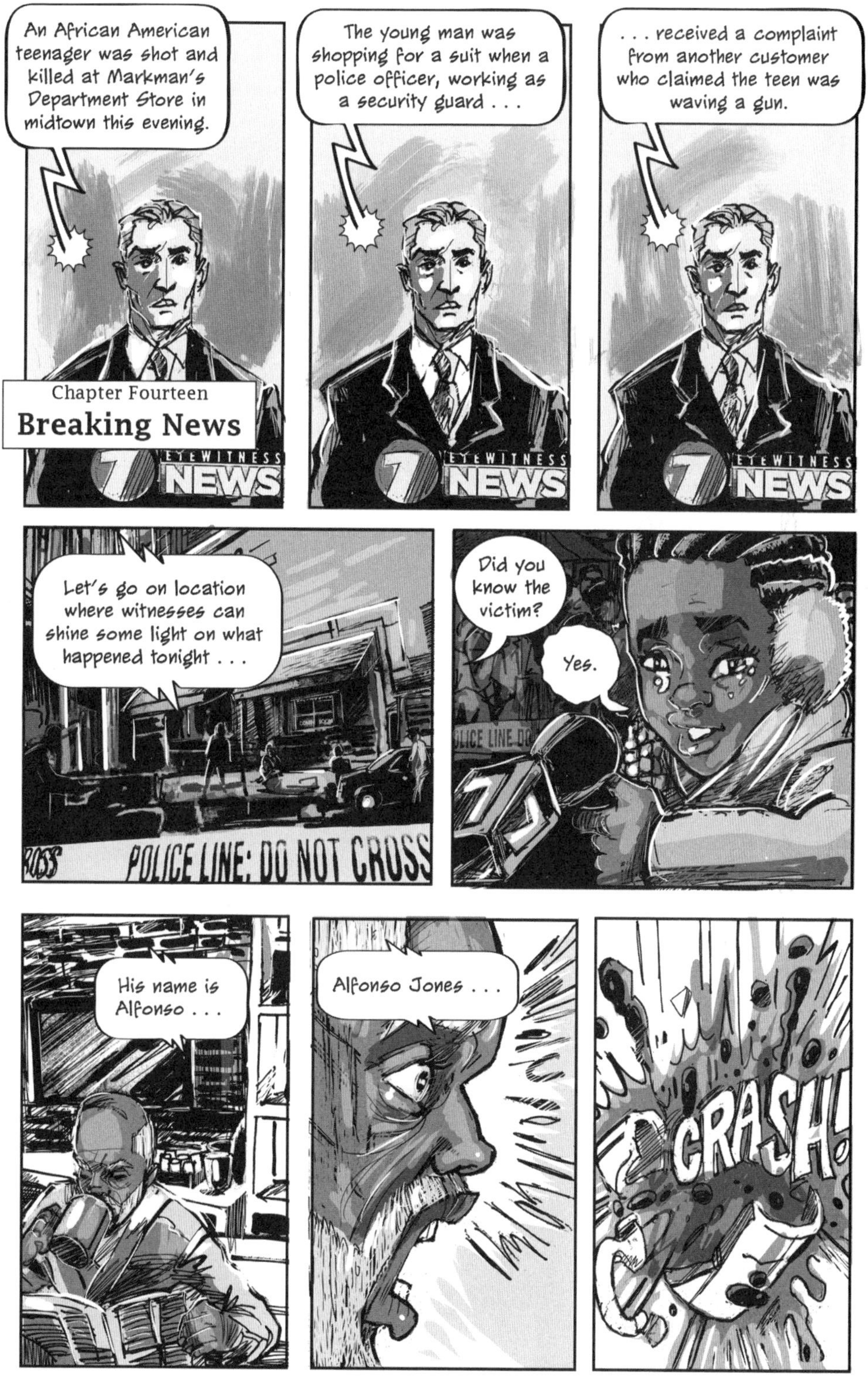

An African American teenager was shot and killed at Markman's Department Store in midtown this evening.
EYEWITNESS 7 NEWS
The young man was shopping for a suit when a police officer, working as a security guard . . .
EYEWITNESS 7 NEWS
. . . received a complaint from another customer who claimed the teen was waving a gun.
EYEWITNESS 7 NEWS
Let's go on location where witnesses can shine some light on what happened tonight . . .
POLICE LINE: DO NOT CROSS
Did you know the victim?
Yes.
His name is Alfonso . . .
Alfonso Jones . . .
CRASH!

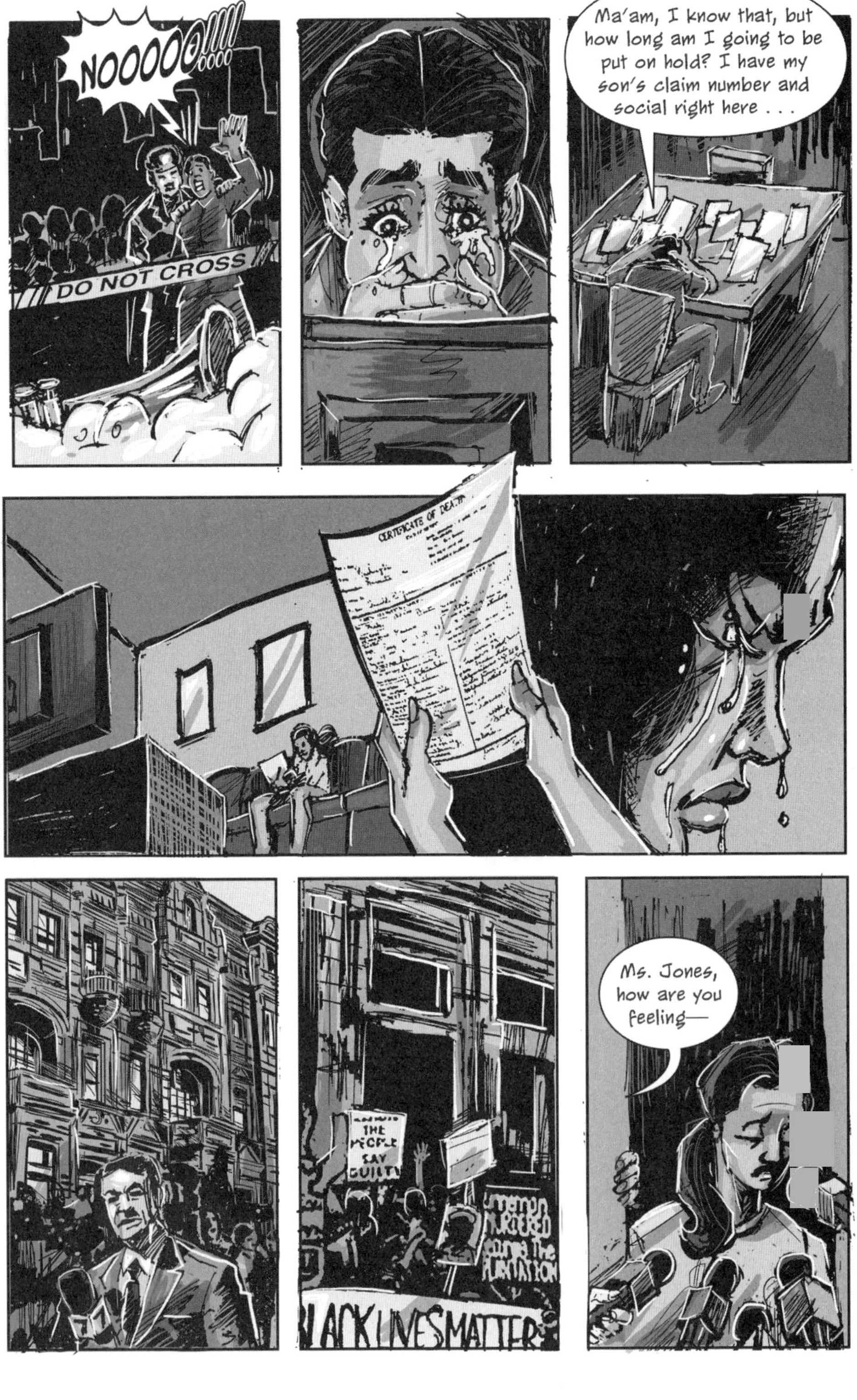
NOOOOO!!!!oooo
DO NOT CROSS
Ma'am, I know that, but how long am I going to be put on hold? I have my son's claim number and social right here . . .
CERTIFICATE OF DEATH
THE PEOPLE SAY GUILTY
BLACK LIVES MATTER
Ms. Jones, how are you feeling—

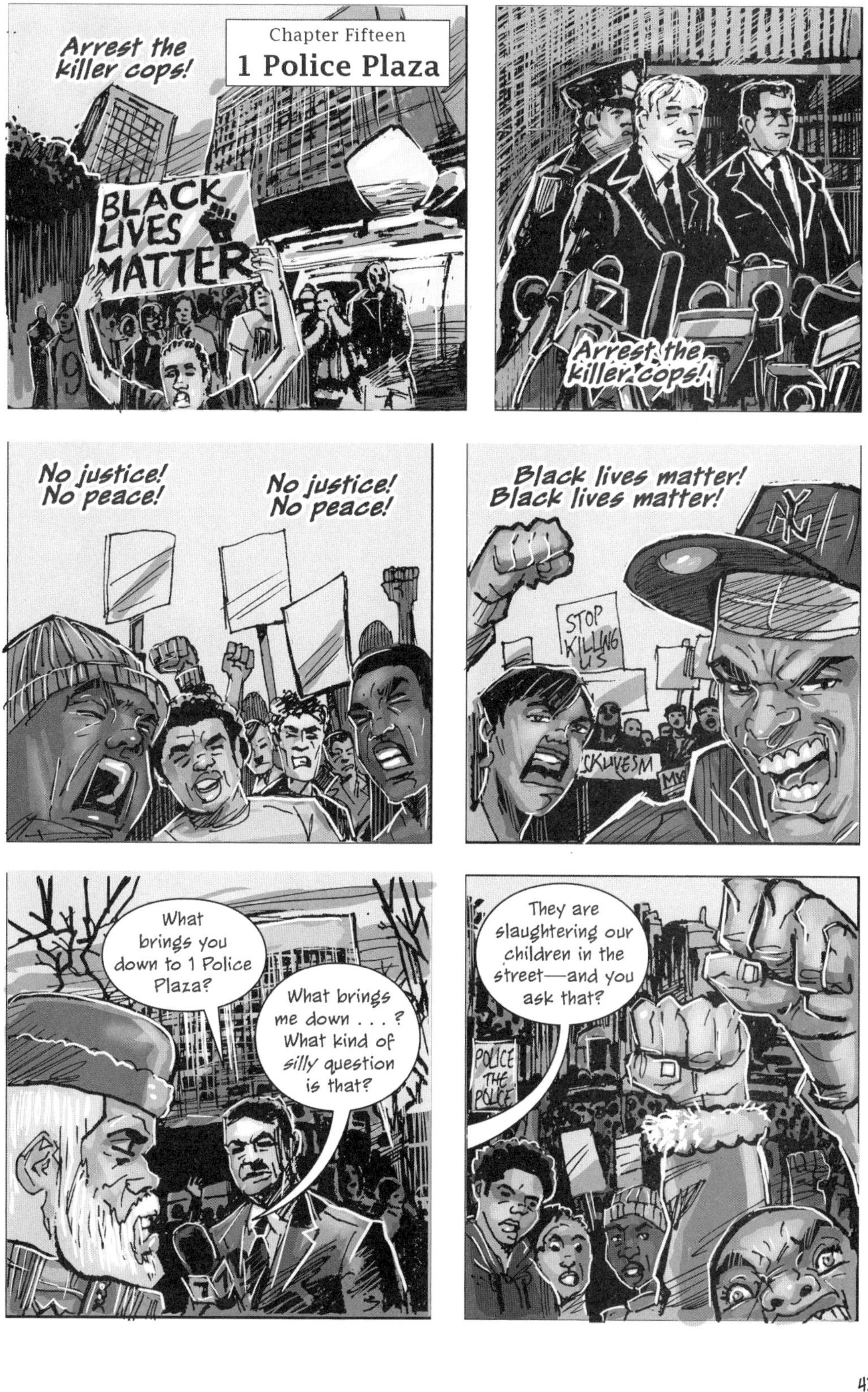
Chapter Fifteen
1 Police Plaza
Arrest the killer cops!
BLACK LIVES MATTER
Arrest the killer cops!
No justice! No peace!
No justice! No peace!
Black lives matter! Black lives matter!
STOP KILLING US
What brings you down to 1 Police Plaza?
What brings me down . . . ? What kind of *silly* question is that?
They are slaughtering our children in the street—and you ask that?
POLICE THE POLICE

Chapter Sixteen

Apollo

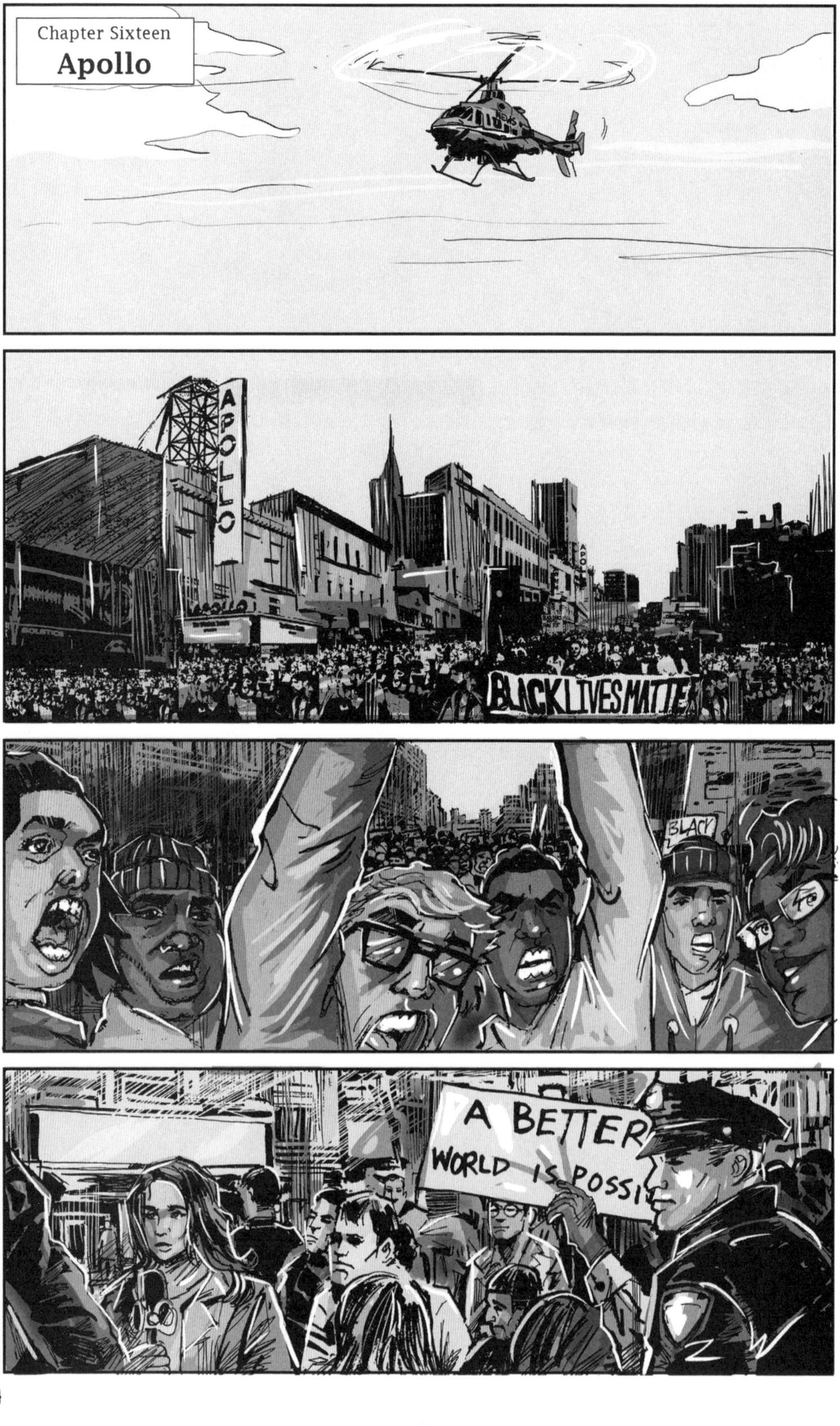
APOLLO
BLACK LIVES MATTE
BLACK
A BETTER
WORLD IS POSSI

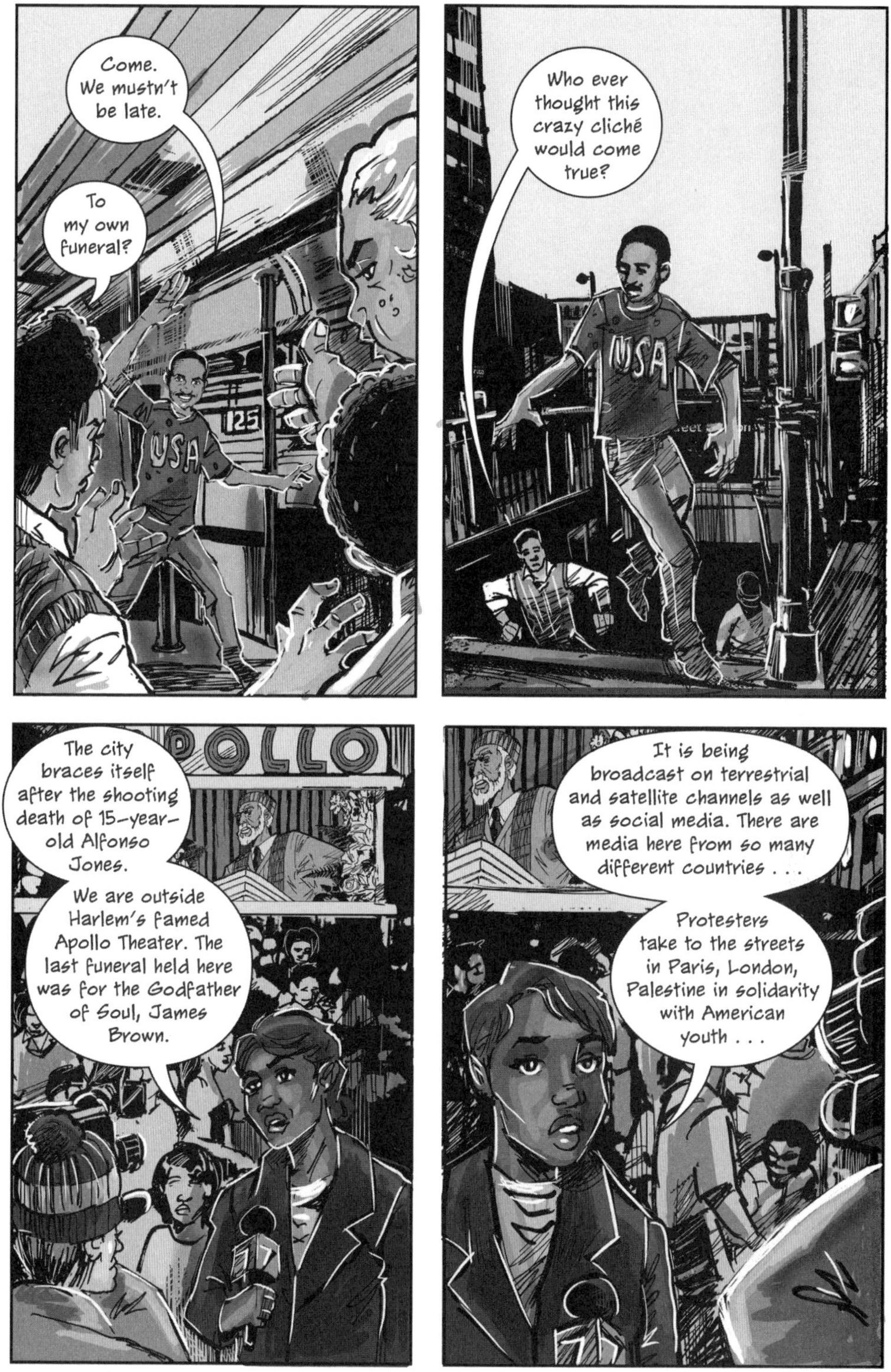
Come. We mustn't be late.
To my own funeral?
Who ever thought this crazy cliché would come true?
The city braces itself after the shooting death of 15-year-old Alfonso Jones.
We are outside Harlem's famed Apollo Theater. The last funeral held here was for the Godfather of Soul, James Brown.
It is being broadcast on terrestrial and satellite channels as well as social media. There are media here from so many different countries . . .
Protesters take to the streets in Paris, London, Palestine in solidarity with American youth . . .

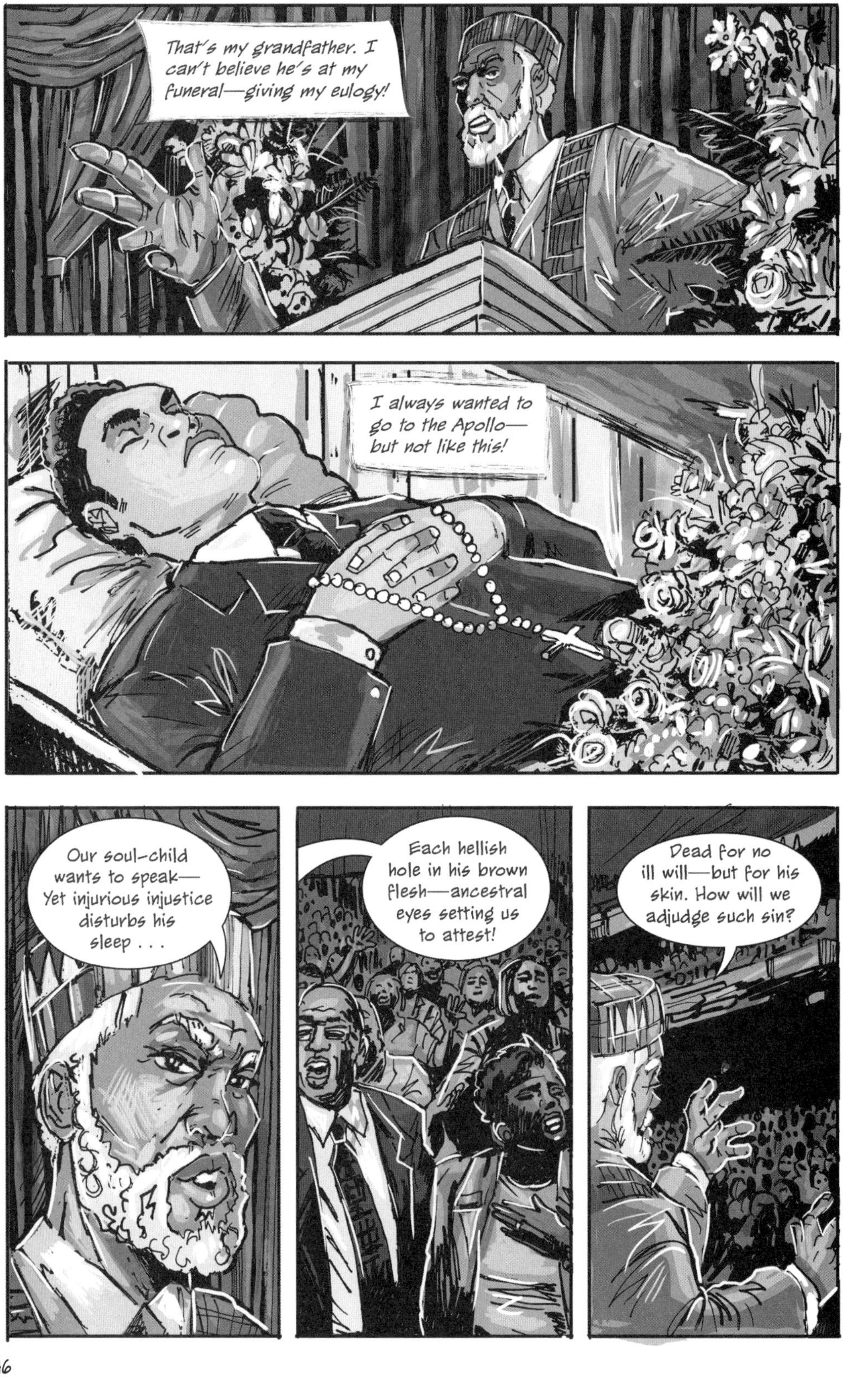
That's my grandfather. I can't believe he's at my funeral—giving my eulogy!
I always wanted to go to the Apollo—but not like this!
Our soul-child wants to speak—Yet injurious injustice disturbs his sleep . . .
Each hellish hole in his brown flesh—ancestral eyes setting us to attest!
Dead for no ill will—but for his skin. How will we adjudge such sin?

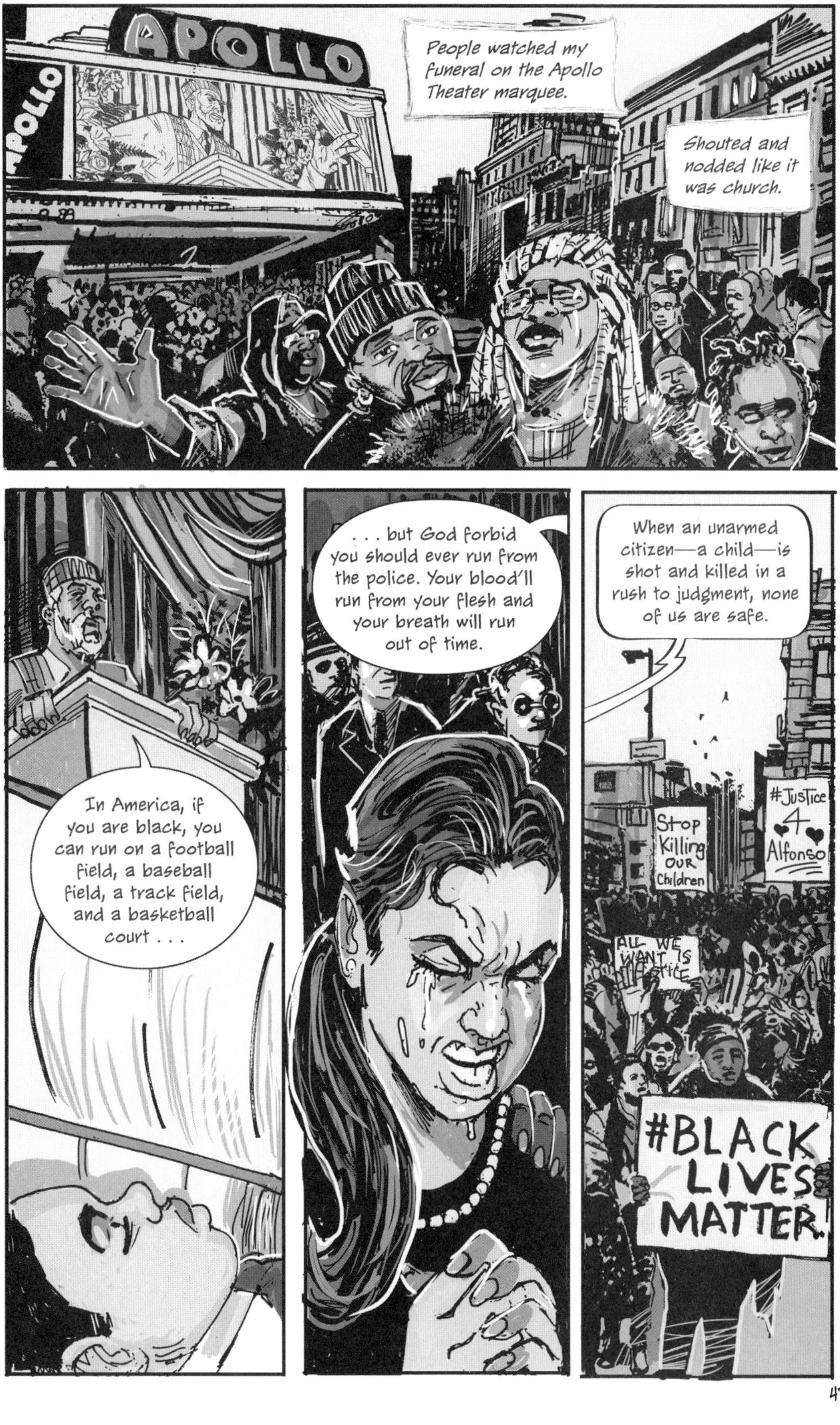
APOLLO
People watched my funeral on the Apollo Theater marquee.
Shouted and nodded like it was church.
In America, if you are black, you can run on a football field, a baseball field, a track field, and a basketball court . . .
. . . but God forbid you should ever run from the police. Your blood'll run from your flesh and your breath will run out of time.
When an unarmed citizen—a child—is shot and killed in a rush to judgment, none of us are safe.
Stop Killing OUR Children
#JUSTICE 4 Alfonso
#BLACK LIVES MATTER

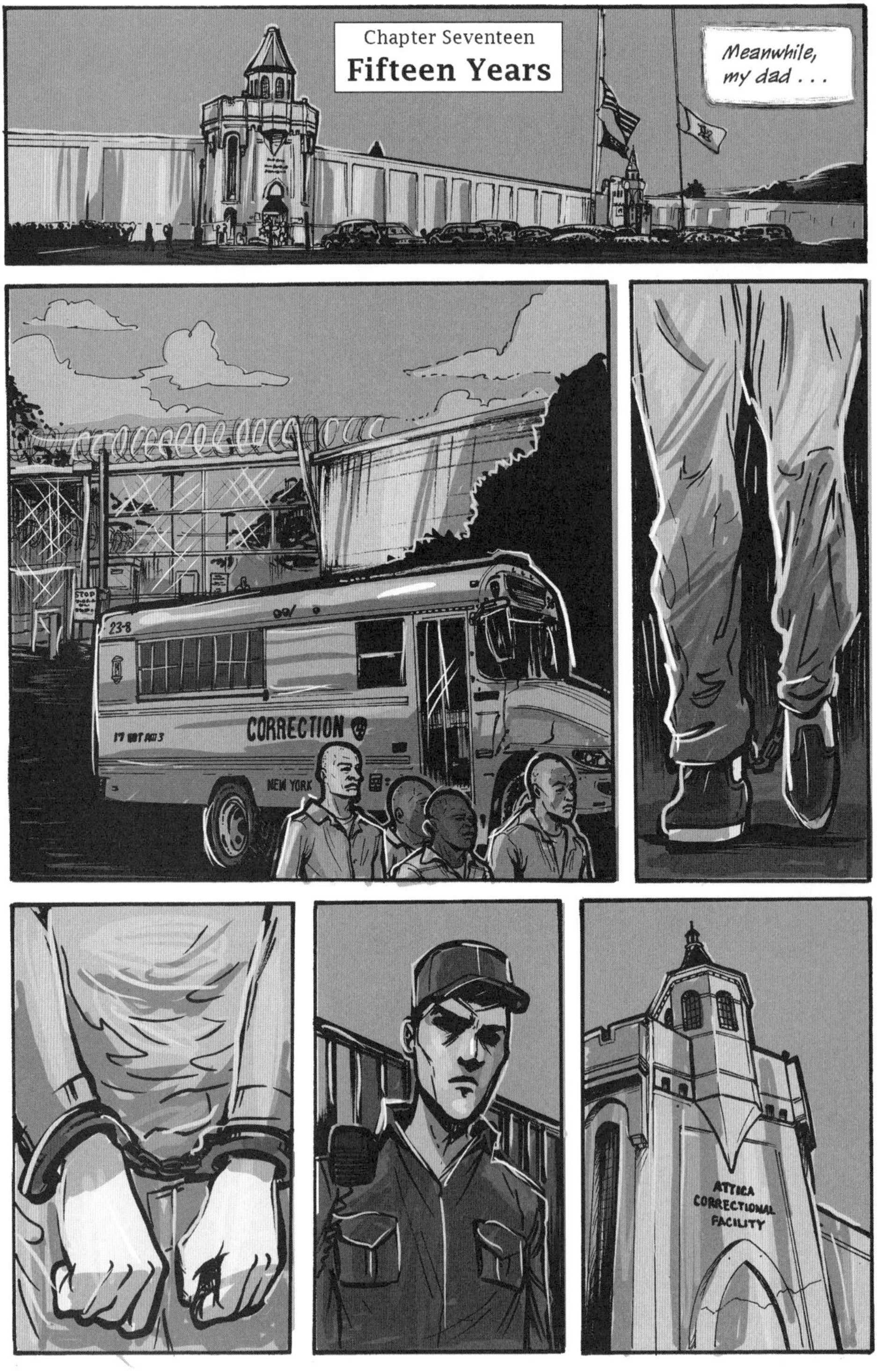
Chapter Seventeen
Fifteen Years
Meanwhile, my dad . . .
23-8
CORRECTION
NEW YORK
ATTICA CORRECTIONAL FACILITY

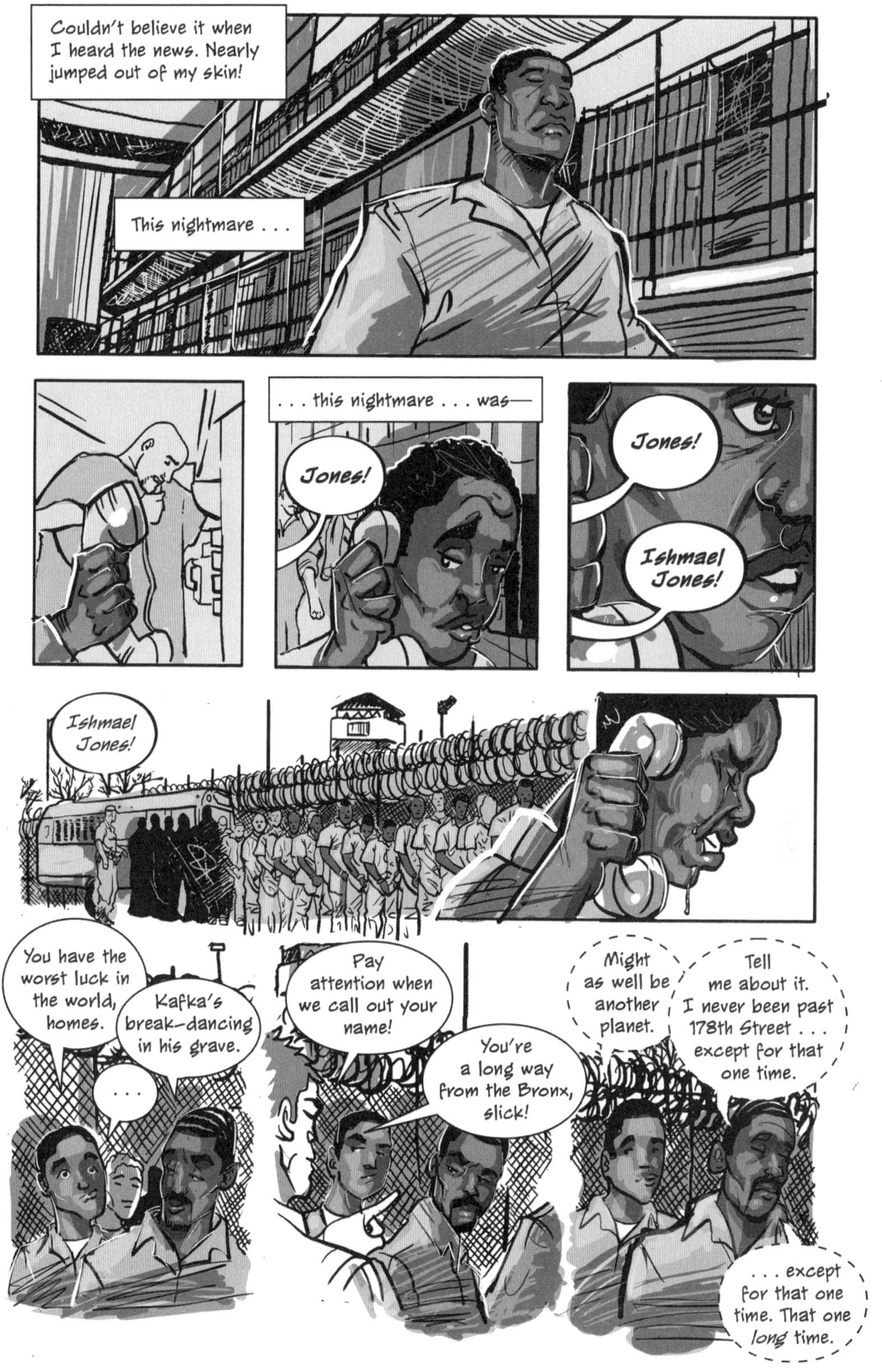

Couldn't believe it when I heard the news. Nearly jumped out of my skin!
This nightmare . . .
. . . this nightmare . . . was—
Jones!
Jones!
Ishmael Jones!
Ishmael Jones!
You have the worst luck in the world, homes.
Kafka's break-dancing in his grave.
. . .
Pay attention when we call out your name!
You're a long way from the Bronx, slick!
Might as well be another planet.
Tell me about it. I never been past 178th Street . . . except for that one time.
. . . except for that one time. That one *long* time.

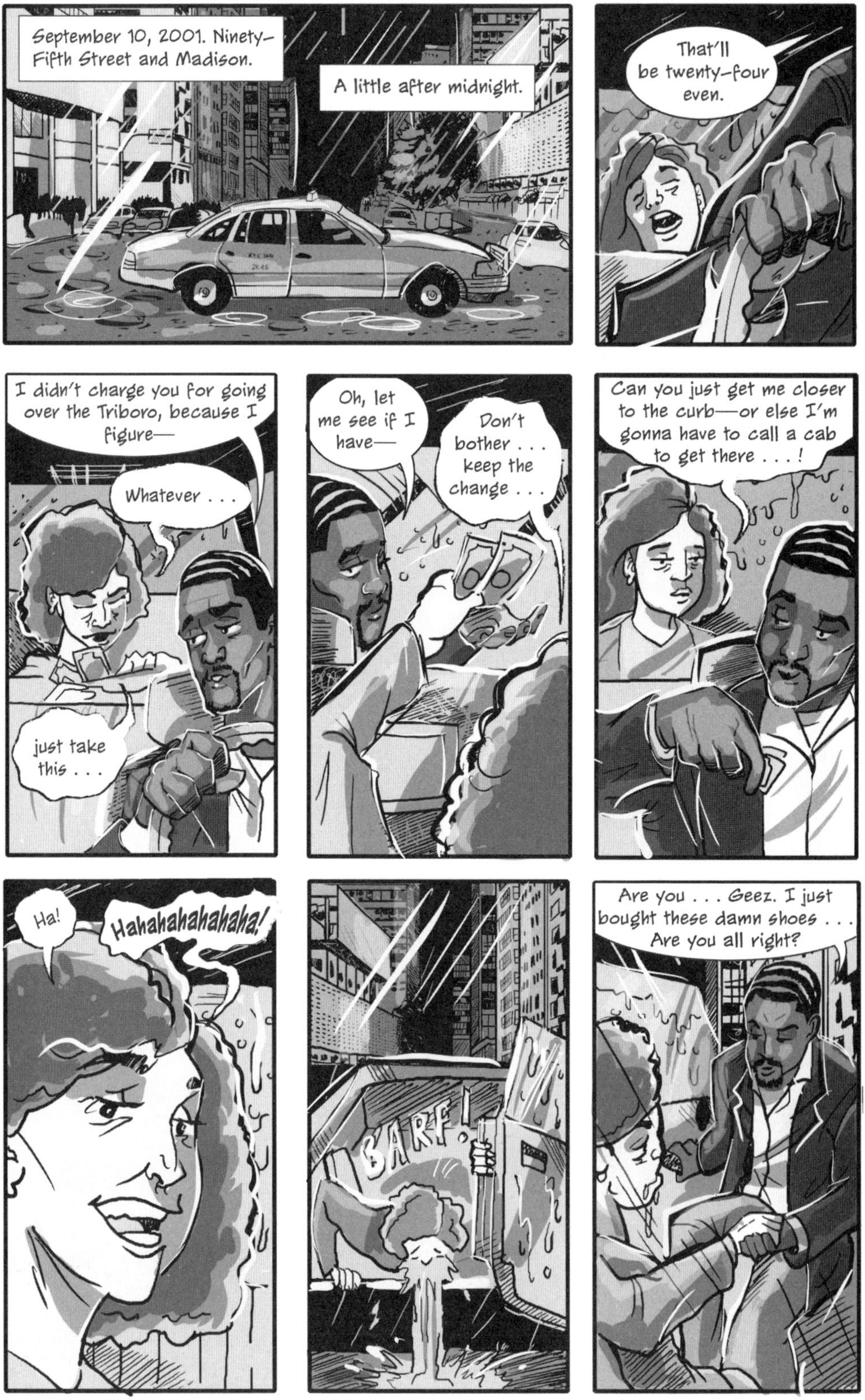
September 10, 2001. Ninety-Fifth Street and Madison.
A little after midnight.
That'll be twenty-four even.
I didn't charge you for going over the Triboro, because I figure—
Whatever . . .
just take this . . .
Oh, let me see if I have—
Don't bother . . . keep the change . . .
Can you just get me closer to the curb—or else I'm gonna have to call a cab to get there . . . !
Ha!
Hahahahahahaha!
BARF!
Are you . . . Geez. I just bought these damn shoes . . . Are you all right?

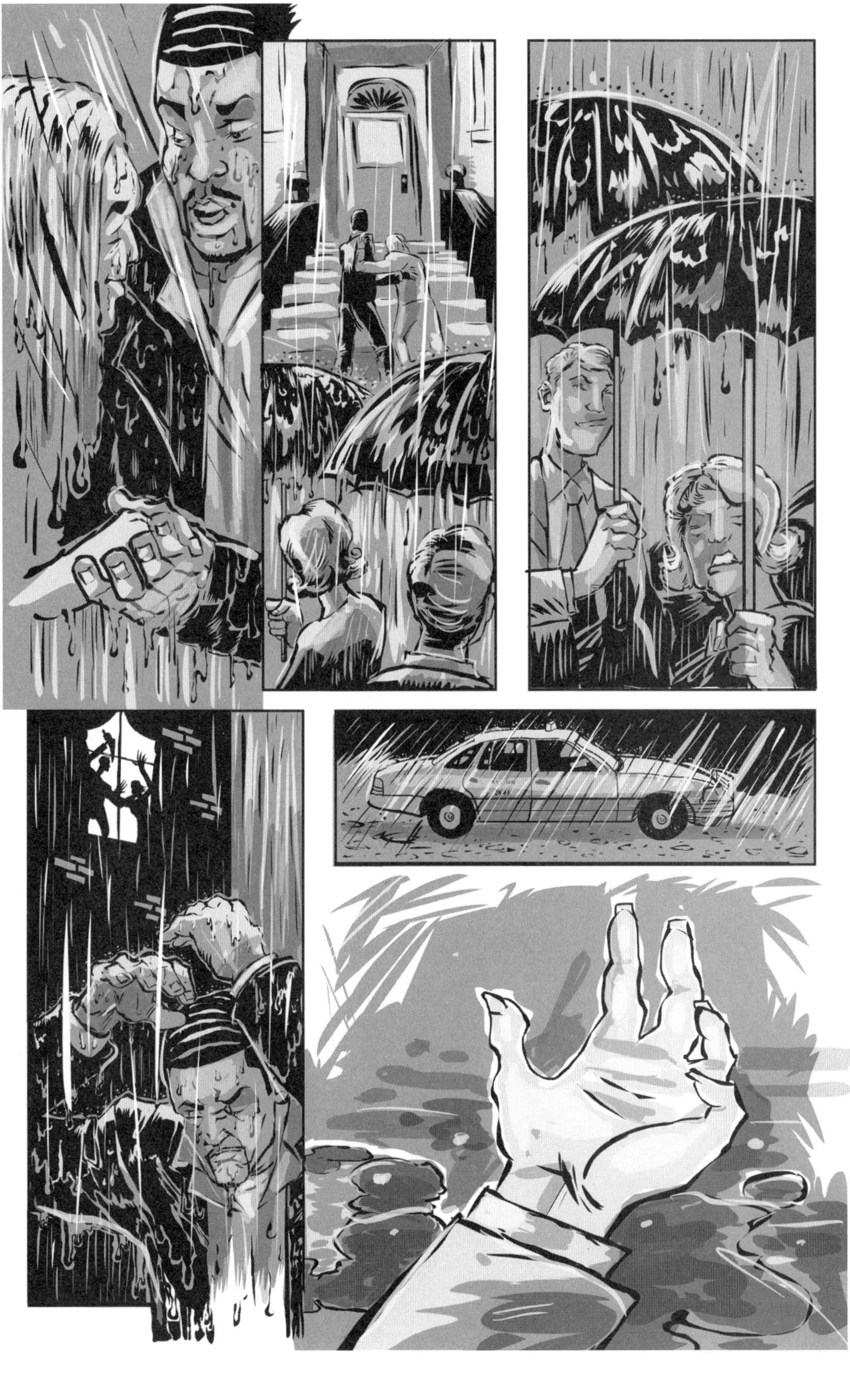

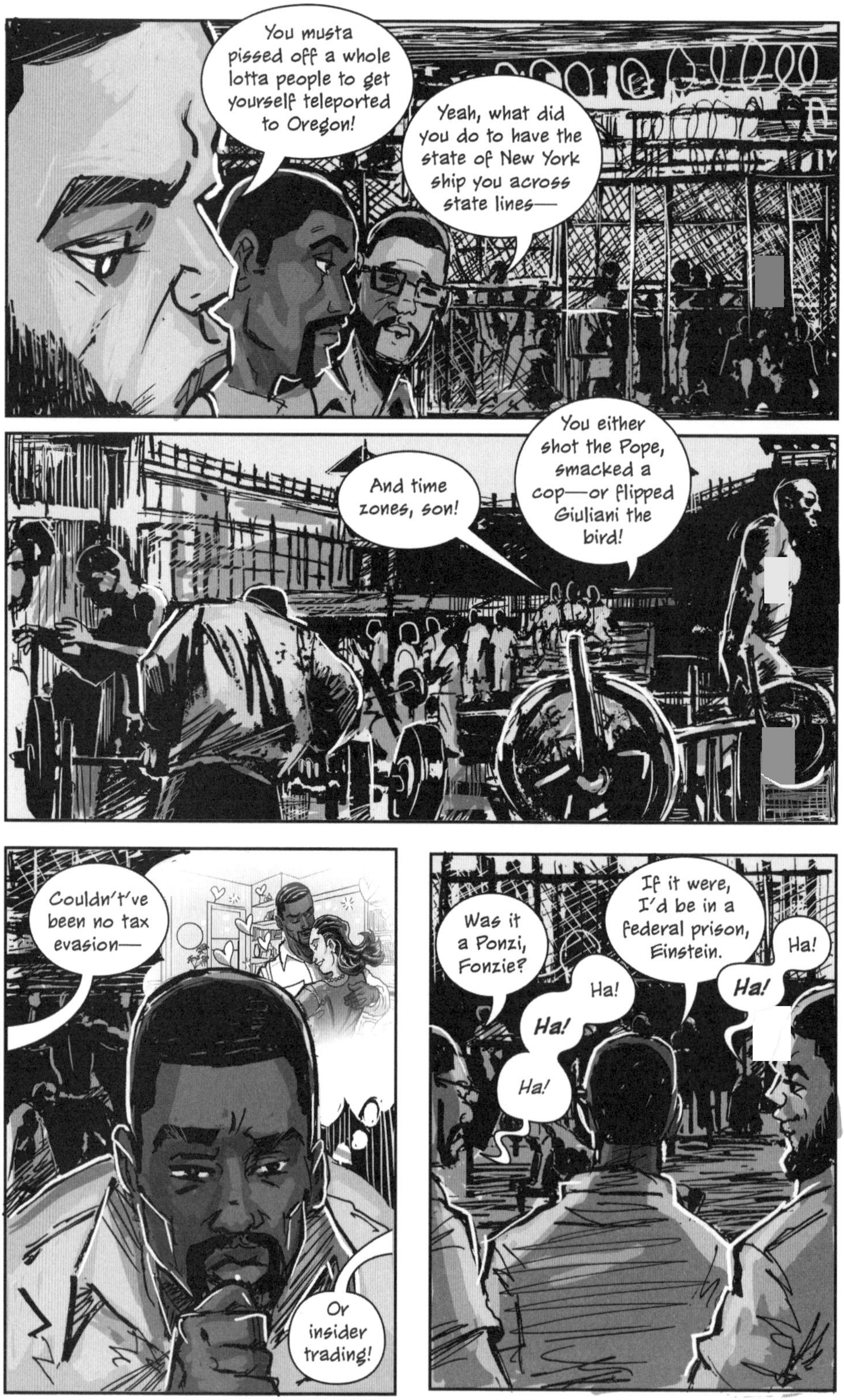
You musta pissed off a whole lotta people to get yourself teleported to Oregon!
Yeah, what did you do to have the state of New York ship you across state lines—
And time zones, son!
You either shot the Pope, smacked a cop—or flipped Giuliani the bird!
Couldn't've been no tax evasion—
Or insider trading!
Was it a Ponzi, Fonzie?
If it were, I'd be in a federal prison, Einstein.
Ha!
Ha!
Ha!
Ha!
Ha!

Chapter Eighteen

Spokes on a Wheel

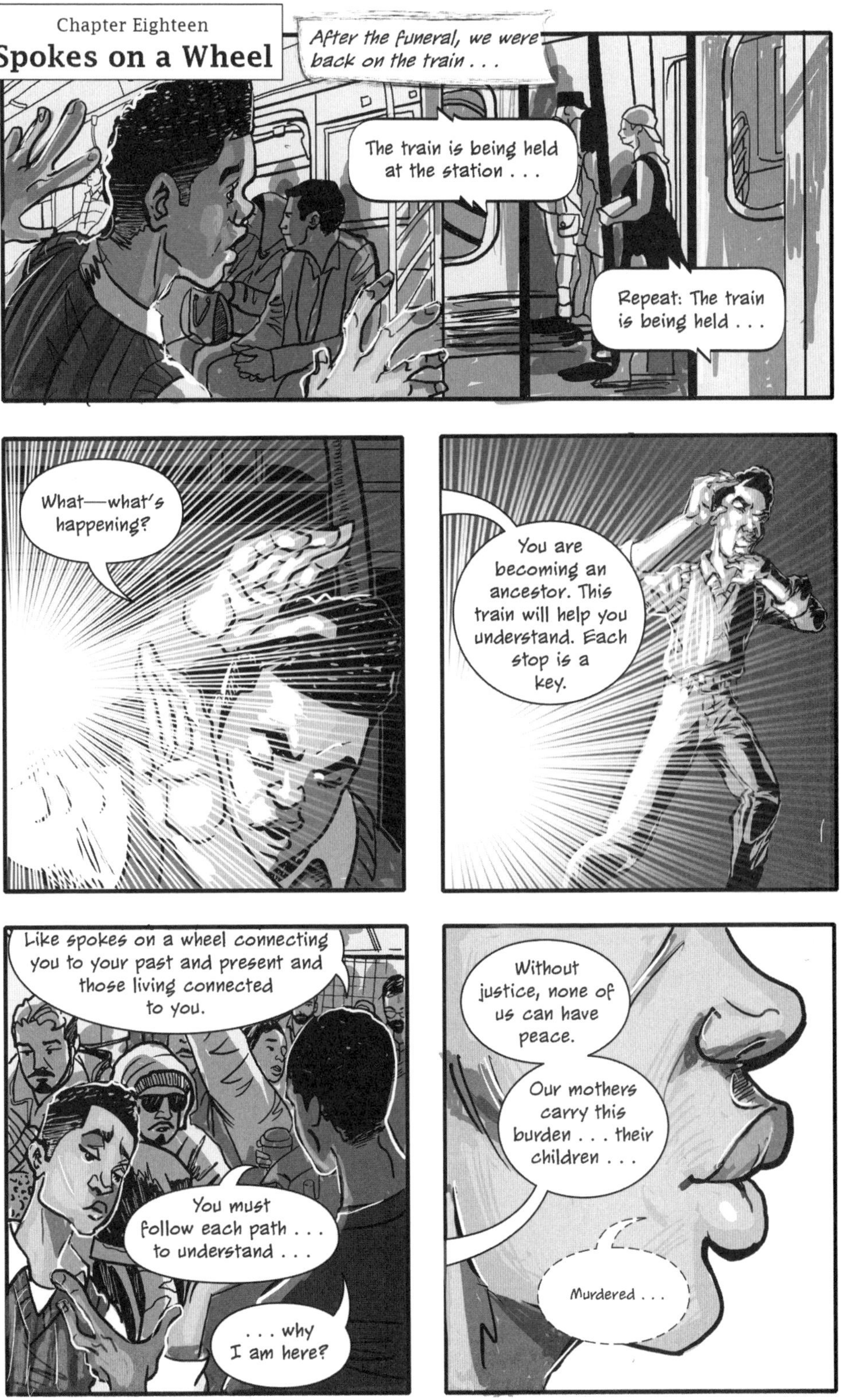
After the funeral, we were back on the train . . .
The train is being held at the station . . .
Repeat: The train is being held . . .
What—what's happening?
You are becoming an ancestor. This train will help you understand. Each stop is a key.
Like spokes on a wheel connecting you to your past and present and those living connected to you.
You must follow each path . . . to understand . . .
. . . why I am here?
Without justice, none of us can have peace.
Our mothers carry this burden . . . their children . . .
Murdered . . .

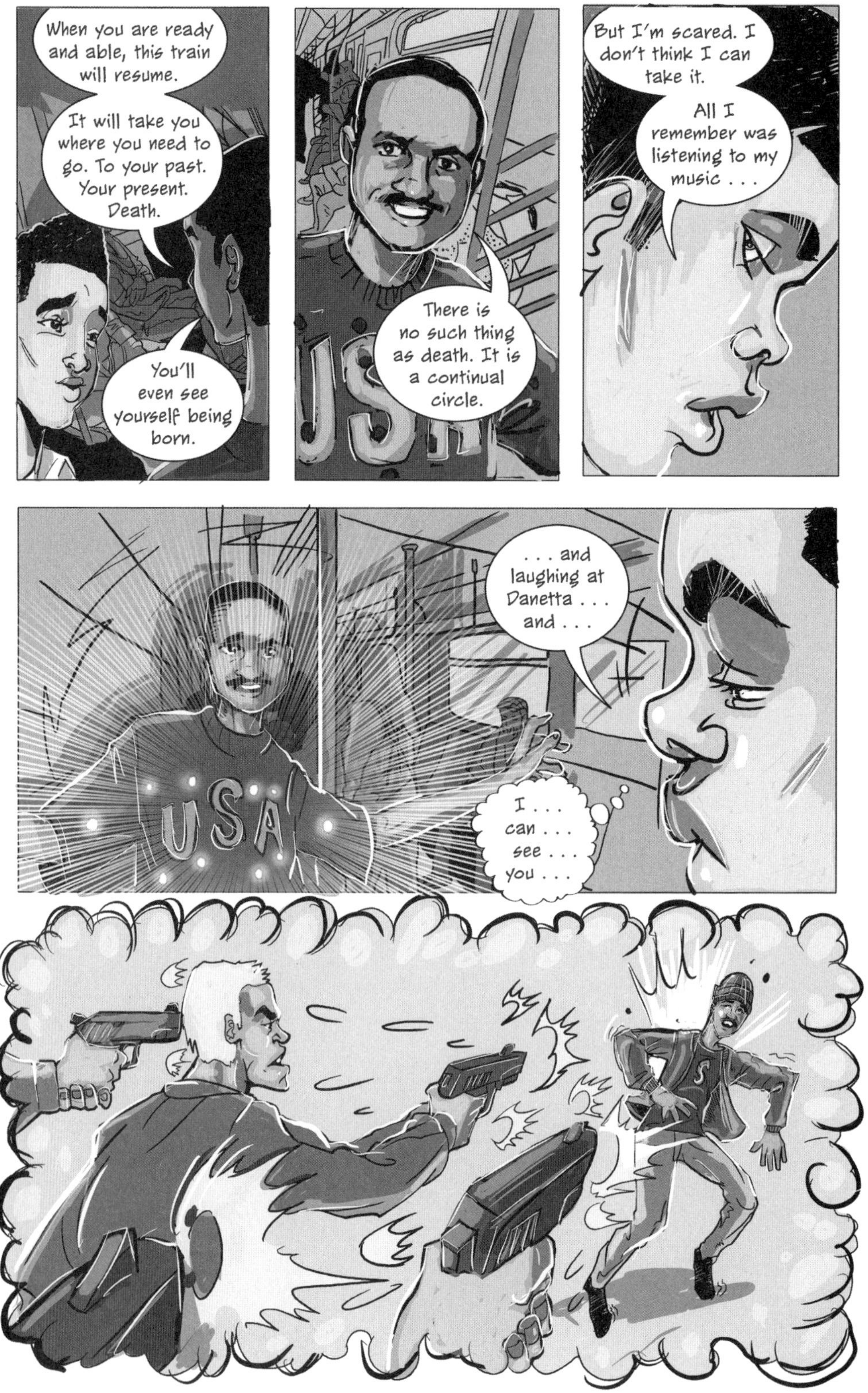
When you are ready and able, this train will resume.
It will take you where you need to go. To your past. Your present. Death.
You'll even see yourself being born.
There is no such thing as death. It is a continual circle.
But I'm scared. I don't think I can take it.
All I remember was listening to my music . . .
. . . and laughing at Danetta . . . and . . .
I . . . can . . . see . . . you . . .

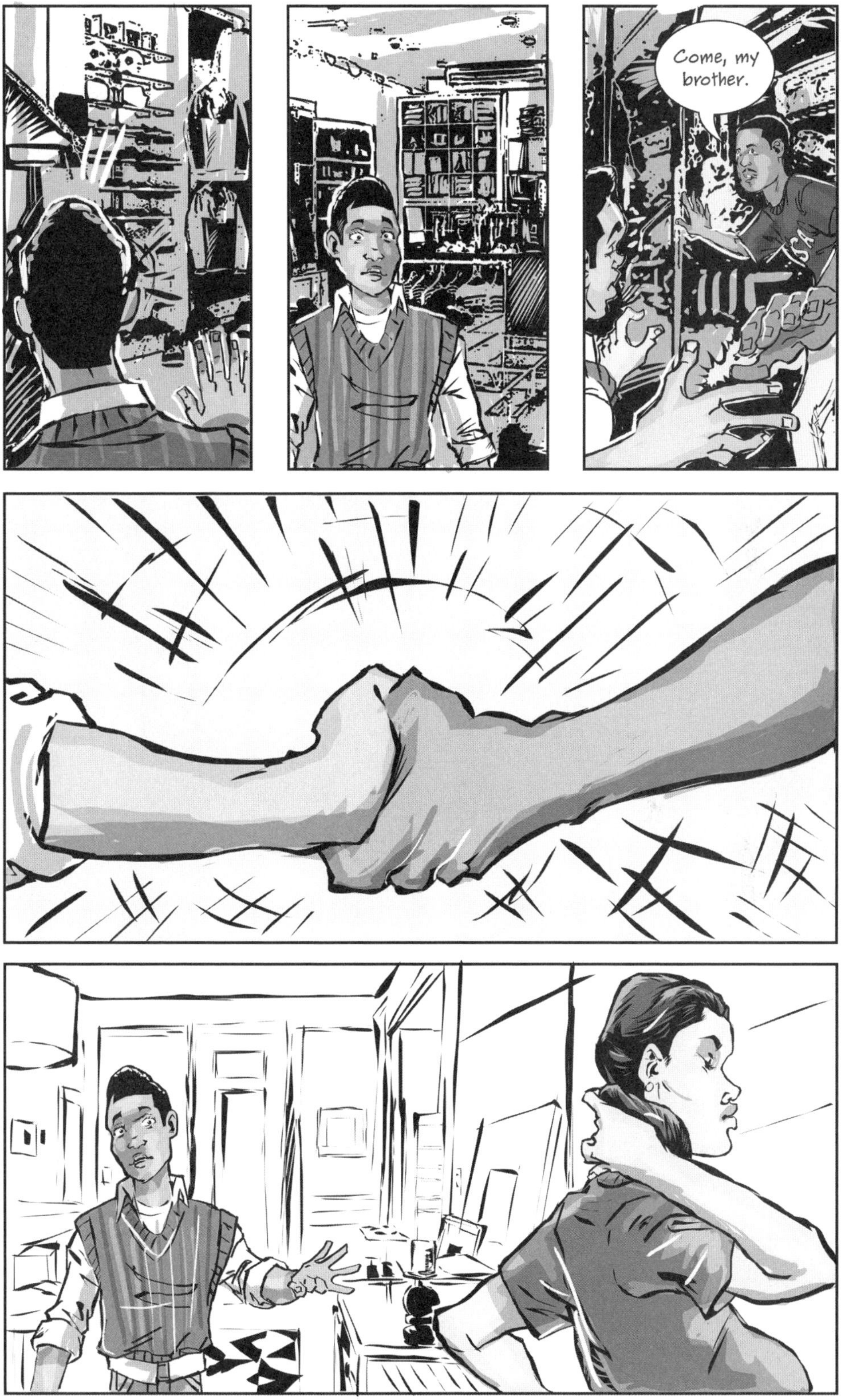
Come, my brother.

Chapter Nineteen

Altar

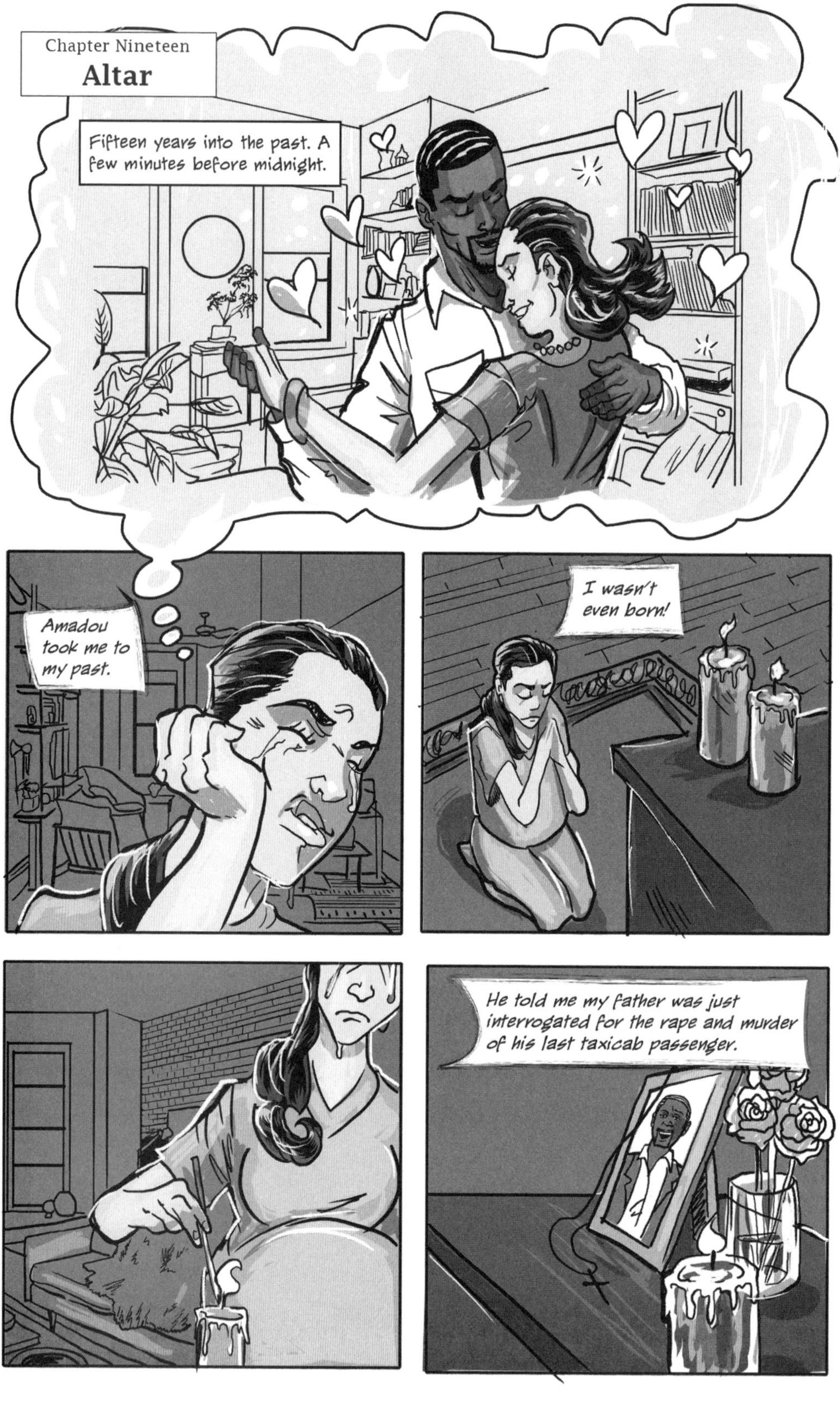

Fifteen years into the past. A few minutes before midnight.
Amadou took me to my past.
I wasn't even born!
He told me my father was just interrogated for the rape and murder of his last taxicab passenger.

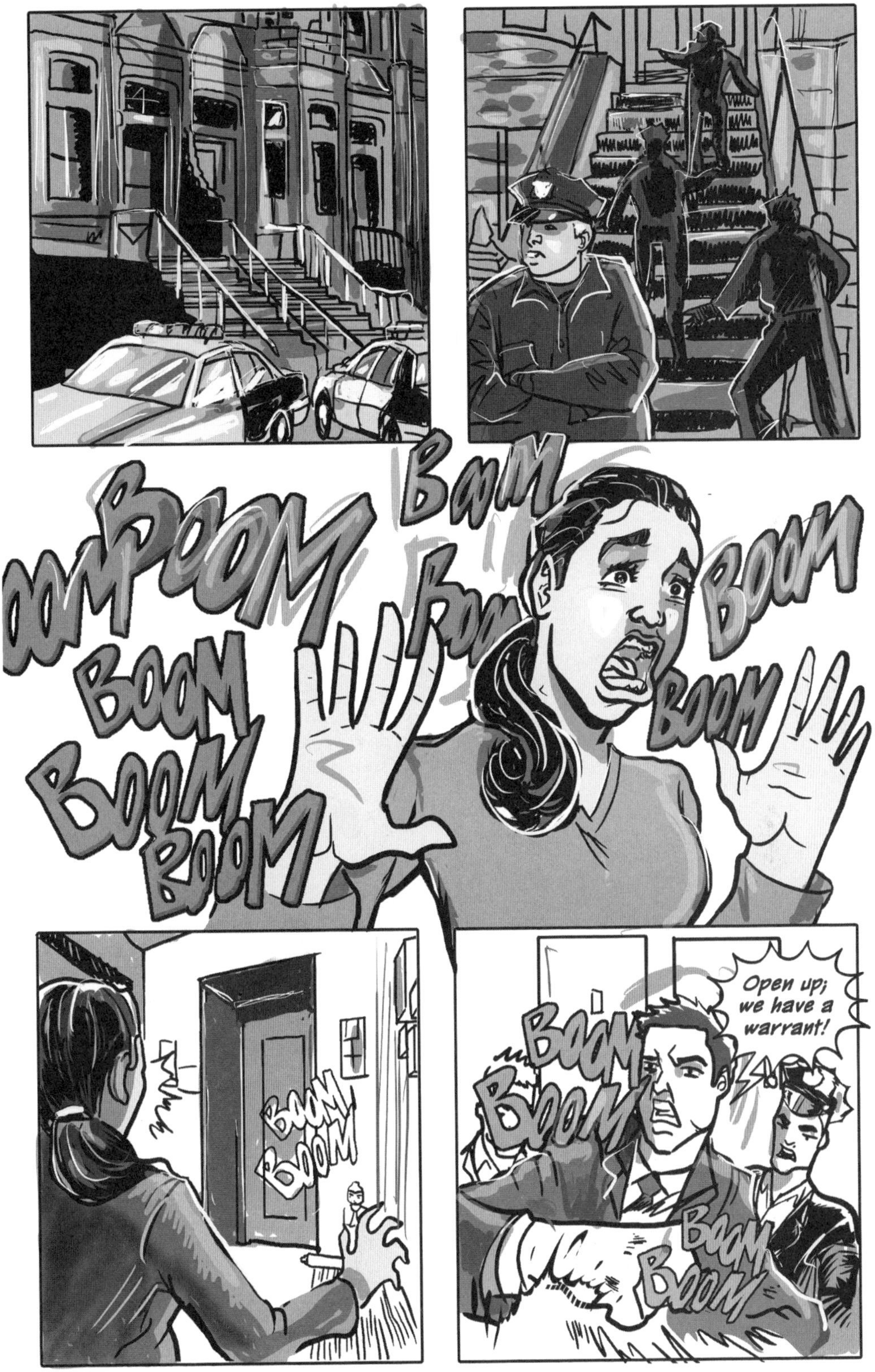
BOOM
BOOM
BOOM
BOOM
BOOM
BOOM
BOOM
BOOM
BOOM
BOOM
Open up; we have a warrant!
BOOM
BOOM

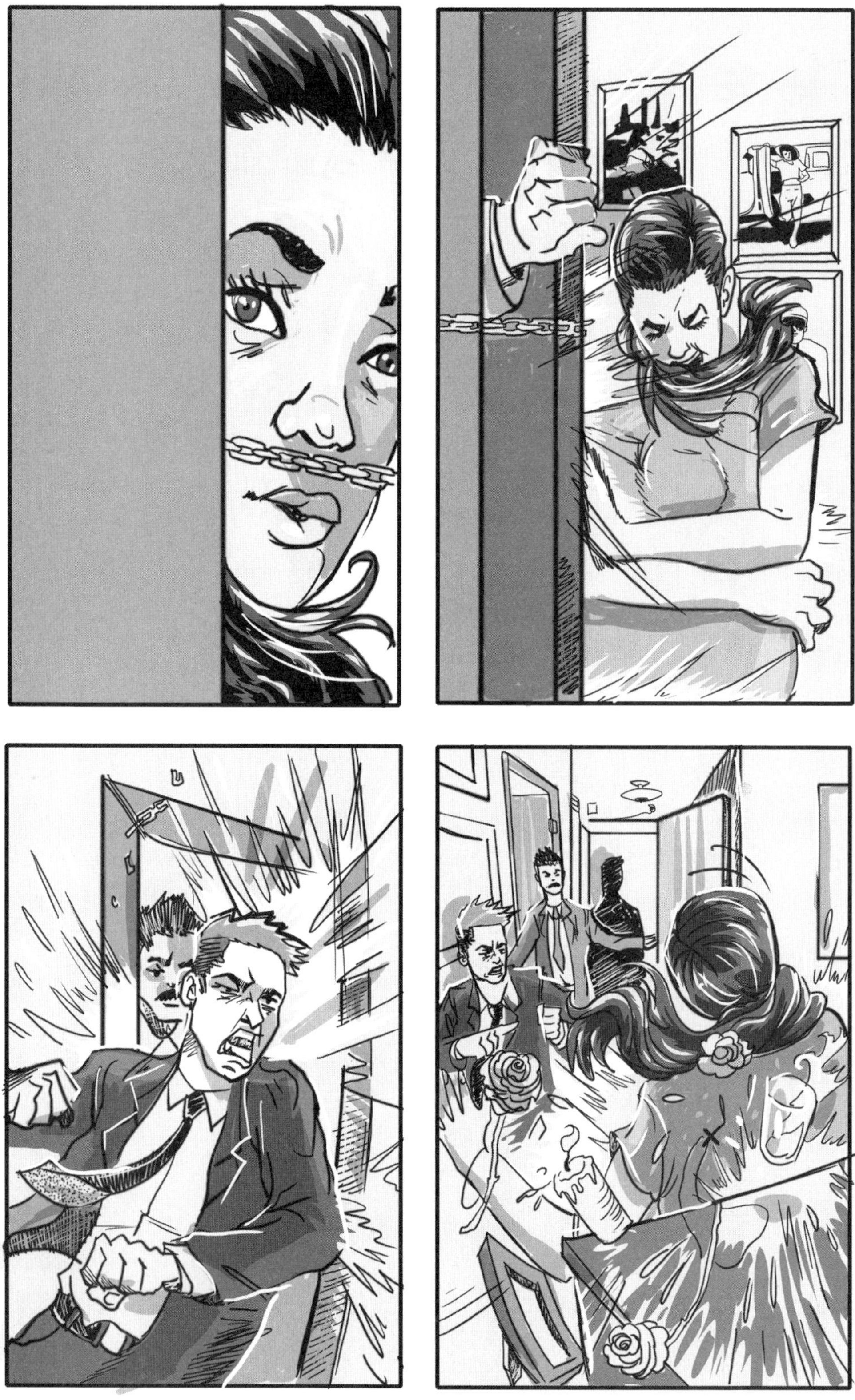

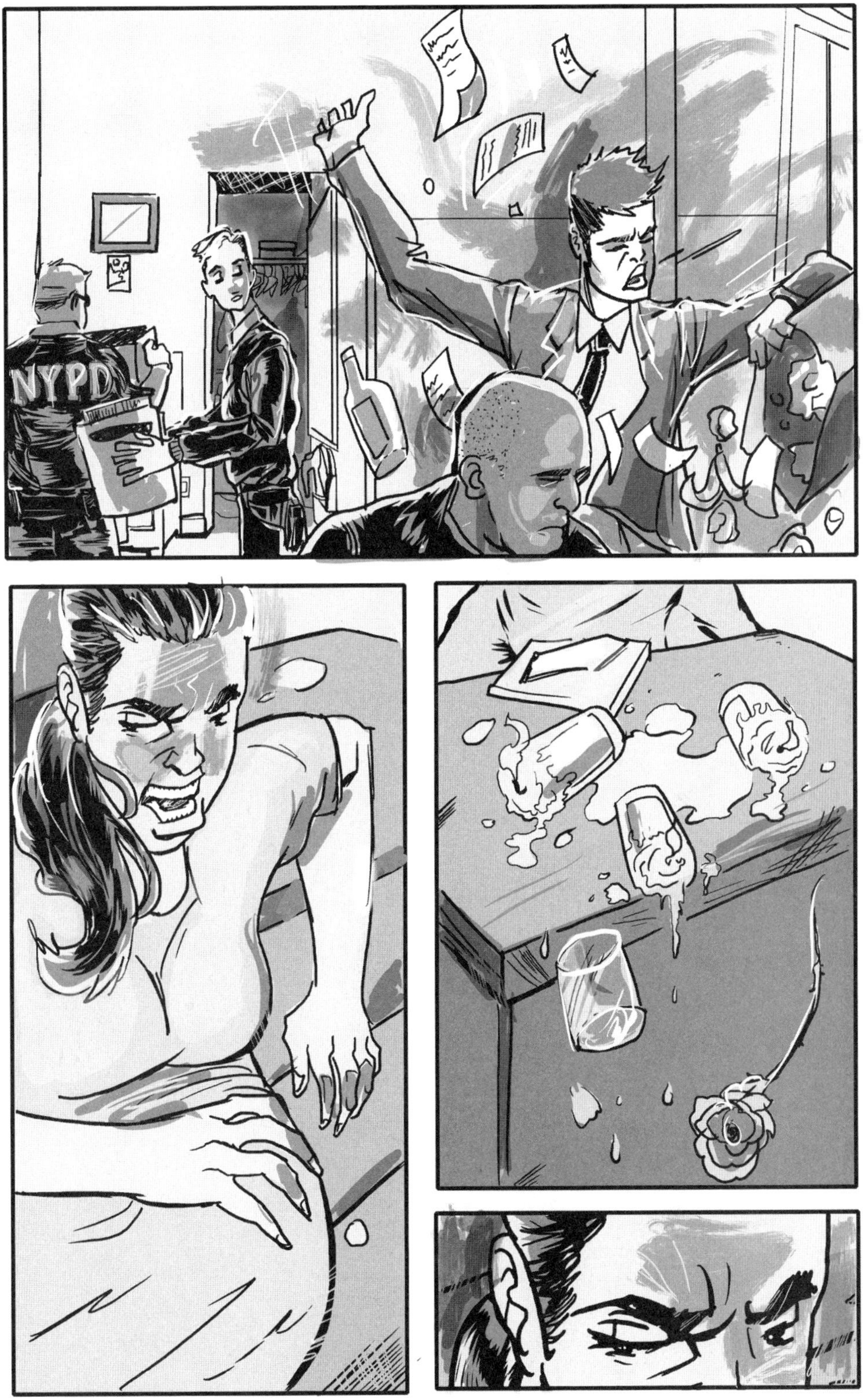
NYPD

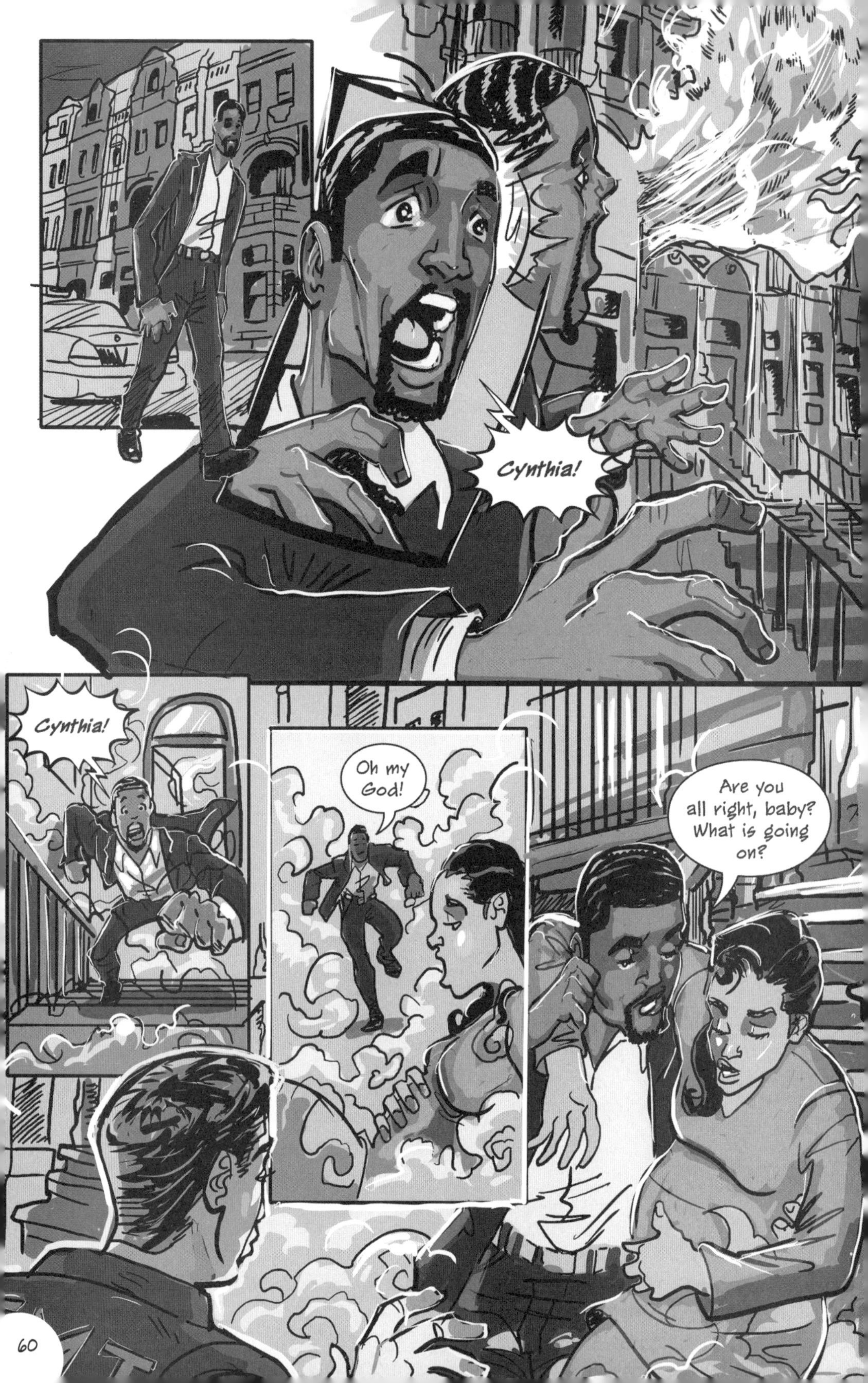
Cynthia!
Cynthia!
Oh my God!
Are you all right, baby? What is going on?

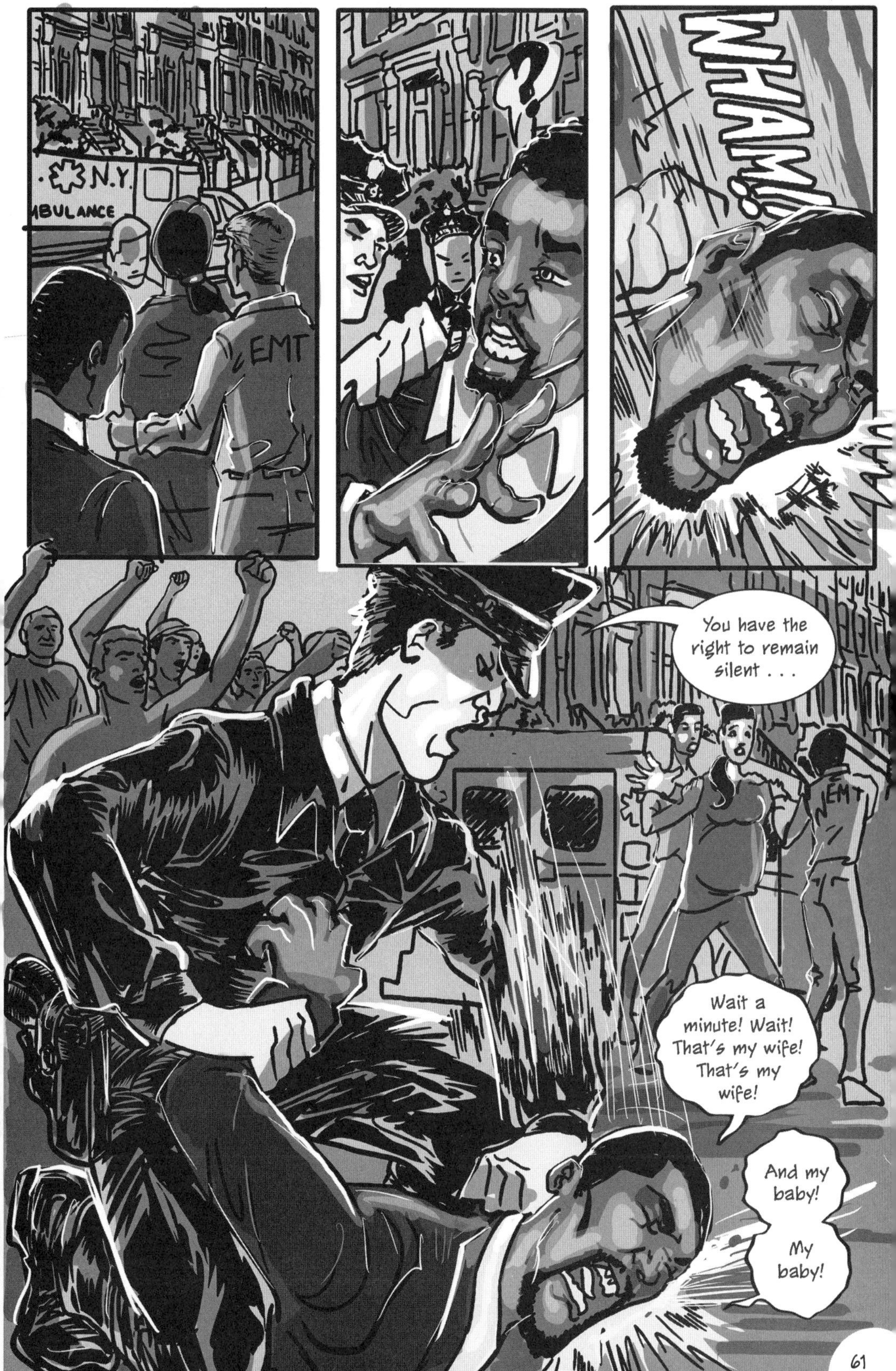
N.Y.
AMBULANCE
EMT
?
WHAM!!
You have the right to remain silent . . .
EMT
Wait a minute! Wait! That's my wife! That's my wife!
And my baby!
My baby!

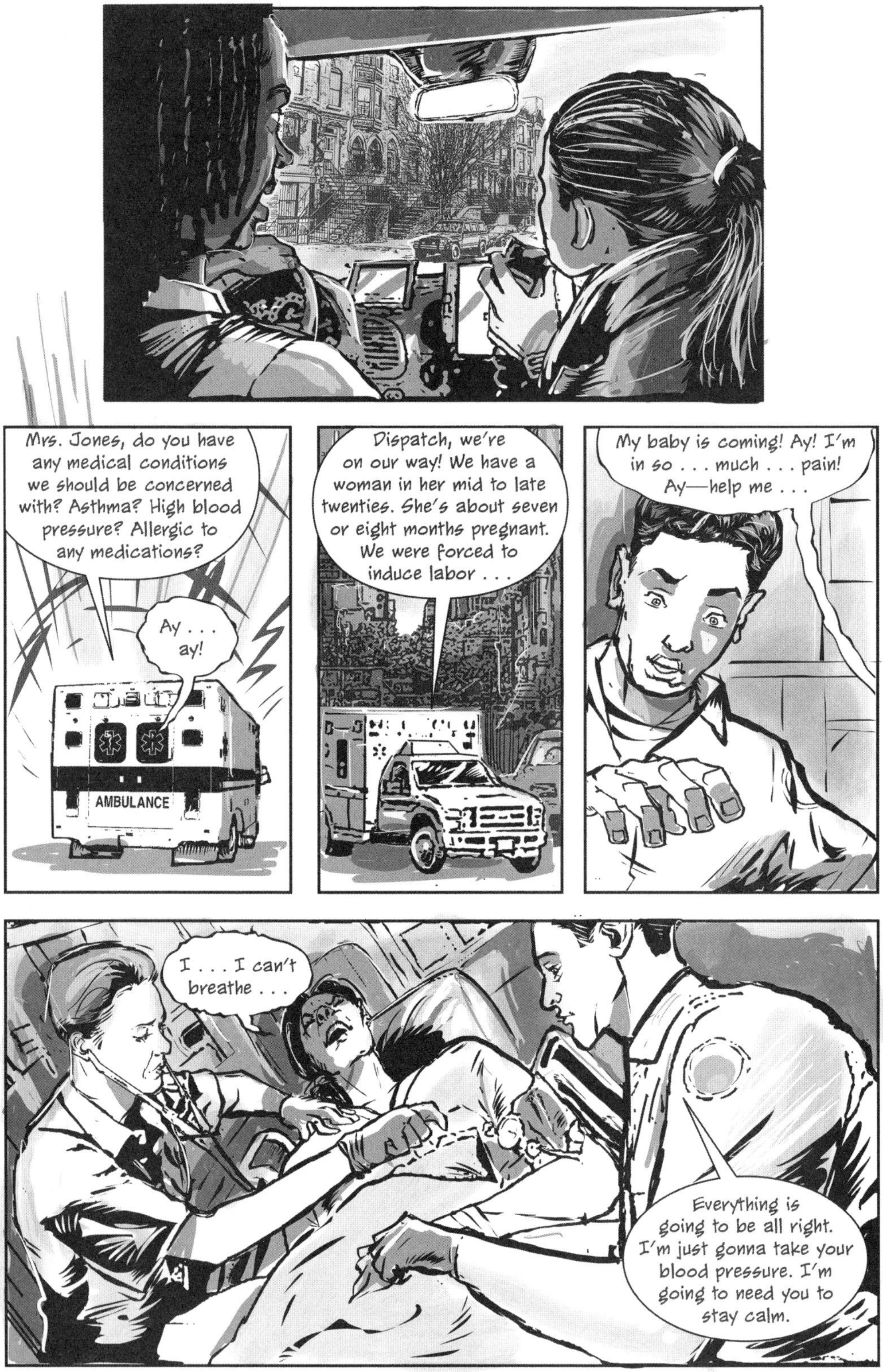
Mrs. Jones, do you have any medical conditions we should be concerned with? Asthma? High blood pressure? Allergic to any medications?
Ay . . . ay!
AMBULANCE
Dispatch, we're on our way! We have a woman in her mid to late twenties. She's about seven or eight months pregnant. We were forced to induce labor . . .
My baby is coming! Ay! I'm in so . . . much . . . pain! Ay—help me . . .
I . . . I can't breathe . . .
Everything is going to be all right. I'm just gonna take your blood pressure. I'm going to need you to stay calm.

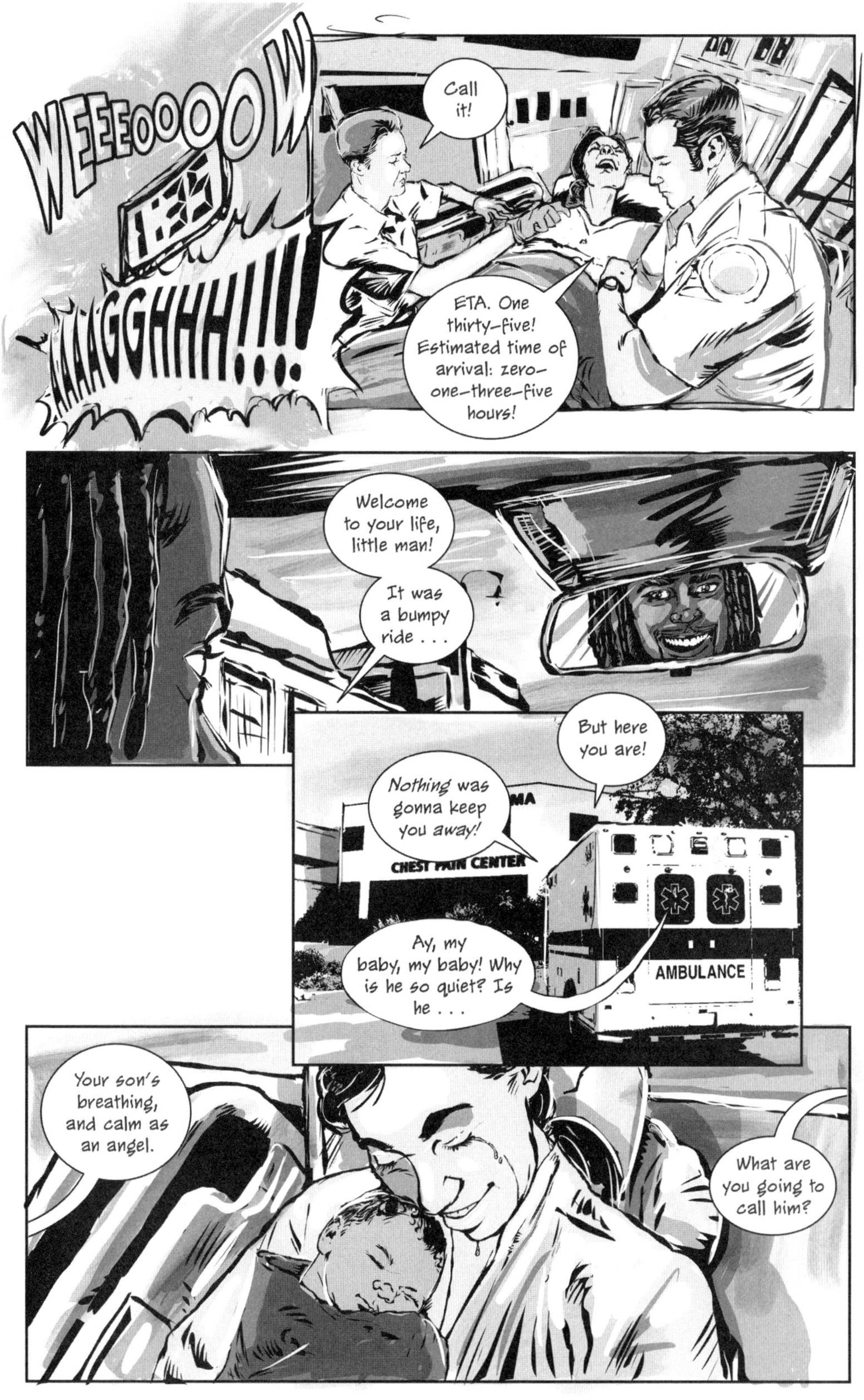
WEEEOOOOW
1:35
AAAGGHHH!!!!
Call it!
ETA. One thirty-five! Estimated time of arrival: zero-one-three-five hours!
Welcome to your life, little man!
It was a bumpy ride . . .
Nothing was gonna keep you away!
But here you are!
CHEST PAIN CENTER
AMBULANCE
Ay, my baby, my baby! Why is he so quiet? Is he . . .
Your son's breathing, and calm as an angel.
What are you going to call him?

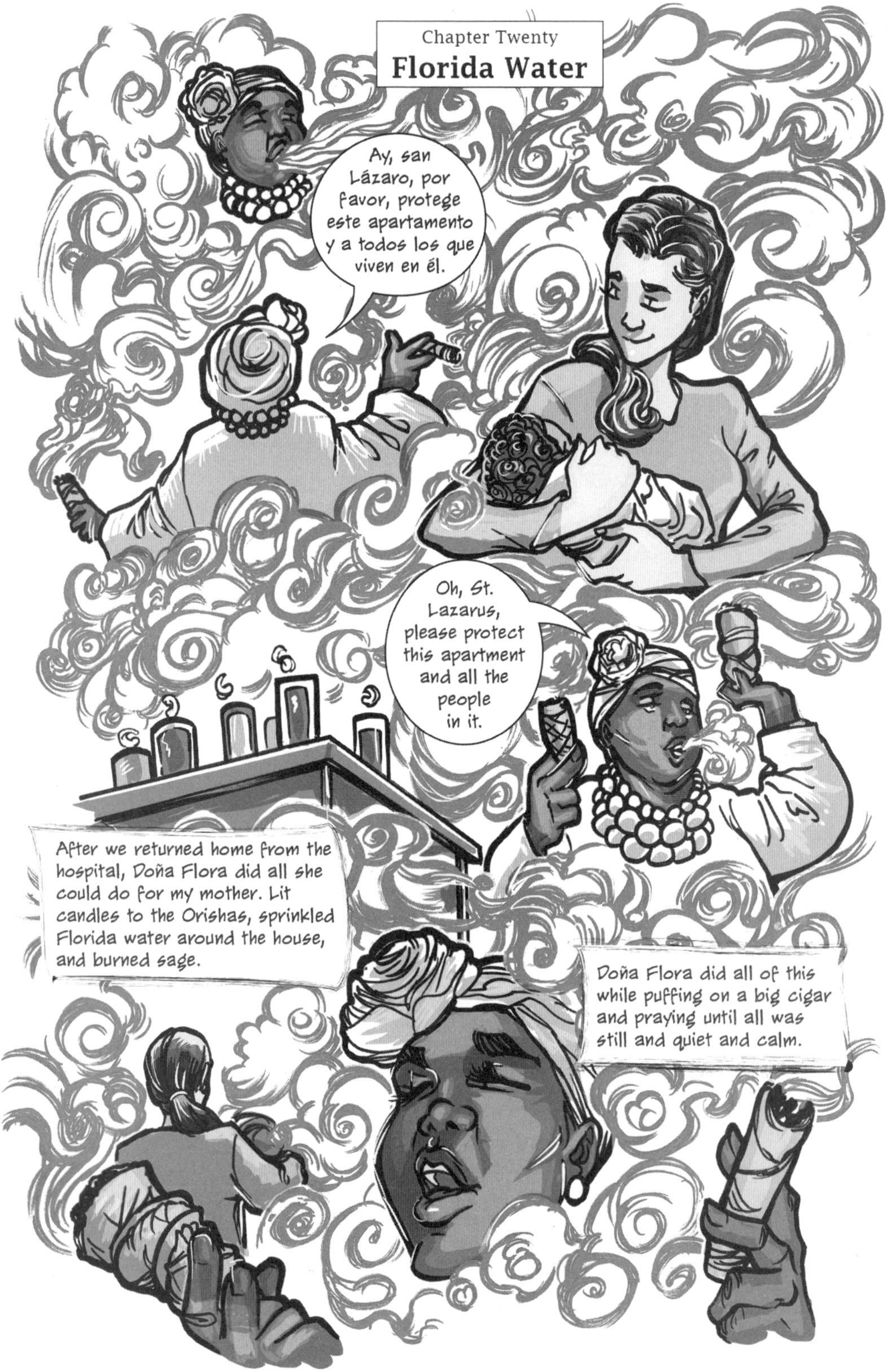
Chapter Twenty
Florida Water
Ay, san Lázaro, por favor, protege este apartamento y a todos los que viven en él.
Oh, St. Lazarus, please protect this apartment and all the people in it.
After we returned home from the hospital, Doña Flora did all she could do for my mother. Lit candles to the Orishas, sprinkled Florida water around the house, and burned sage.
Doña Flora did all of this while puffing on a big cigar and praying until all was still and quiet and calm.

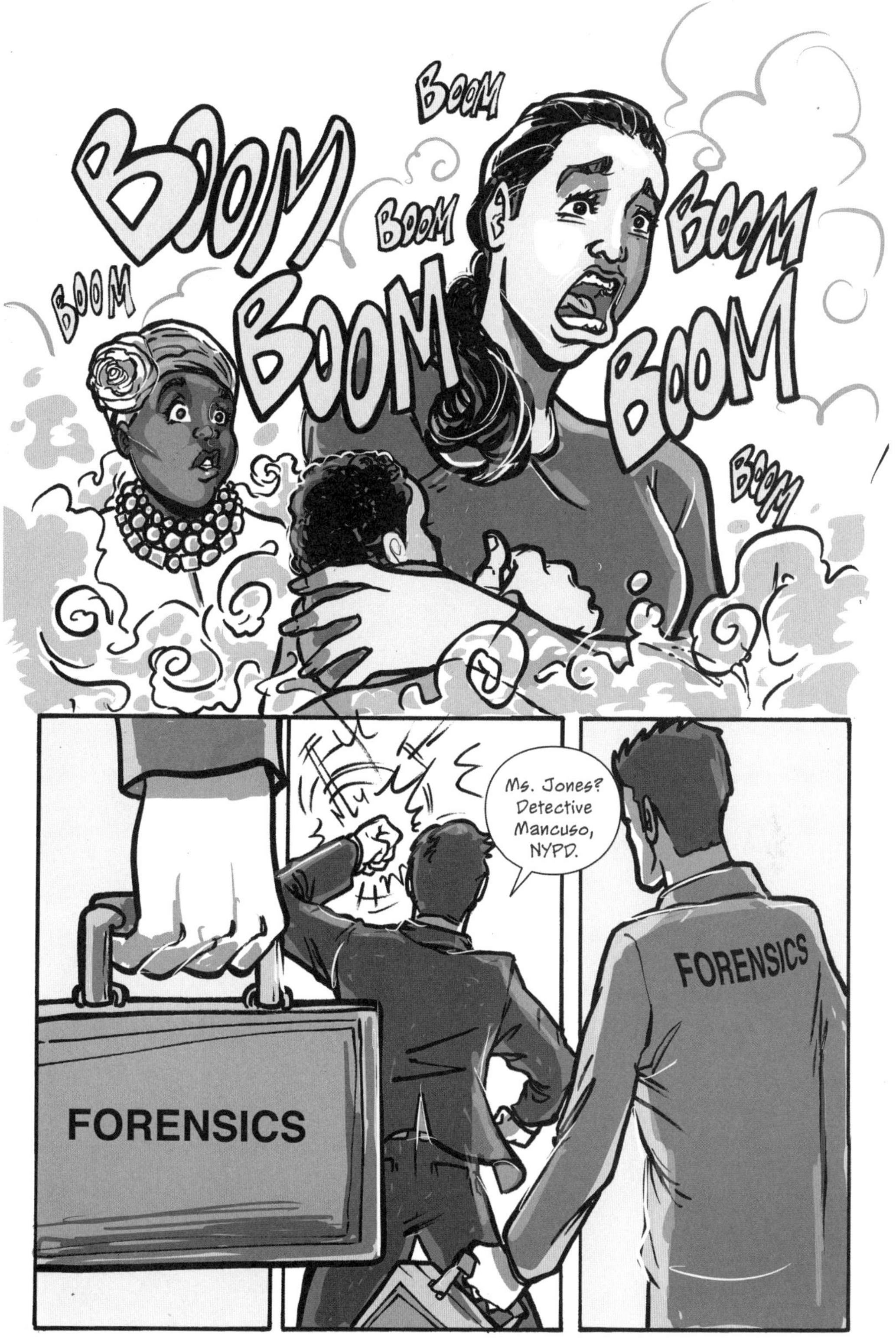
BOOM
BOOM
BOOM
BOOM
BOOM
BOOM
BOOM
BOOM
Ms. Jones? Detective Mancuso, NYPD.
FORENSICS
FORENSICS

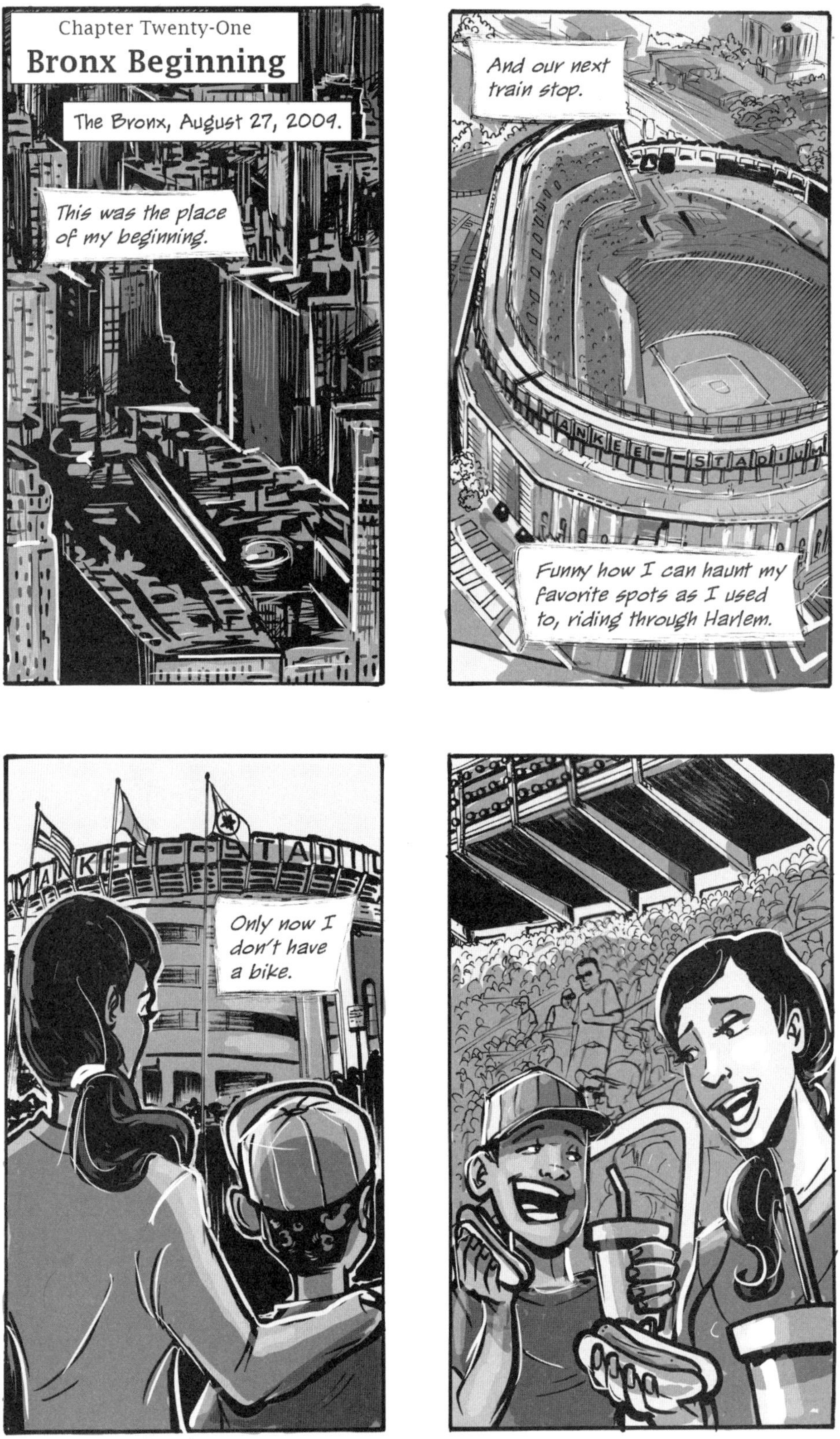
Chapter Twenty-One
Bronx Beginning
The Bronx, August 27, 2009.
This was the place of my beginning.
And our next train stop.
YANKEE STADIUM
Funny how I can haunt my favorite spots as I used to, riding through Harlem.
Only now I don't have a bike.

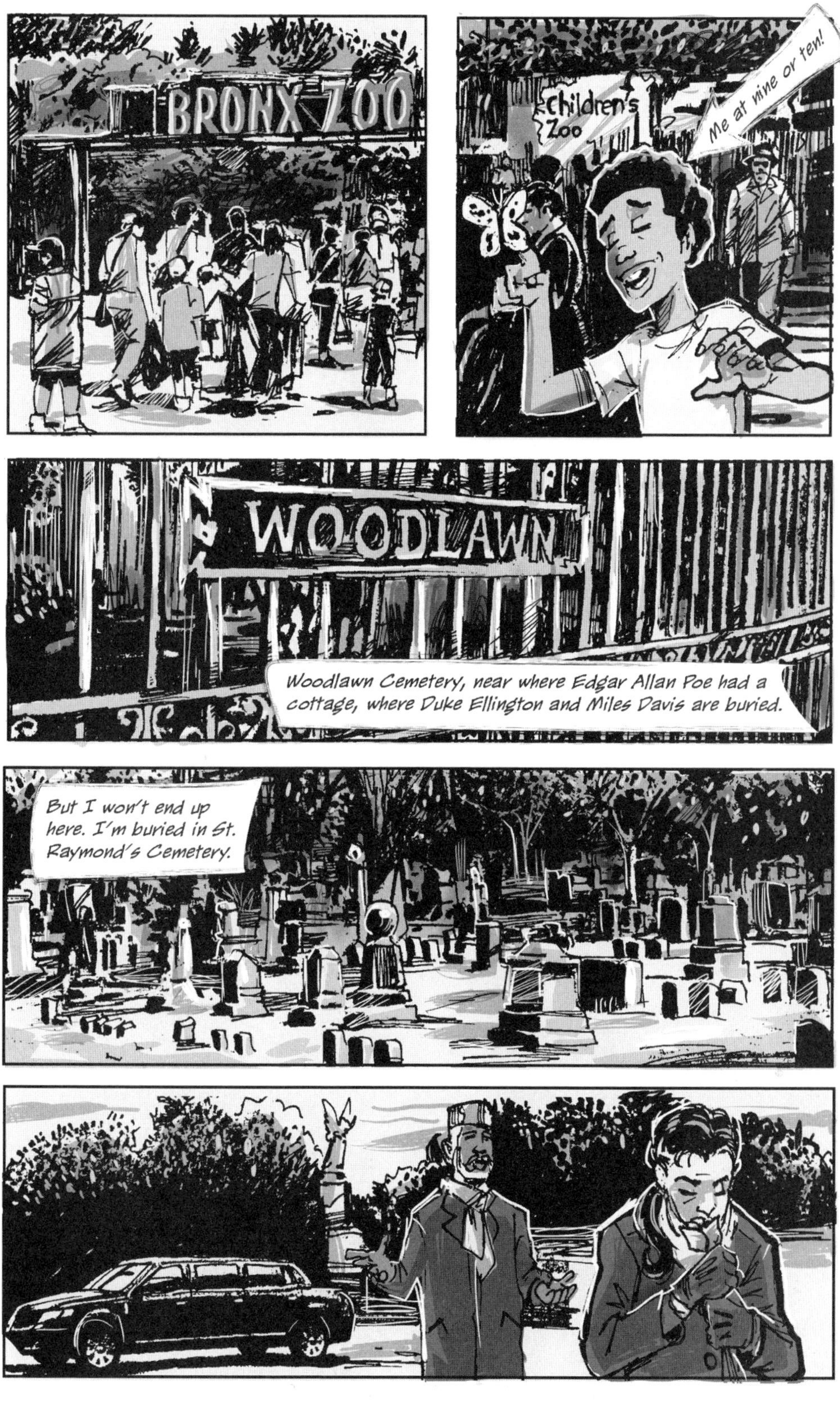
BRONX ZOO
Children's Zoo
Me at nine or ten!
WOODLAWN
Woodlawn Cemetery, near where Edgar Allan Poe had a cottage, where Duke Ellington and Miles Davis are buried.
But I won't end up here. I'm buried in St. Raymond's Cemetery.

Chapter Twenty-Two

Bronx Beirut

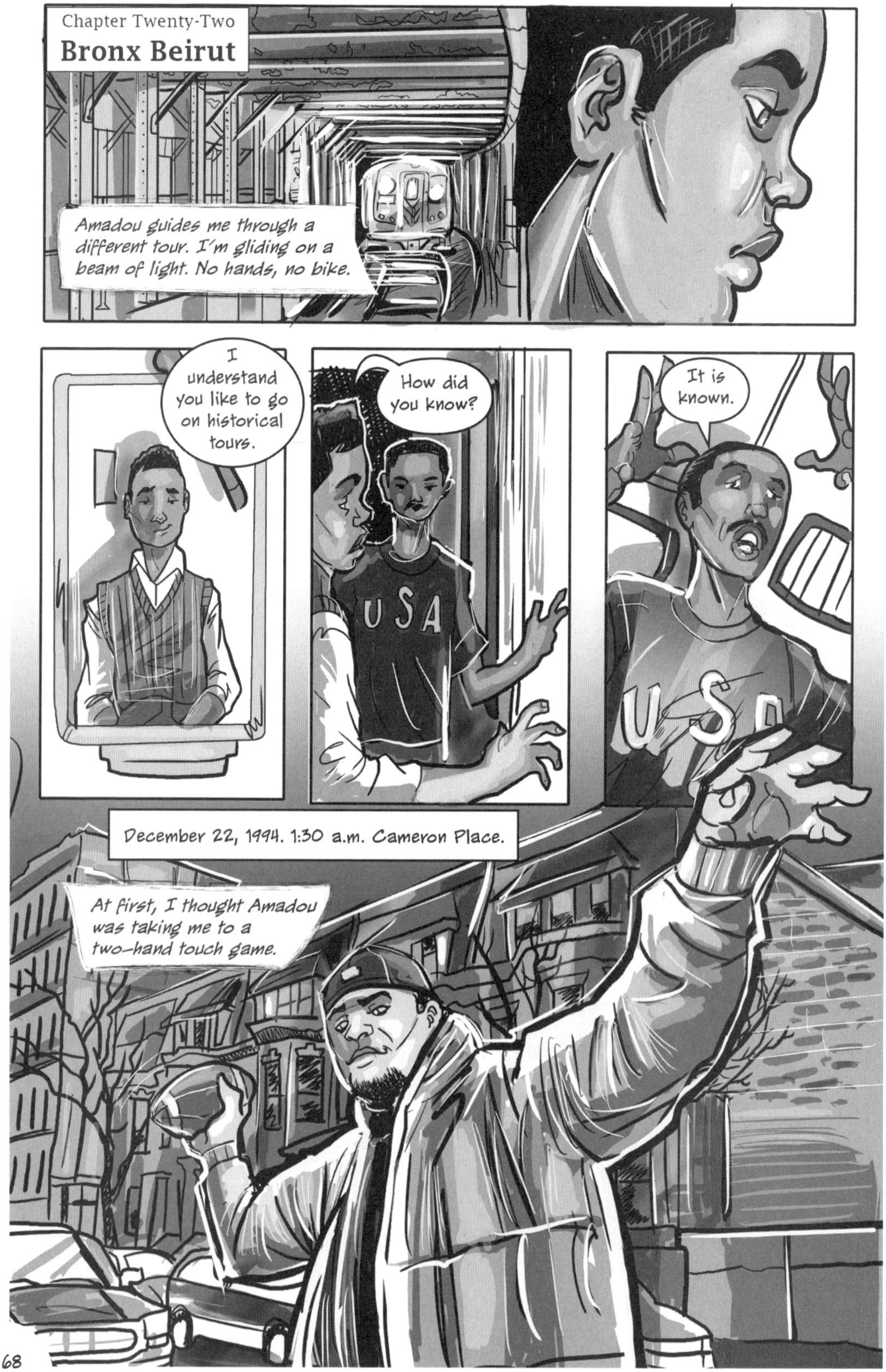
Amadou guides me through a different tour. I'm gliding on a beam of light. No hands, no bike.
I understand you like to go on historical tours.
How did you know?
It is known.
USA
December 22, 1994. 1:30 a.m. Cameron Place.
At first, I thought Amadou was taking me to a two-hand touch game.

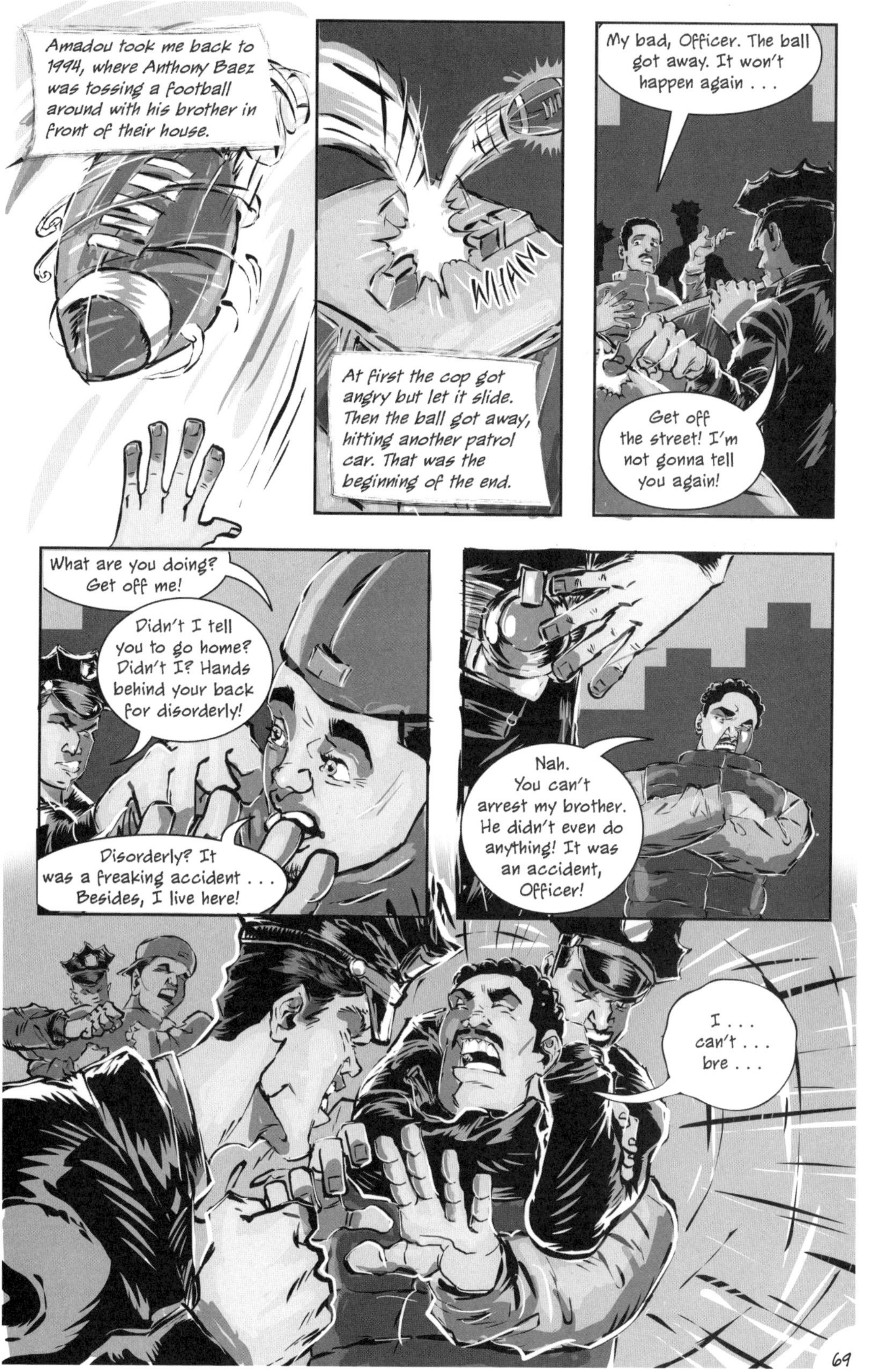
Amadou took me back to 1994, where Anthony Baez was tossing a football around with his brother in front of their house.
WHAM
At first the cop got angry but let it slide. Then the ball got away, hitting another patrol car. That was the beginning of the end.
My bad, Officer. The ball got away. It won't happen again . . .
Get off the street! I'm not gonna tell you again!
What are you doing? Get off me!
Didn't I tell you to go home? Didn't I? Hands behind your back for disorderly!
Disorderly? It was a freaking accident . . . Besides, I live here!
Nah. You can't arrest my brother. He didn't even do anything! It was an accident, Officer!
I . . . can't . . . bre . . .

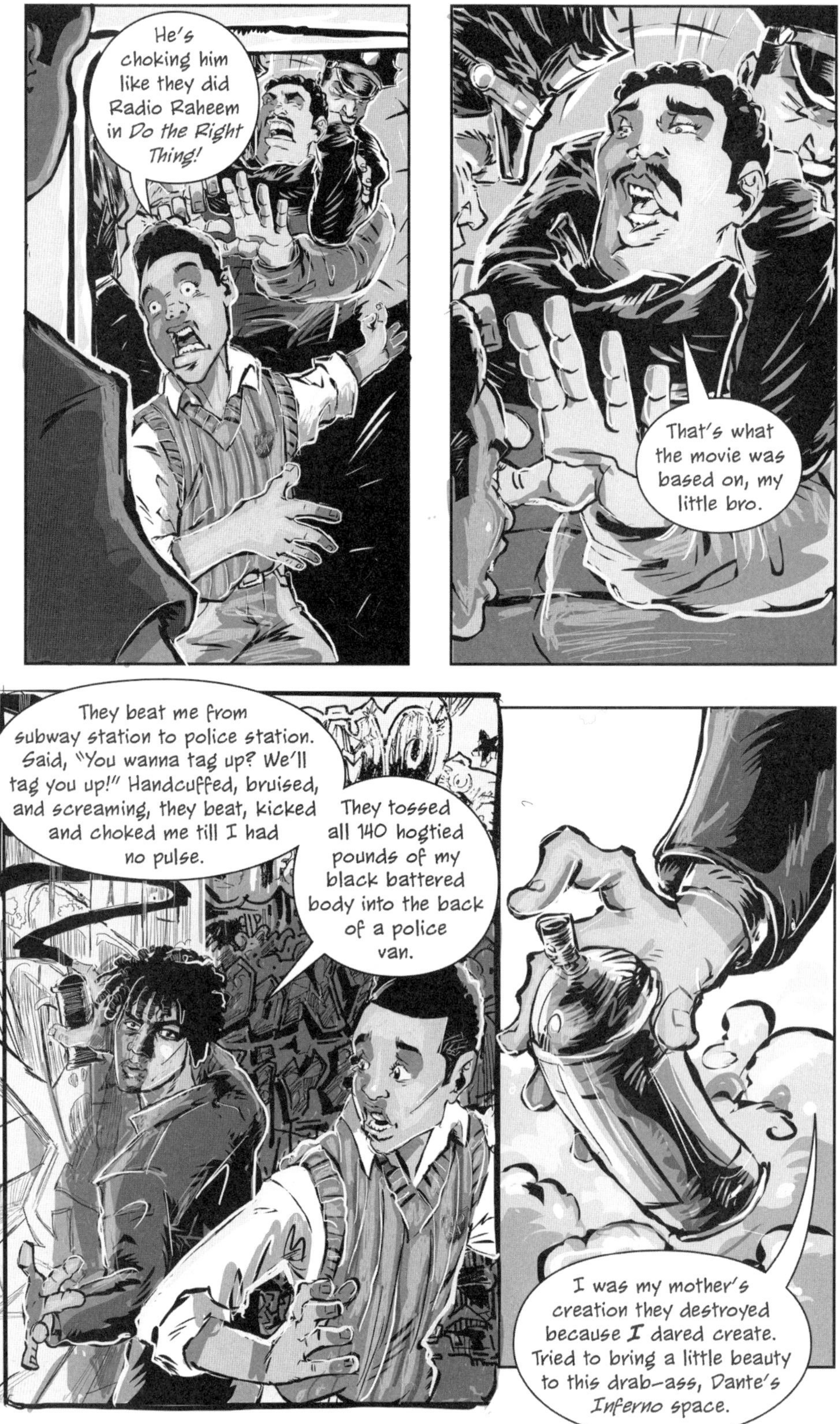
He's choking him like they did Radio Raheem in *Do the Right Thing!*
That's what the movie was based on, my little bro.
They beat me from subway station to police station. Said, "You wanna tag up? We'll tag you up!" Handcuffed, bruised, and screaming, they beat, kicked and choked me till I had no pulse.
They tossed all 140 hogtied pounds of my black battered body into the back of a police van.
I was my mother's creation they destroyed because ***I*** dared create. Tried to bring a little beauty to this drab-ass, Dante's *Inferno* space.

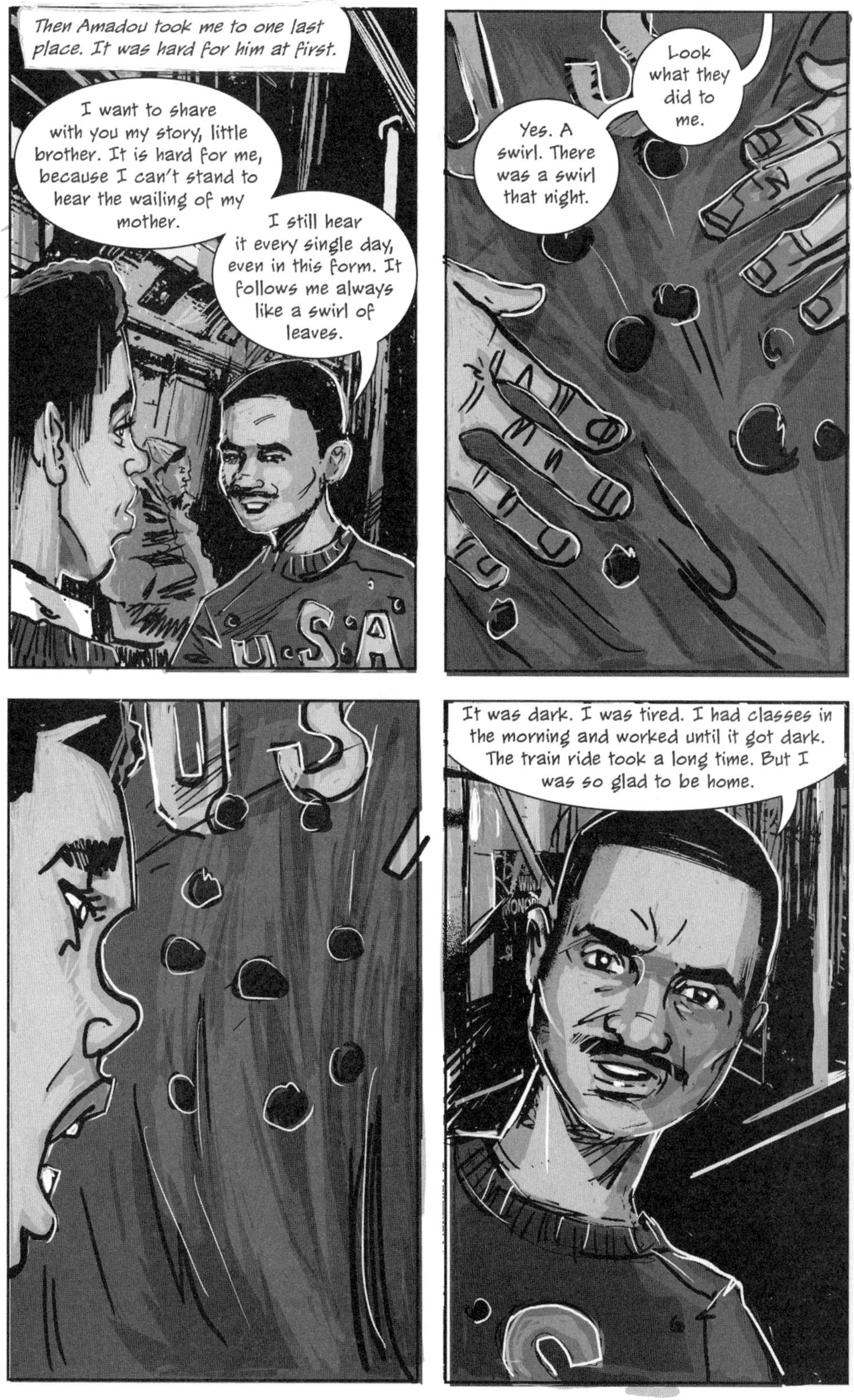
Then Amadou took me to one last place. It was hard for him at first.
I want to share with you my story, little brother. It is hard for me, because I can't stand to hear the wailing of my mother.
I still hear it every single day, even in this form. It follows me always like a swirl of leaves.
U.S.A
Look what they did to me.
Yes. A swirl. There was a swirl that night.
It was dark. I was tired. I had classes in the morning and worked until it got dark. The train ride took a long time. But I was so glad to be home.

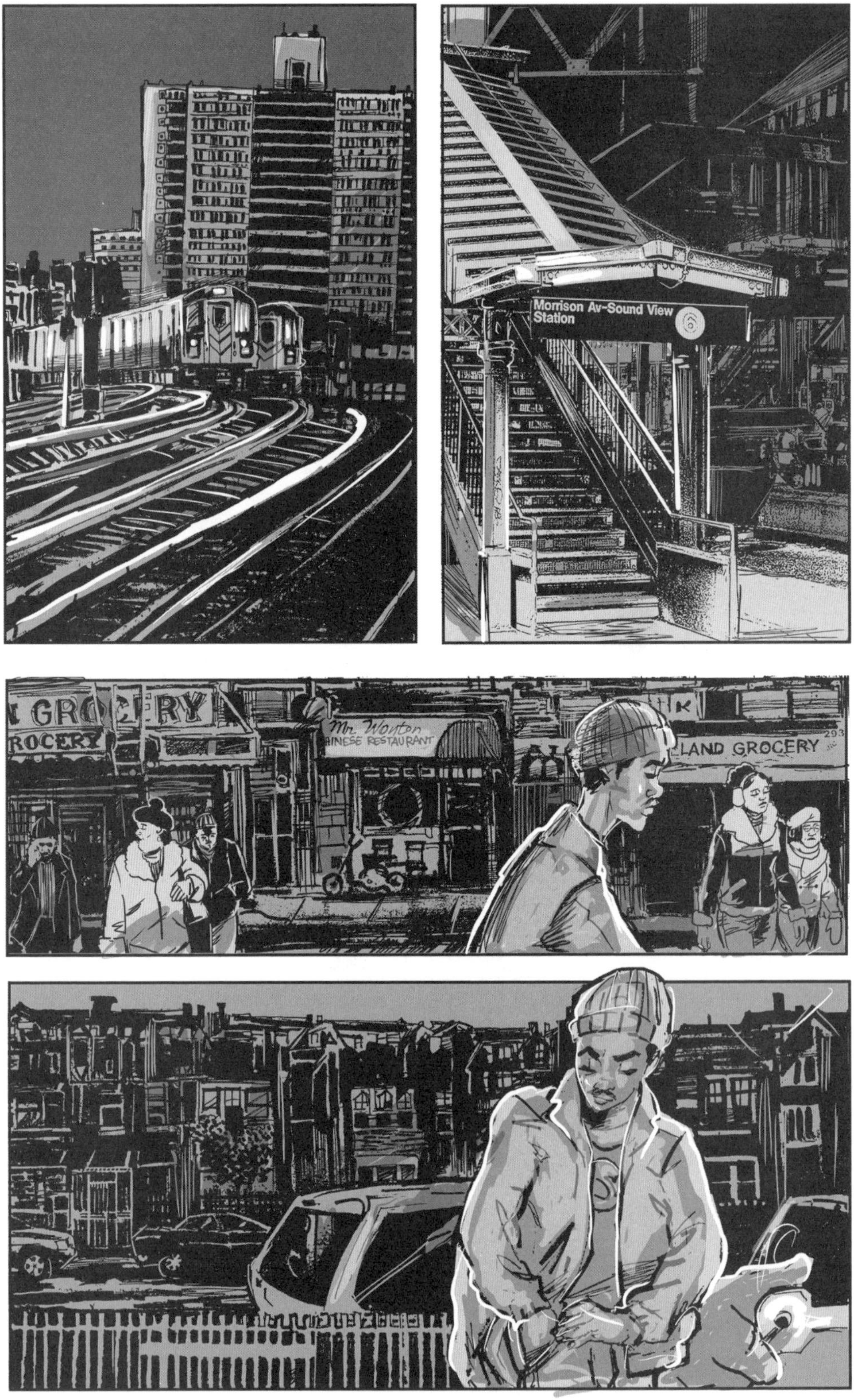
Morrison Av-Sound View Station
6
GROCERY
ROCERY
Mr. Wonton
INESE RESTAURANT
LAND GROCERY
293

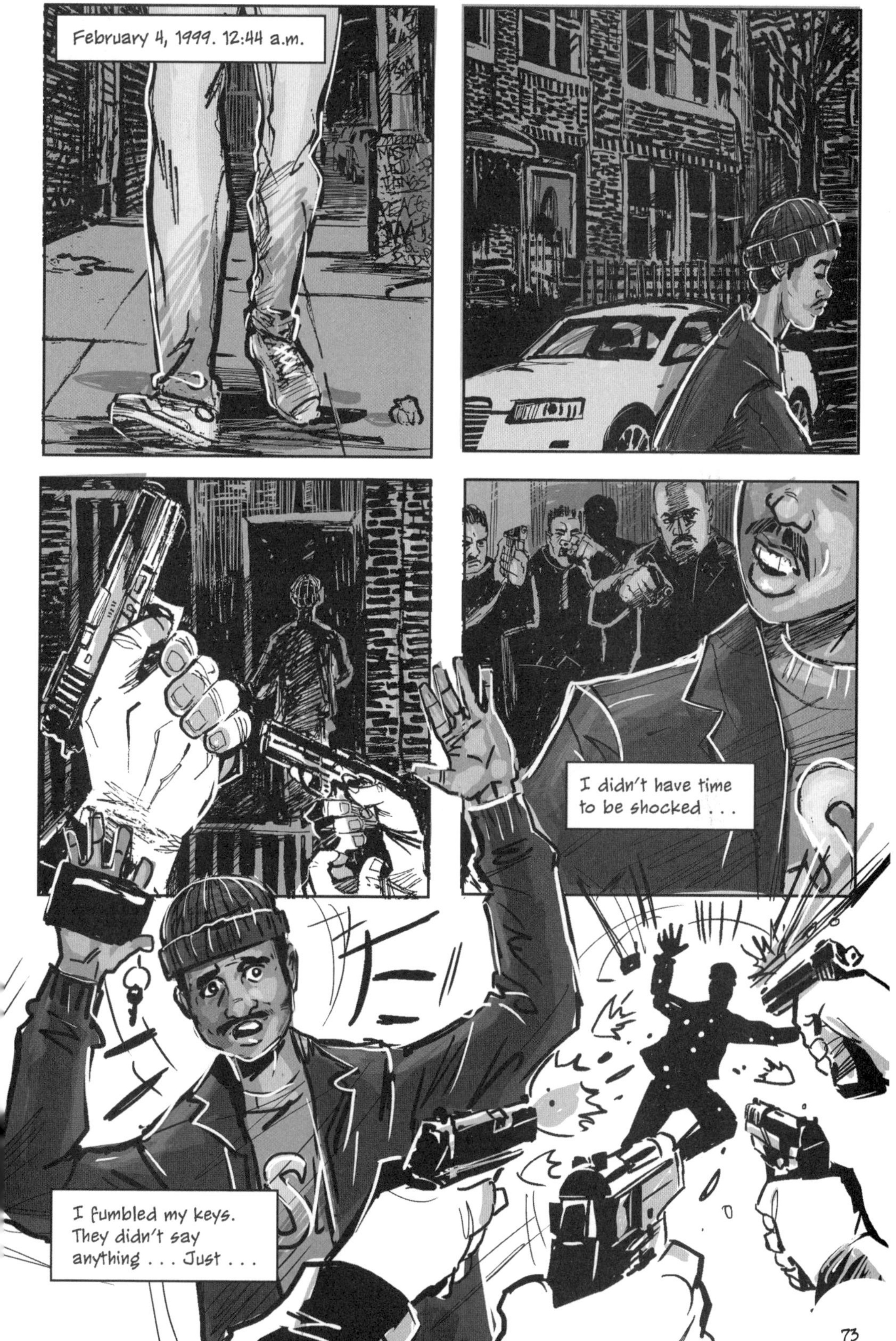
February 4, 1999. 12:44 a.m.
I didn't have time to be shocked . . .
I fumbled my keys. They didn't say anything . . . Just . . .

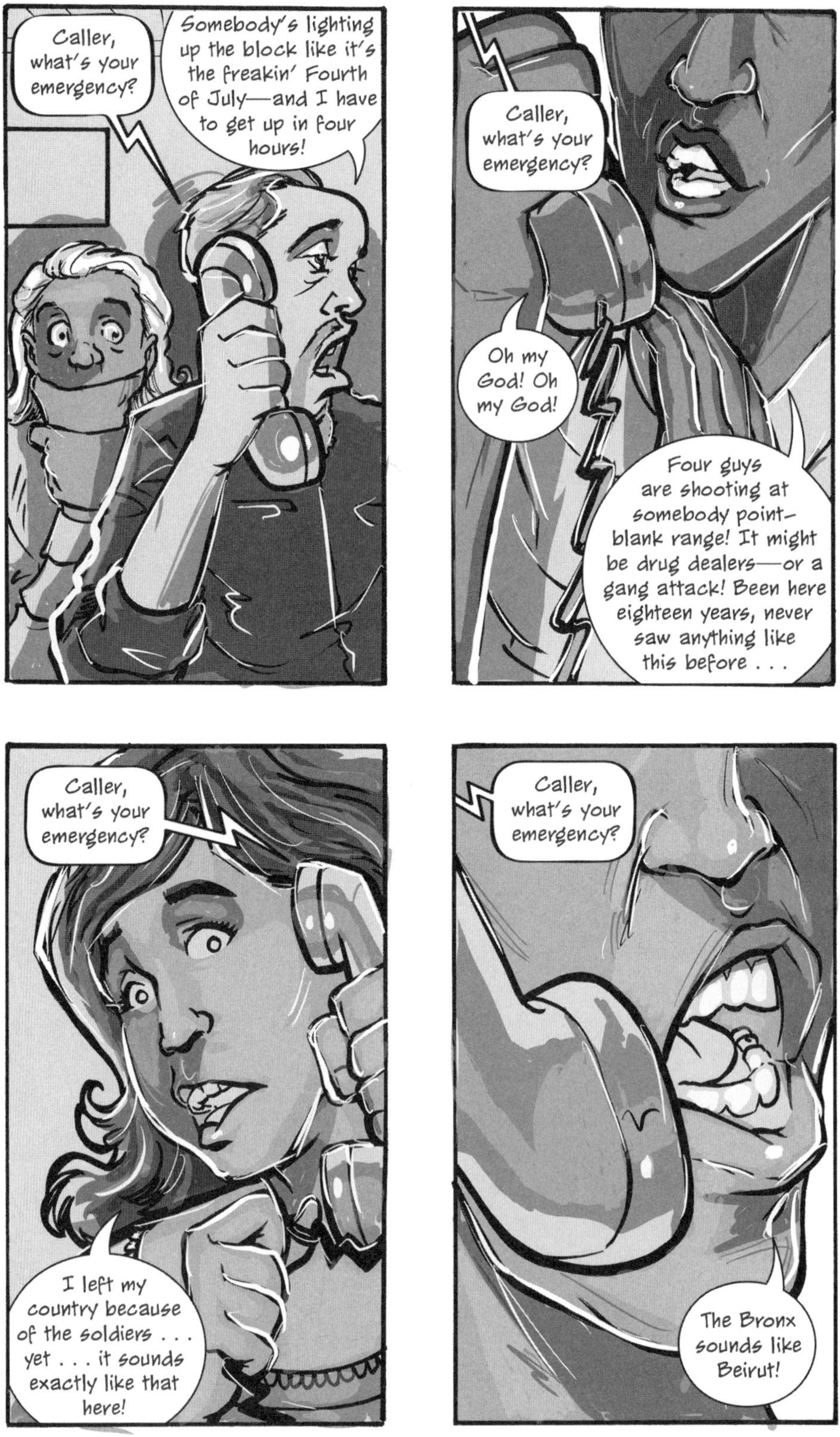
Caller, what's your emergency?
Somebody's lighting up the block like it's the freakin' Fourth of July—and I have to get up in four hours!
Caller, what's your emergency?
Oh my God! Oh my God!
Four guys are shooting at somebody point-blank range! It might be drug dealers—or a gang attack! Been here eighteen years, never saw anything like this before . . .
Caller, what's your emergency?
I left my country because of the soldiers . . . yet . . . it sounds exactly like that here!
Caller, what's your emergency?
The Bronx sounds like Beirut!

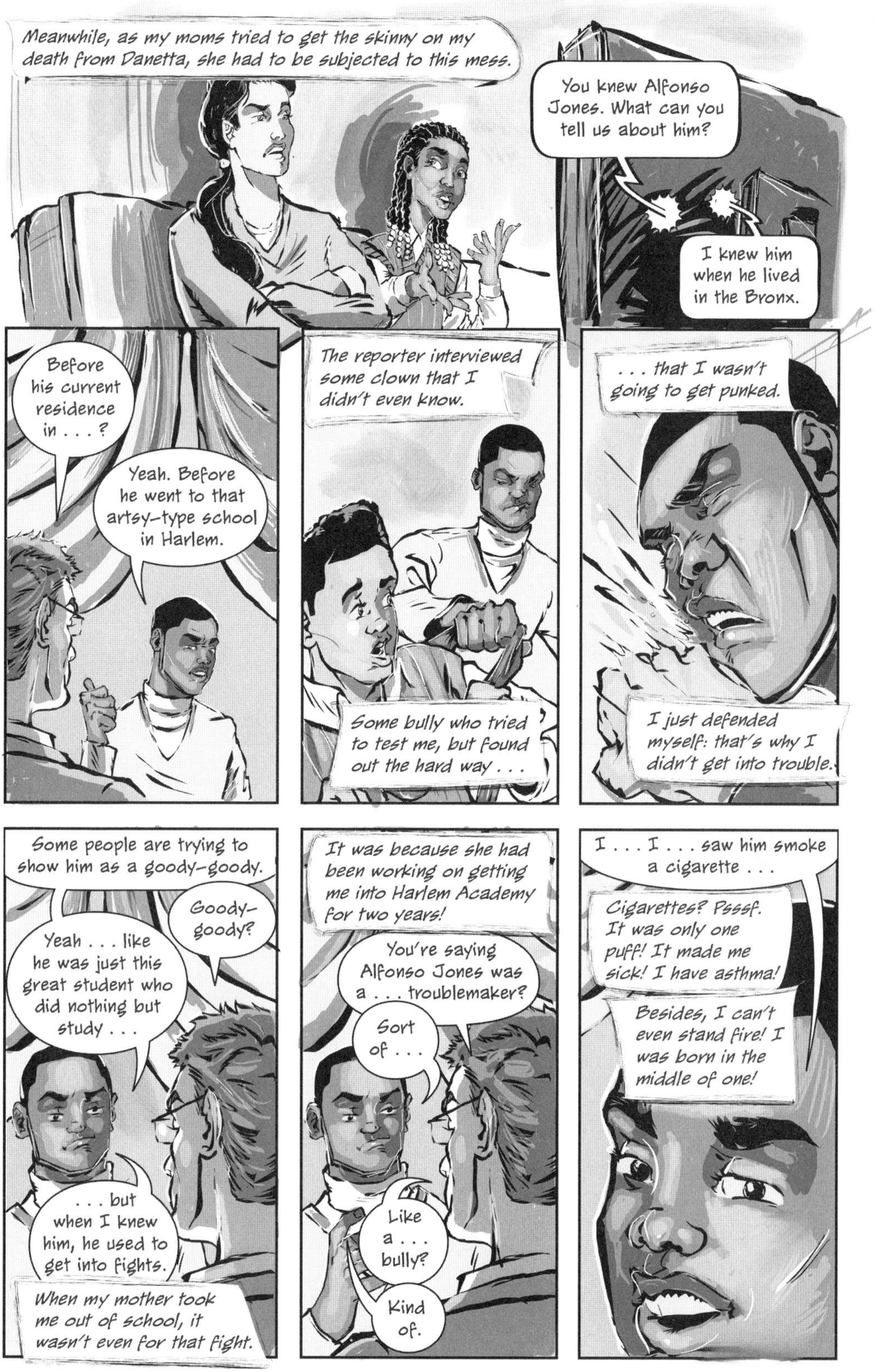

Meanwhile, as my moms tried to get the skinny on my death from Danetta, she had to be subjected to this mess.
You knew Alfonso Jones. What can you tell us about him?
I knew him when he lived in the Bronx.
Before his current residence in . . . ?
Yeah. Before he went to that artsy-type school in Harlem.
The reporter interviewed some clown that I didn't even know.
Some bully who tried to test me, but found out the hard way . . .
. . . that I wasn't going to get punked.
I just defended myself: that's why I didn't get into trouble.
Some people are trying to show him as a goody-goody.
Goody-goody?
Yeah . . . like he was just this great student who did nothing but study . . .
. . . but when I knew him, he used to get into fights.
When my mother took me out of school, it wasn't even for that fight.
It was because she had been working on getting me into Harlem Academy for two years!
You're saying Alfonso Jones was a . . . troublemaker?
Sort of . . .
Like a . . . bully?
Kind of.
I . . . I . . . saw him smoke a cigarette . . .
Cigarettes? Psssf. It was only one puff! It made me sick! I have asthma!
Besides, I can't even stand fire! I was born in the middle of one!

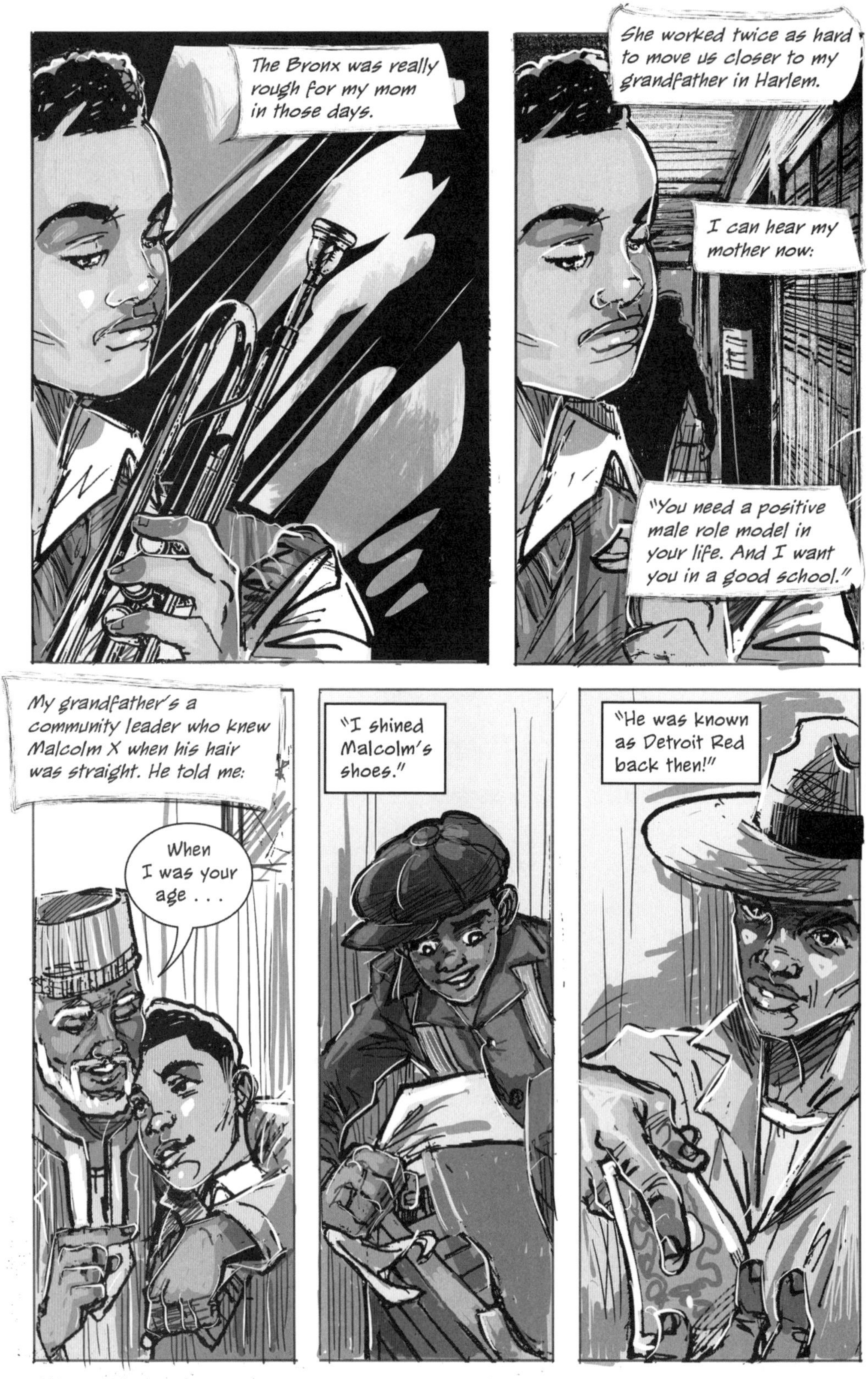
The Bronx was really rough for my mom in those days.
She worked twice as hard to move us closer to my grandfather in Harlem.
I can hear my mother now:
"You need a positive male role model in your life. And I want you in a good school."
My grandfather's a community leader who knew Malcolm X when his hair was straight. He told me:
When I was your age . . .
"I shined Malcolm's shoes."
"He was known as Detroit Red back then!"

Chapter Twenty-Three

New School

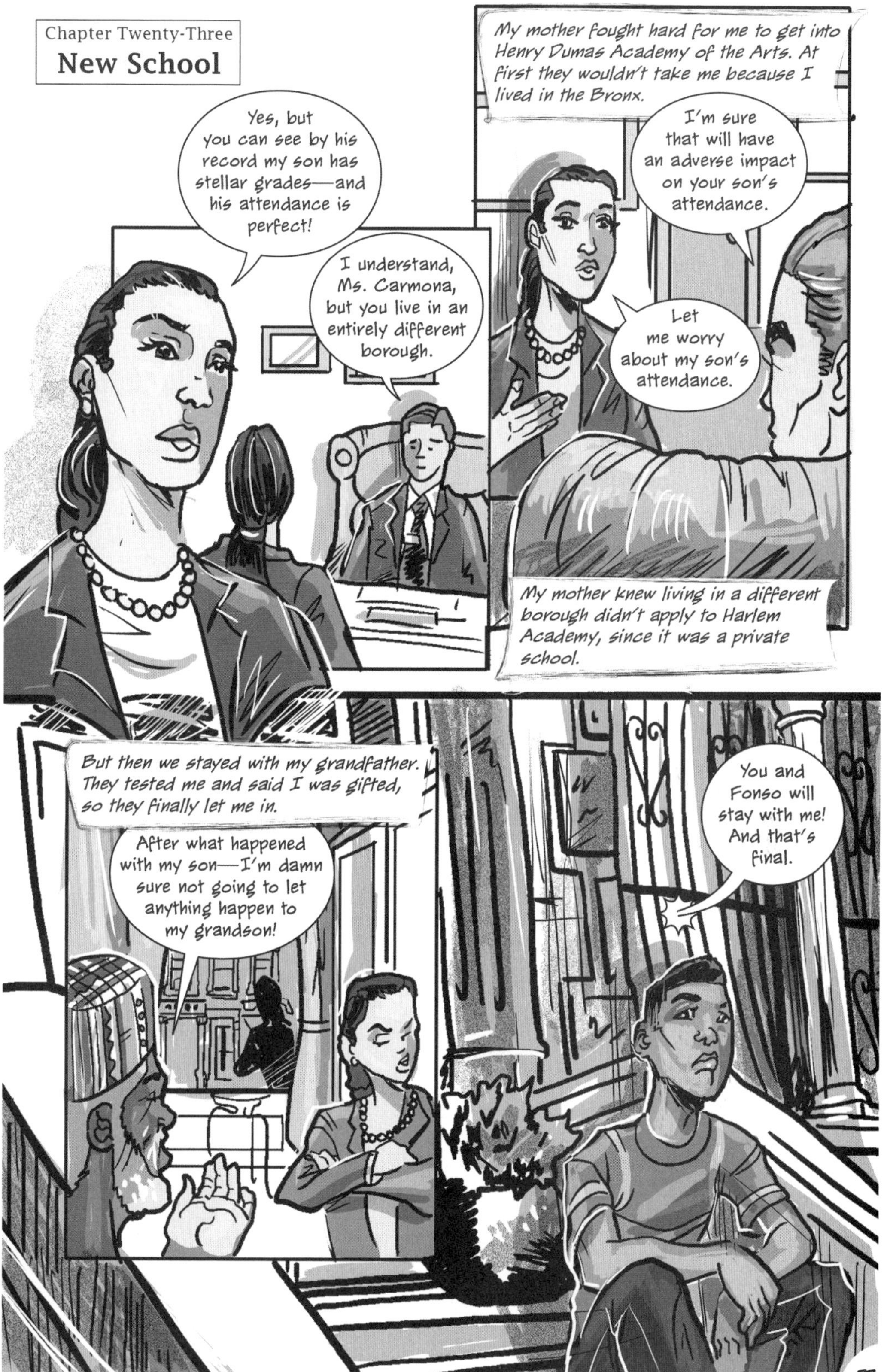
Yes, but you can see by his record my son has stellar grades—and his attendance is perfect!
I understand, Ms. Carmona, but you live in an entirely different borough.
My mother fought hard for me to get into Henry Dumas Academy of the Arts. At first they wouldn't take me because I lived in the Bronx.
I'm sure that will have an adverse impact on your son's attendance.
Let me worry about my son's attendance.
My mother knew living in a different borough didn't apply to Harlem Academy, since it was a private school.
But then we stayed with my grandfather. They tested me and said I was gifted, so they finally let me in.
After what happened with my son—I'm damn sure not going to let anything happen to my grandson!
You and Fonso will stay with me! And that's final.

Chapter Twenty-Four
King Hamlet

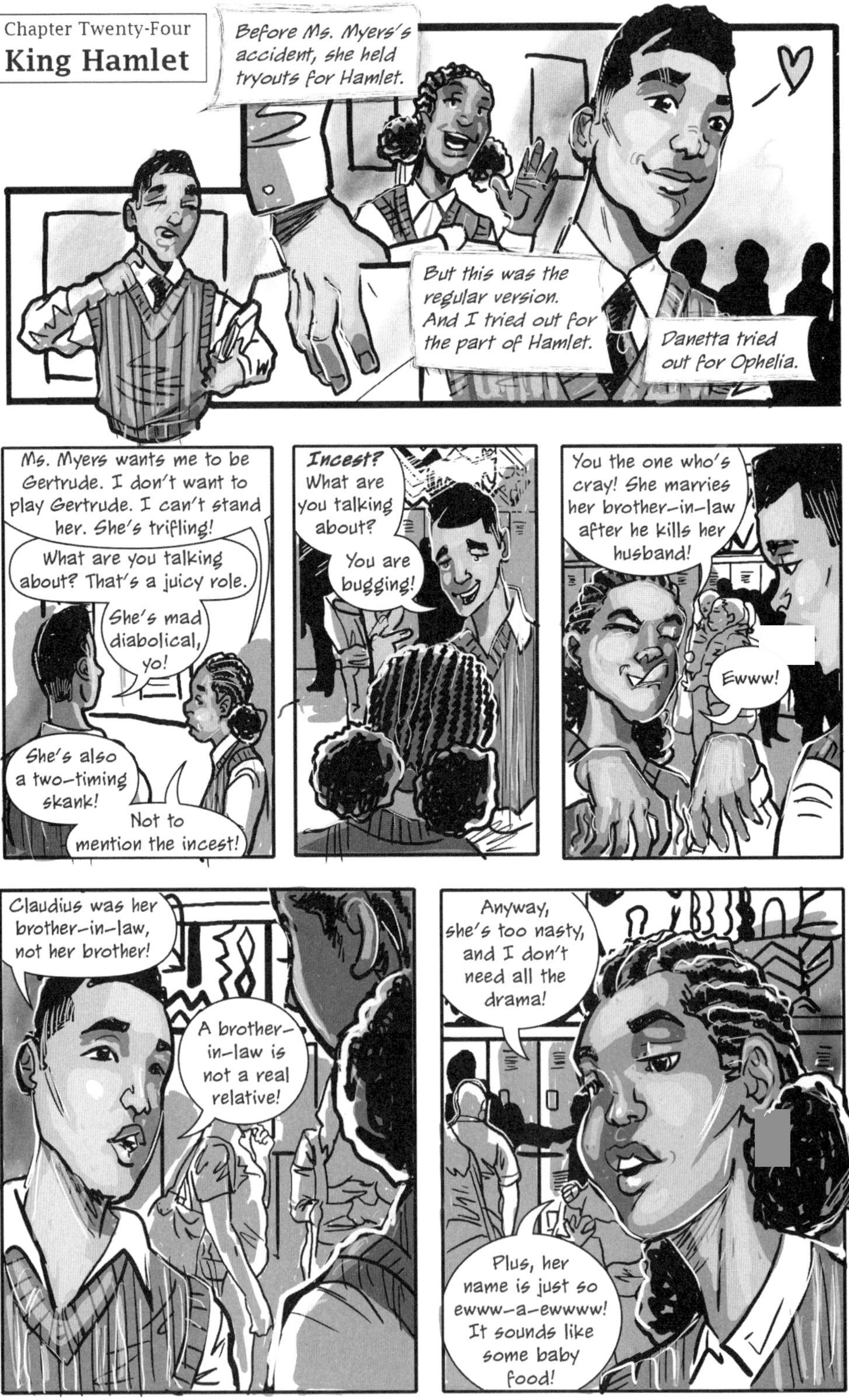

Before Ms. Myers's accident, she held tryouts for Hamlet.
But this was the regular version. And I tried out for the part of Hamlet.
Danetta tried out for Ophelia.
Ms. Myers wants me to be Gertrude. I don't want to play Gertrude. I can't stand her. She's trifling!
What are you talking about? That's a juicy role.
She's mad diabolical, yo!
She's also a two-timing skank!
Not to mention the incest!
Incest? What are you talking about?
You are bugging!
You the one who's cray! She marries her brother-in-law after he kills her husband!
Ewww!
Claudius was her brother-in-law, not her brother!
A brother-in-law is not a real relative!
Anyway, she's too nasty, and I don't need all the drama!
Plus, her name is just so ewww-a-ewwww! It sounds like some baby food!

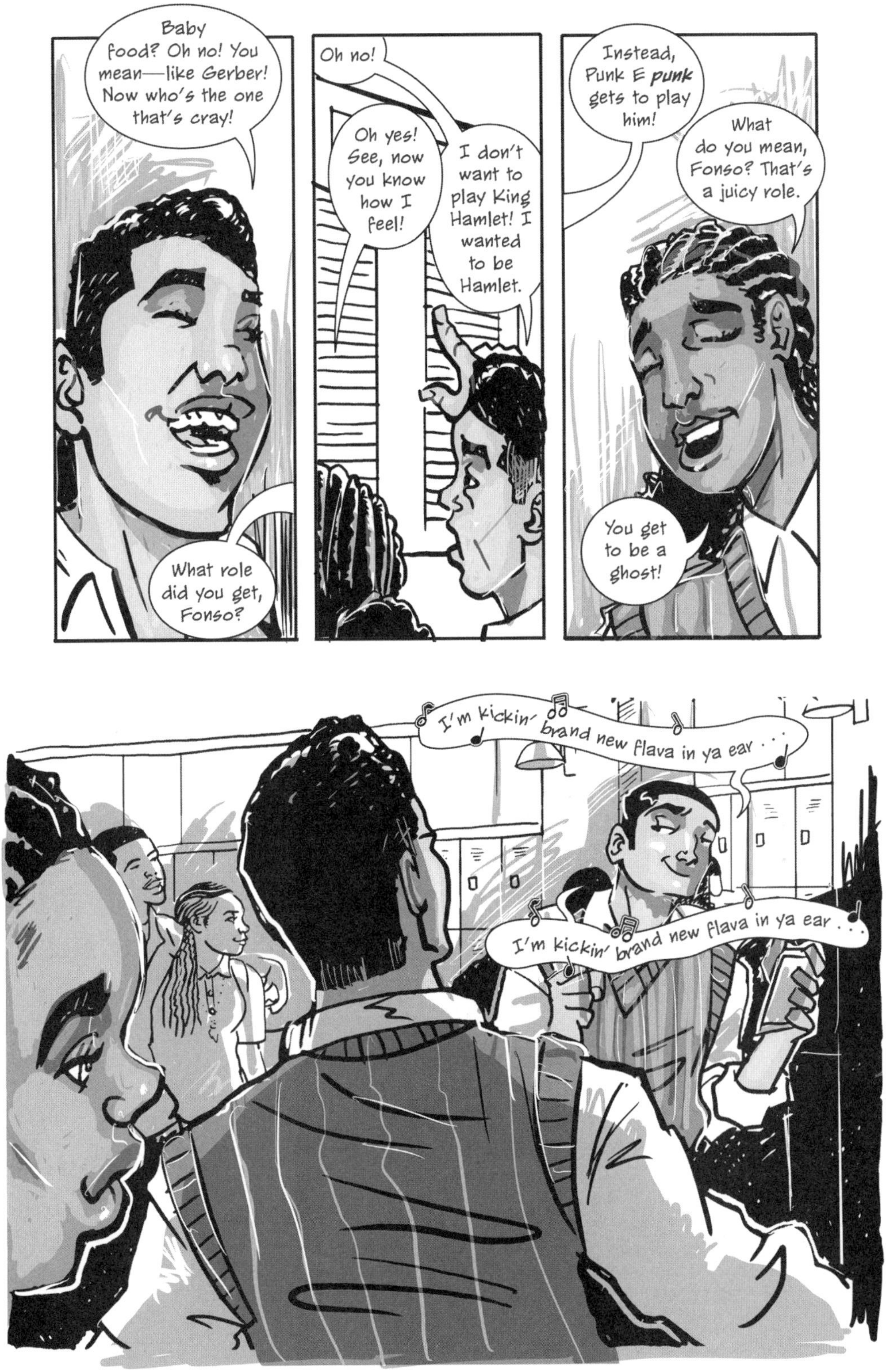
Baby food? Oh no! You mean—like Gerber! Now who's the one that's cray!
What role did you get, Fonso?
Oh no!
Oh yes! See, now you know how I feel!
I don't want to play King Hamlet! I wanted to be Hamlet.
Instead, Punk E **punk** gets to play him!
What do you mean, Fonso? That's a juicy role.
You get to be a ghost!
I'm kickin' brand new flava in ya ear . . .
I'm kickin' brand new flava in ya ear . . .

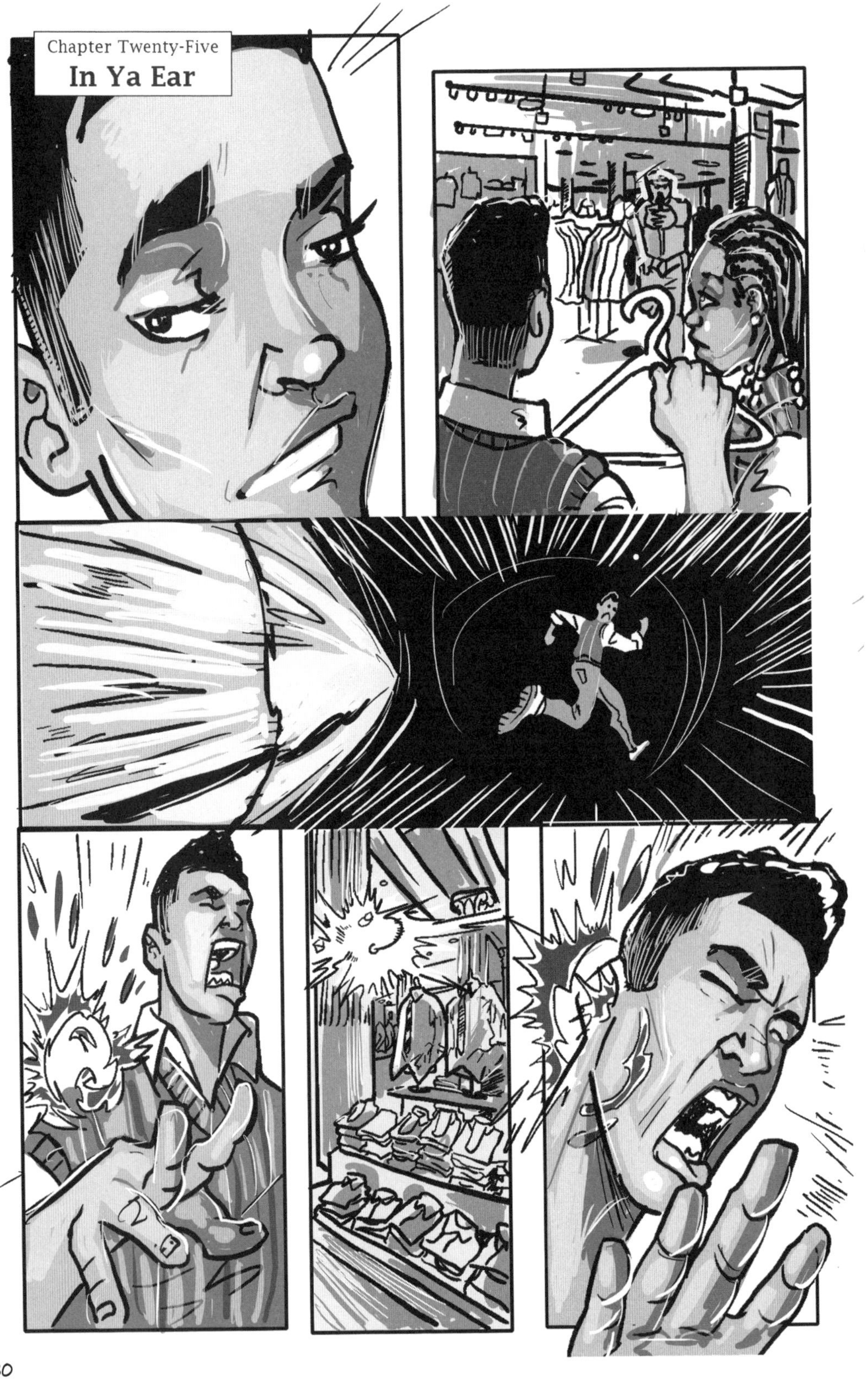
Chapter Twenty-Five
In Ya Ear

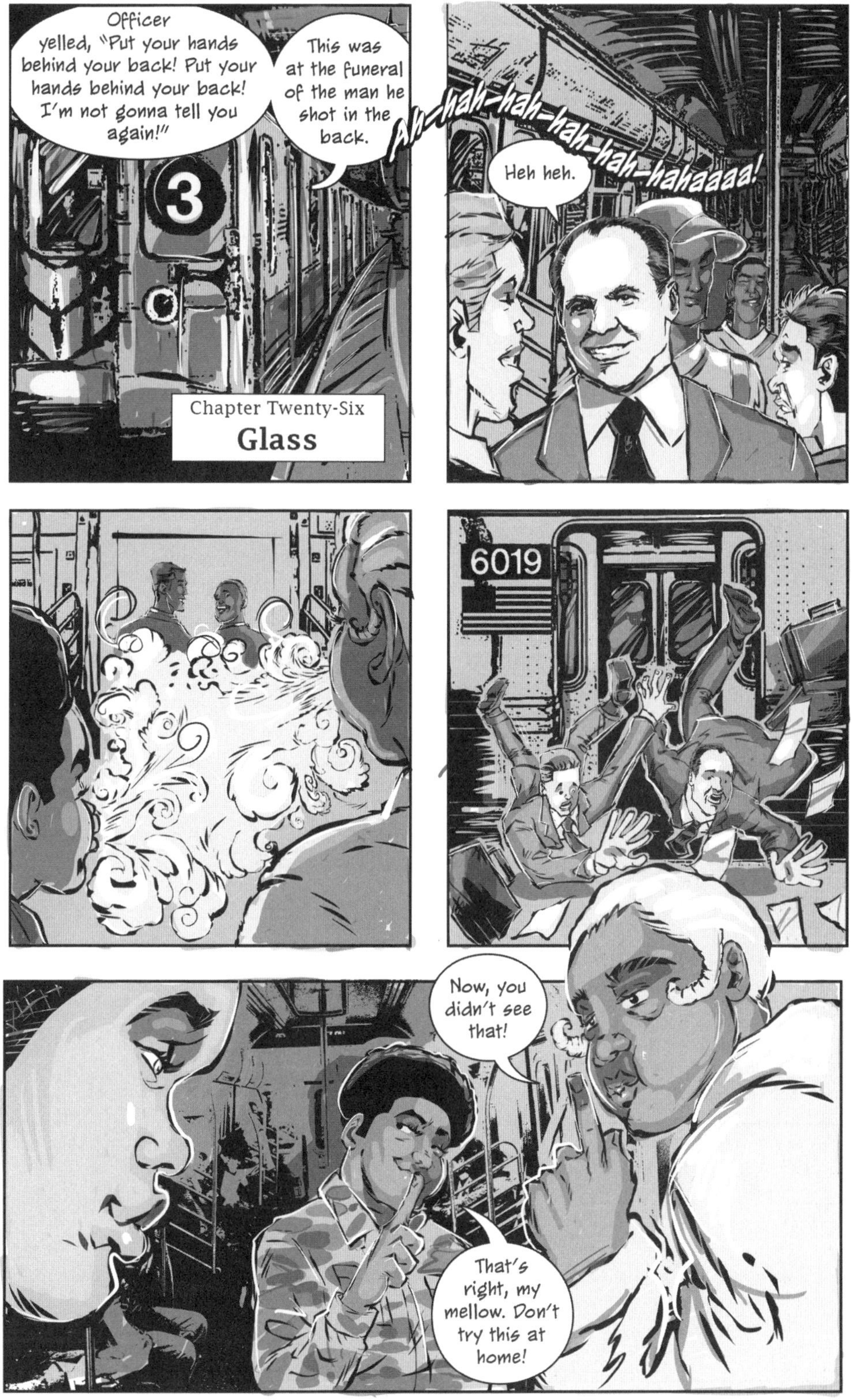
Officer yelled, "Put your hands behind your back! Put your hands behind your back! I'm not gonna tell you again!"
This was at the funeral of the man he shot in the back.
3
Chapter Twenty-Six
Glass
Ah-hah-hah-hah-hah-hahaaaa!
Heh heh.
6019
Now, you didn't see that!
That's right, my mellow. Don't try this at home!

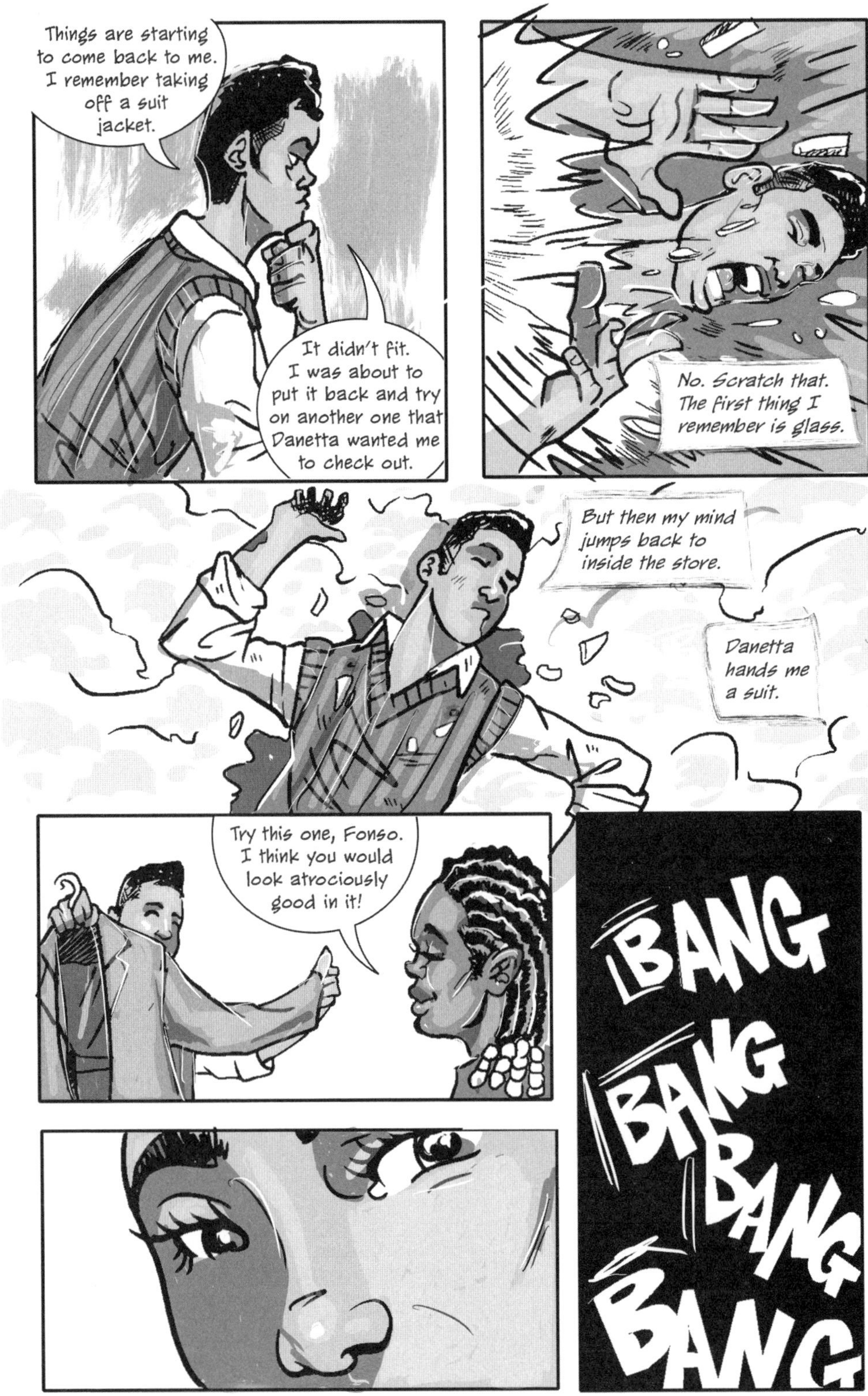
Things are starting to come back to me. I remember taking off a suit jacket.
It didn't fit. I was about to put it back and try on another one that Danetta wanted me to check out.
No. Scratch that. The first thing I remember is glass.
But then my mind jumps back to inside the store.
Danetta hands me a suit.
Try this one, Fonso. I think you would look atrociously good in it!
BANG
BANG
BANG
BANG

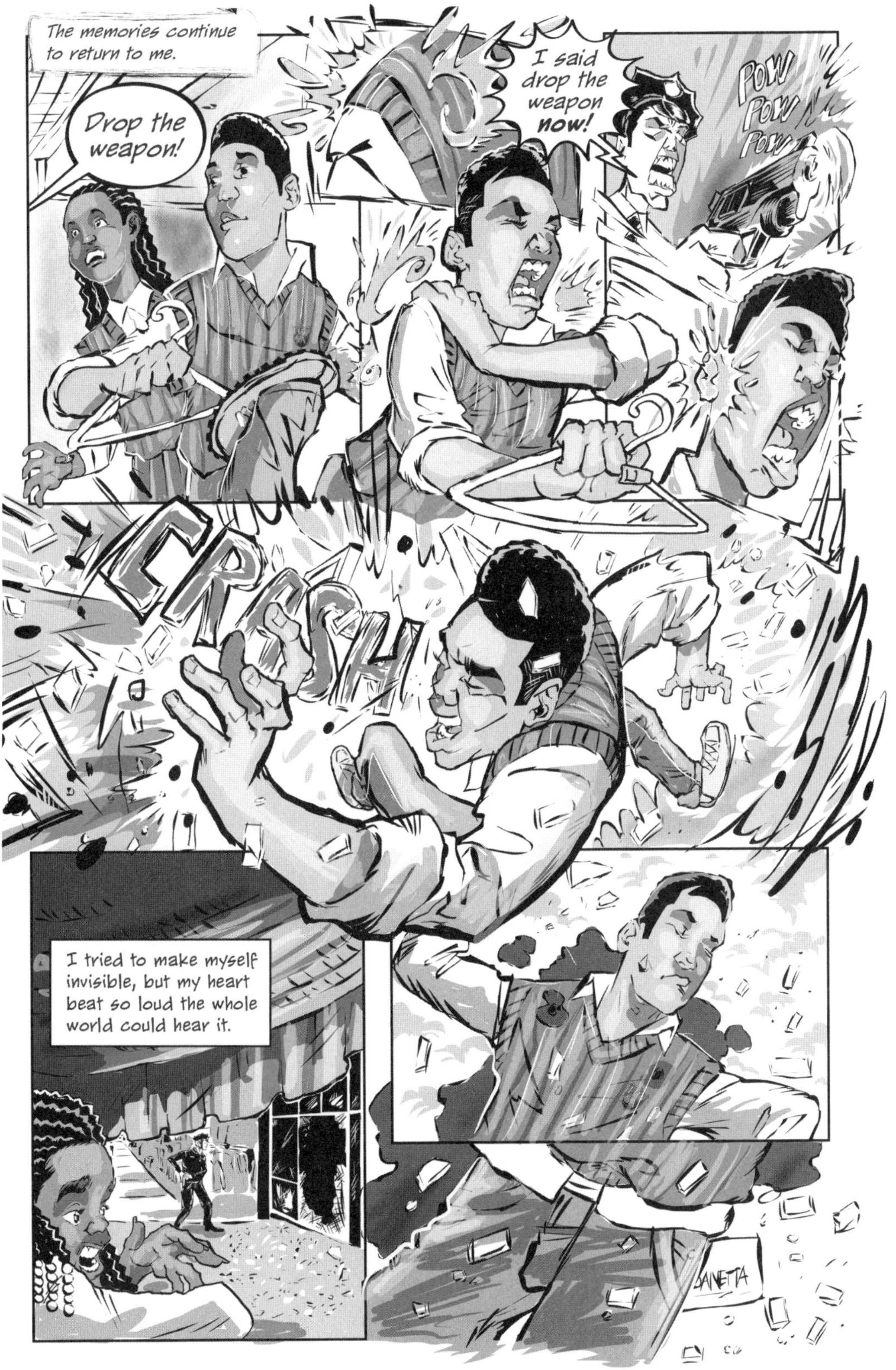
The memories continue to return to me.
Drop the weapon!
I said drop the weapon now!
POW POW POW
CRASH!
I tried to make myself invisible, but my heart beat so loud the whole world could hear it.
JANETTA

Chapter Twenty-Seven
Invisibility Blues

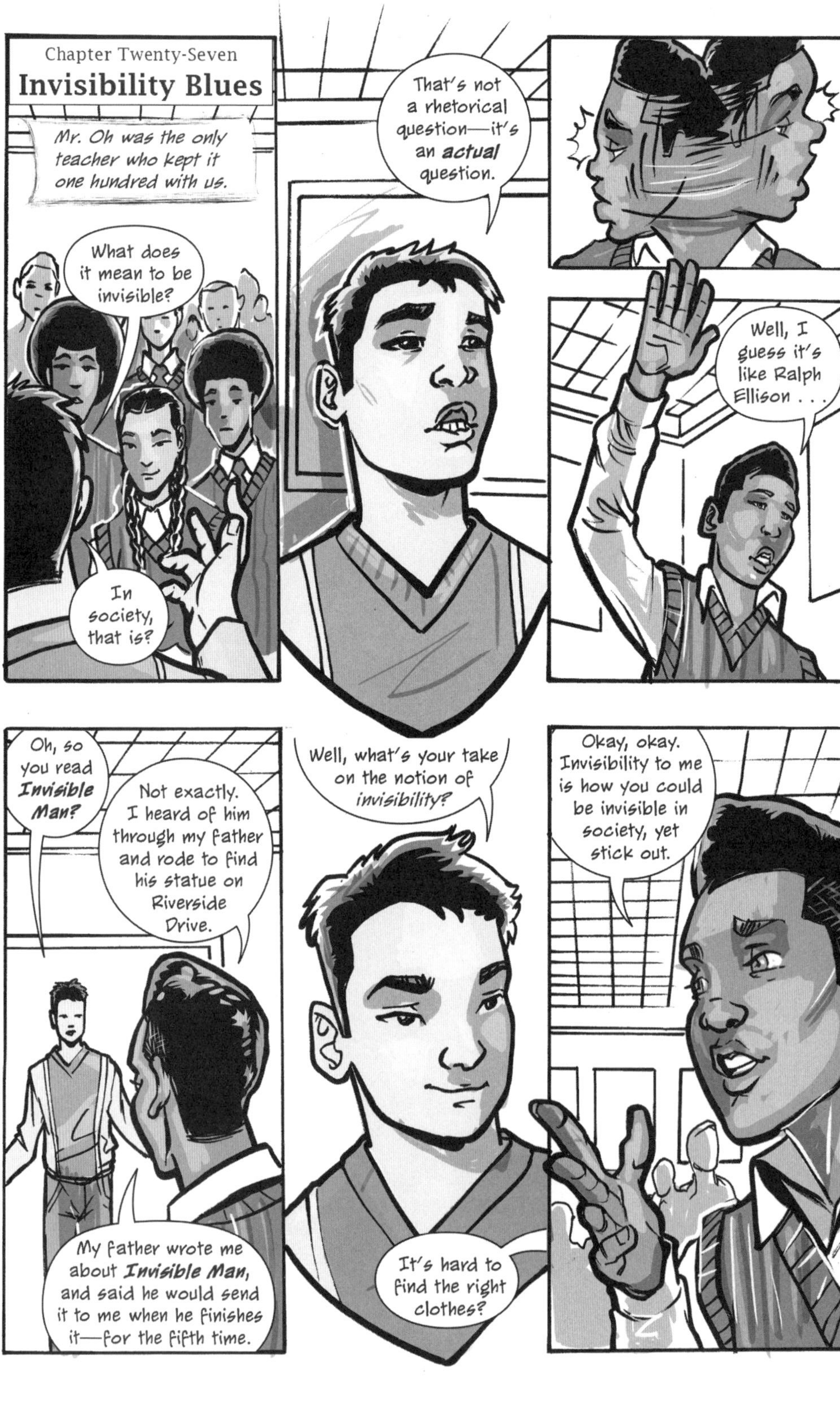
Mr. Oh was the only teacher who kept it one hundred with us.
What does it mean to be invisible?
In society, that is?
That's not a rhetorical question—it's an *actual* question.
Well, I guess it's like Ralph Ellison . . .
Oh, so you read ***Invisible Man?***
Not exactly. I heard of him through my father and rode to find his statue on Riverside Drive.
My father wrote me about ***Invisible Man,*** and said he would send it to me when he finishes it—for the fifth time.
Well, what's your take on the notion of *invisibility?*
It's hard to find the right clothes?
Okay, okay. Invisibility to me is how you could be invisible in society, yet stick out.

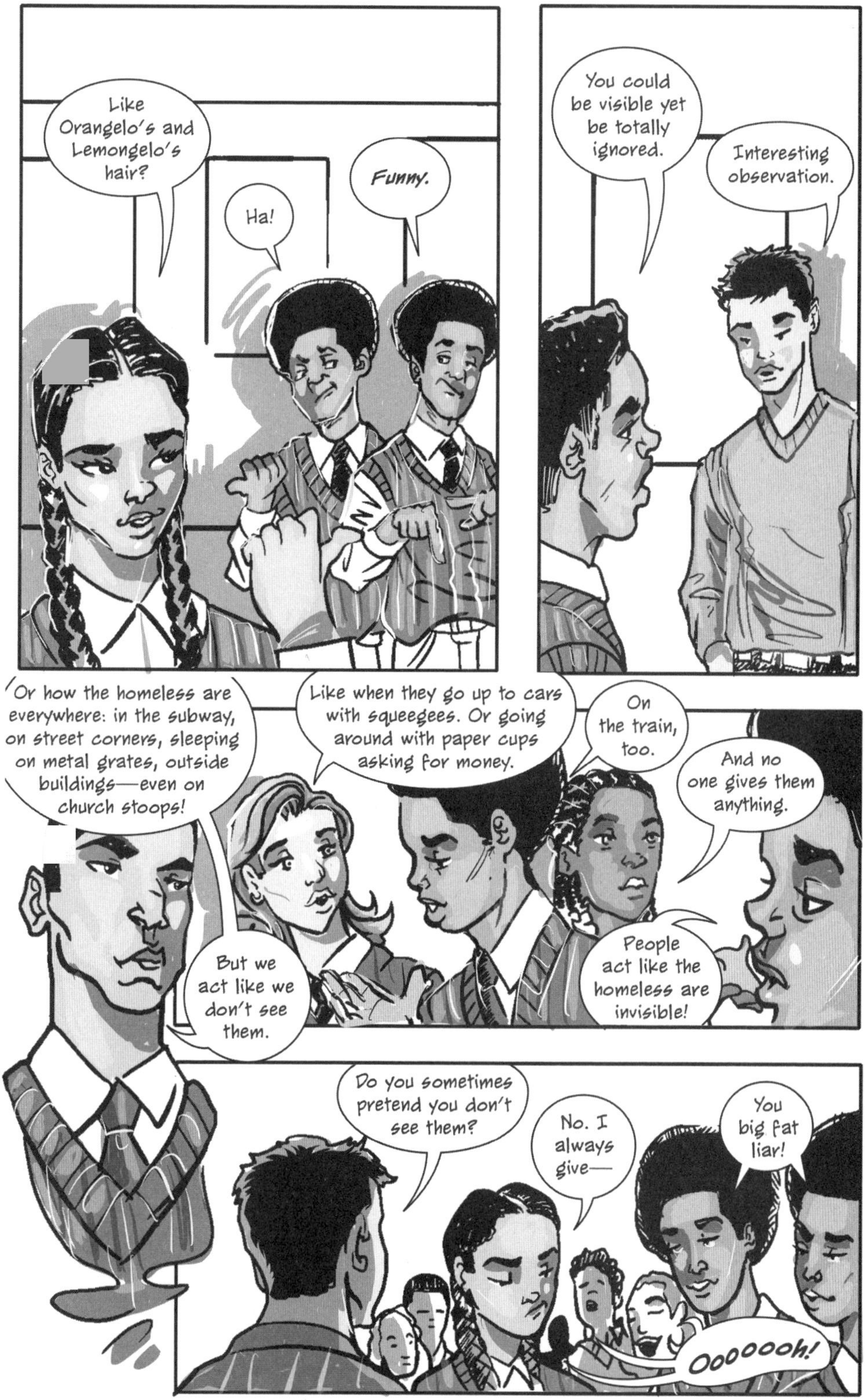
Like Orangelo's and Lemongelo's hair?
Ha!
Funny.
You could be visible yet be totally ignored.
Interesting observation.
Or how the homeless are everywhere: in the subway, on street corners, sleeping on metal grates, outside buildings—even on church stoops!
Like when they go up to cars with squeegees. Or going around with paper cups asking for money.
On the train, too.
And no one gives them anything.
But we act like we don't see them.
People act like the homeless are invisible!
Do you sometimes pretend you don't see them?
No. I always give—
You big fat liar!
Oooooooh!

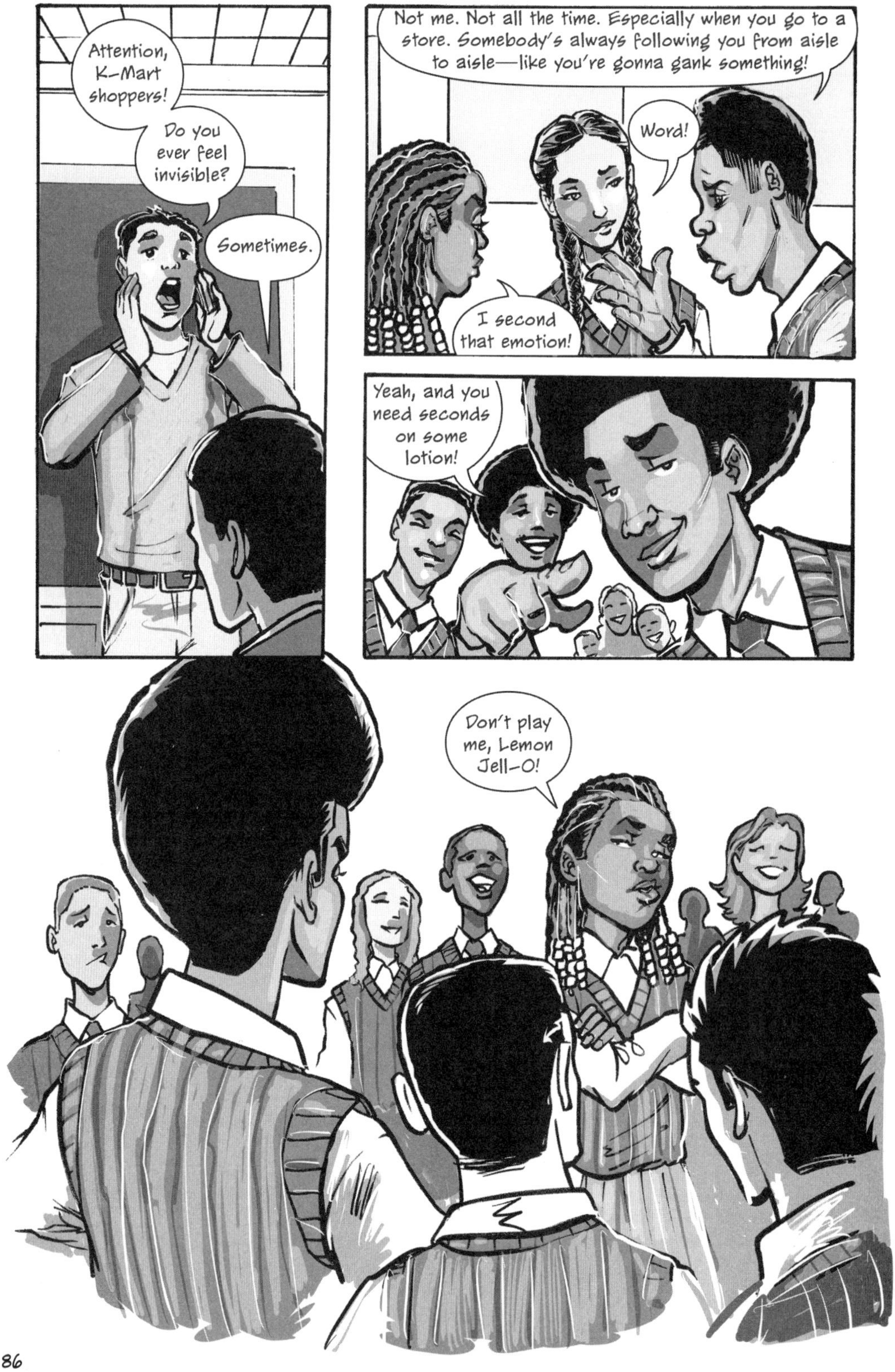
Attention, K-Mart shoppers!
Do you ever feel invisible?
Sometimes.
Not me. Not all the time. Especially when you go to a store. Somebody's always following you from aisle to aisle—like you're gonna gank something!
Word!
I second that emotion!
Yeah, and you need seconds on some lotion!
Don't play me, Lemon Jell-O!

Chapter Twenty-Eight

No Man Is an Island

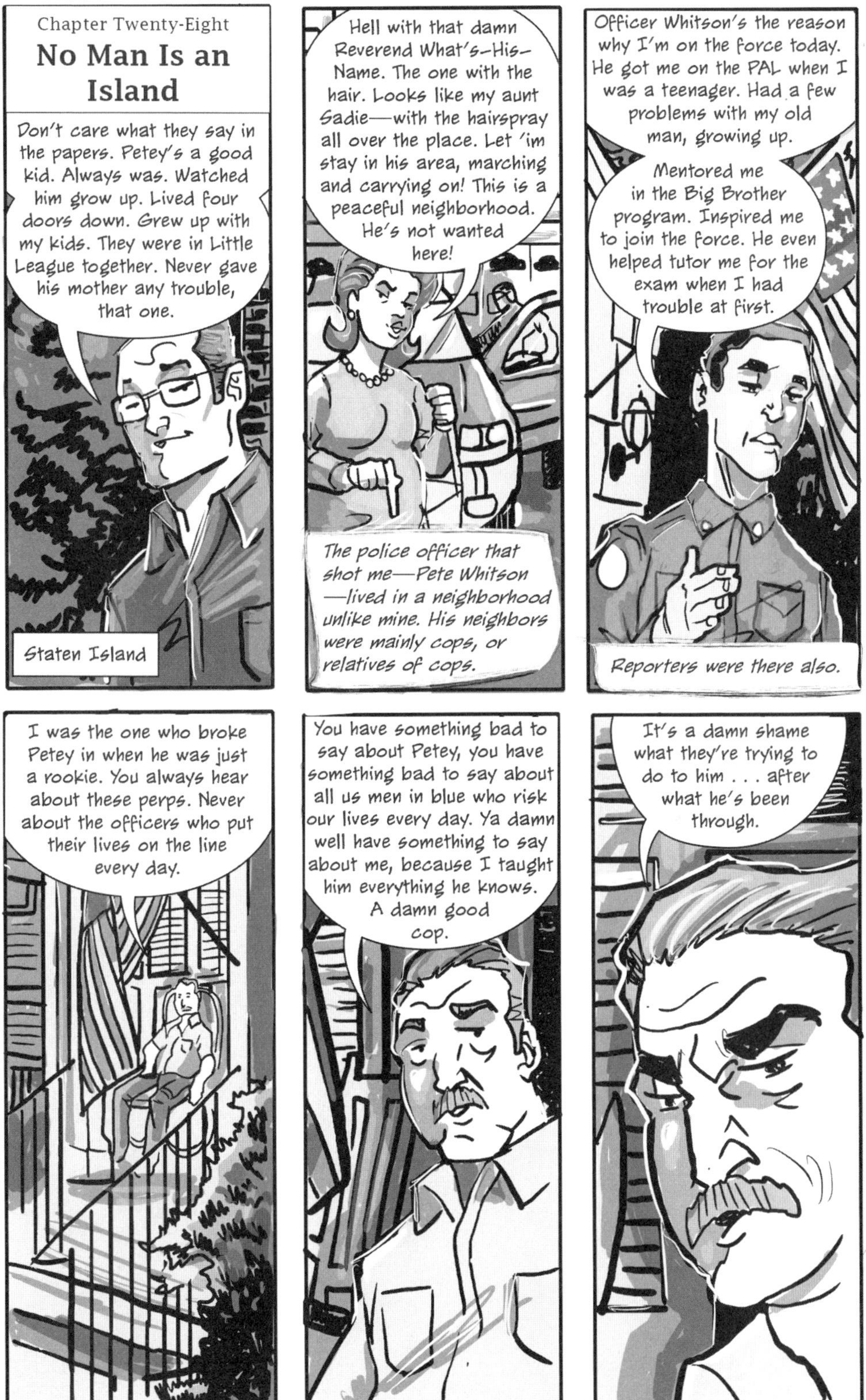

Don't care what they say in the papers. Petey's a good kid. Always was. Watched him grow up. Lived four doors down. Grew up with my kids. They were in Little League together. Never gave his mother any trouble, that one.
Staten Island
Hell with that damn Reverend What's-His-Name. The one with the hair. Looks like my aunt Sadie—with the hairspray all over the place. Let 'im stay in his area, marching and carrying on! This is a peaceful neighborhood. He's not wanted here!
The police officer that shot me—Pete Whitson—lived in a neighborhood unlike mine. His neighbors were mainly cops, or relatives of cops.
Officer Whitson's the reason why I'm on the force today. He got me on the PAL when I was a teenager. Had a few problems with my old man, growing up.
Mentored me in the Big Brother program. Inspired me to join the force. He even helped tutor me for the exam when I had trouble at first.
Reporters were there also.
I was the one who broke Petey in when he was just a rookie. You always hear about these perps. Never about the officers who put their lives on the line every day.
You have something bad to say about Petey, you have something bad to say about all us men in blue who risk our lives every day. Ya damn well have something to say about me, because I taught him everything he knows. A damn good cop.
It's a damn shame what they're trying to do to him . . . after what he's been through.

Chapter Twenty-Nine
Wrestling with Reality

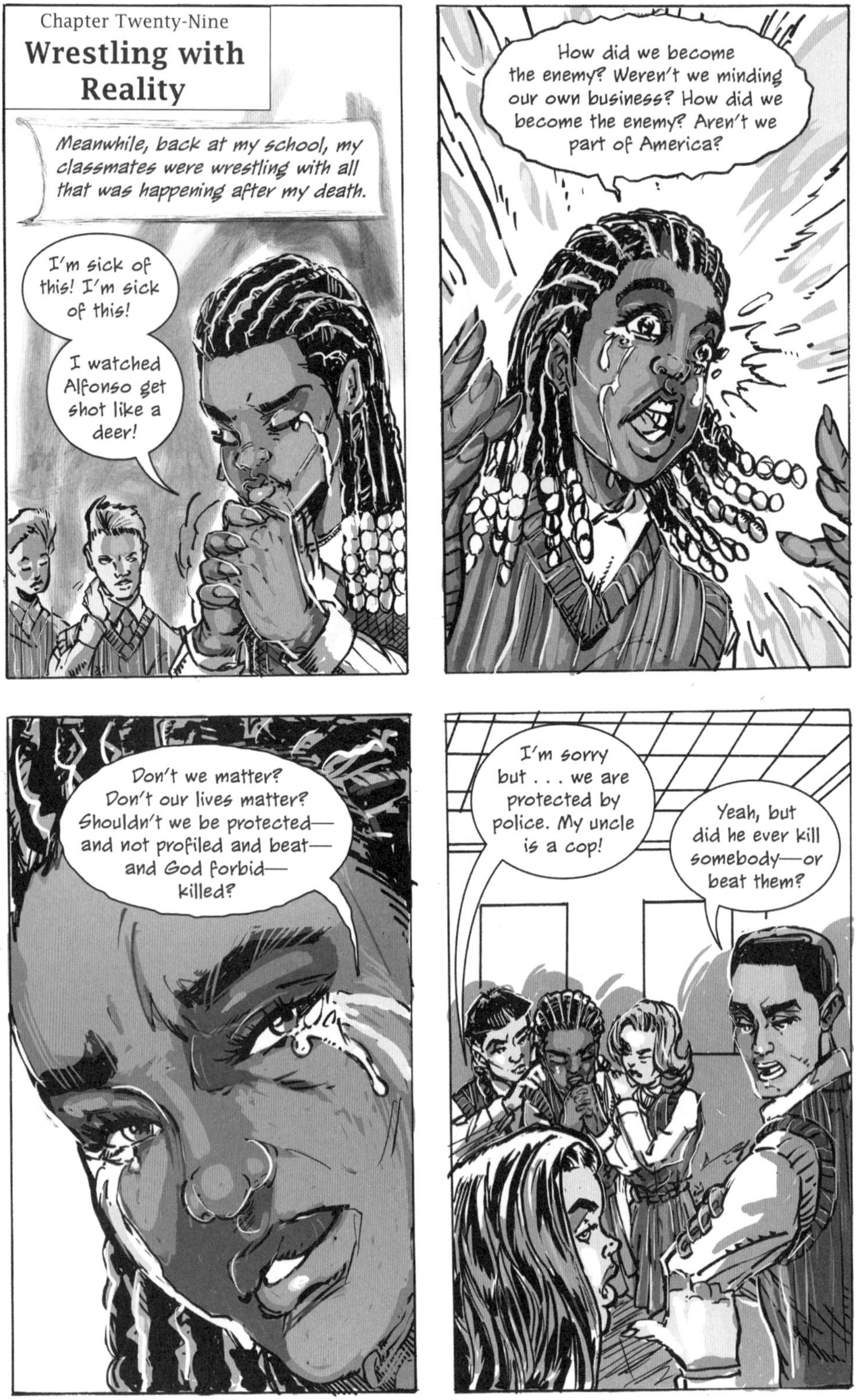
Meanwhile, back at my school, my classmates were wrestling with all that was happening after my death.
I'm sick of this! I'm sick of this!
I watched Alfonso get shot like a deer!
How did we become the enemy? Weren't we minding our own business? How did we become the enemy? Aren't we part of America?
Don't we matter? Don't our lives matter? Shouldn't we be protected—and not profiled and beat—and God forbid—killed?
I'm sorry but . . . we are protected by police. My uncle is a cop!
Yeah, but did he ever kill somebody—or beat them?

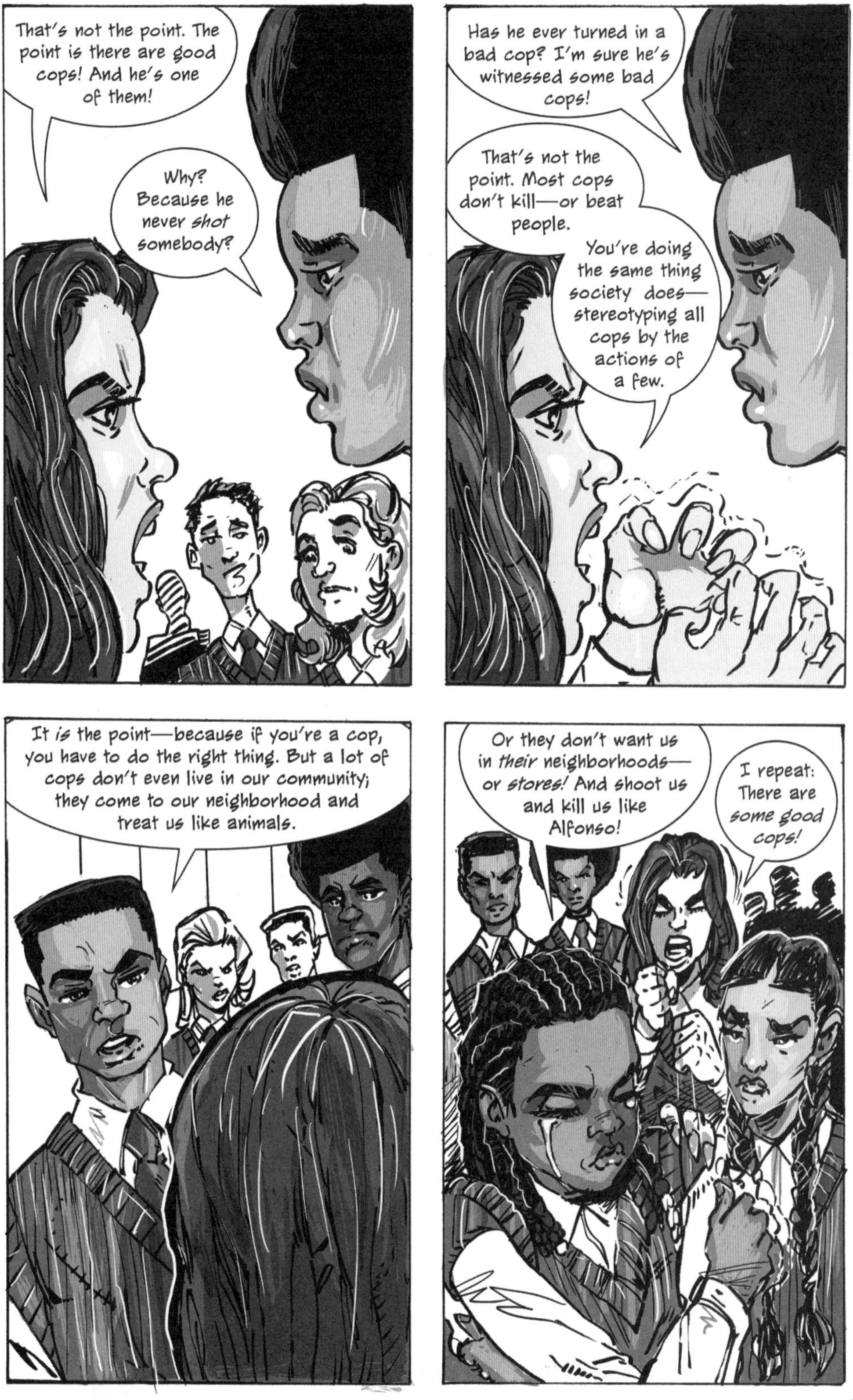

That's not the point. The point is there are good cops! And he's one of them!
Why? Because he never *shot* somebody?
Has he ever turned in a bad cop? I'm sure he's witnessed some bad cops!
That's not the point. Most cops don't kill—or beat people.
You're doing the same thing society does—stereotyping all cops by the actions of a few.
It *is* the point—because if you're a cop, you have to do the right thing. But a lot of cops don't even live in our community; they come to our neighborhood and treat us like animals.
Or they don't want us in *their* neighborhoods—or *stores!* And shoot us and kill us like Alfonso!
I repeat: There are *some good* cops!

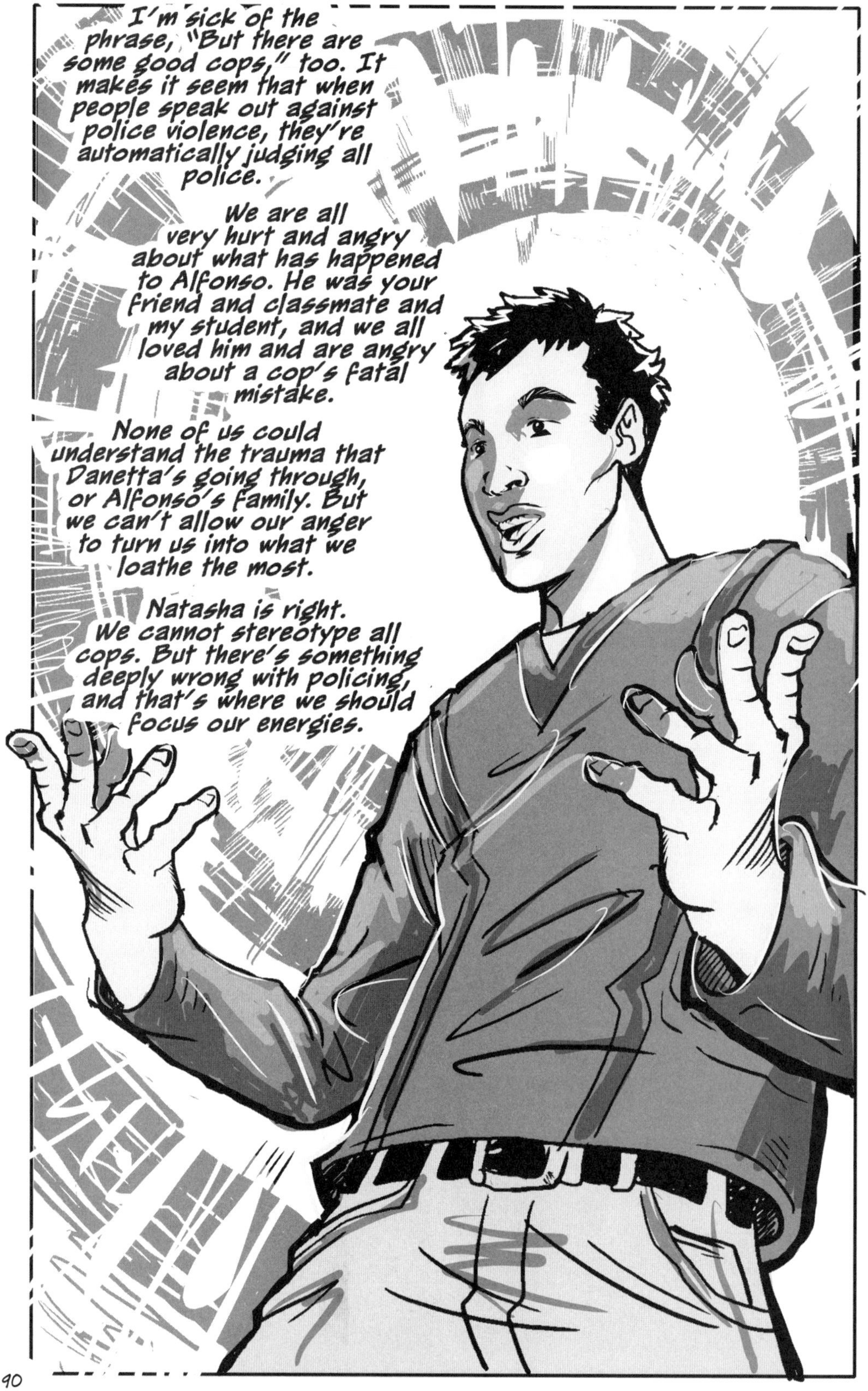
I'm sick of the phrase, "But there are some good cops," too. It makes it seem that when people speak out against police violence, they're automatically judging all police.
We are all very hurt and angry about what has happened to Alfonso. He was your friend and classmate and my student, and we all loved him and are angry about a cop's fatal mistake.
None of us could understand the trauma that Danetta's going through, or Alfonso's family. But we can't allow our anger to turn us into what we loathe the most.
Natasha is right. We cannot stereotype all cops. But there's something deeply wrong with policing, and that's where we should focus our energies.

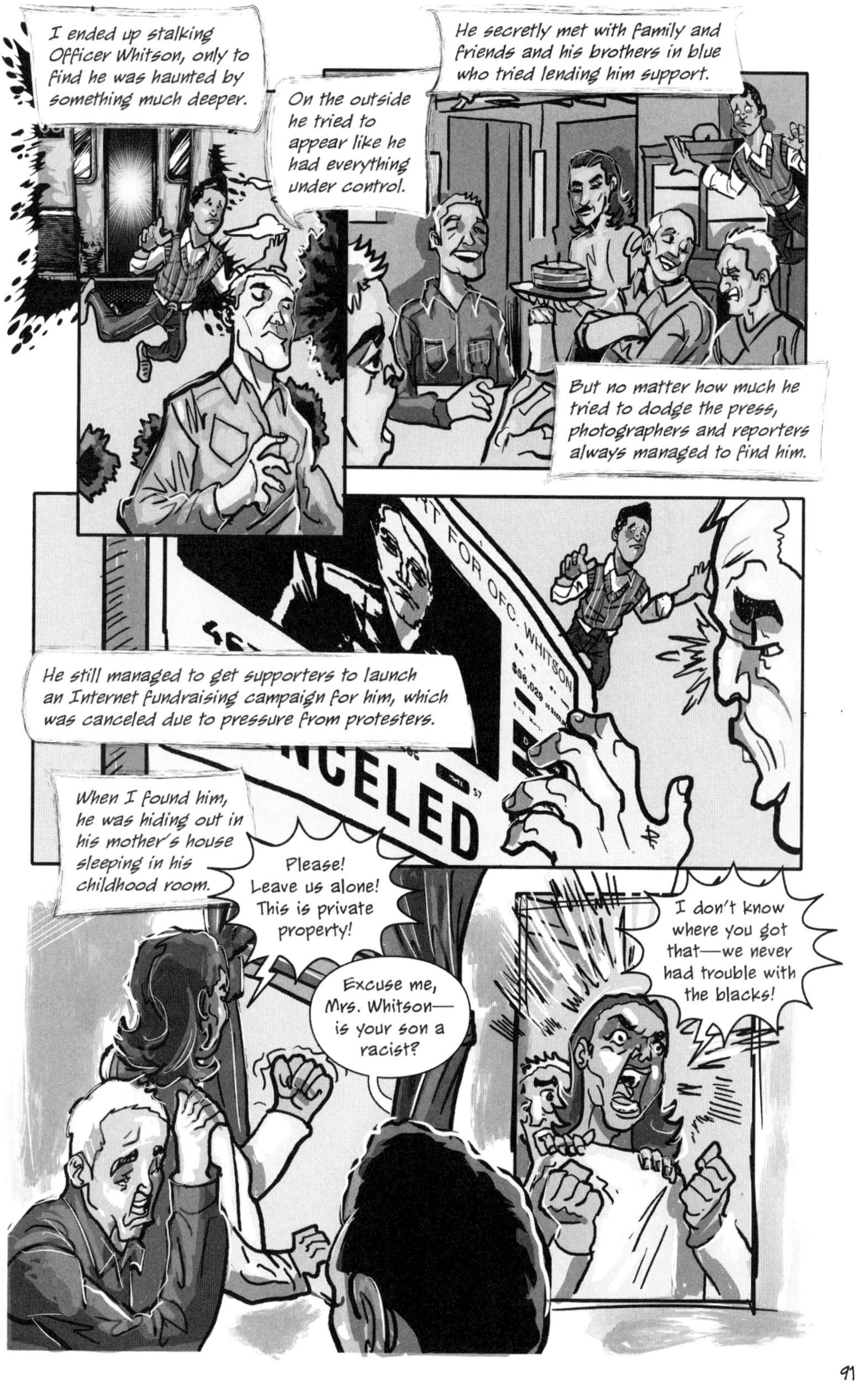
I ended up stalking Officer Whitson, only to find he was haunted by something much deeper.
On the outside he tried to appear like he had everything under control.
He secretly met with family and friends and his brothers in blue who tried lending him support.
But no matter how much he tried to dodge the press, photographers and reporters always managed to find him.
FOR OFC. WHITSON
$56,029
He still managed to get supporters to launch an Internet fundraising campaign for him, which was canceled due to pressure from protesters.
When I found him, he was hiding out in his mother's house sleeping in his childhood room.
Please! Leave us alone! This is private property!
Excuse me, Mrs. Whitson—is your son a racist?
I don't know where you got that—we never had trouble with the blacks!

I followed Officer Whitson around as he hid in his 'hood, because I had to look into his eyes.

When I did, it was like looking at a deer in headlights.

We were face-to-face for the first time. I could see him, but he could not see me.

Yet I wondered if he could feel my presence.

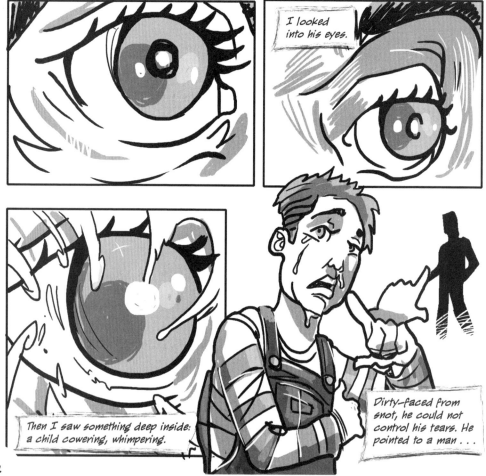

I looked into his eyes.

Then I saw something deep inside: a child cowering, whimpering.

Dirty-faced from snot, he could not control his tears. He pointed to a man . . .

Frank!
Frank!
BANG!!!!

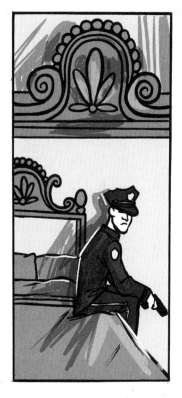

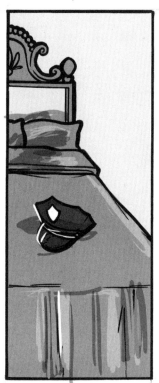

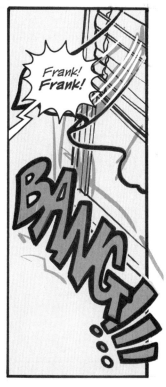

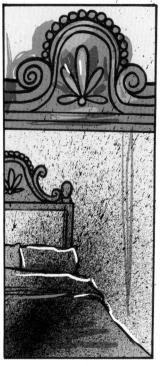

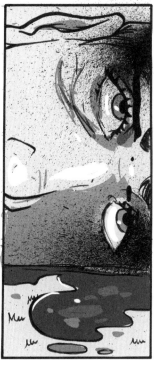

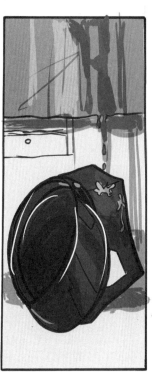

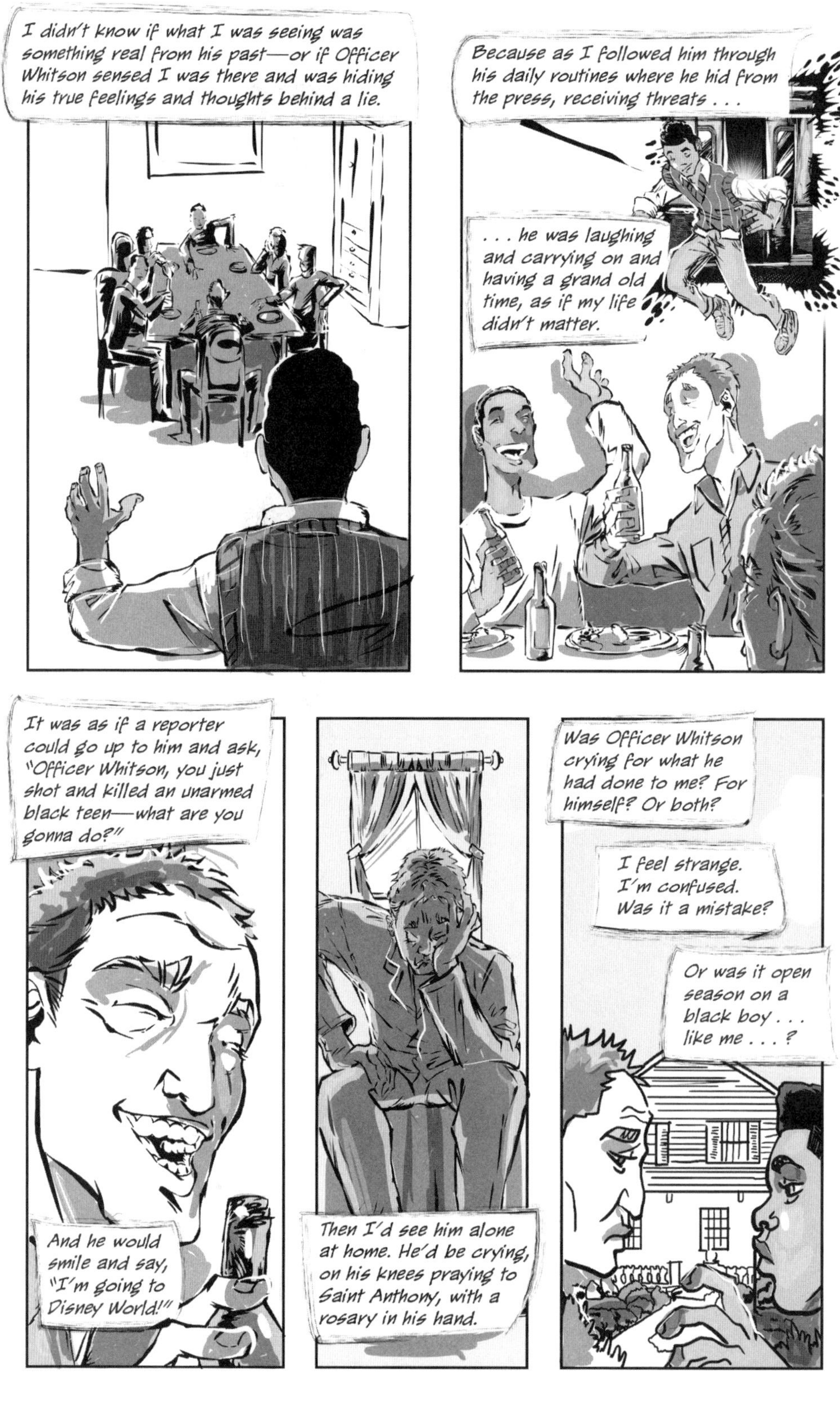
I didn't know if what I was seeing was something real from his past—or if Officer Whitson sensed I was there and was hiding his true feelings and thoughts behind a lie.
Because as I followed him through his daily routines where he hid from the press, receiving threats . . .
. . . he was laughing and carrying on and having a grand old time, as if my life didn't matter.
It was as if a reporter could go up to him and ask, "Officer Whitson, you just shot and killed an unarmed black teen—what are you gonna do?"
And he would smile and say, "I'm going to Disney World!"
Then I'd see him alone at home. He'd be crying, on his knees praying to Saint Anthony, with a rosary in his hand.
Was Officer Whitson crying for what he had done to me? For himself? Or both?
I feel strange. I'm confused. Was it a mistake?
Or was it open season on a black boy . . . like me . . . ?

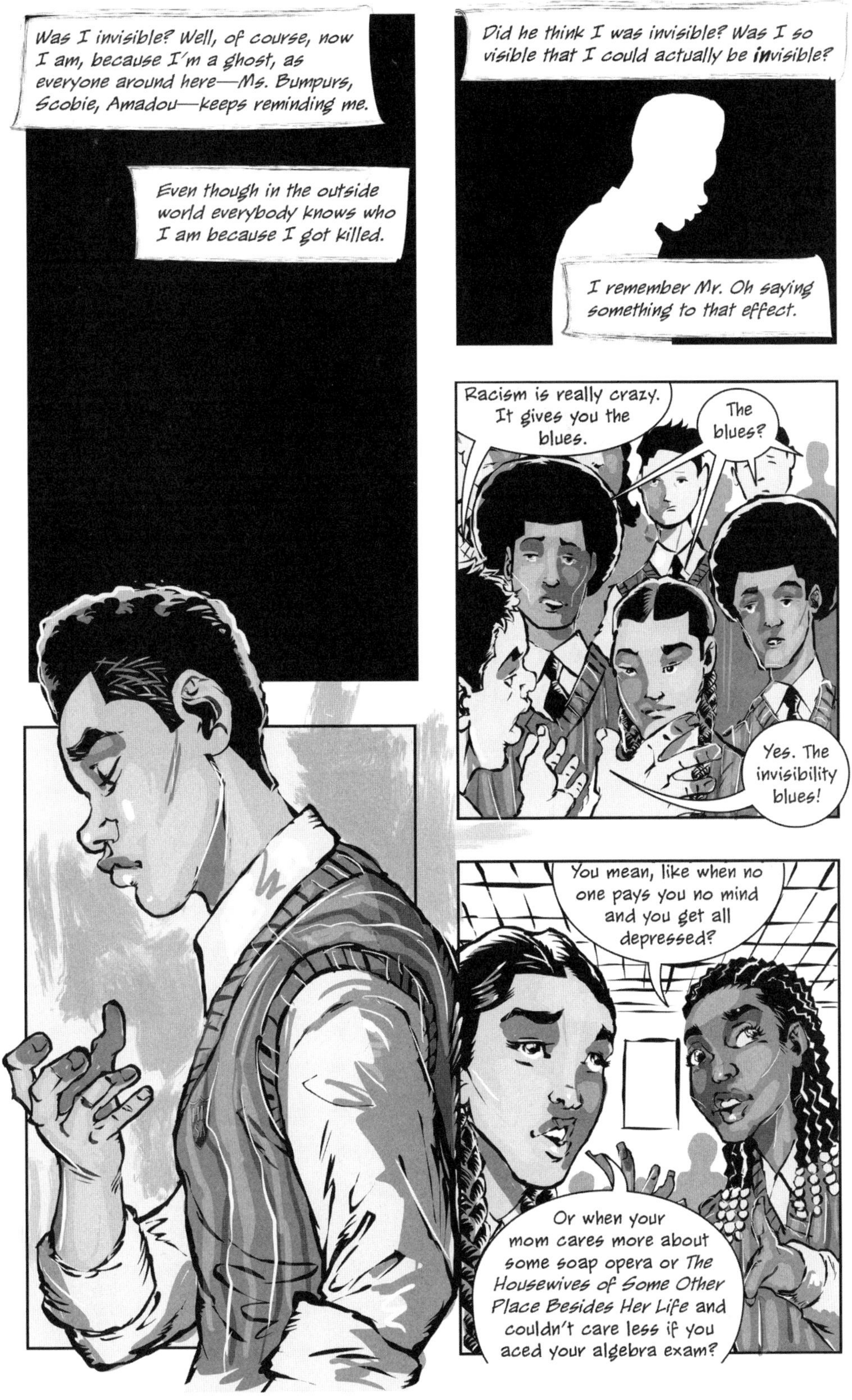
Was I invisible? Well, of course, now I am, because I'm a ghost, as everyone around here—Ms. Bumpurs, Scobie, Amadou—keeps reminding me.
Even though in the outside world everybody knows who I am because I got killed.
Did he think I was invisible? Was I so visible that I could actually be invisible?
I remember Mr. Oh saying something to that effect.
Racism is really crazy. It gives you the blues.
The blues?
Yes. The invisibility blues!
You mean, like when no one pays you no mind and you get all depressed?
Or when your mom cares more about some soap opera or *The Housewives of Some Other Place Besides Her Life* and couldn't care less if you aced your algebra exam?

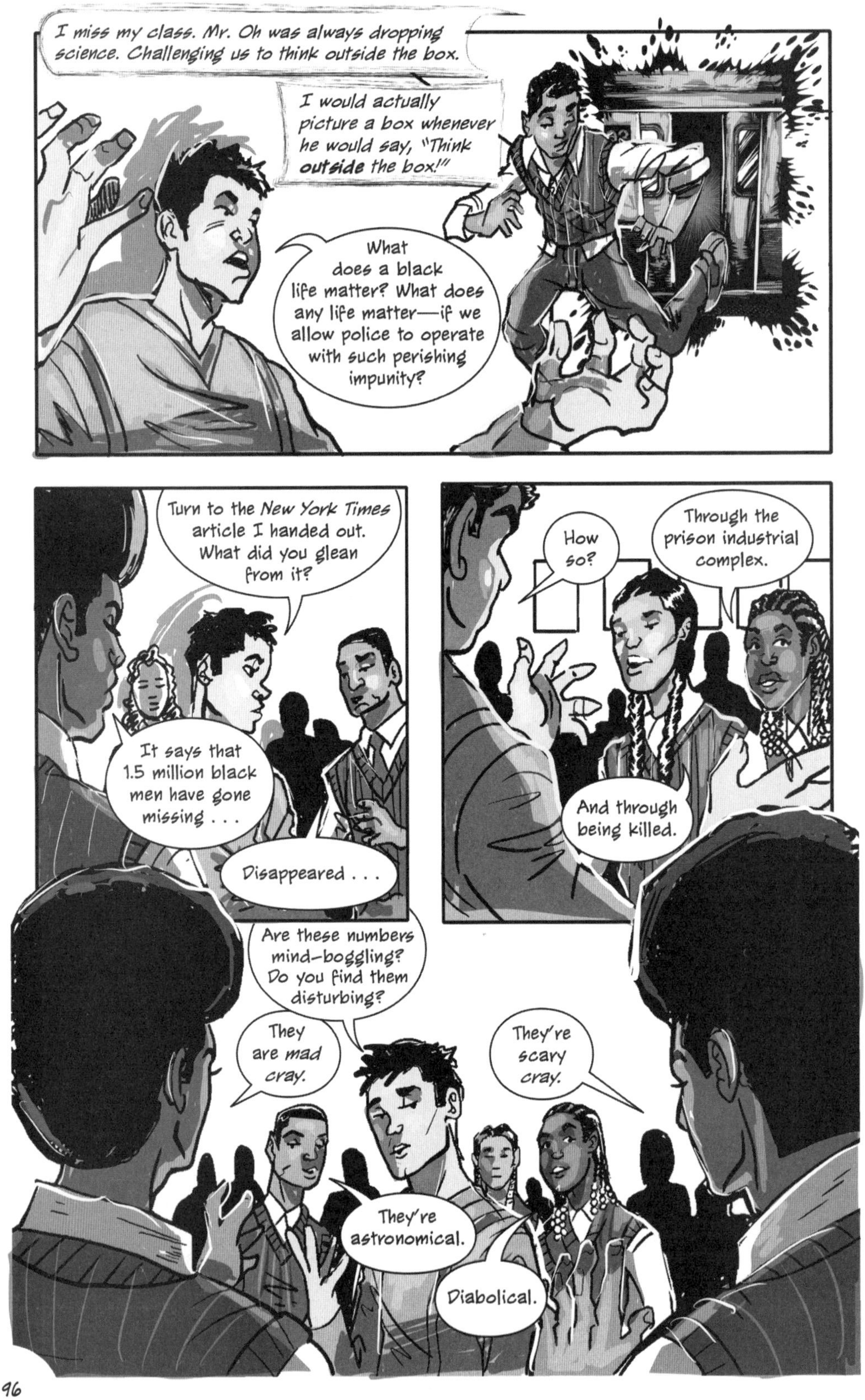
I miss my class. Mr. Oh was always dropping science. Challenging us to think outside the box.
I would actually picture a box whenever he would say, "Think **outside** the box!"
What does a black life matter? What does any life matter—if we allow police to operate with such perishing impunity?
Turn to the *New York Times* article I handed out. What did you glean from it?
It says that 1.5 million black men have gone missing . . .
Disappeared . . .
How so?
Through the prison industrial complex.
And through being killed.
Are these numbers mind-boggling? Do you find them disturbing?
They are *mad* cray.
They're scary cray.
They're astronomical.
Diabolical.

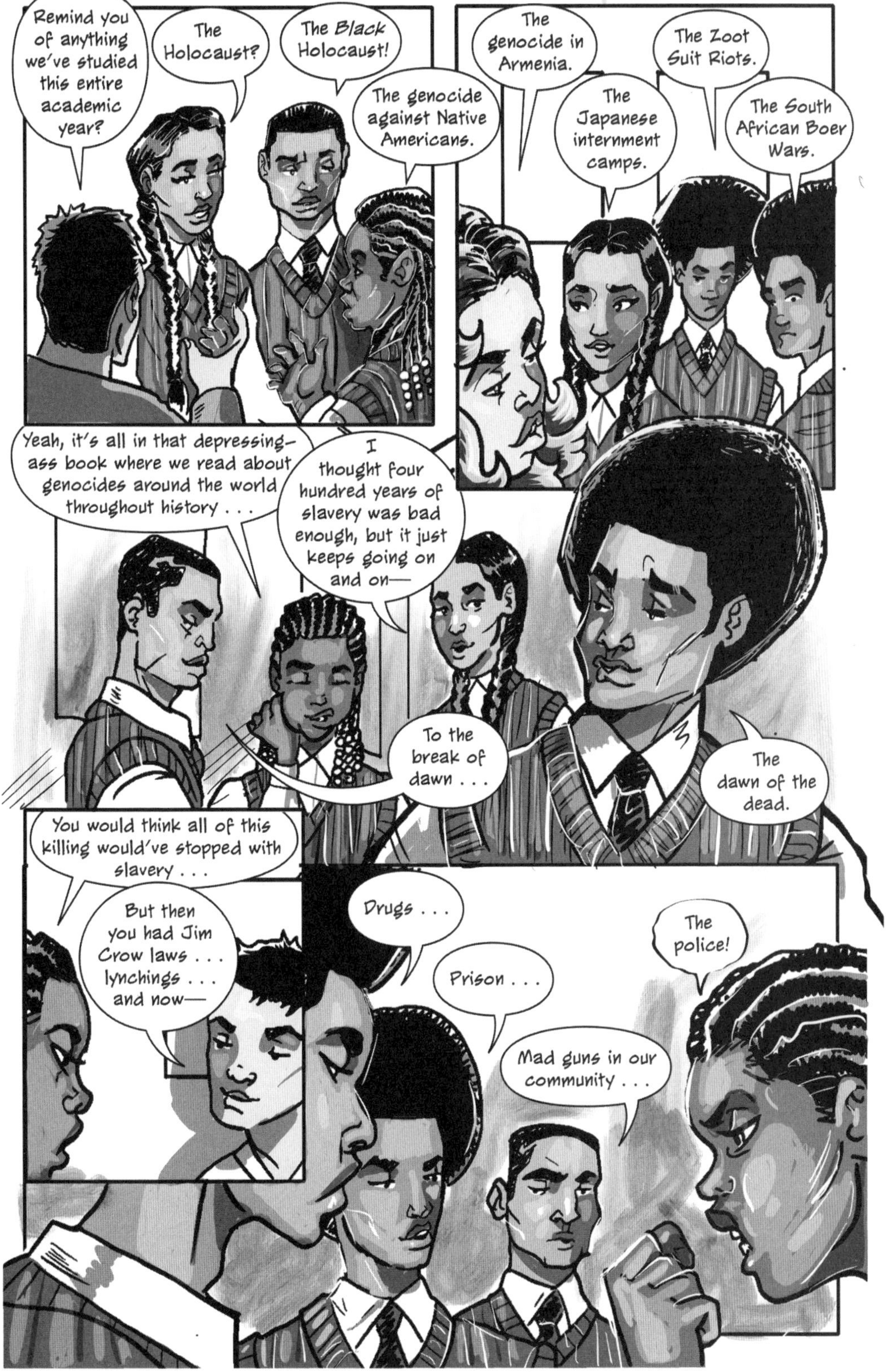
Remind you of anything we've studied this entire academic year?
The Holocaust?
The *Black* Holocaust!
The genocide against Native Americans.
The genocide in Armenia.
The Japanese internment camps.
The Zoot Suit Riots.
The South African Boer Wars.
Yeah, it's all in that depressing-ass book where we read about genocides around the world throughout history . . .
I thought four hundred years of slavery was bad enough, but it just keeps going on and on—
To the break of dawn . . .
The dawn of the dead.
You would think all of this killing would've stopped with slavery . . .
But then you had Jim Crow laws . . . lynchings . . . and now—
Drugs . . .
Prison . . .
The police!
Mad guns in our community . . .

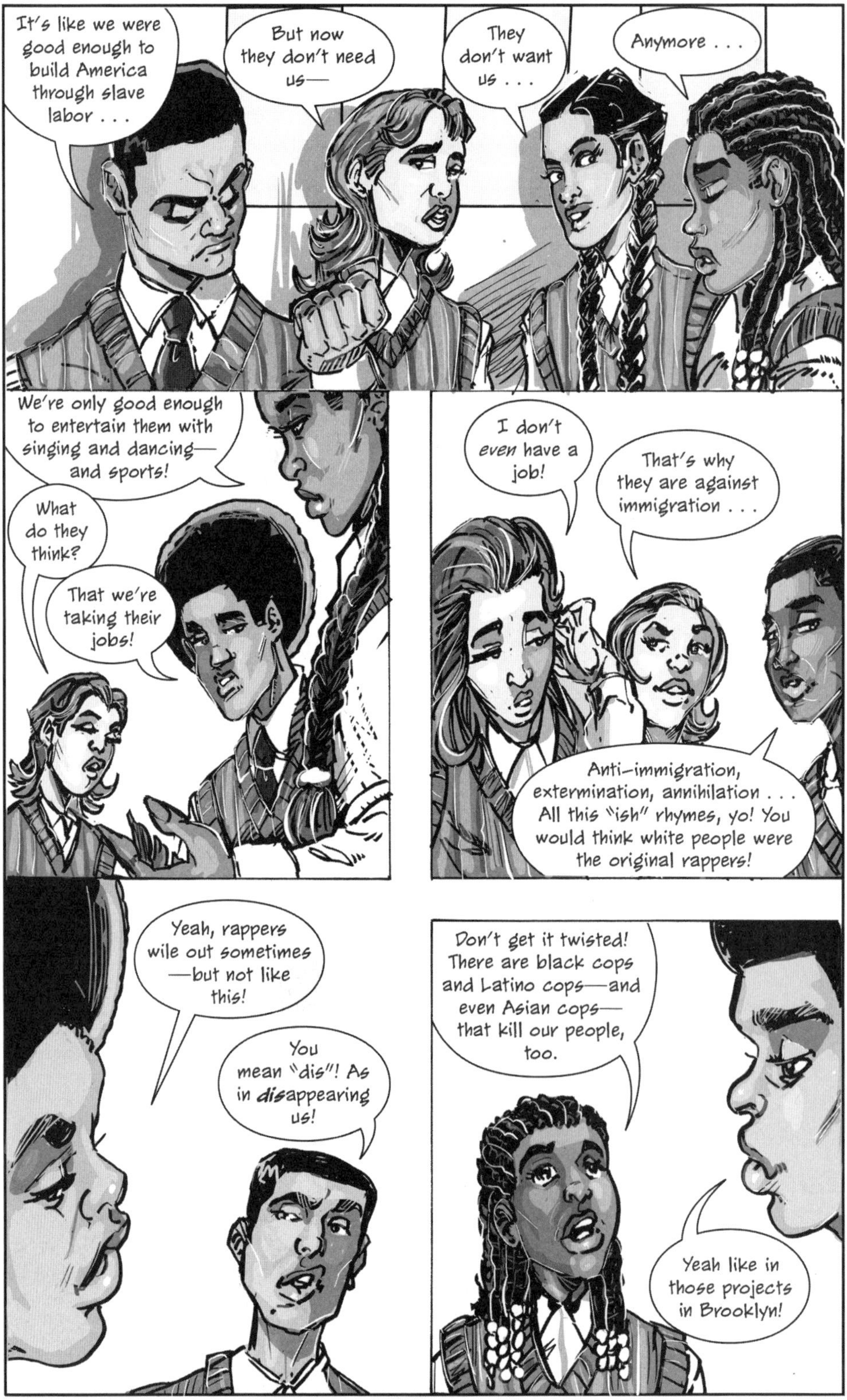
It's like we were good enough to build America through slave labor . . .
But now they don't need us—
They don't want us . . .
Anymore . . .
We're only good enough to entertain them with singing and dancing—and sports!
What do they think?
That we're taking their jobs!
I don't *even* have a job!
That's why they are against immigration . . .
Anti-immigration, extermination, annihilation . . . All this "ish" rhymes, yo! You would think white people were the original rappers!
Yeah, rappers wile out sometimes—but not like this!
You mean "dis"! As in ***dis***appearing us!
Don't get it twisted! There are black cops and Latino cops—and even Asian cops—that kill our people, too.
Yeah like in those projects in Brooklyn!

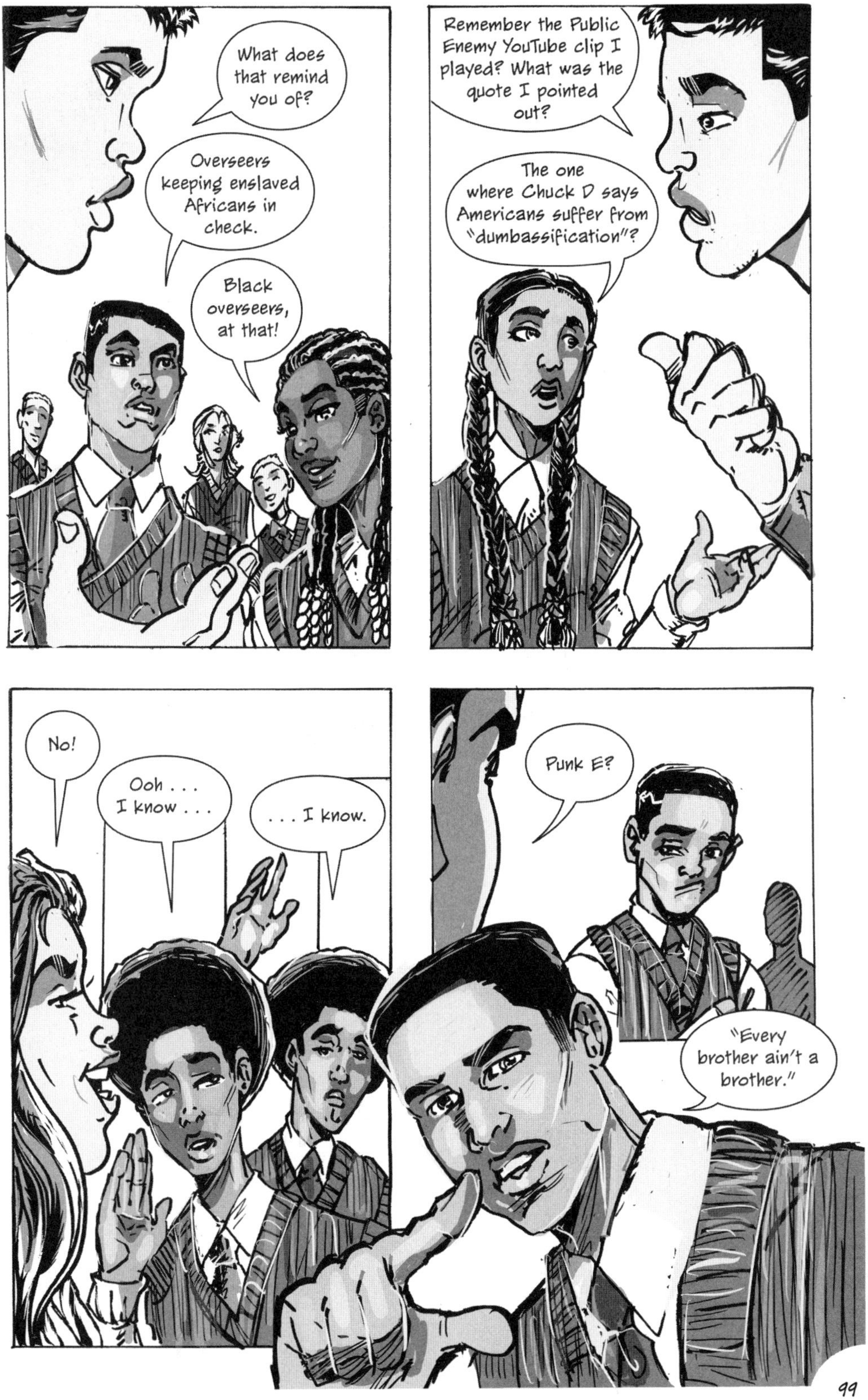
What does that remind you of?
Overseers keeping enslaved Africans in check.
Black overseers, at that!
Remember the Public Enemy YouTube clip I played? What was the quote I pointed out?
The one where Chuck D says Americans suffer from "dumbassification"?
No!
Ooh . . . I know . . .
. . . I know.
Punk E?
"Every brother ain't a brother."

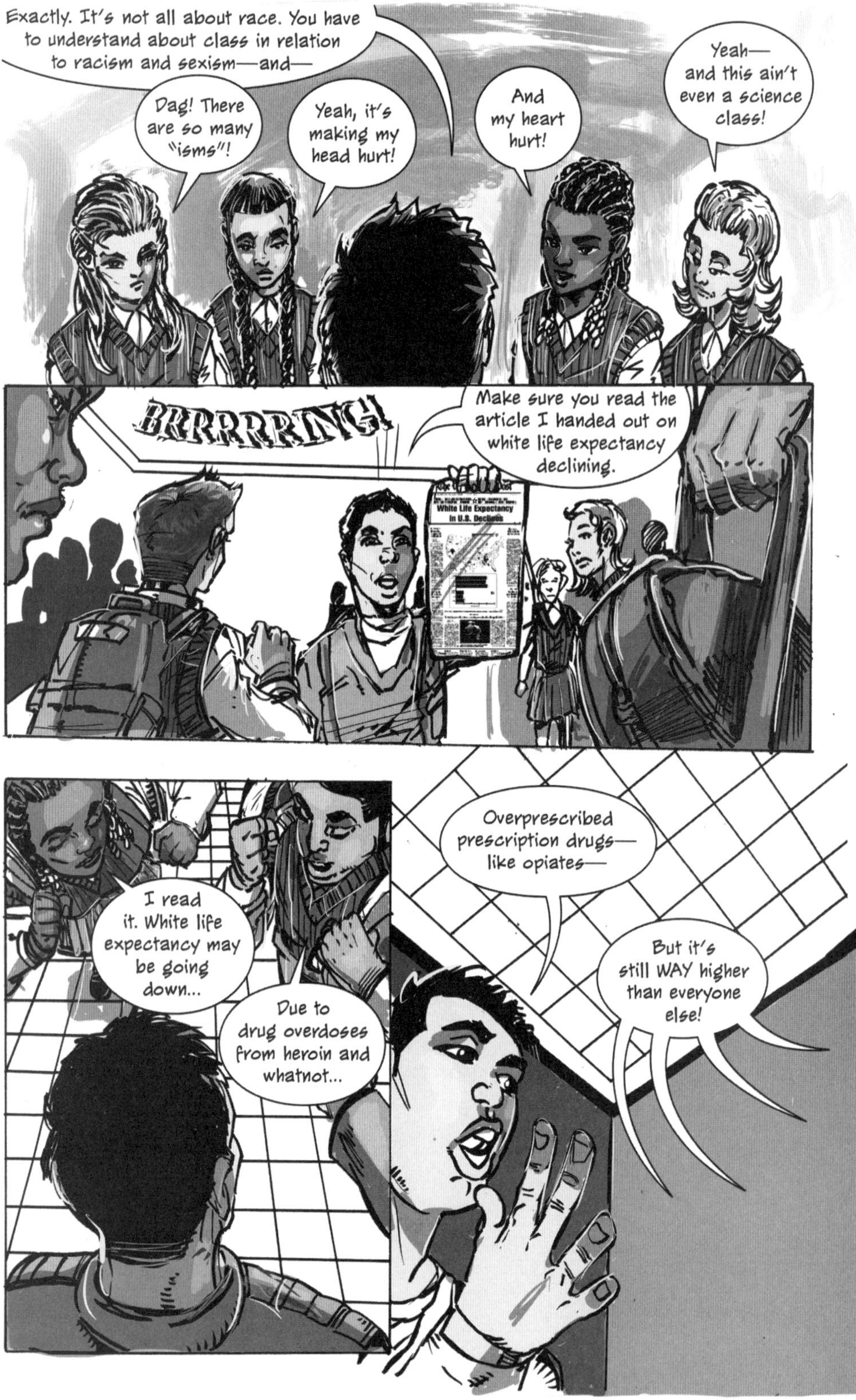
Exactly. It's not all about race. You have to understand about class in relation to racism and sexism—and—
Dag! There are so many "isms"!
Yeah, it's making my head hurt!
And my heart hurt!
Yeah— and this ain't even a science class!
BRRRRRING!
Make sure you read the article I handed out on white life expectancy declining.
White Life Expectancy in U.S. Declines
I read it. White life expectancy may be going down...
Due to drug overdoses from heroin and whatnot...
Overprescribed prescription drugs— like opiates—
But it's still WAY higher than everyone else!

Chapter Thirty

Field Trip

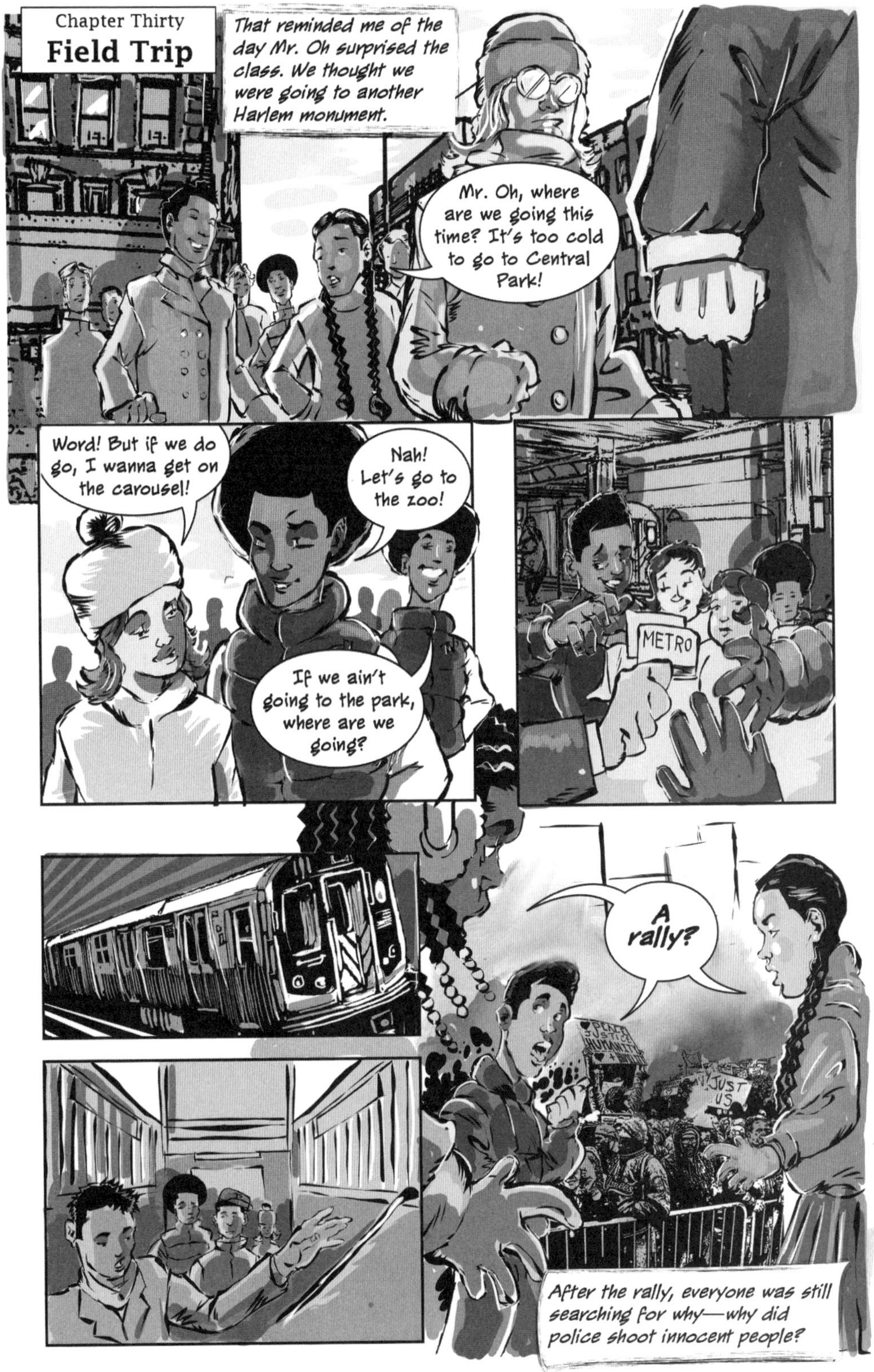

That reminded me of the day Mr. Oh surprised the class. We thought we were going to another Harlem monument.
Mr. Oh, where are we going this time? It's too cold to go to Central Park!
Word! But if we do go, I wanna get on the carousel!
Nah! Let's go to the zoo!
If we ain't going to the park, where are we going?
METRO
A rally?
After the rally, everyone was still searching for why—why did police shoot innocent people?

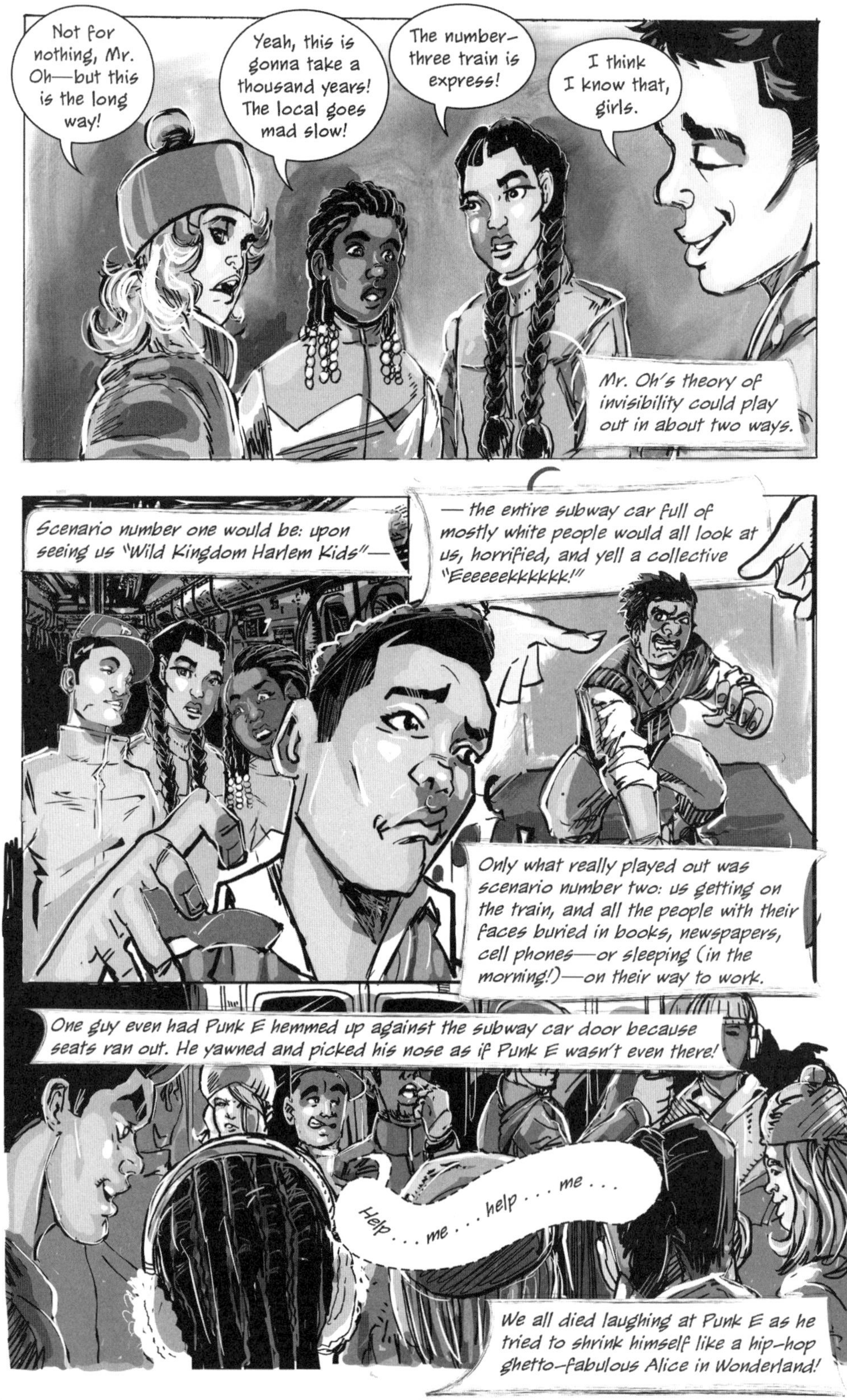
Not for nothing, Mr. Oh—but this is the long way!
Yeah, this is gonna take a thousand years! The local goes mad slow!
The number-three train is express!
I think I know that, girls.
Mr. Oh's theory of invisibility could play out in about two ways.
Scenario number one would be: upon seeing us "Wild Kingdom Harlem Kids"—
— the entire subway car full of mostly white people would all look at us, horrified, and yell a collective "Eeeeeekkkkkk!"
Only what really played out was scenario number two: us getting on the train, and all the people with their faces buried in books, newspapers, cell phones—or sleeping (in the morning!)—on their way to work.
One guy even had Punk E hemmed up against the subway car door because seats ran out. He yawned and picked his nose as if Punk E wasn't even there!
Help . . . me . . . help . . . me . . .
We all died laughing at Punk E as he tried to shrink himself like a hip-hop ghetto-fabulous Alice in Wonderland!

Chapter Thirty-One
Faux News

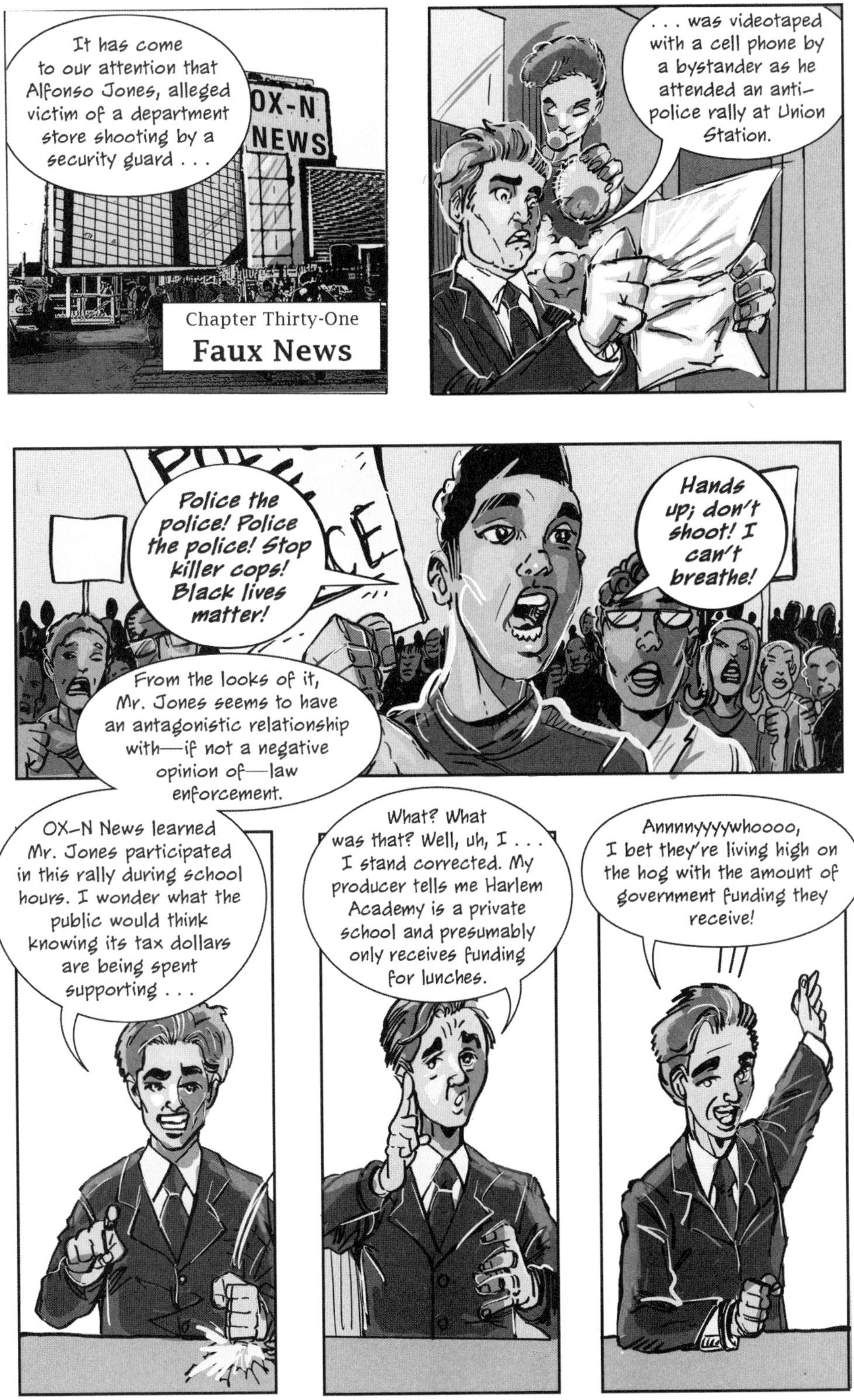

It has come to our attention that Alfonso Jones, alleged victim of a department store shooting by a security guard . . .
OX-N NEWS
. . . was videotaped with a cell phone by a bystander as he attended an anti-police rally at Union Station.
Police the police! Police the police! Stop killer cops! Black lives matter!
Hands up; don't shoot! I can't breathe!
From the looks of it, Mr. Jones seems to have an antagonistic relationship with—if not a negative opinion of—law enforcement.
OX-N News learned Mr. Jones participated in this rally during school hours. I wonder what the public would think knowing its tax dollars are being spent supporting . . .
What? What was that? Well, uh, I . . . I stand corrected. My producer tells me Harlem Academy is a private school and presumably only receives funding for lunches.
Annnnyyyywhoooo, I bet they're living high on the hog with the amount of government funding they receive!

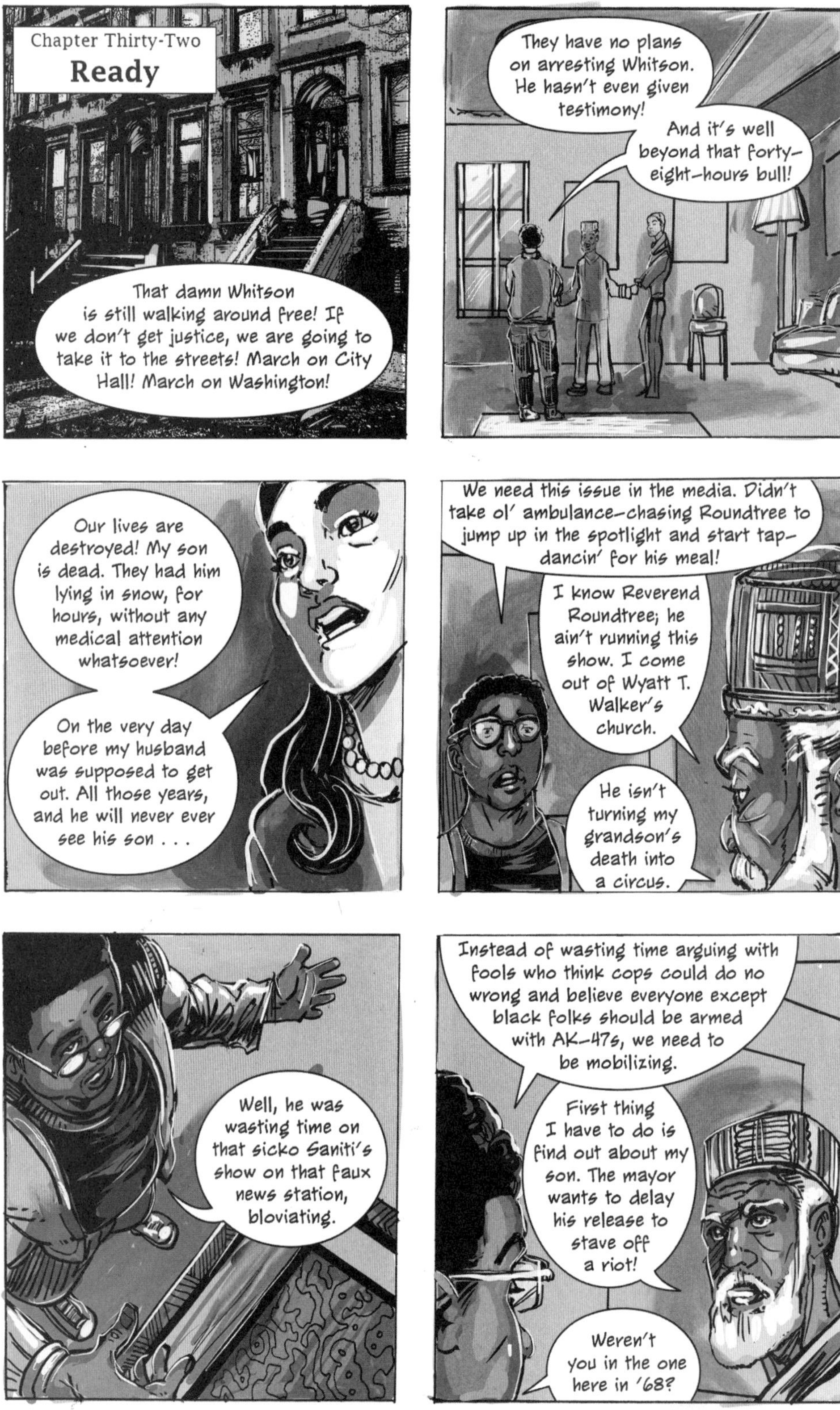
Chapter Thirty-Two
Ready
That damn Whitson is still walking around free! If we don't get justice, we are going to take it to the streets! March on City Hall! March on Washington!
They have no plans on arresting Whitson. He hasn't even given testimony!
And it's well beyond that forty-eight-hours bull!
Our lives are destroyed! My son is dead. They had him lying in snow, for hours, without any medical attention whatsoever!
On the very day before my husband was supposed to get out. All those years, and he will never ever see his son . . .
We need this issue in the media. Didn't take ol' ambulance-chasing Roundtree to jump up in the spotlight and start tap-dancin' for his meal!
I know Reverend Roundtree; he ain't running this show. I come out of Wyatt T. Walker's church.
He isn't turning my grandson's death into a circus.
Well, he was wasting time on that sicko Saniti's show on that faux news station, bloviating.
Instead of wasting time arguing with fools who think cops could do no wrong and believe everyone except black folks should be armed with AK-47s, we need to be mobilizing.
First thing I have to do is find out about my son. The mayor wants to delay his release to stave off a riot!
Weren't you in the one here in '68?

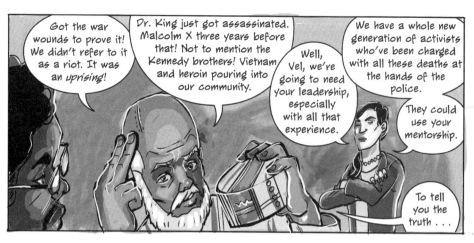

Got the war wounds to prove it! We didn't refer to it as a riot. It was an *uprising*!

Dr. King just got assassinated. Malcolm X three years before that! Not to mention the Kennedy brothers! Vietnam and heroin pouring into our community.

Well, Vel, we're going to need your leadership, especially with all that experience.

We have a whole new generation of activists who've been charged with all these deaths at the hands of the police.

They could use your mentorship.

To tell you the truth . . .

. . . I think these young activists like Black Lives Matter are doing wonderful work that we couldn't possibly have, with all this new technology.

They're keeping these politicians on their toes, pushing for criminal justice reform. But we need to join together and mobilize around Alfonso for the sake of the cause.

That's why we're here, my dear. Ol' Rev. don't need to be leading nobody no how! It's time for a new generation to be heard! I'm here to listen to you all!

Wonderful, because I invited someone from Black Lives Matter New York and a leader from the LGBT community.

The who what when and where?

The lesbian, gay, bisexual, and transgender community!

What in the bejeezus?

Now, Vel. You're supposed to be a progressive!

Well, I'm a *little* conservative. But I do believe in liberation theology.

DING DONG

They're here.

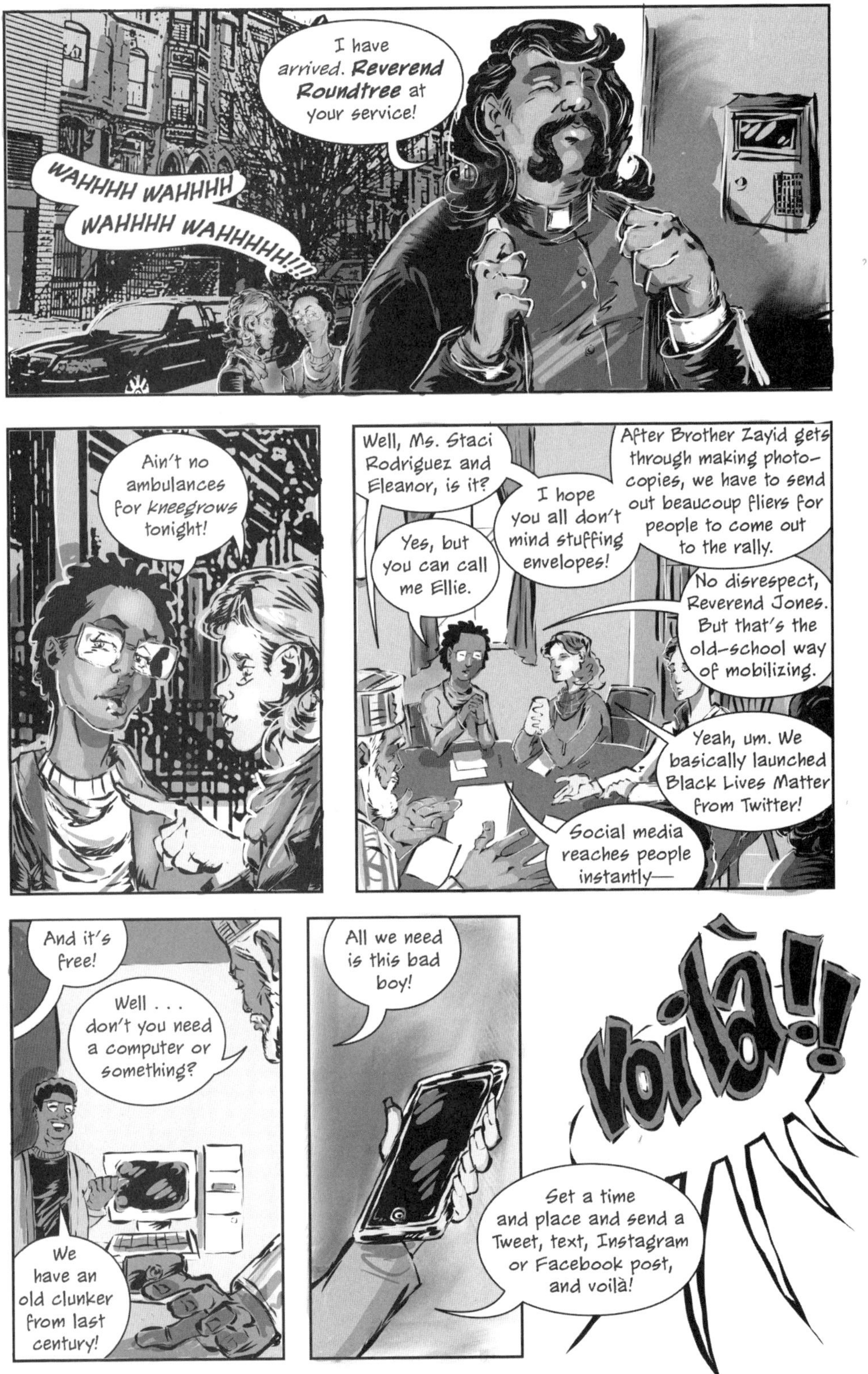
I have arrived. Reverend Roundtree at your service!
WAHHHH WAHHHH WAHHHH WAHHHHH!!!
Ain't no ambulances for kneegrows tonight!
Well, Ms. Staci Rodriguez and Eleanor, is it?
Yes, but you can call me Ellie.
I hope you all don't mind stuffing envelopes!
After Brother Zayid gets through making photocopies, we have to send out beaucoup fliers for people to come out to the rally.
No disrespect, Reverend Jones. But that's the old-school way of mobilizing.
Yeah, um. We basically launched Black Lives Matter from Twitter!
Social media reaches people instantly—
And it's free!
Well . . . don't you need a computer or something?
We have an old clunker from last century!
All we need is this bad boy!
Set a time and place and send a Tweet, text, Instagram or Facebook post, and voilà!
voilà!!

Chapter Thirty-Three

Cry

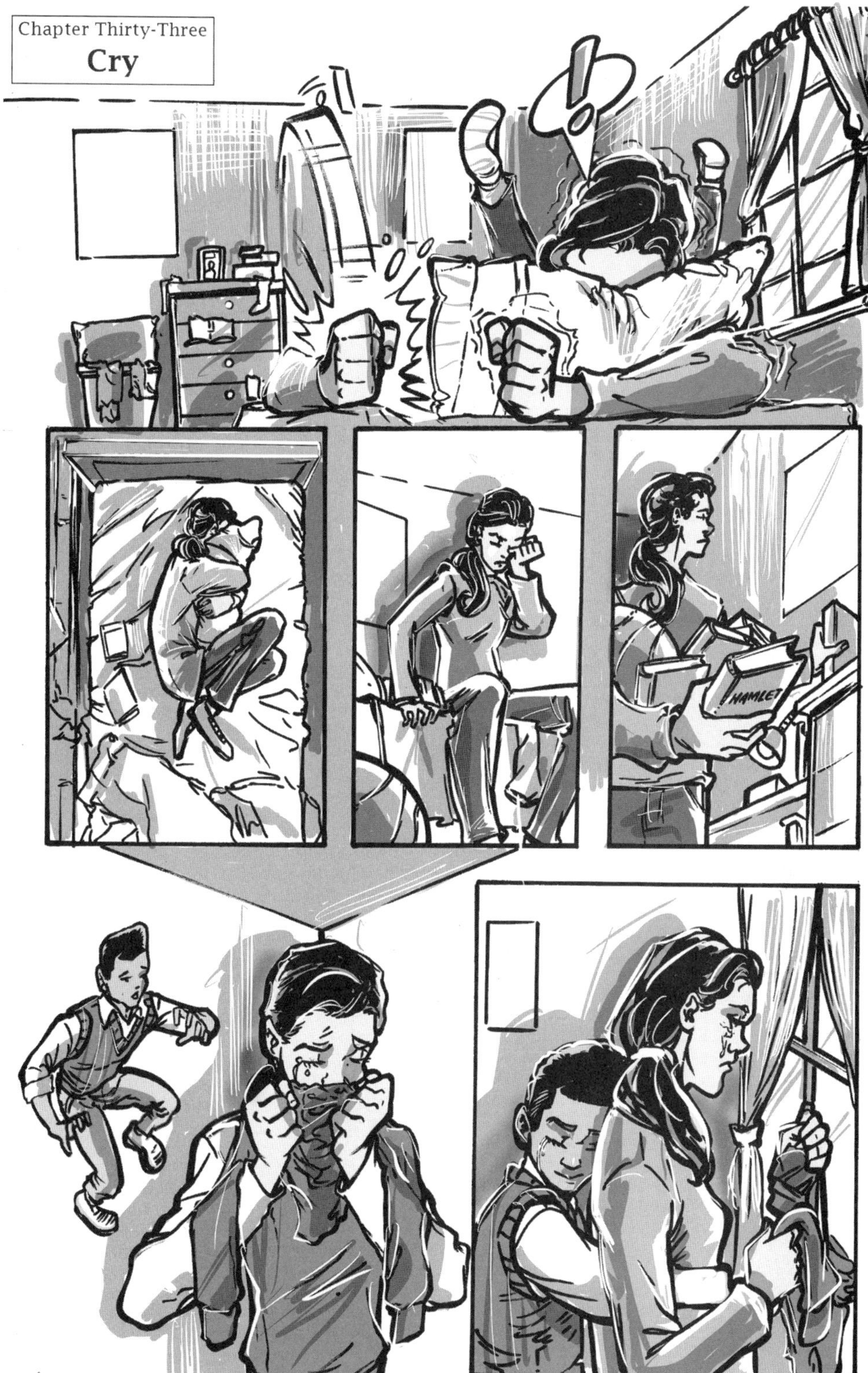
!
HAMLET

Scobie and Mrs. Bumpurs said, "Don't try this at home"—but ha ha, there has to be a real reason my letter still ended up with me, and not some forensics nerd or the clumsy cops stepping all over my blood in the snow.

Mom— it's me!

I tried whispering in my mom's ear.

I couldn't get her to budge. She kept shooing me away like a fly.

Mom, it's me, Fonso! Can you hear me?

I even tried blowing as hard as I could. I was surprised to find I didn't have trouble because of my asthma.

Did my lungs get bigger or stronger? Or was it because I really didn't have none?

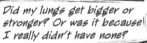

That security guard cop did get a few bullets into them.

All I did was bring my mom chills— and . . . to tears.

Chapter Thirty-Four

Videotape

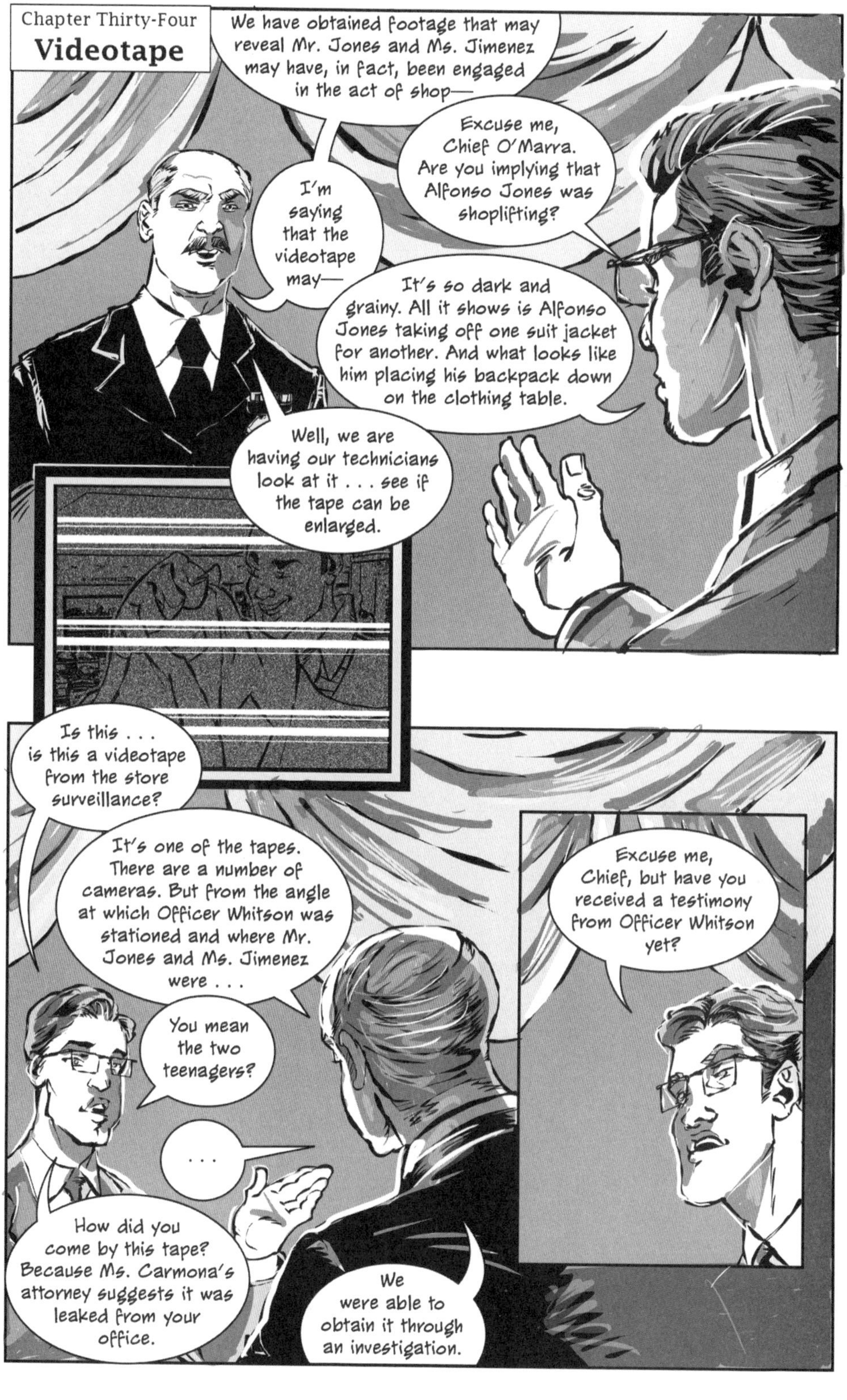
We have obtained footage that may reveal Mr. Jones and Ms. Jimenez may have, in fact, been engaged in the act of shop—
Excuse me, Chief O'Marra. Are you implying that Alfonso Jones was shoplifting?
I'm saying that the videotape may—
It's so dark and grainy. All it shows is Alfonso Jones taking off one suit jacket for another. And what looks like him placing his backpack down on the clothing table.
Well, we are having our technicians look at it . . . see if the tape can be enlarged.
Is this . . . is this a videotape from the store surveillance?
It's one of the tapes. There are a number of cameras. But from the angle at which Officer Whitson was stationed and where Mr. Jones and Ms. Jimenez were . . .
You mean the two teenagers?
. . .
Excuse me, Chief, but have you received a testimony from Officer Whitson yet?
How did you come by this tape? Because Ms. Carmona's attorney suggests it was leaked from your office.
We were able to obtain it through an investigation.

Chapter Thirty-Five

Born to Trauma

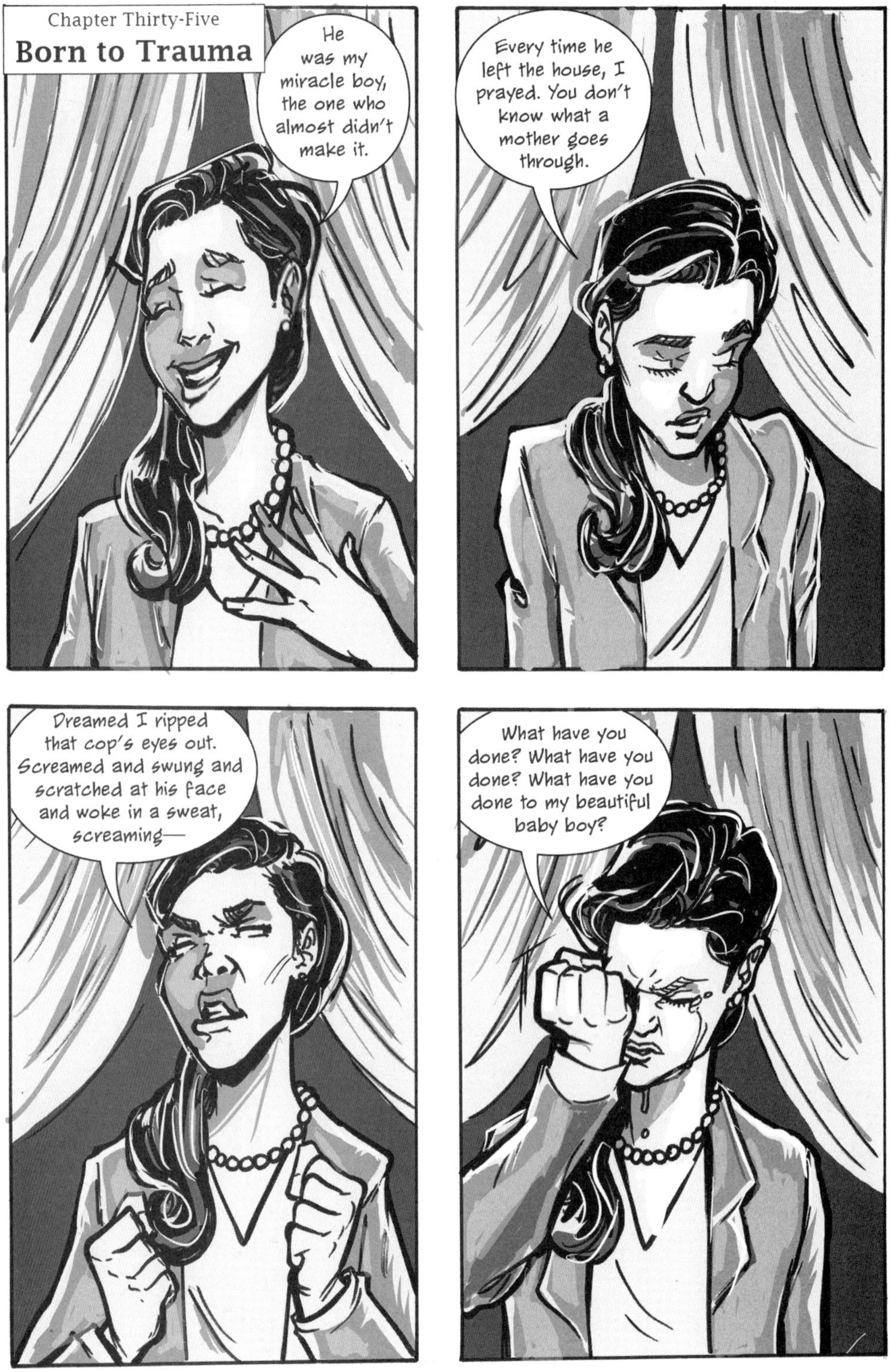
He was my miracle boy, the one who almost didn't make it.
Every time he left the house, I prayed. You don't know what a mother goes through.
Dreamed I ripped that cop's eyes out. Screamed and swung and scratched at his face and woke in a sweat, screaming—
What have you done? What have you done? What have you done to my beautiful baby boy?

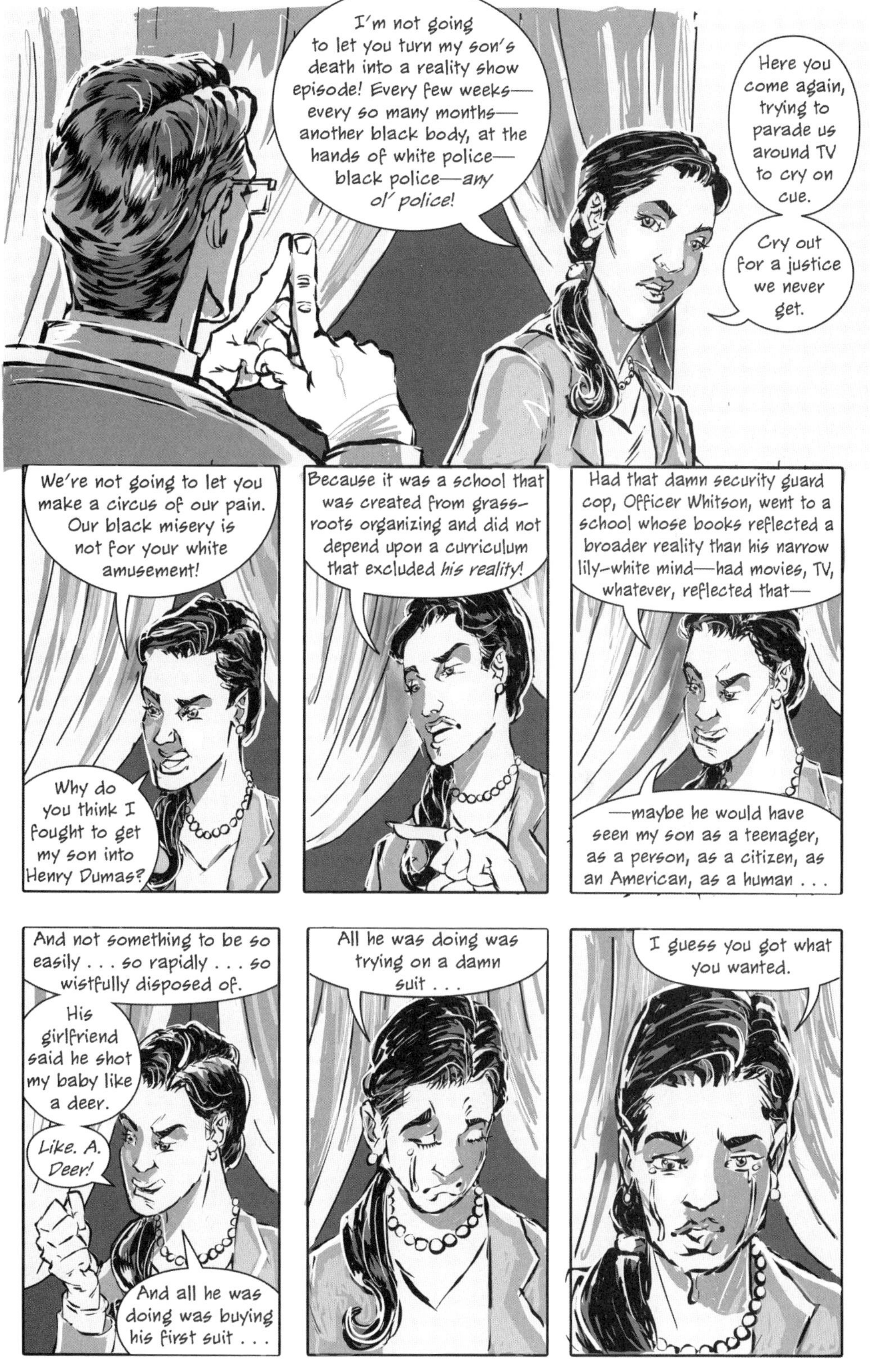
I'm not going to let you turn my son's death into a reality show episode! Every few weeks— every so many months— another black body, at the hands of white police— black police—*any ol' police!*
Here you come again, trying to parade us around TV to cry on cue.
Cry out for a justice we never get.
We're not going to let you make a circus of our pain. Our black misery is not for your white amusement!
Why do you think I fought to get my son into Henry Dumas?
Because it was a school that was created from grass-roots organizing and did not depend upon a curriculum that excluded *his reality!*
Had that damn security guard cop, Officer Whitson, went to a school whose books reflected a broader reality than his narrow lily-white mind—had movies, TV, whatever, reflected that—
—maybe he would have seen my son as a teenager, as a person, as a citizen, as an American, as a human . . .
And not something to be so easily . . . so rapidly . . . so wistfully disposed of.
His girlfriend said he shot my baby like a deer.
Like. A. Deer!
And all he was doing was buying his first suit . . .
All he was doing was trying on a damn suit . . .
I guess you got what you wanted.

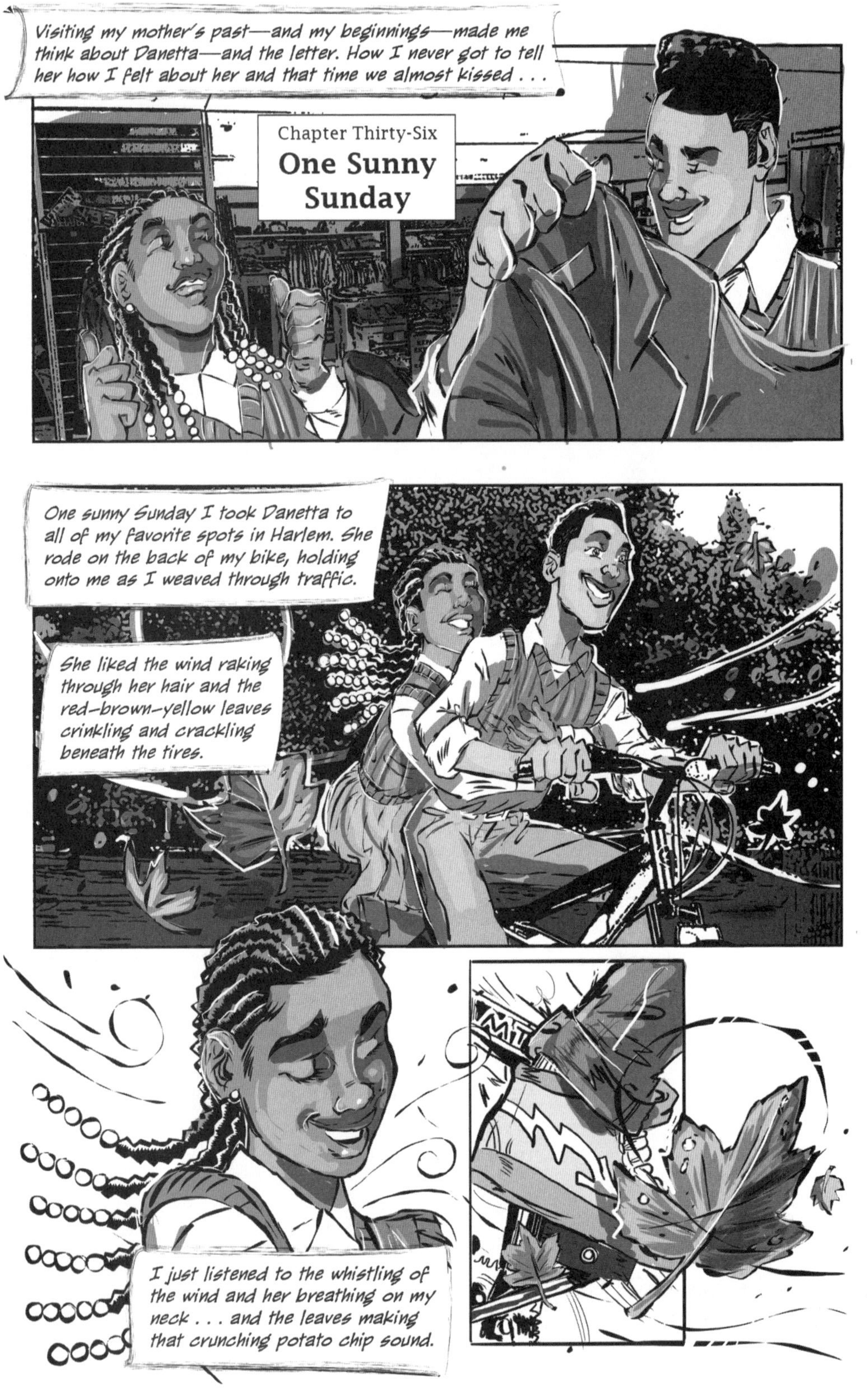
Visiting my mother's past—and my beginnings—made me think about Danetta—and the letter. How I never got to tell her how I felt about her and that time we almost kissed . . .
Chapter Thirty-Six
One Sunny Sunday
One sunny Sunday I took Danetta to all of my favorite spots in Harlem. She rode on the back of my bike, holding onto me as I weaved through traffic.
She liked the wind raking through her hair and the red-brown-yellow leaves crinkling and crackling beneath the tires.
I just listened to the whistling of the wind and her breathing on my neck . . . and the leaves making that crunching potato chip sound.

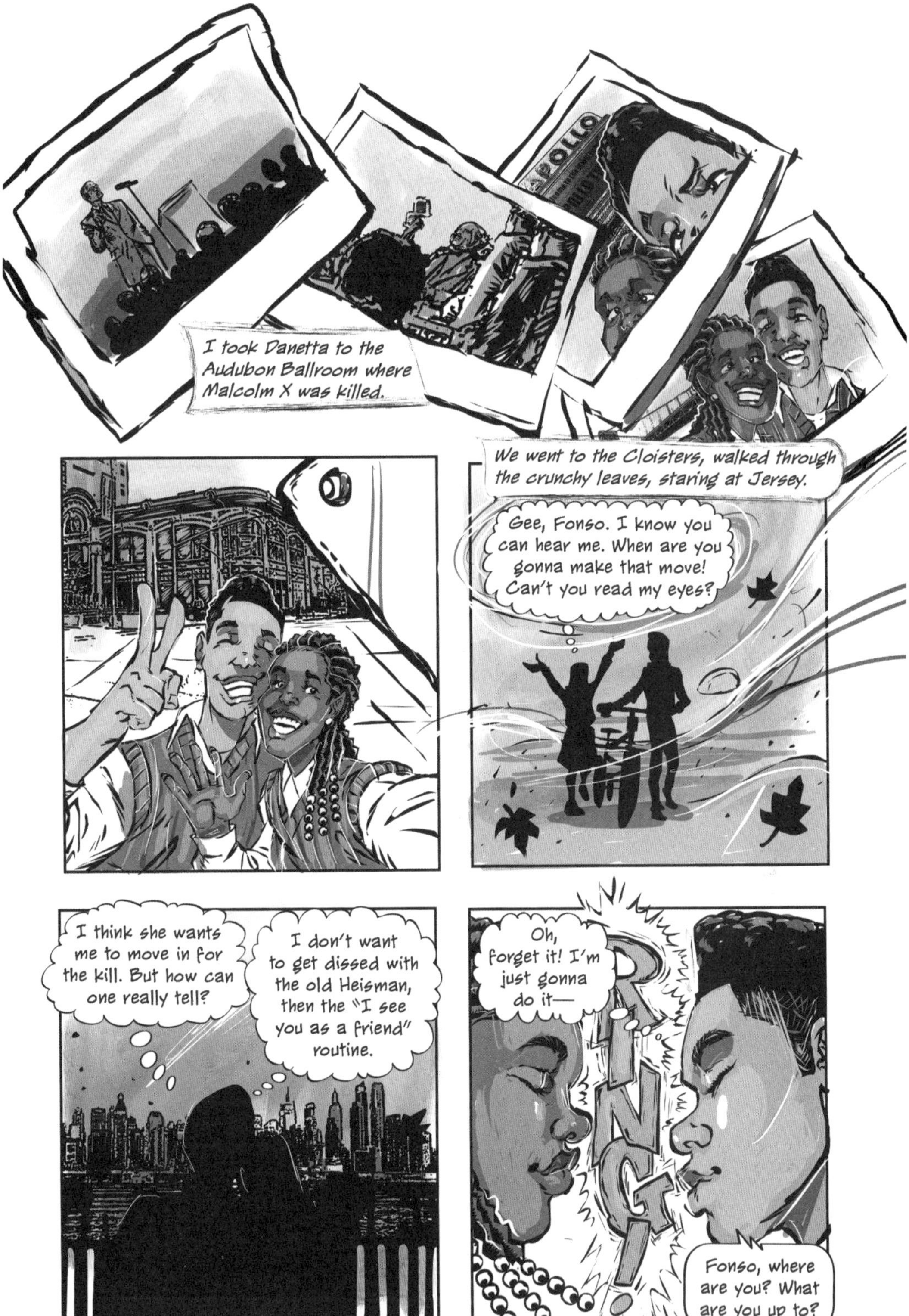
I took Danetta to the Audubon Ballroom where Malcolm X was killed.
We went to the Cloisters, walked through the crunchy leaves, staring at Jersey.
Gee, Fonso. I know you can hear me. When are you gonna make that move! Can't you read my eyes?
I think she wants me to move in for the kill. But how can one really tell?
I don't want to get dissed with the old Heisman, then the "I see you as a friend" routine.
Oh, forget it! I'm just gonna do it—
Fonso, where are you? What are you up to?

Chapter Thirty-Seven

Poem Depot

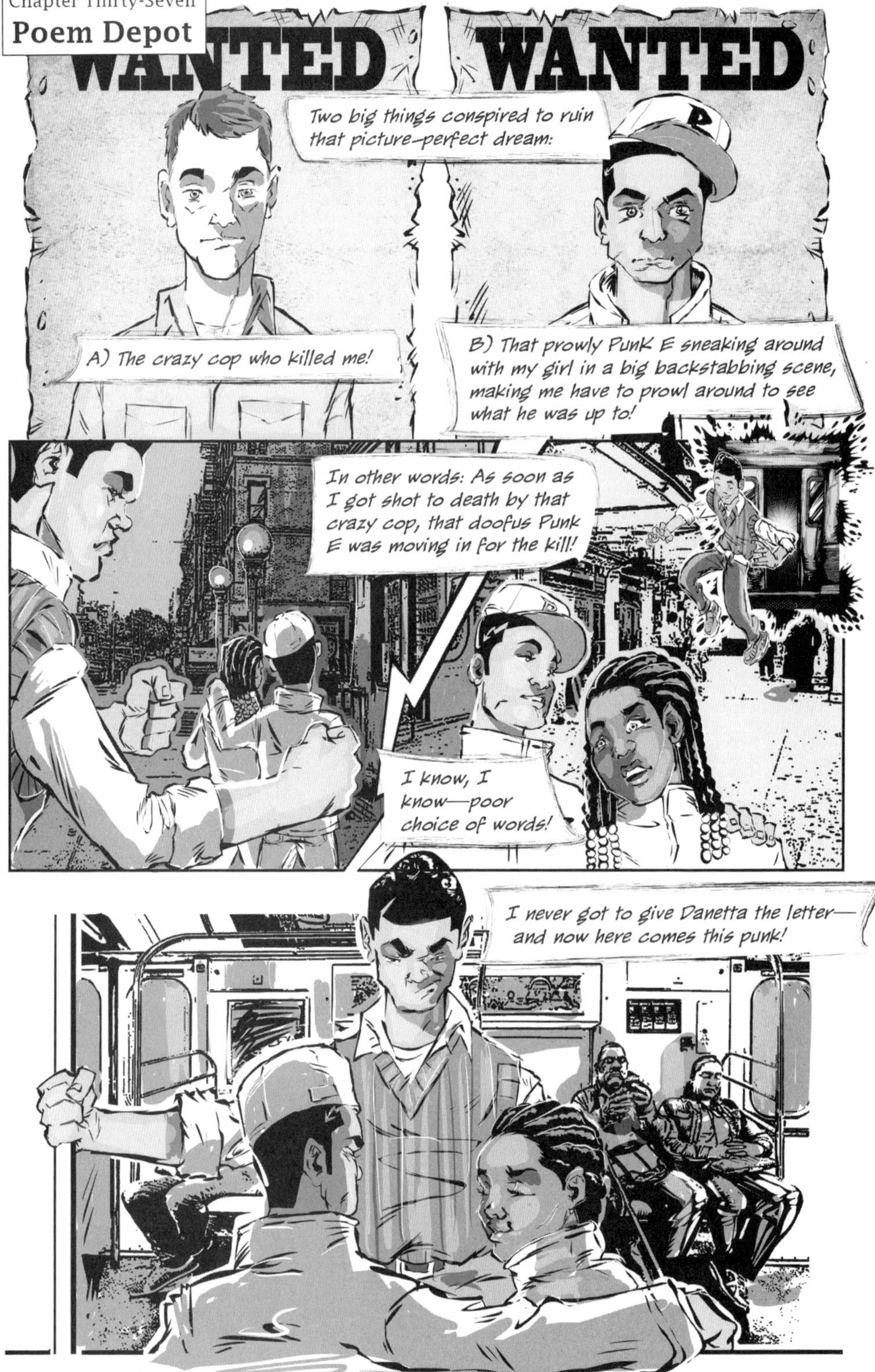

WANTED
WANTED
Two big things conspired to ruin that picture-perfect dream:
A) The crazy cop who killed me!
B) That prowly Punk E sneaking around with my girl in a big backstabbing scene, making me have to prowl around to see what he was up to!
In other words: As soon as I got shot to death by that crazy cop, that doofus Punk E was moving in for the kill!
I know, I know—poor choice of words!
I never got to give Danetta the letter—and now here comes this punk!

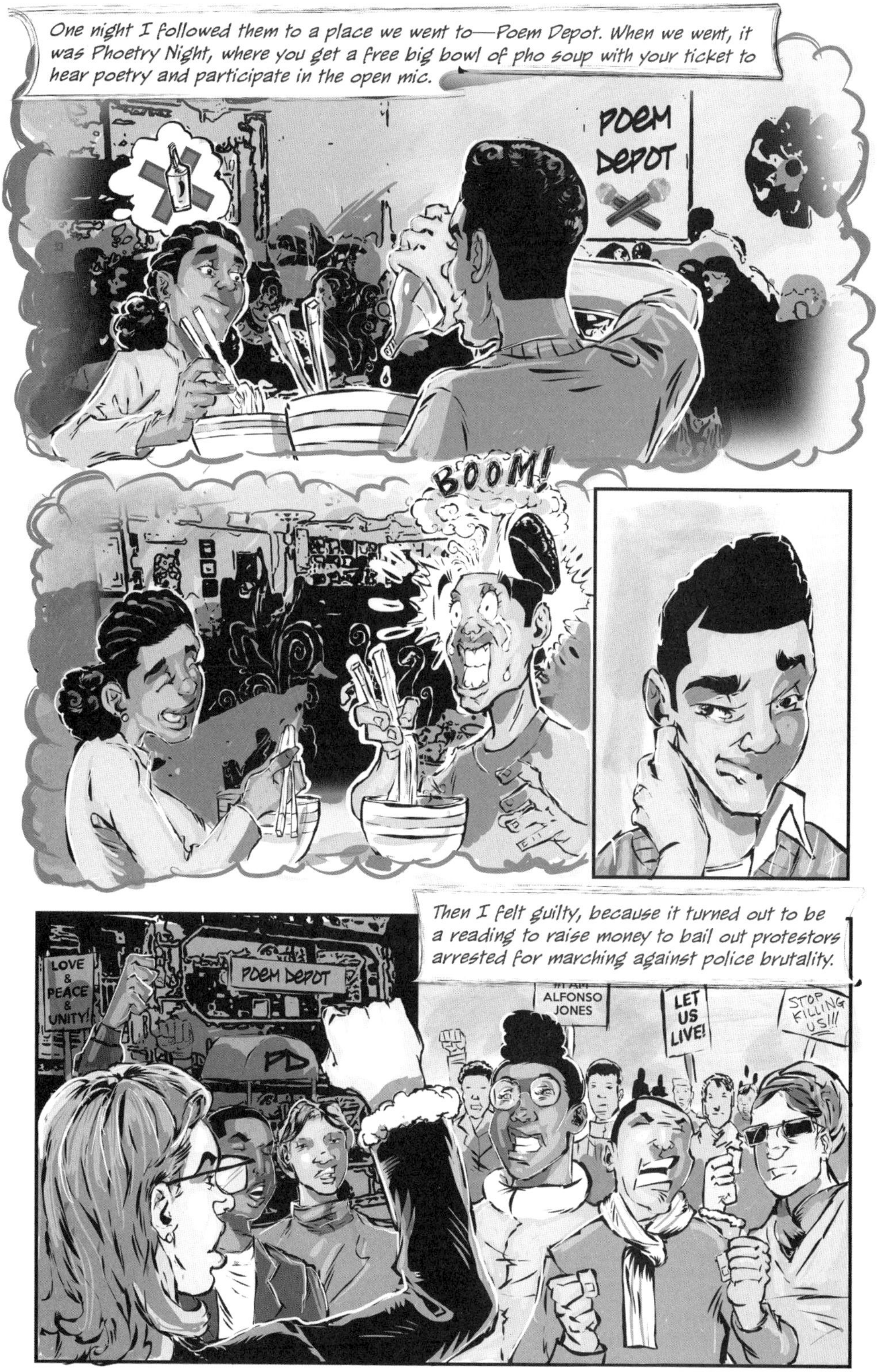
One night I followed them to a place we went to—Poem Depot. When we went, it was Phoetry Night, where you get a free big bowl of pho soup with your ticket to hear poetry and participate in the open mic.
POEM DEPOT
BOOM!
Then I felt guilty, because it turned out to be a reading to raise money to bail out protestors arrested for marching against police brutality.
LOVE & PEACE & UNITY!
POEM DEPOT
#I AM ALFONSO JONES
LET US LIVE!
STOP KILLING US!!!
PD

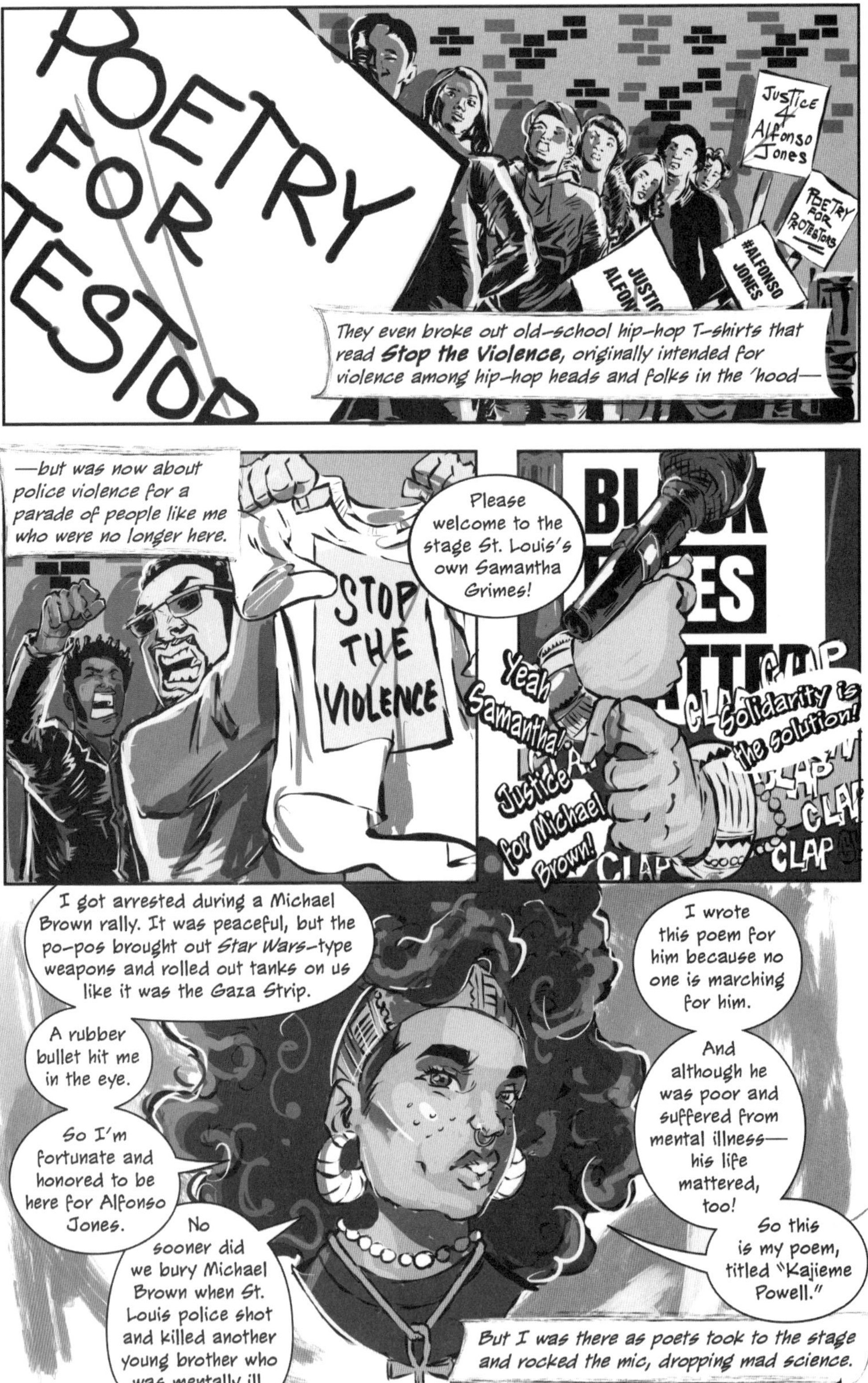

POETRY FOR PROTESTOR
JUSTICE 4 Alfonso Jones
POETRY FOR PROTESTORS
#ALFONSO JONES
They even broke out old-school hip-hop T-shirts that read **Stop the Violence**, originally intended for violence among hip-hop heads and folks in the 'hood—
—but was now about police violence for a parade of people like me who were no longer here.
STOP THE VIOLENCE
Please welcome to the stage St. Louis's own Samantha Grimes!
Yeah Samantha!
Justice for Michael Brown!
Solidarity is the solution!
CLAP
CLAP
CLAP
CLAP
I got arrested during a Michael Brown rally. It was peaceful, but the po-pos brought out *Star Wars*-type weapons and rolled out tanks on us like it was the Gaza Strip.
A rubber bullet hit me in the eye.
So I'm fortunate and honored to be here for Alfonso Jones.
No sooner did we bury Michael Brown when St. Louis police shot and killed another young brother who was mentally ill.
I wrote this poem for him because no one is marching for him.
And although he was poor and suffered from mental illness—his life mattered, too!
So this is my poem, titled "Kajieme Powell."
But I was there as poets took to the stage and rocked the mic, dropping mad science.

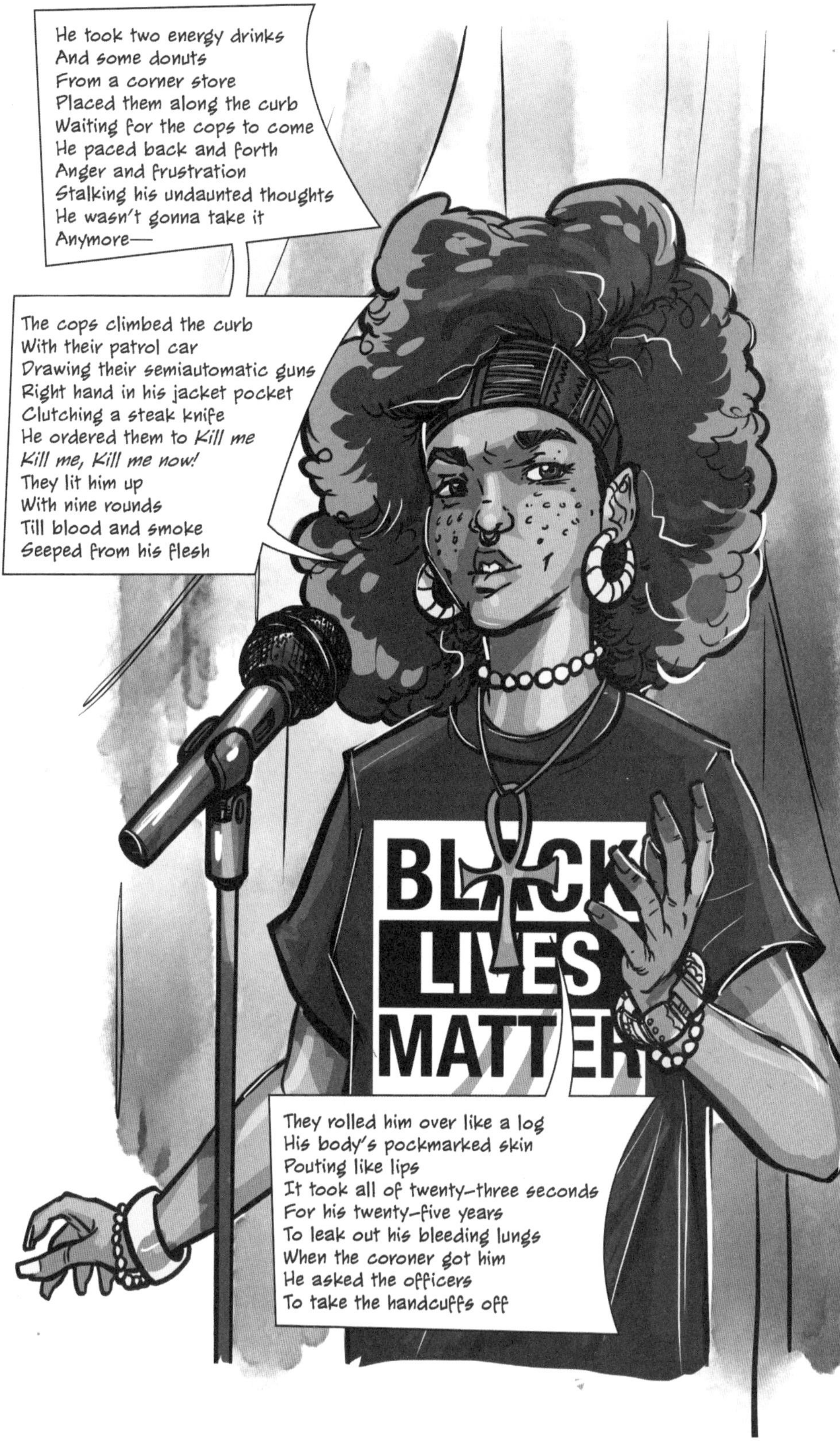
He took two energy drinks And some donuts From a corner store Placed them along the curb Waiting for the cops to come He paced back and forth Anger and frustration Stalking his undaunted thoughts He wasn't gonna take it Anymore—
The cops climbed the curb With their patrol car Drawing their semiautomatic guns Right hand in his jacket pocket Clutching a steak knife He ordered them to *Kill me Kill me, Kill me now!* They lit him up With nine rounds Till blood and smoke Seeped from his flesh
BLACK LIVES MATTER
They rolled him over like a log His body's pockmarked skin Pouting like lips It took all of twenty-three seconds For his twenty-five years To leak out his bleeding lungs When the coroner got him He asked the officers To take the handcuffs off

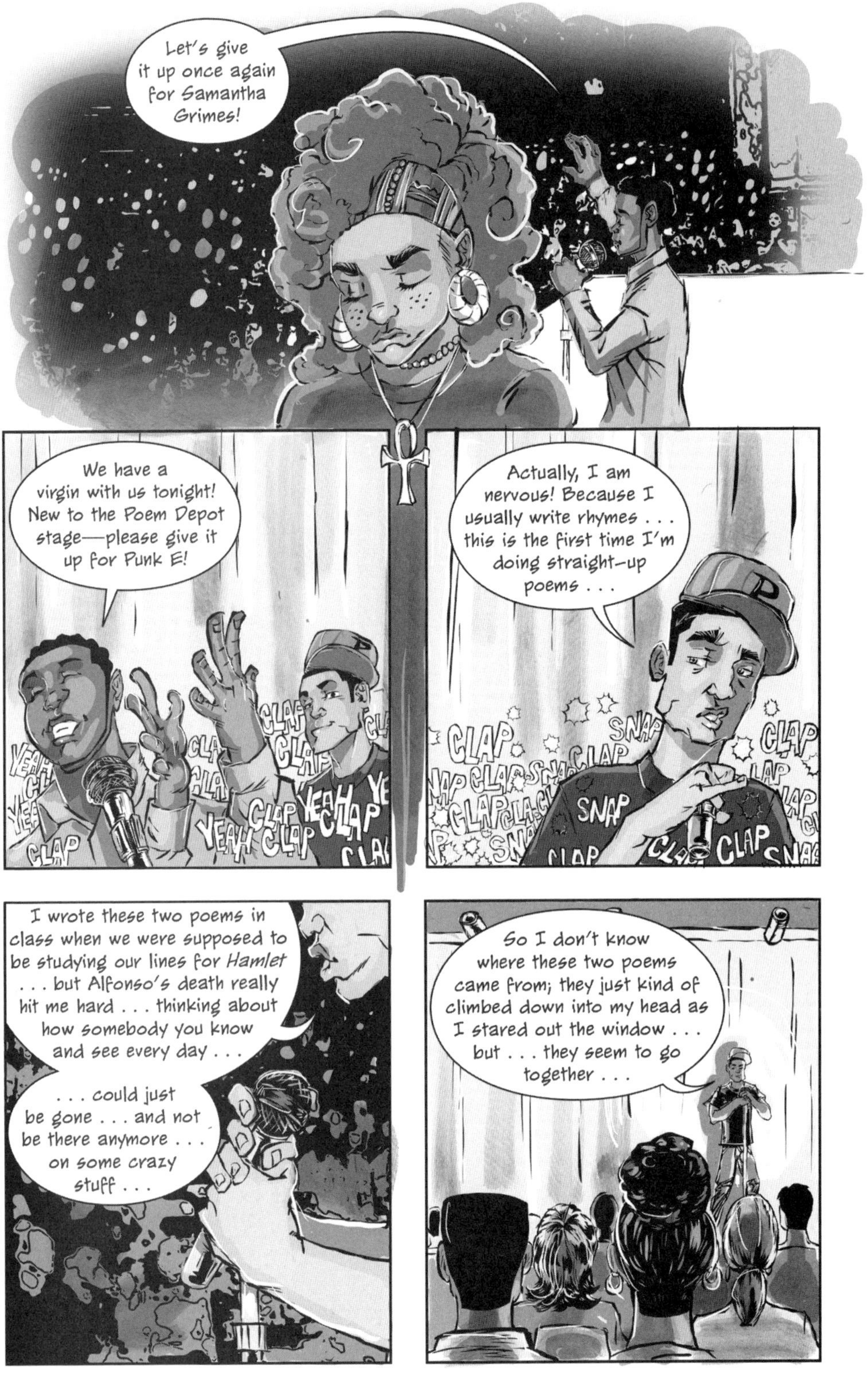
Let's give it up once again for Samantha Grimes!
We have a virgin with us tonight! New to the Poem Depot stage—please give it up for Punk E!
CLAP YEAH CLAP
Actually, I am nervous! Because I usually write rhymes . . . this is the first time I'm doing straight-up poems . . .
CLAP SNAP CLAP SNAP
I wrote these two poems in class when we were supposed to be studying our lines for *Hamlet* . . . but Alfonso's death really hit me hard . . . thinking about how somebody you know and see every day . . .
. . . could just be gone . . . and not be there anymore . . . on some crazy stuff . . .
So I don't know where these two poems came from; they just kind of climbed down into my head as I stared out the window . . . but . . . they seem to go together . . .

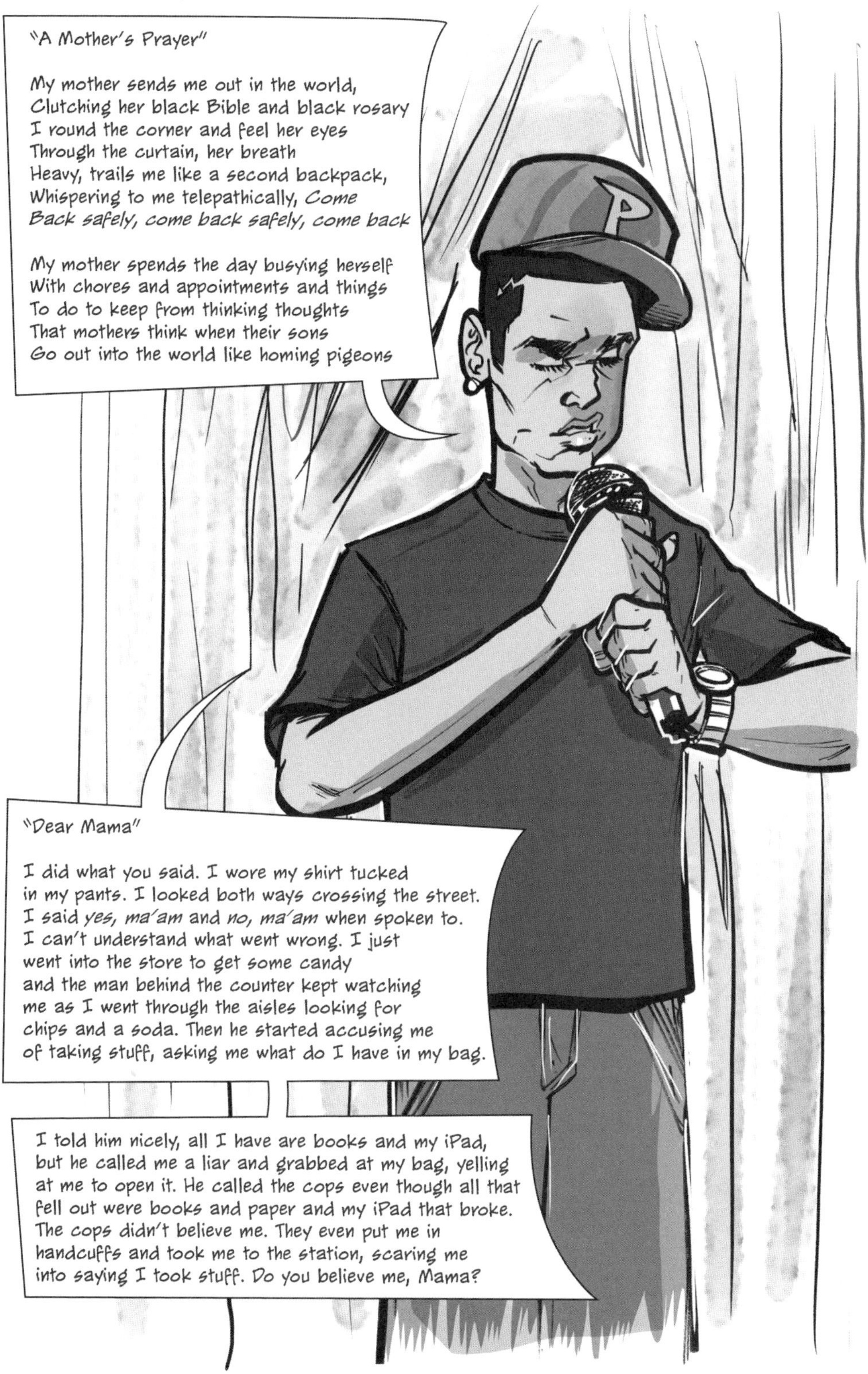
"A Mother's Prayer"
My mother sends me out in the world, Clutching her black Bible and black rosary I round the corner and feel her eyes Through the curtain, her breath Heavy, trails me like a second backpack, Whispering to me telepathically, *Come Back safely, come back safely, come back*
My mother spends the day busying herself With chores and appointments and things To do to keep from thinking thoughts That mothers think when their sons Go out into the world like homing pigeons
"Dear Mama"
I did what you said. I wore my shirt tucked in my pants. I looked both ways crossing the street. I said *yes, ma'am* and *no, ma'am* when spoken to. I can't understand what went wrong. I just went into the store to get some candy and the man behind the counter kept watching me as I went through the aisles looking for chips and a soda. Then he started accusing me of taking stuff, asking me what do I have in my bag.
I told him nicely, all I have are books and my iPad, but he called me a liar and grabbed at my bag, yelling at me to open it. He called the cops even though all that fell out were books and paper and my iPad that broke. The cops didn't believe me. They even put me in handcuffs and took me to the station, scaring me into saying I took stuff. Do you believe me, Mama?

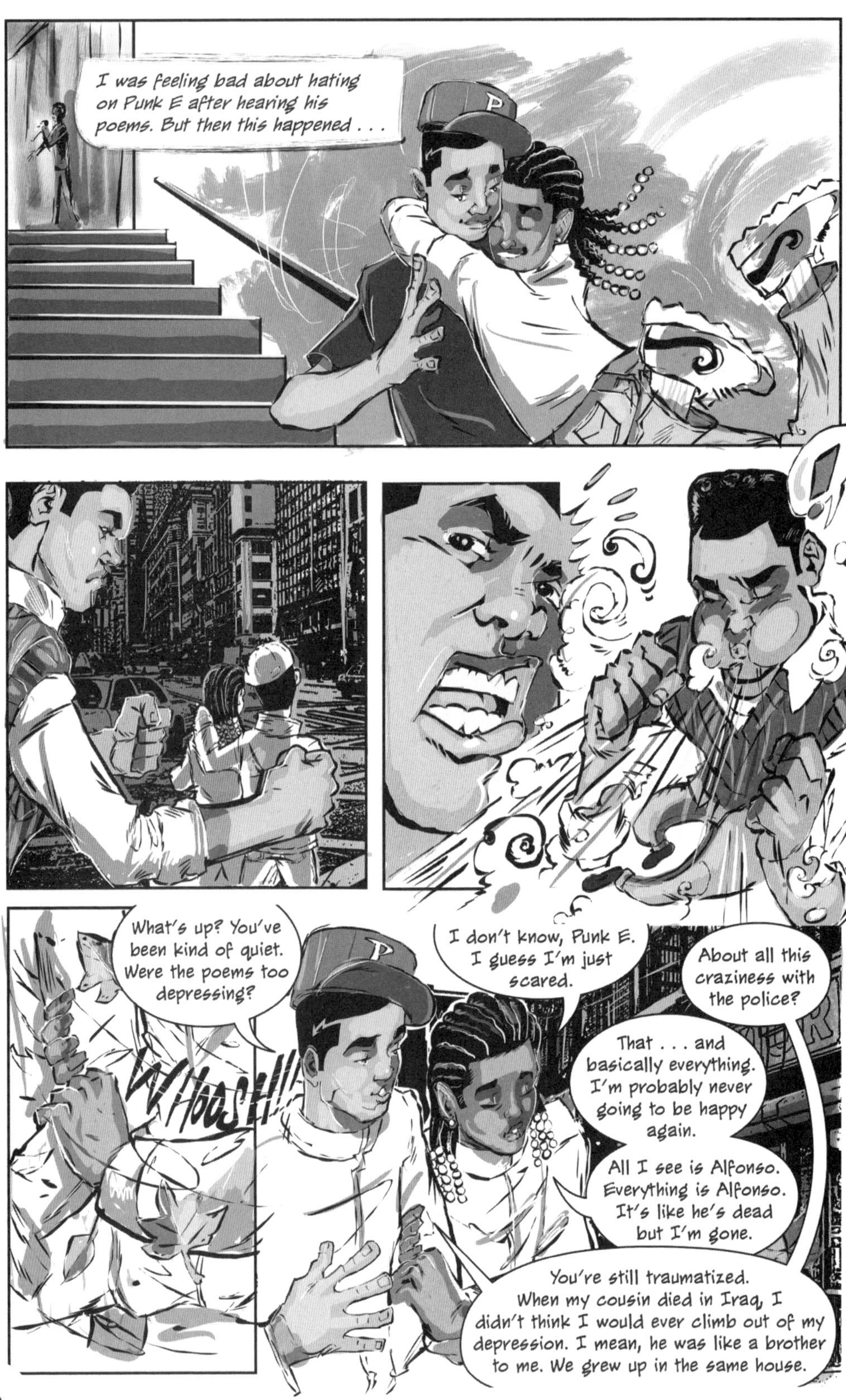
I was feeling bad about hating on Punk E after hearing his poems. But then this happened . . .
What's up? You've been kind of quiet. Were the poems too depressing?
WHOOSH!!
I don't know, Punk E. I guess I'm just scared.
About all this craziness with the police?
That . . . and basically everything. I'm probably never going to be happy again.
All I see is Alfonso. Everything is Alfonso. It's like he's dead but I'm gone.
You're still traumatized. When my cousin died in Iraq, I didn't think I would ever climb out of my depression. I mean, he was like a brother to me. We grew up in the same house.

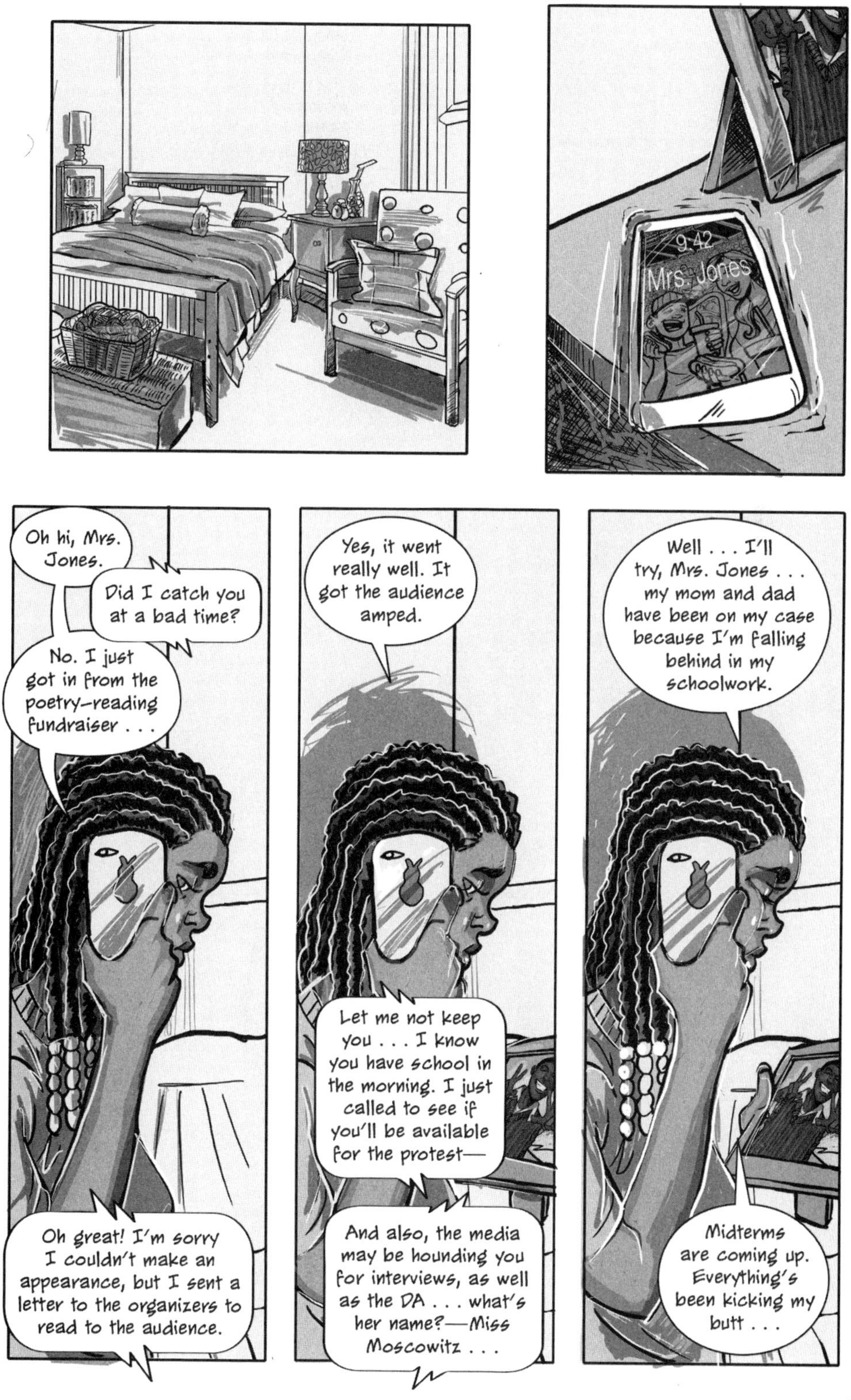
9:42
Mrs. Jones
Oh hi, Mrs. Jones.
Did I catch you at a bad time?
No. I just got in from the poetry-reading fundraiser . . .
Oh great! I'm sorry I couldn't make an appearance, but I sent a letter to the organizers to read to the audience.
Yes, it went really well. It got the audience amped.
Let me not keep you . . . I know you have school in the morning. I just called to see if you'll be available for the protest—
And also, the media may be hounding you for interviews, as well as the DA . . . what's her name?—Miss Moscowitz . . .
Well . . . I'll try, Mrs. Jones . . . my mom and dad have been on my case because I'm falling behind in my schoolwork.
Midterms are coming up. Everything's been kicking my butt . . .

Chapter Thirty-Eight

Rehearsal

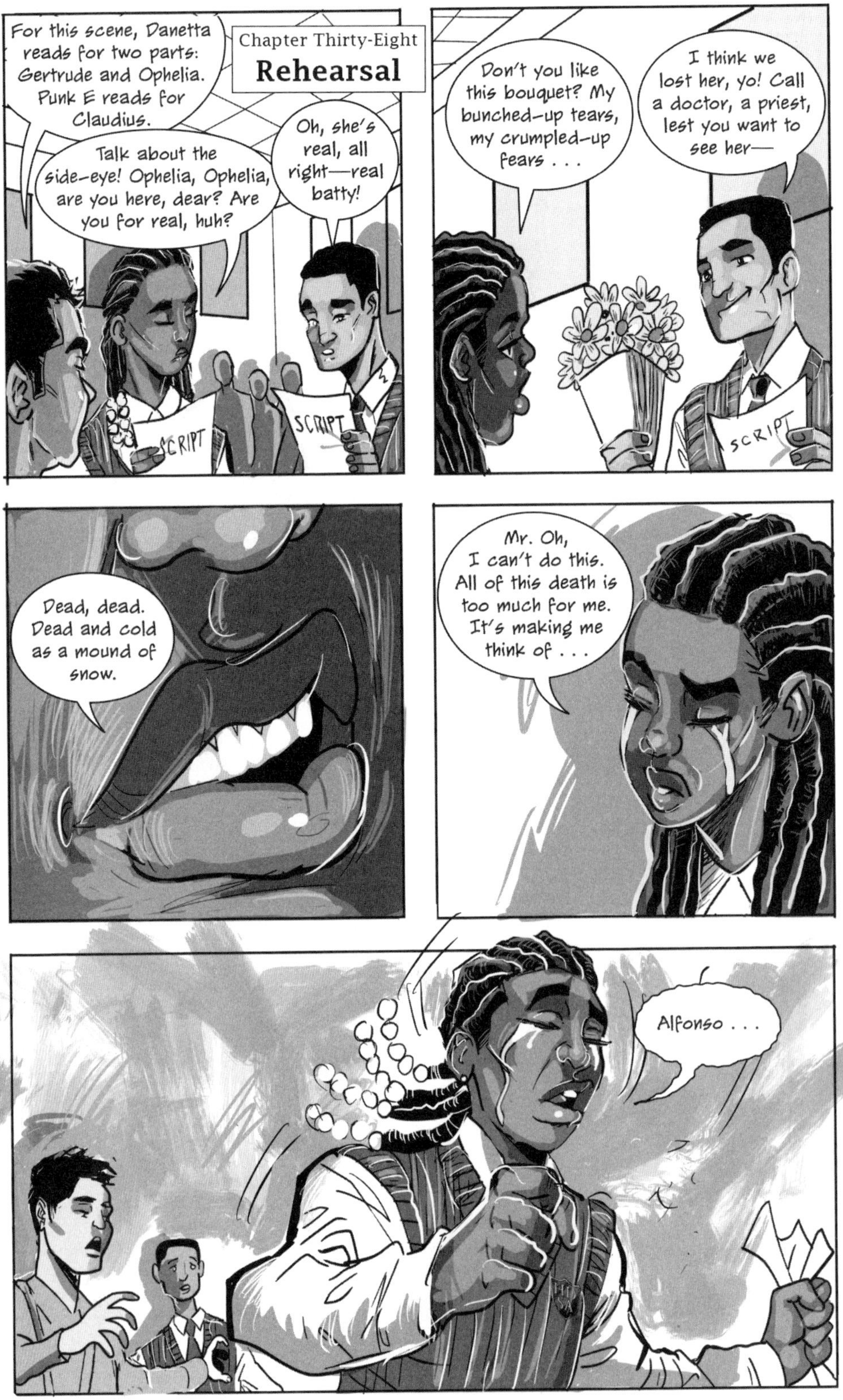
For this scene, Danetta reads for two parts: Gertrude and Ophelia. Punk E reads for Claudius.
Talk about the side-eye! Ophelia, Ophelia, are you here, dear? Are you for real, huh?
Oh, she's real, all right—real batty!
SCRIPT
SCRIPT
Don't you like this bouquet? My bunched-up tears, my crumpled-up fears . . .
I think we lost her, yo! Call a doctor, a priest, lest you want to see her—
SCRIPT
Dead, dead. Dead and cold as a mound of snow.
Mr. Oh, I can't do this. All of this death is too much for me. It's making me think of . . .
Alfonso . . .

Chapter Thirty-Nine

Call

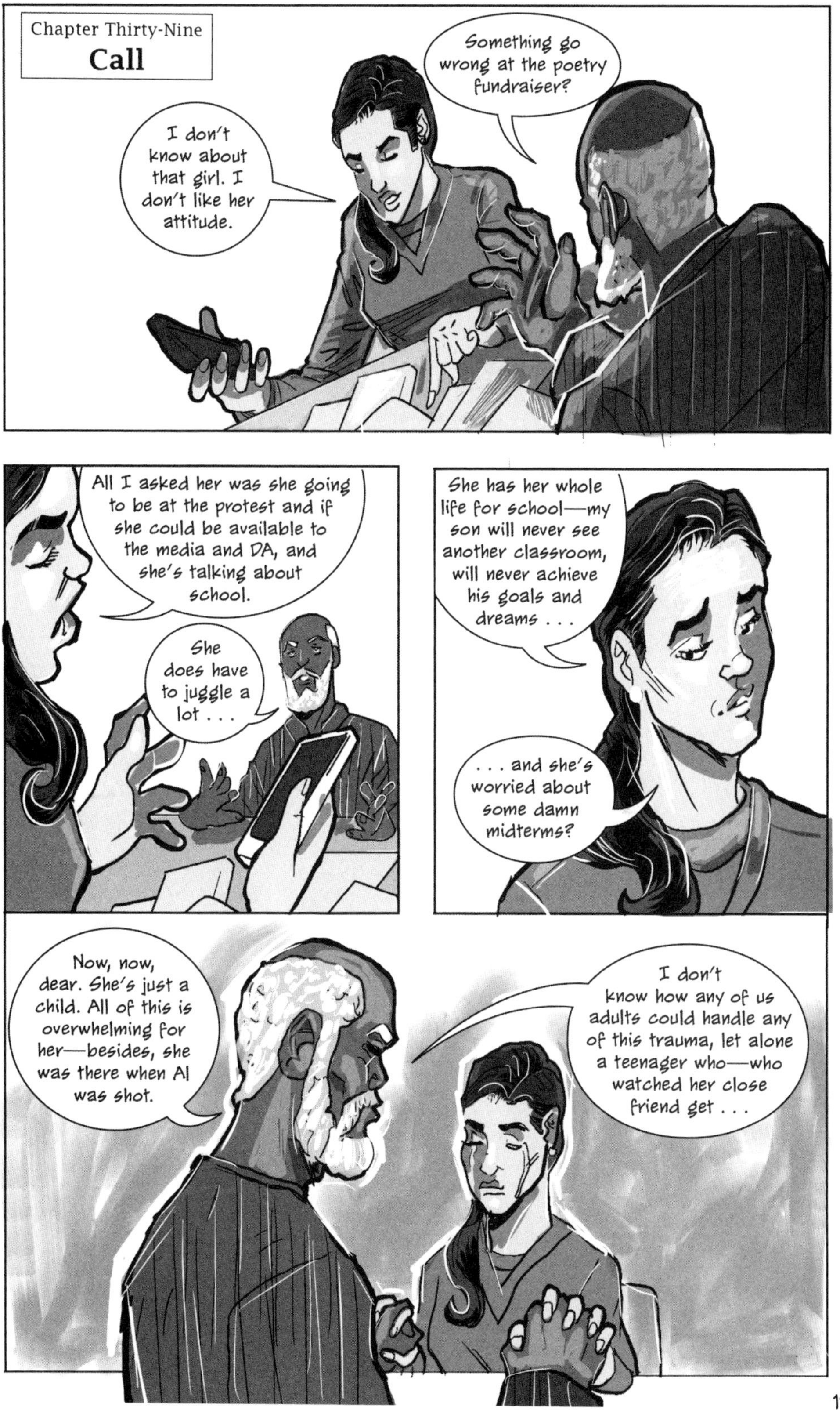
Something go wrong at the poetry fundraiser?
I don't know about that girl. I don't like her attitude.
All I asked her was she going to be at the protest and if she could be available to the media and DA, and she's talking about school.
She does have to juggle a lot . . .
She has her whole life for school—my son will never see another classroom, will never achieve his goals and dreams . . .
. . . and she's worried about some damn midterms?
Now, now, dear. She's just a child. All of this is overwhelming for her—besides, she was there when Al was shot.
I don't know how any of us adults could handle any of this trauma, let alone a teenager who—who watched her close friend get . . .

Chapter Forty

Auditions

My grandfather was right. What he told my mother reminded me of when Danetta auditioned for the part of Ophelia.

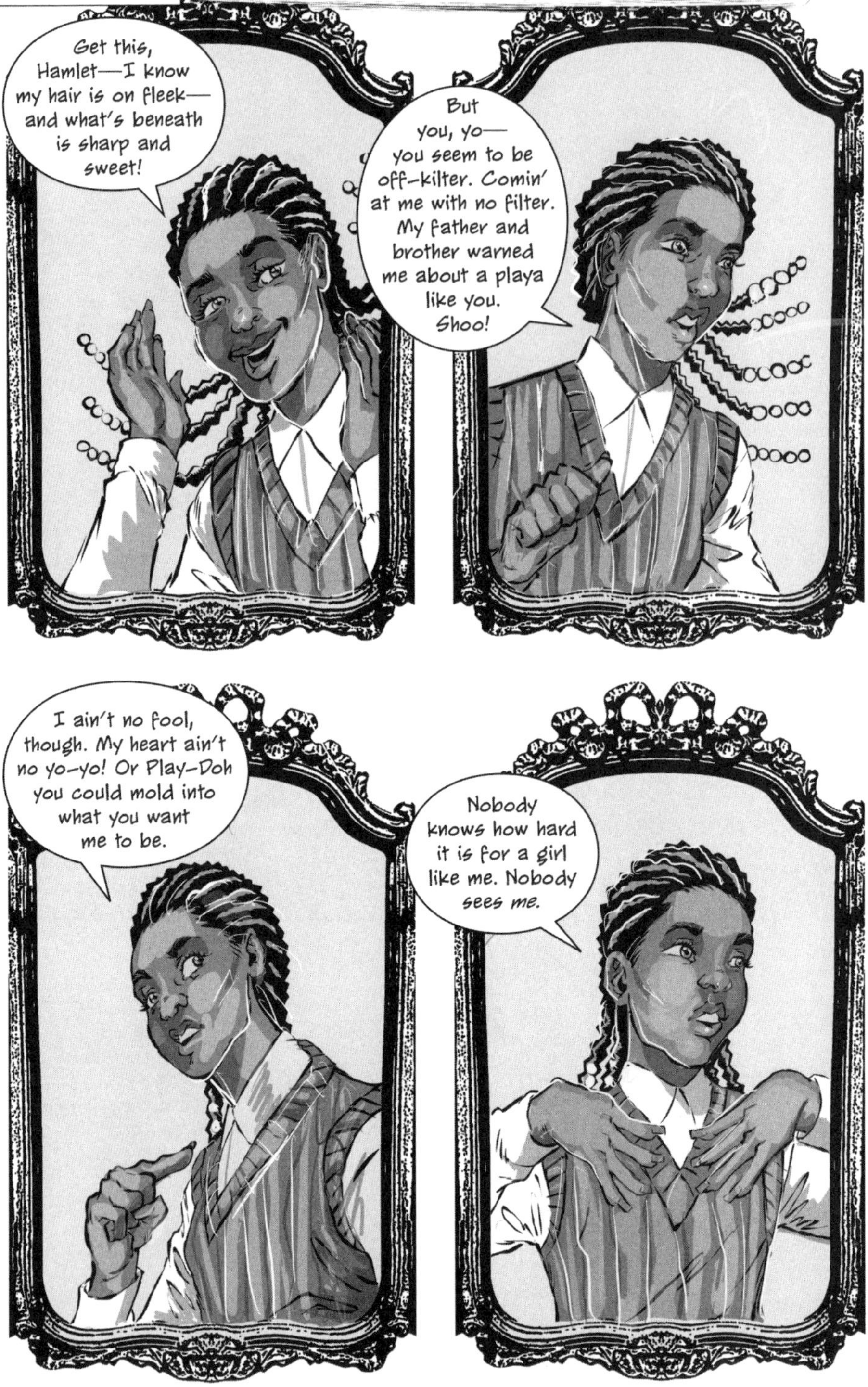
Get this, Hamlet—I know my hair is on fleek—and what's beneath is sharp and sweet!
But you, yo—you seem to be off-kilter. Comin' at me with no filter. My father and brother warned me about a playa like you. Shoo!
I ain't no fool, though. My heart ain't no yo-yo! Or Play-Doh you could mold into what you want me to be.
Nobody knows how hard it is for a girl like me. Nobody sees me.

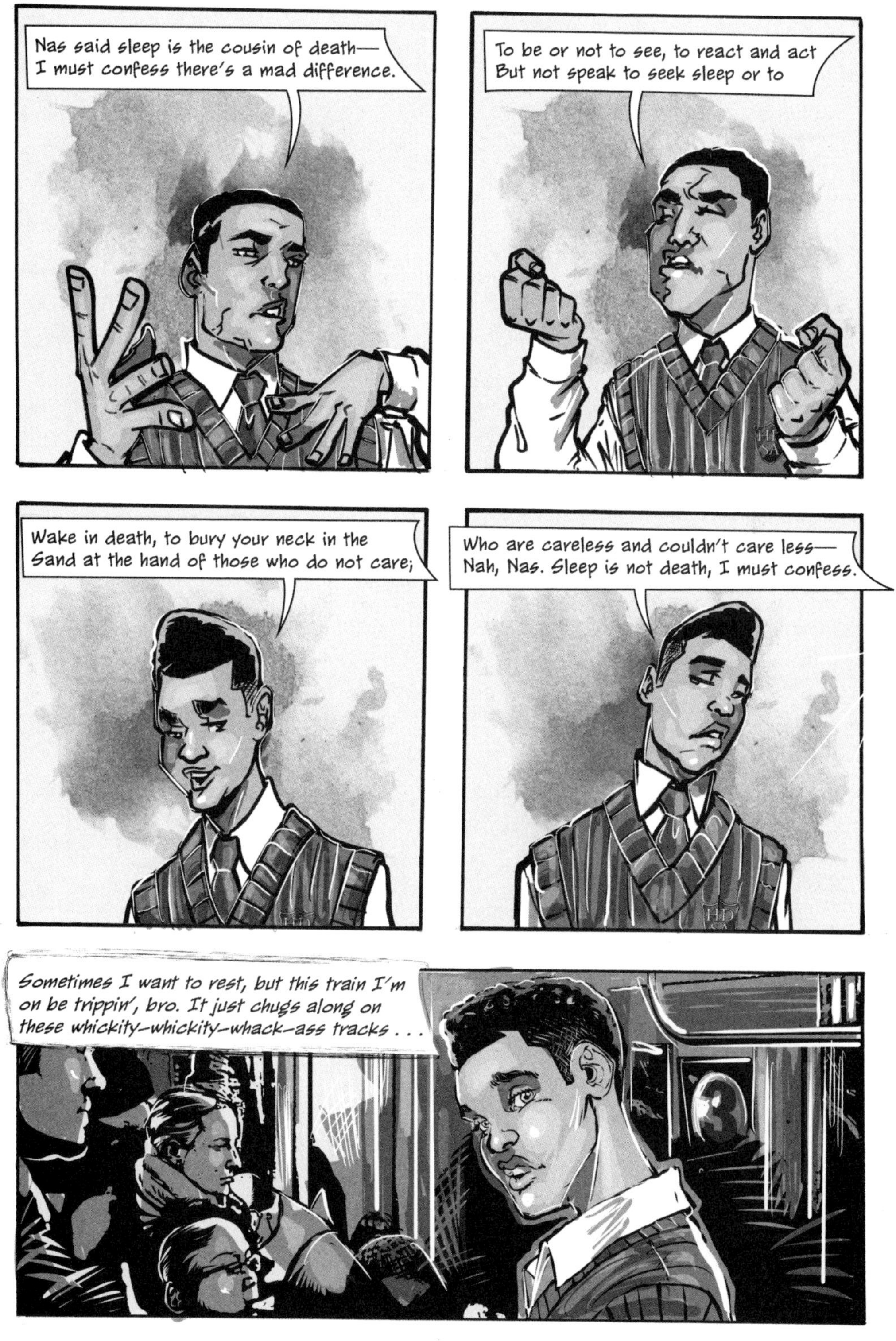
Nas said sleep is the cousin of death—
I must confess there's a mad difference.
To be or not to see, to react and act
But not speak to seek sleep or to
Wake in death, to bury your neck in the
Sand at the hand of those who do not care;
Who are careless and couldn't care less—
Nah, Nas. Sleep is not death, I must confess.
Sometimes I want to rest, but this train I'm on be trippin', bro. It just chugs along on these whickity-whickity-whack-ass tracks . . .
3

Chapter Forty-One
Explode

My father's release from prison was held back because of me. The warden convinced him to stay a little longer, even though he had a release date after he was cleared through DNA testing.

The mayor and the warden believed my father's release—on the day I was murdered by a cop—would cause the city to explode.

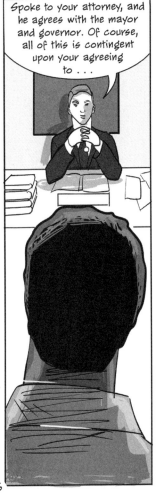

Spoke to your attorney, and he agrees with the mayor and governor. Of course, all of this is contingent upon your agreeing to . . .

. . . to being away from my wife, away from my son. Are you crazy, Warden? Your system has delayed—destroyed—my life, my family, long enough . . .

More lives could be lost. New York—and other parts—could explode.

126

Chapter Forty-Two
Lies

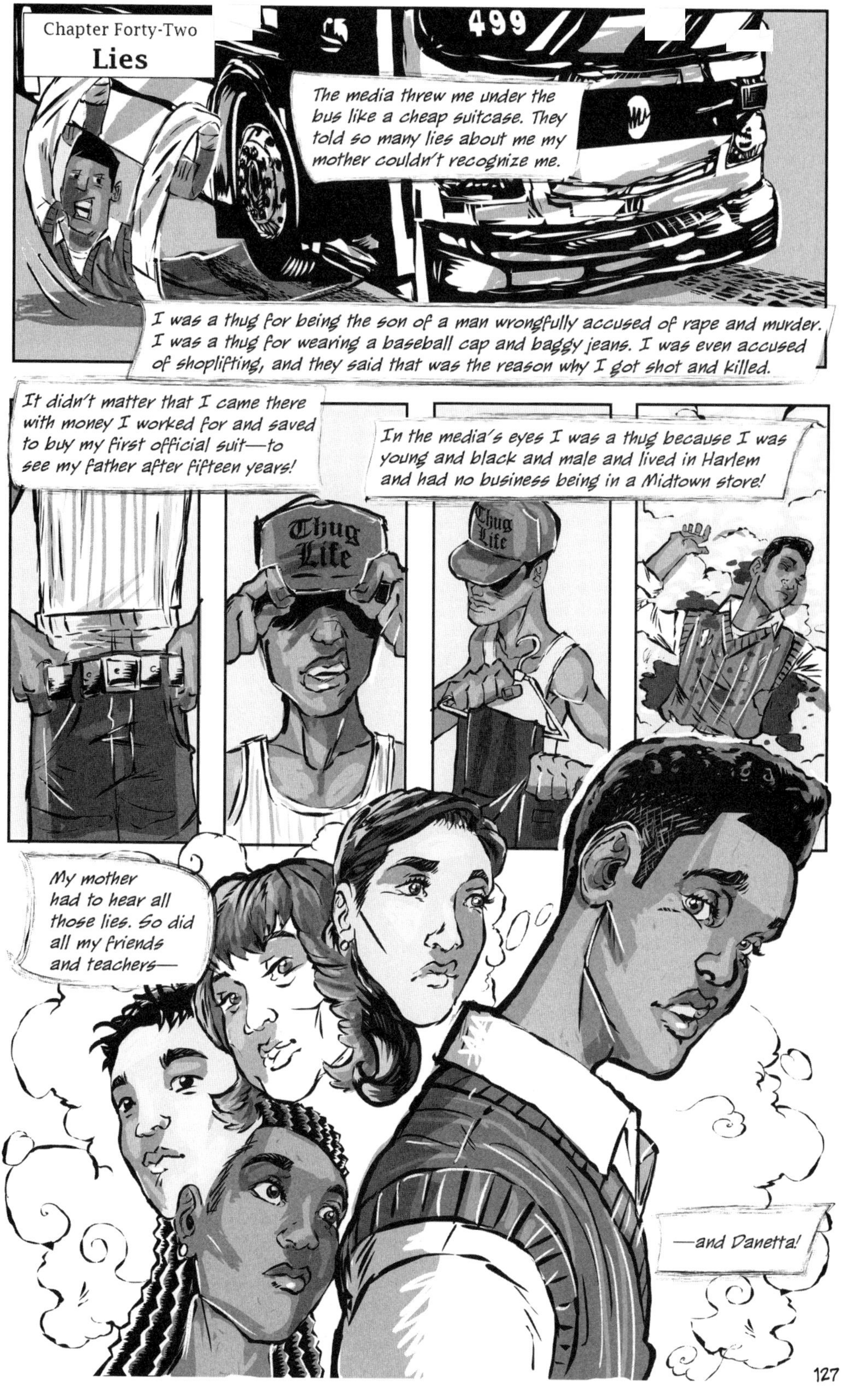
499
The media threw me under the bus like a cheap suitcase. They told so many lies about me my mother couldn't recognize me.
I was a thug for being the son of a man wrongfully accused of rape and murder. I was a thug for wearing a baseball cap and baggy jeans. I was even accused of shoplifting, and they said that was the reason why I got shot and killed.
It didn't matter that I came there with money I worked for and saved to buy my first official suit—to see my father after fifteen years!
In the media's eyes I was a thug because I was young and black and male and lived in Harlem and had no business being in a Midtown store!
Thug Life
Thug Life
My mother had to hear all those lies. So did all my friends and teachers—
—and Danetta!

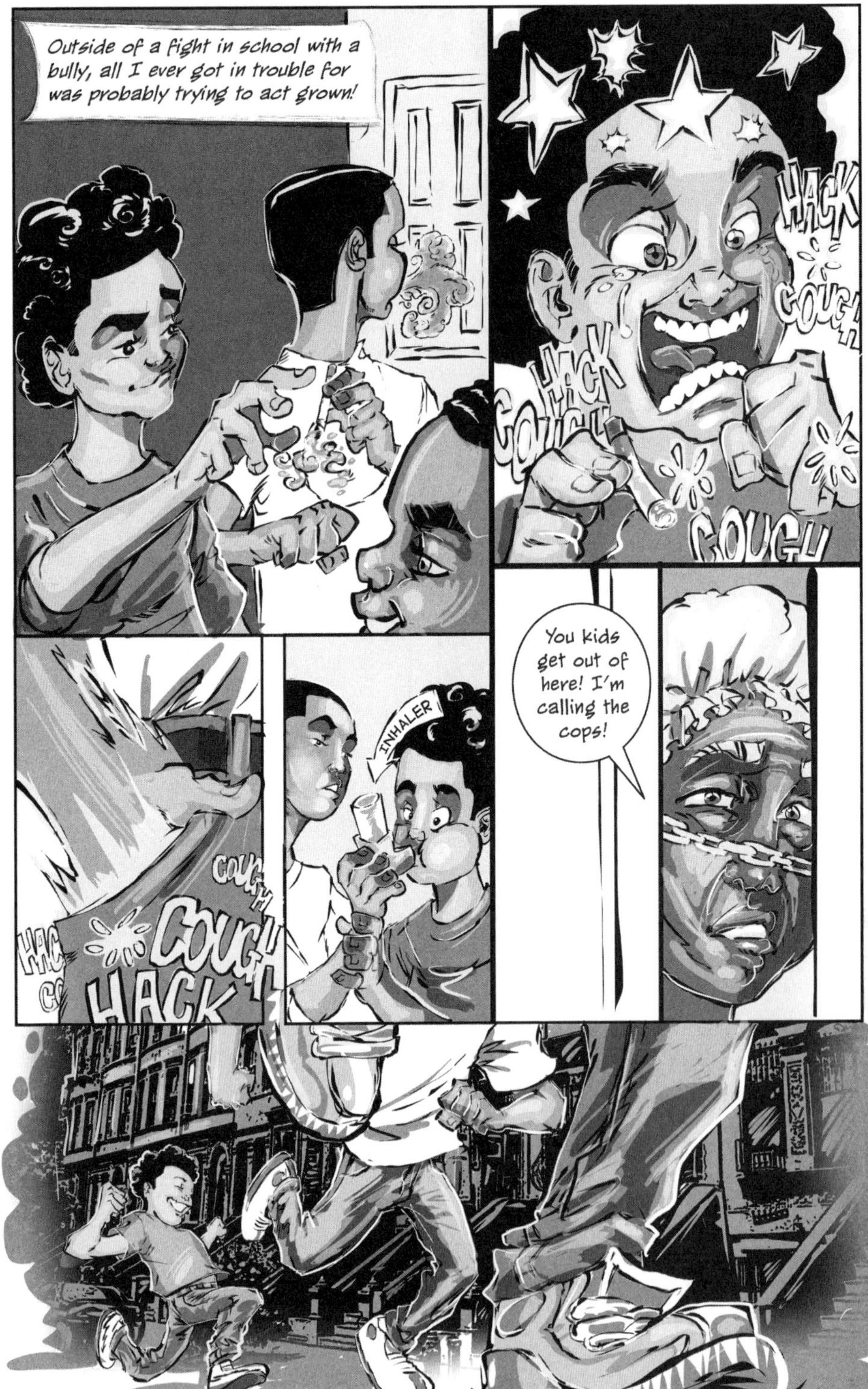

Outside of a fight in school with a bully, all I ever got in trouble for was probably trying to act grown!
HACK
COUGH
HACK
COUGH
COUGH
COUGH
COUGH
HACK
INHALER
You kids get out of here! I'm calling the cops!

Chapter Forty-Three

Birthday Cards and Letters

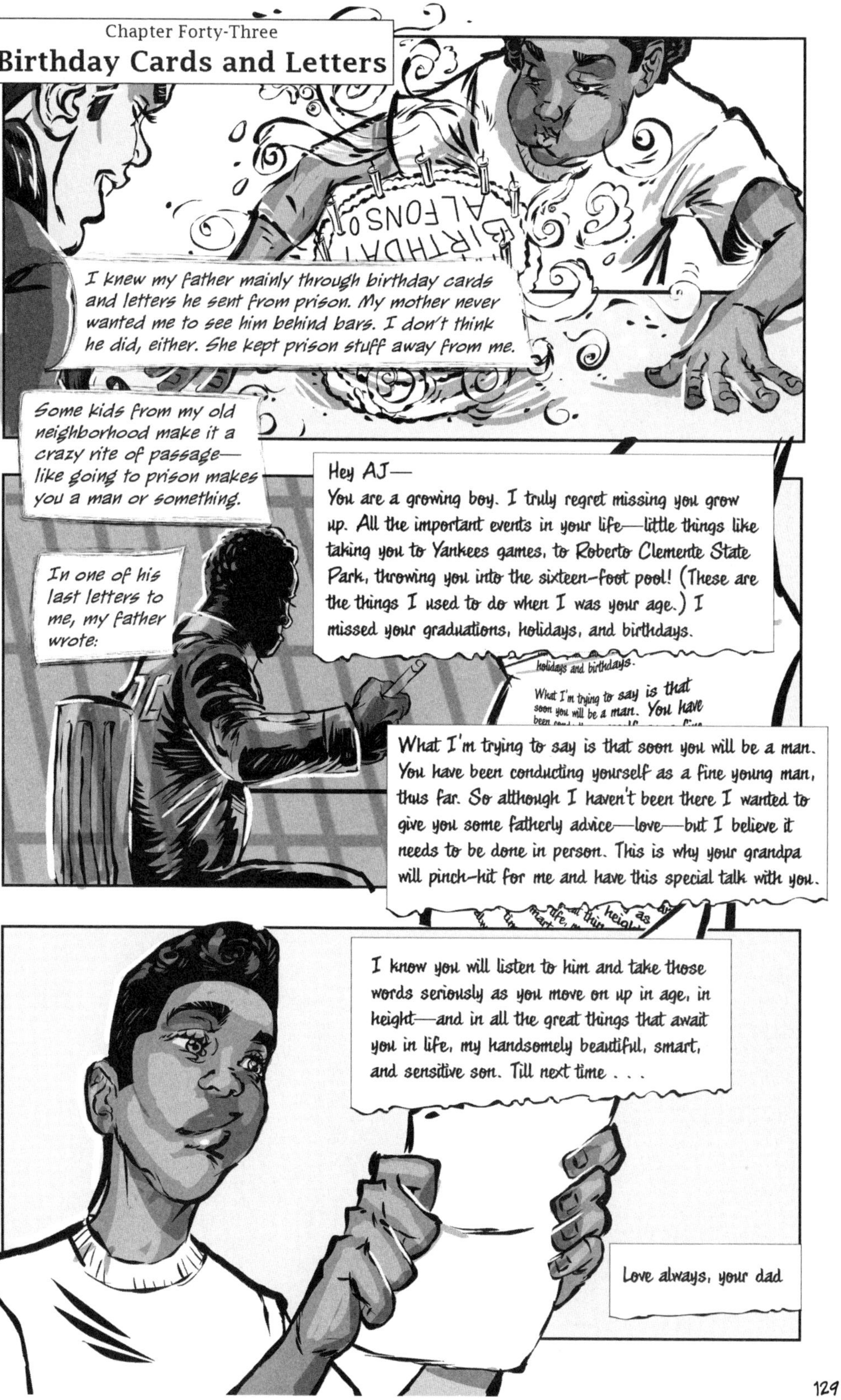

I knew my father mainly through birthday cards and letters he sent from prison. My mother never wanted me to see him behind bars. I don't think he did, either. She kept prison stuff away from me.
Some kids from my old neighborhood make it a crazy rite of passage—like going to prison makes you a man or something.
In one of his last letters to me, my father wrote:
Hey AJ—
You are a growing boy. I truly regret missing you grow up. All the important events in your life—little things like taking you to Yankees games, to Roberto Clemente State Park, throwing you into the sixteen-foot pool! (These are the things I used to do when I was your age.) I missed your graduations, holidays, and birthdays.
holidays and birthdays.
What I'm trying to say is that soon you will be a man. You have
What I'm trying to say is that soon you will be a man. You have been conducting yourself as a fine young man, thus far. So although I haven't been there I wanted to give you some fatherly advice—love—but I believe it needs to be done in person. This is why your grandpa will pinch-hit for me and have this special talk with you.
I know you will listen to him and take those words seriously as you move on up in age, in height—and in all the great things that await you in life, my handsomely beautiful, smart, and sensitive son. Till next time . . .
Love always, your dad

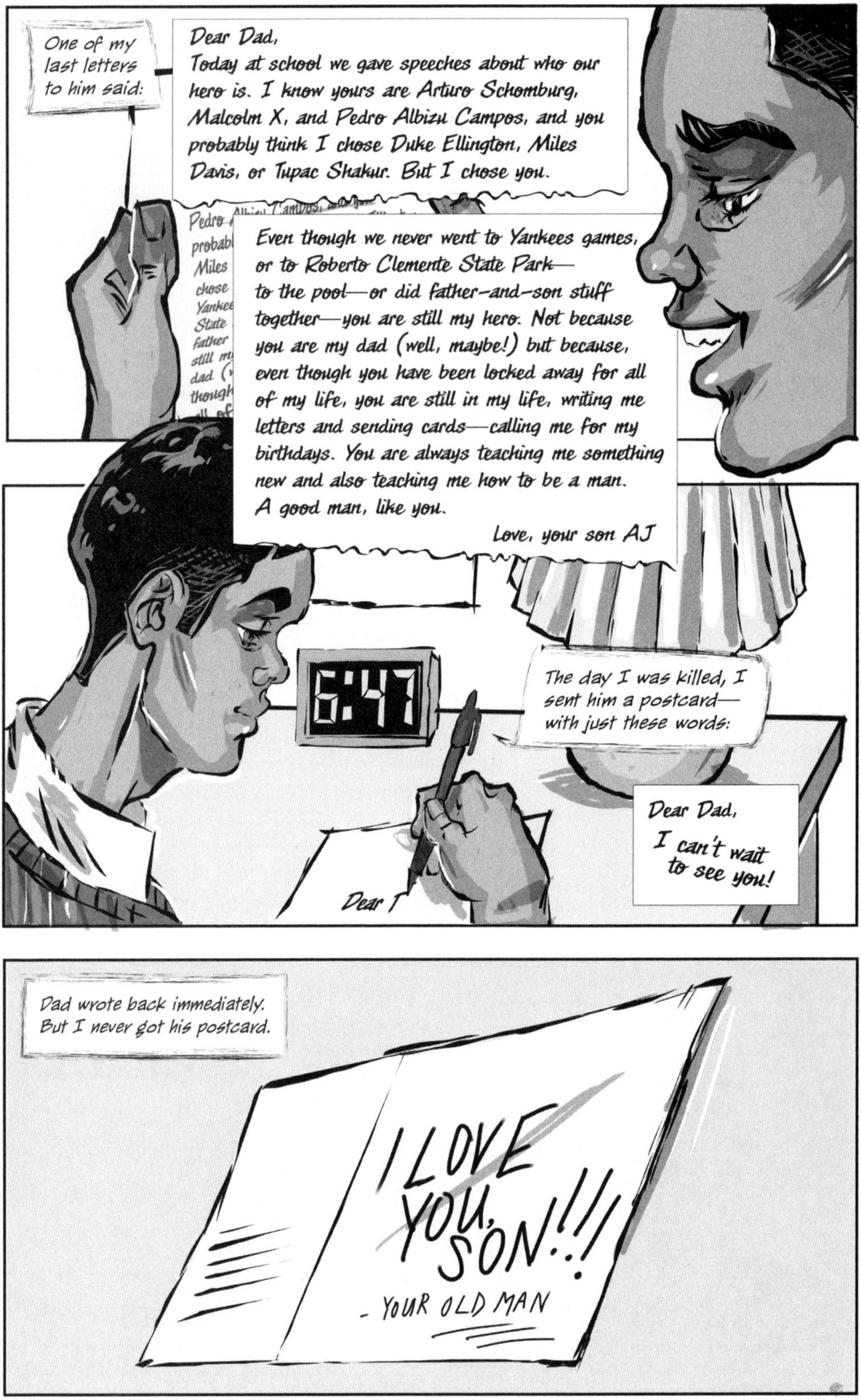
One of my last letters to him said:
Dear Dad,
Today at school we gave speeches about who our hero is. I know yours are Arturo Schomburg, Malcolm X, and Pedro Albizu Campos, and you probably think I chose Duke Ellington, Miles Davis, or Tupac Shakur. But I chose you.
Even though we never went to Yankees games, or to Roberto Clemente State Park—to the pool—or did father-and-son stuff together—you are still my hero. Not because you are my dad (well, maybe!) but because, even though you have been locked away for all of my life, you are still in my life, writing me letters and sending cards—calling me for my birthdays. You are always teaching me something new and also teaching me how to be a man. A good man, like you.
Love, your son AJ
6:47
The day I was killed, I sent him a postcard—with just these words:
Dear Dad,
I can't wait to see you!
Dear
Dad wrote back immediately. But I never got his postcard.
I LOVE YOU, SON!!!
- YOUR OLD MAN

Chapter Forty-Four

The Talk

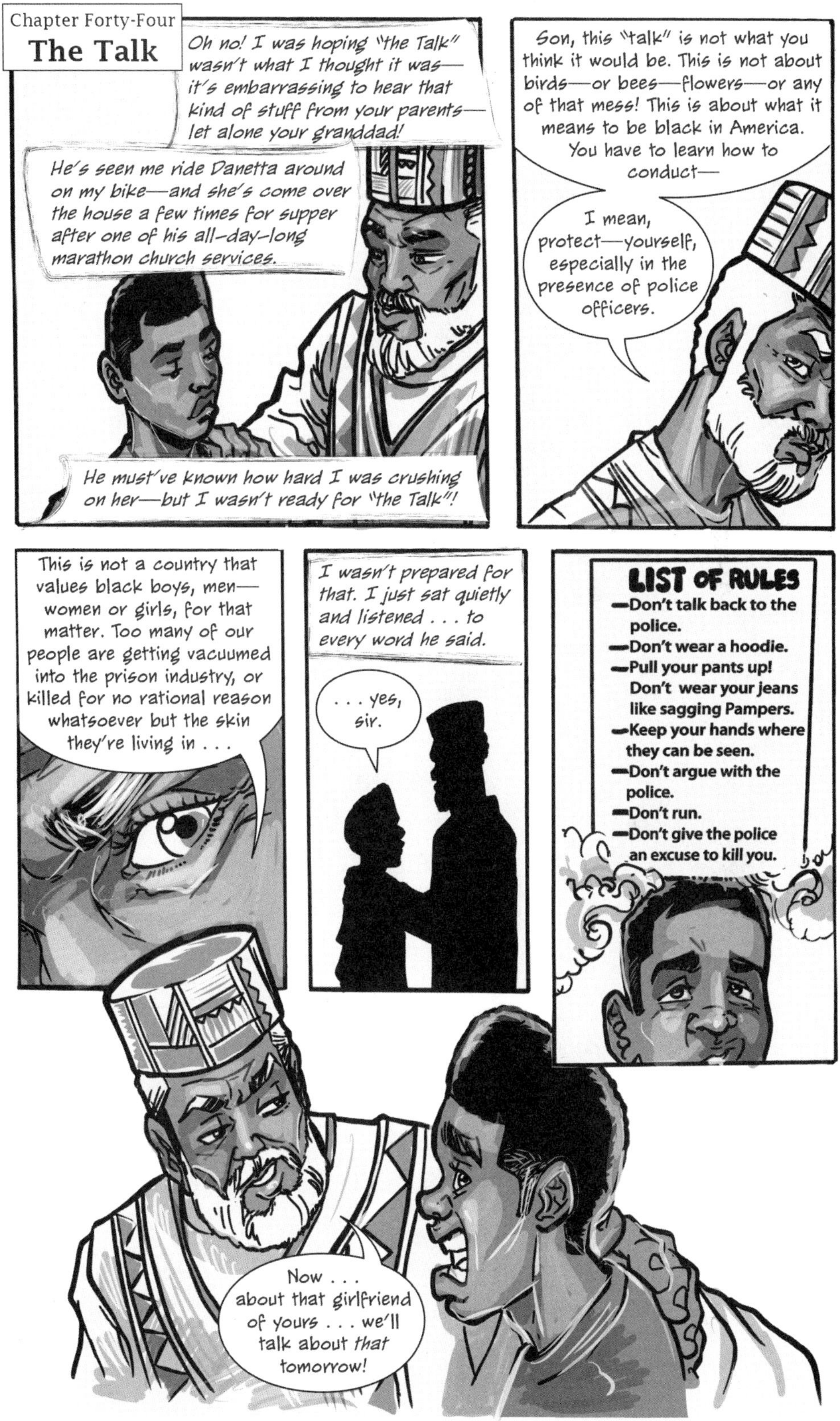
Oh no! I was hoping "the Talk" wasn't what I thought it was—it's embarrassing to hear that kind of stuff from your parents—let alone your granddad!
He's seen me ride Danetta around on my bike—and she's come over the house a few times for supper after one of his all-day-long marathon church services.
He must've known how hard I was crushing on her—but I wasn't ready for "the Talk"!
Son, this "talk" is not what you think it would be. This is not about birds—or bees—flowers—or any of that mess! This is about what it means to be black in America. You have to learn how to conduct—
I mean, protect—yourself, especially in the presence of police officers.
This is not a country that values black boys, men—women or girls, for that matter. Too many of our people are getting vacuumed into the prison industry, or killed for no rational reason whatsoever but the skin they're living in . . .
I wasn't prepared for that. I just sat quietly and listened . . . to every word he said.
. . . yes, sir.
LIST OF RULES
—Don't talk back to the police.
—Don't wear a hoodie.
—Pull your pants up! Don't wear your jeans like sagging Pampers.
—Keep your hands where they can be seen.
—Don't argue with the police.
—Don't run.
—Don't give the police an excuse to kill you.
Now . . . about that girlfriend of yours . . . we'll talk about that tomorrow!

Chapter Forty-Five

Hanger

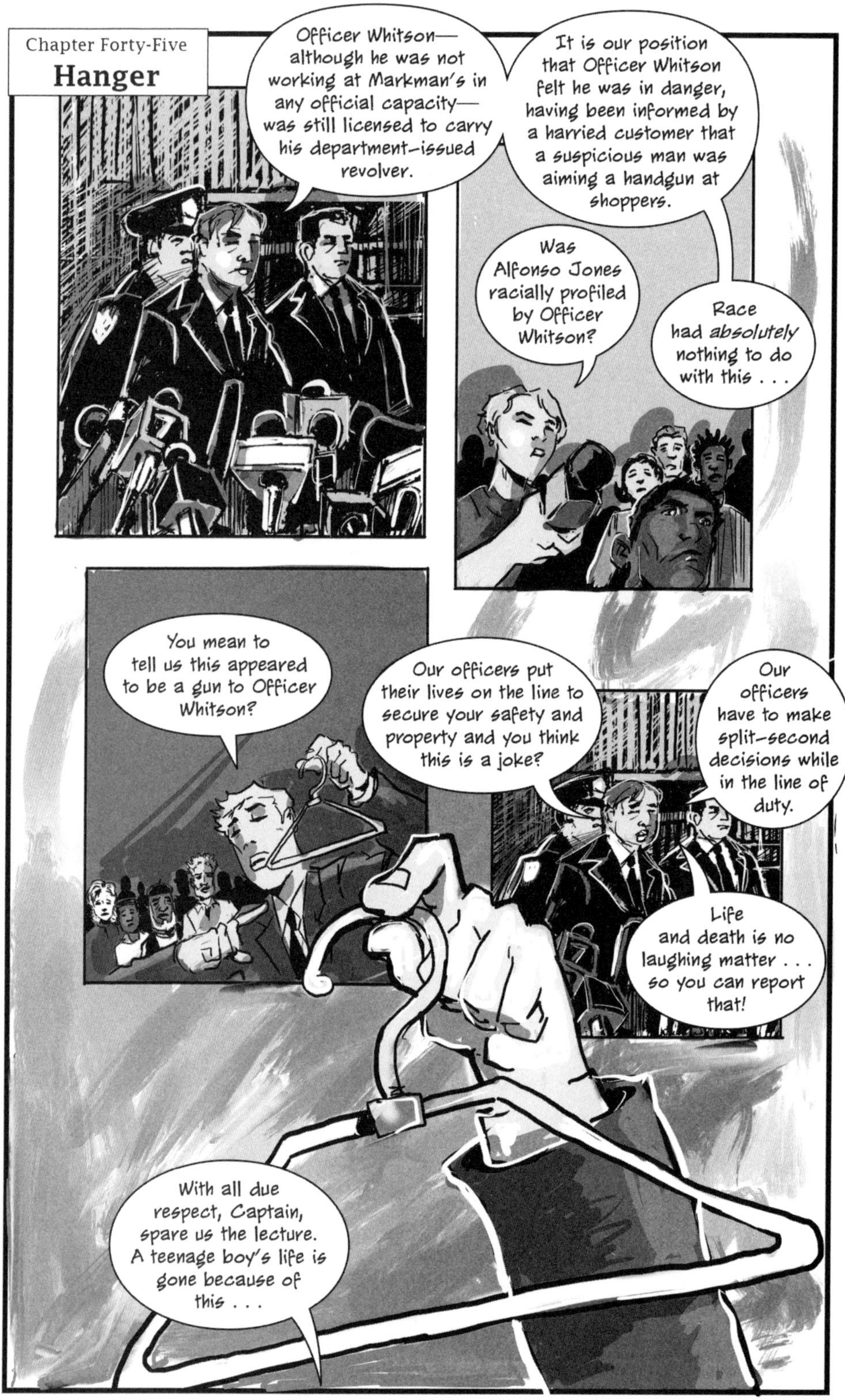

Officer Whitson—although he was not working at Markman's in any official capacity—was still licensed to carry his department-issued revolver.
It is our position that Officer Whitson felt he was in danger, having been informed by a harried customer that a suspicious man was aiming a handgun at shoppers.
Was Alfonso Jones racially profiled by Officer Whitson?
Race had *absolutely* nothing to do with this . . .
You mean to tell us this appeared to be a gun to Officer Whitson?
Our officers put their lives on the line to secure your safety and property and you think this is a joke?
Our officers have to make split-second decisions while in the line of duty.
Life and death is no laughing matter . . . so you can report that!
With all due respect, Captain, spare us the lecture. A teenage boy's life is gone because of this . . .

Chapter Forty-Six

If Only

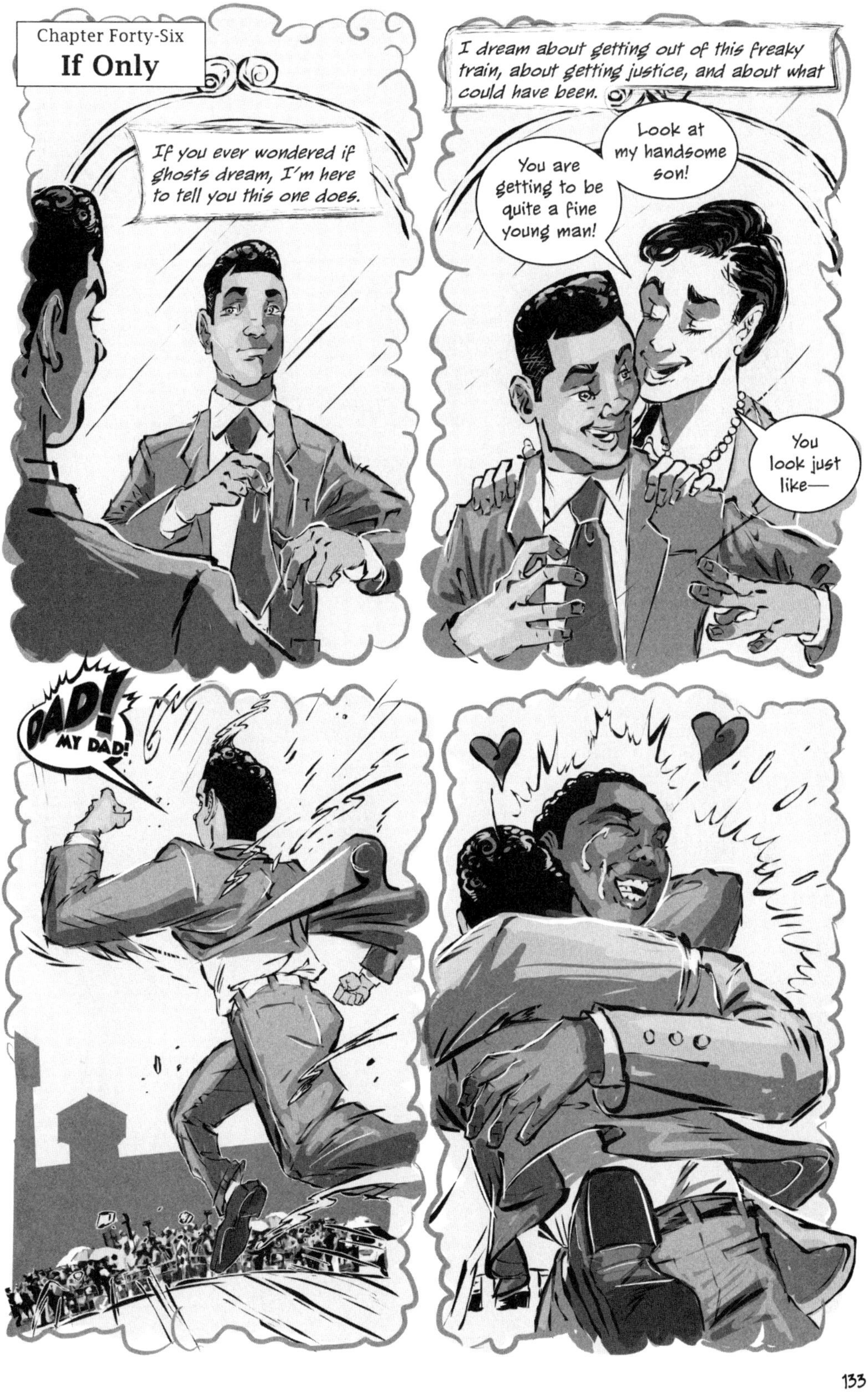

If you ever wondered if ghosts dream, I'm here to tell you this one does.
I dream about getting out of this freaky train, about getting justice, and about what could have been.
Look at my handsome son!
You are getting to be quite a fine young man!
You look just like—
DAD! MY DAD!

Chapter Forty-Seven
BB Gun

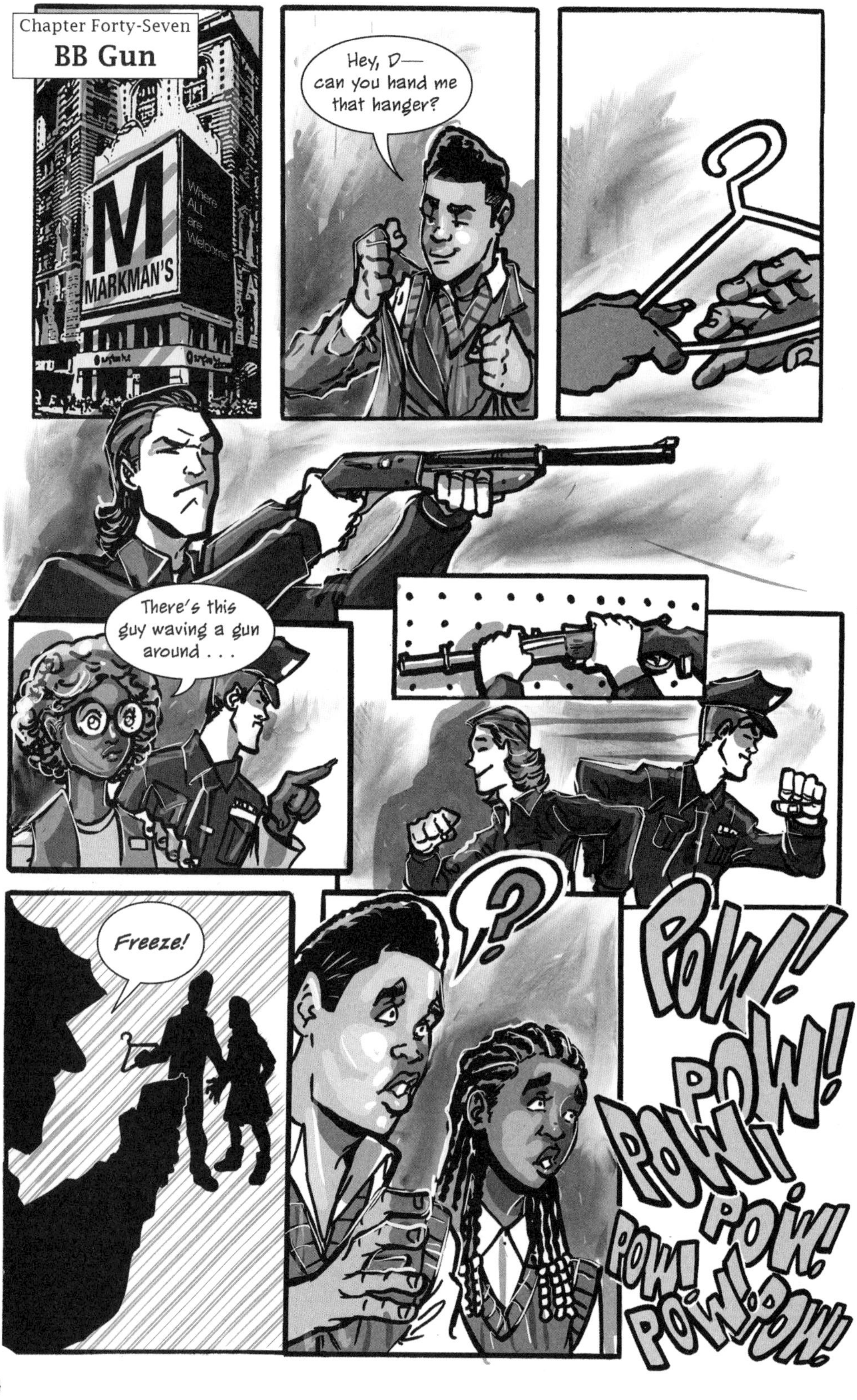
MARKMAN'S
Where ALL are Welcome
Hey, D— can you hand me that hanger?
There's this guy waving a gun around . . .
Freeze!
?
POW! POW! POW! POW! POW! POW! POW!

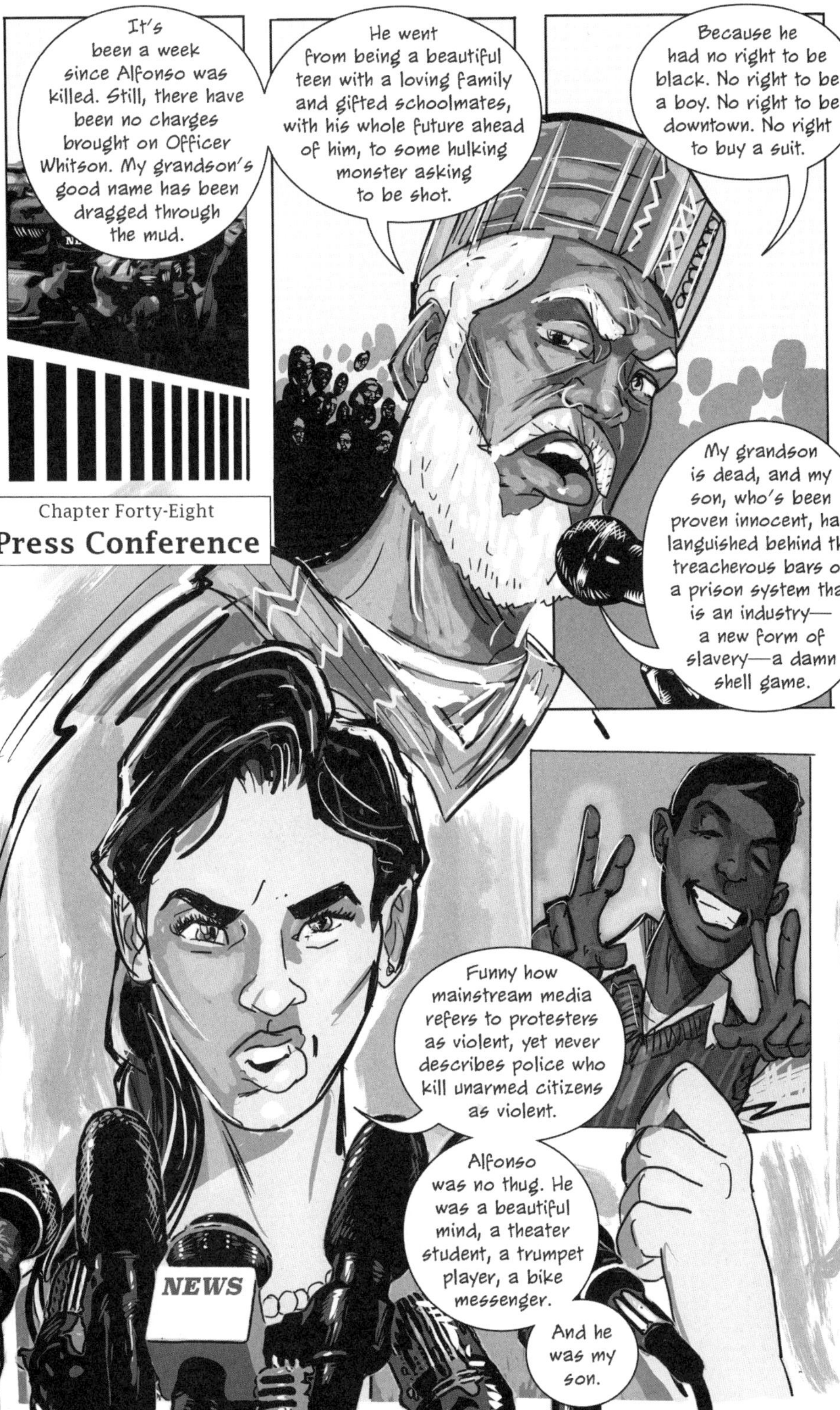
It's been a week since Alfonso was killed. Still, there have been no charges brought on Officer Whitson. My grandson's good name has been dragged through the mud.
He went from being a beautiful teen with a loving family and gifted schoolmates, with his whole future ahead of him, to some hulking monster asking to be shot.
Because he had no right to be black. No right to be a boy. No right to be downtown. No right to buy a suit.
My grandson is dead, and my son, who's been proven innocent, has languished behind the treacherous bars of a prison system that is an industry— a new form of slavery—a damn shell game.
Chapter Forty-Eight
Press Conference
Funny how mainstream media refers to protesters as violent, yet never describes police who kill unarmed citizens as violent.
NEWS
Alfonso was no thug. He was a beautiful mind, a theater student, a trumpet player, a bike messenger.
And he was my son.

Chapter Forty-Nine
Spinning and Spinning

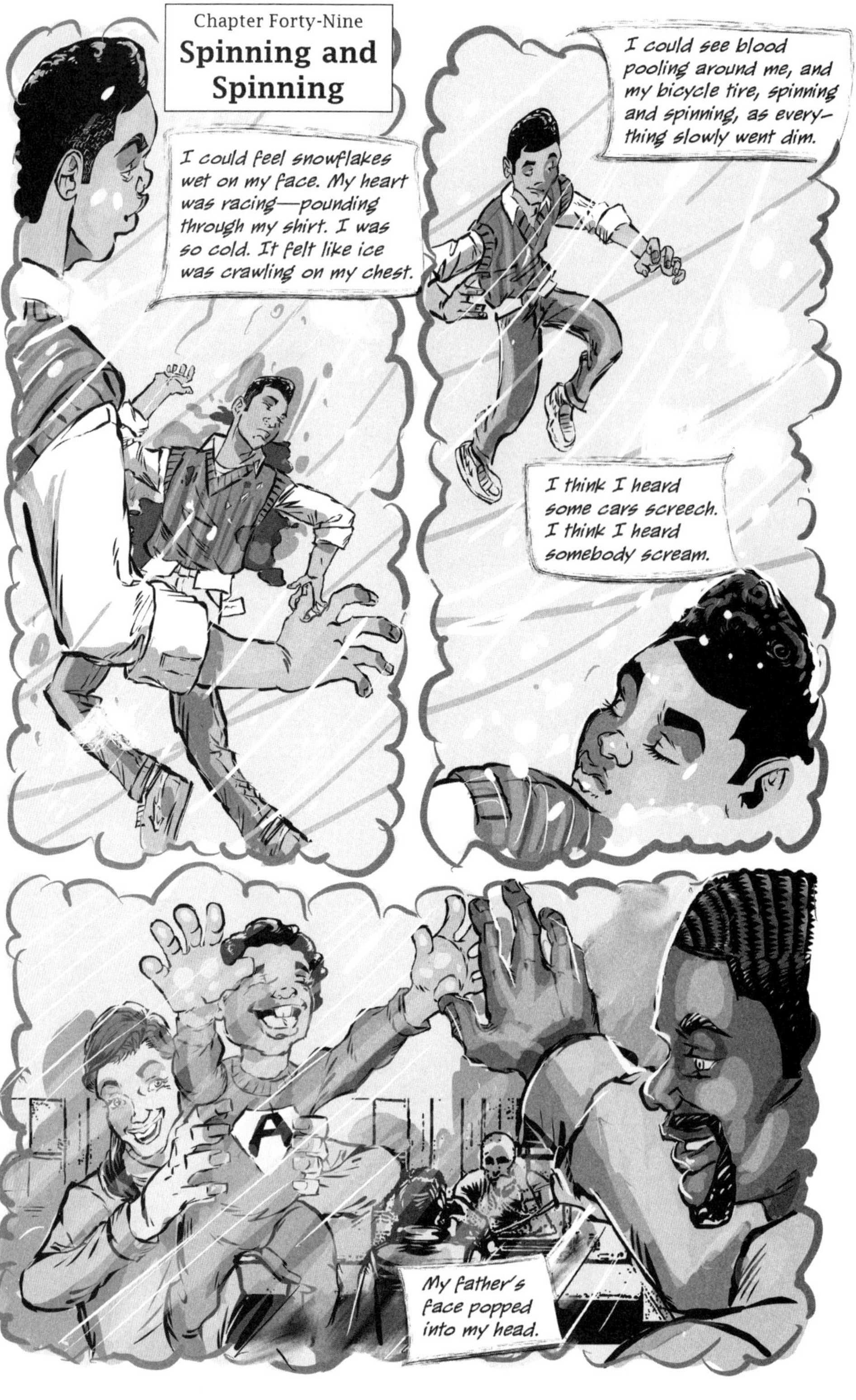
I could feel snowflakes wet on my face. My heart was racing—pounding through my shirt. I was so cold. It felt like ice was crawling on my chest.
I could see blood pooling around me, and my bicycle tire, spinning and spinning, as everything slowly went dim.
I think I heard some cars screech. I think I heard somebody scream.
My father's face popped into my head.

Chapter Fifty

Hip-Hop Hamlet

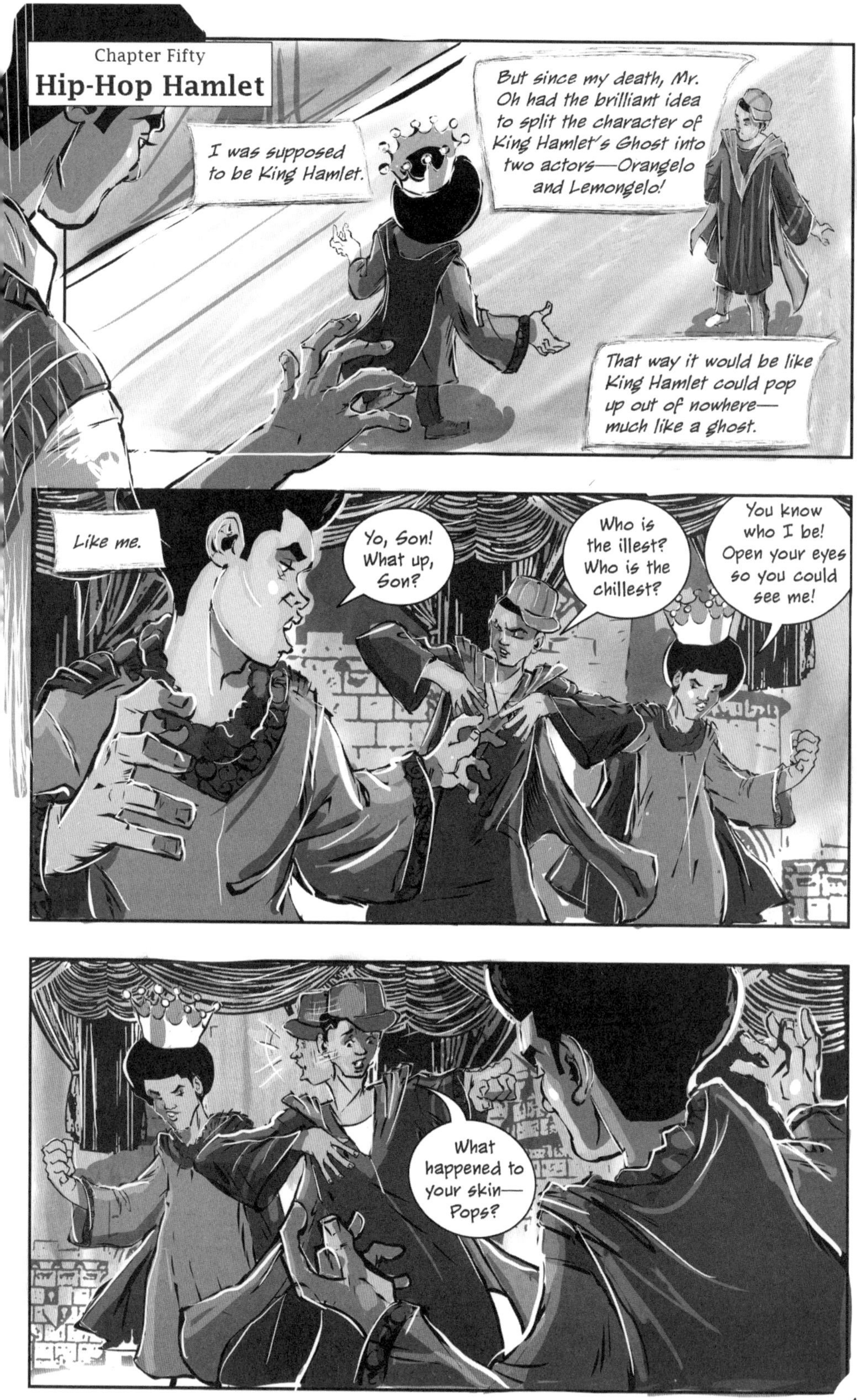
I was supposed to be King Hamlet.
But since my death, Mr. Oh had the brilliant idea to split the character of King Hamlet's Ghost into two actors—Orangelo and Lemongelo!
That way it would be like King Hamlet could pop up out of nowhere—much like a ghost.
Like me.
Yo, Son! What up, Son?
Who is the illest? Who is the chillest?
You know who I be! Open your eyes so you could see me!
What happened to your skin—Pops?

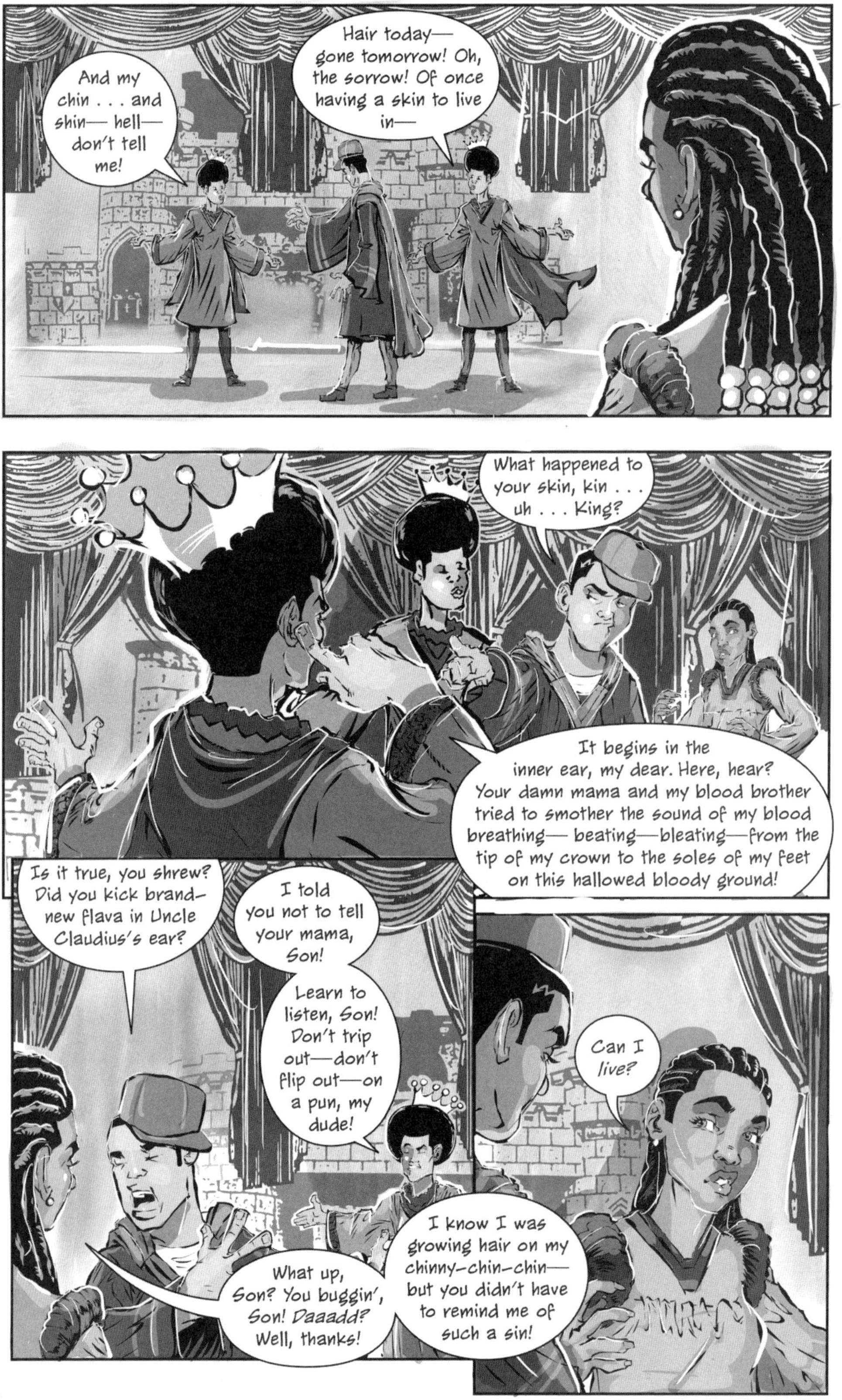

And my chin . . . and shin— hell— don't tell me!
Hair today— gone tomorrow! Oh, the sorrow! Of once having a skin to live in—
What happened to your skin, kin . . . uh . . . King?
It begins in the inner ear, my dear. Here, hear? Your damn mama and my blood brother tried to smother the sound of my blood breathing— beating—bleating—from the tip of my crown to the soles of my feet on this hallowed bloody ground!
Is it true, you shrew? Did you kick brand-new flava in Uncle Claudius's ear?
I told you not to tell your mama, Son!
Learn to listen, Son! Don't trip out—don't flip out—on a pun, my dude!
What up, Son? You buggin', Son! *Daaadd?* Well, thanks!
I know I was growing hair on my chinny-chin-chin— but you didn't have to remind me of such a sin!
Can I *live?*

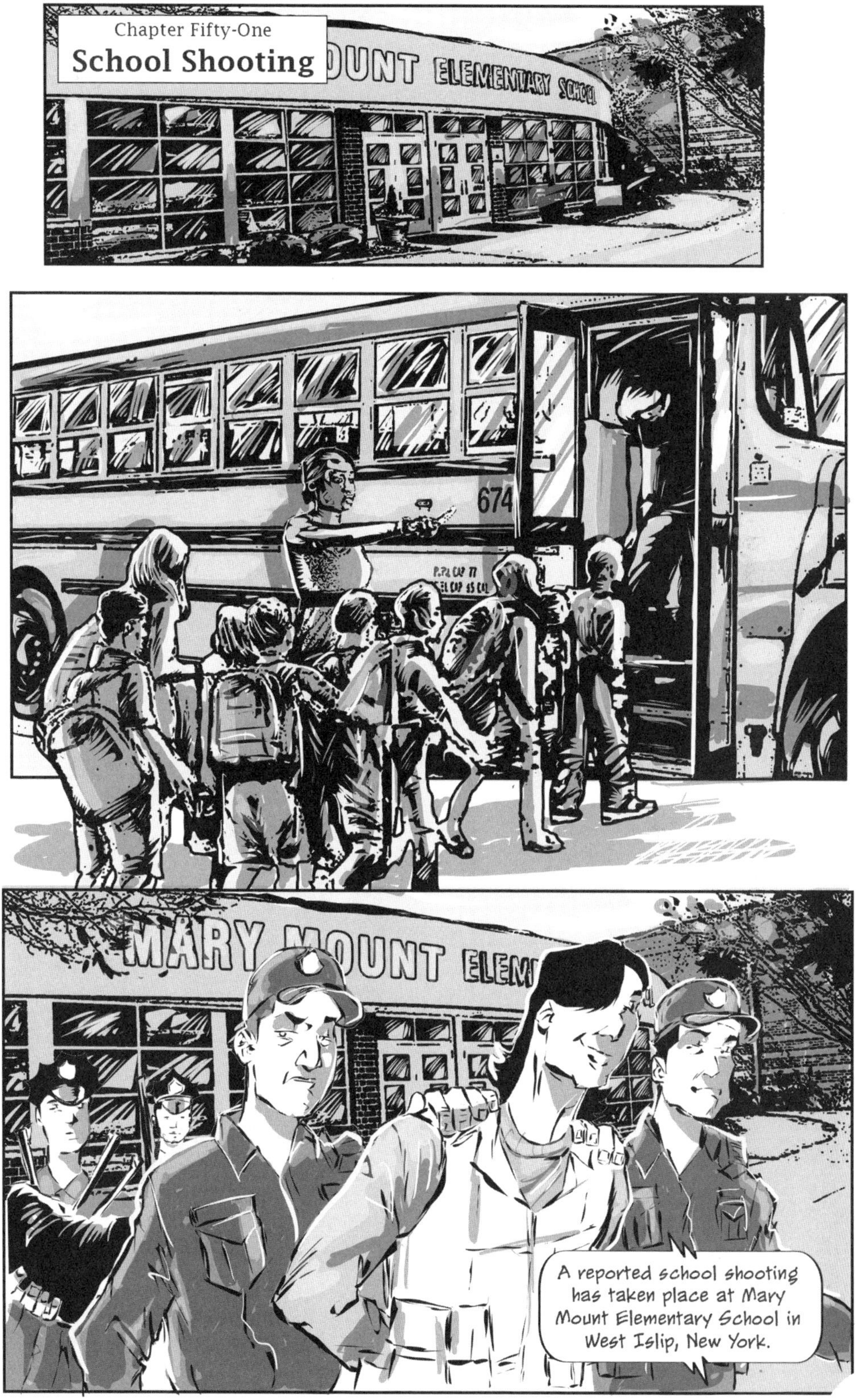
Chapter Fifty-One
School Shooting
OUNT ELEMENTARY SCHOOL
674
MARY MOUNT ELEM
A reported school shooting has taken place at Mary Mount Elementary School in West Islip, New York.

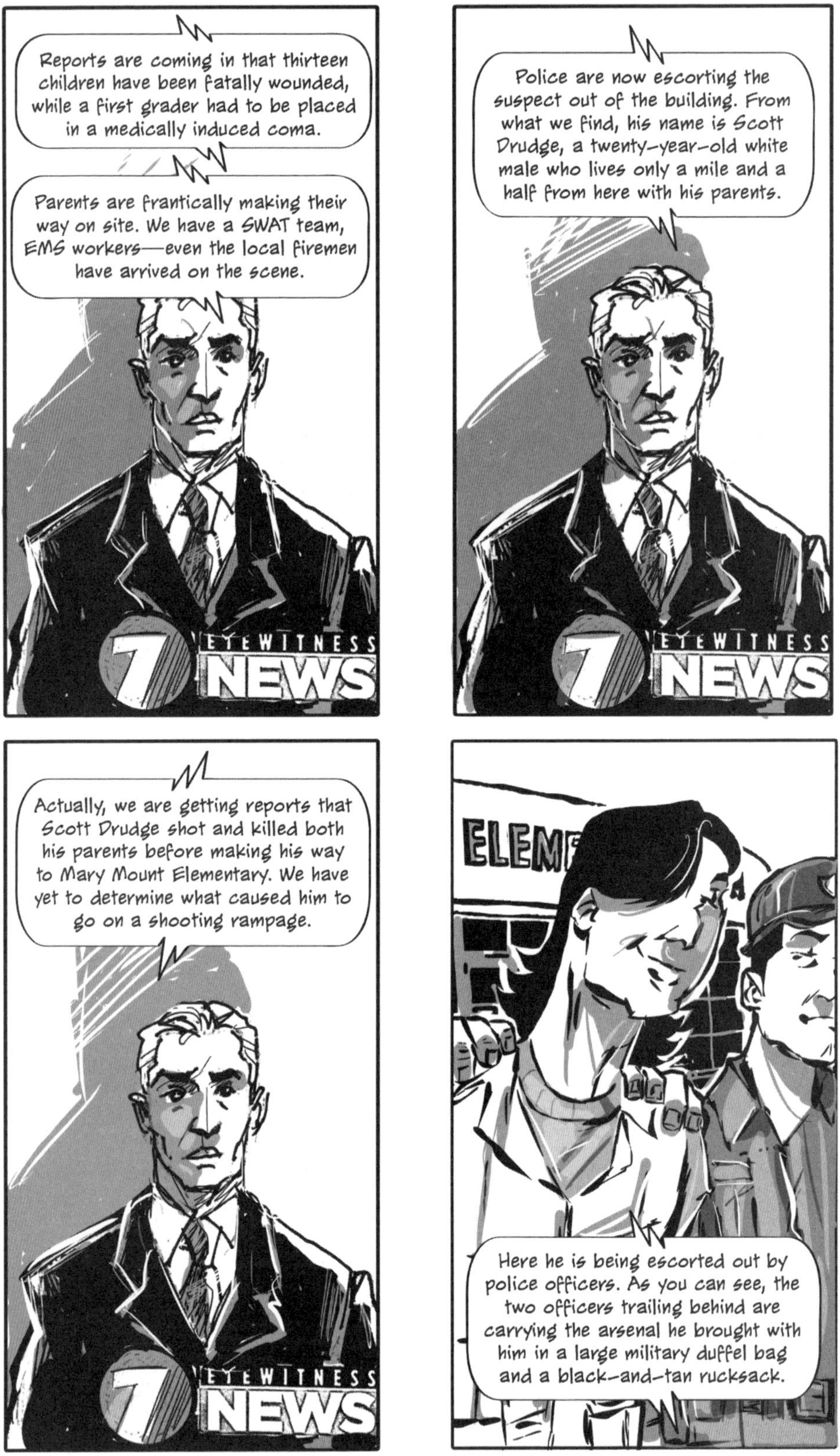
Reports are coming in that thirteen children have been fatally wounded, while a first grader had to be placed in a medically induced coma.
Parents are frantically making their way on site. We have a SWAT team, EMS workers—even the local firemen have arrived on the scene.
7 EYEWITNESS NEWS
Police are now escorting the suspect out of the building. From what we find, his name is Scott Drudge, a twenty-year-old white male who lives only a mile and a half from here with his parents.
7 EYEWITNESS NEWS
Actually, we are getting reports that Scott Drudge shot and killed both his parents before making his way to Mary Mount Elementary. We have yet to determine what caused him to go on a shooting rampage.
7 EYEWITNESS NEWS
ELEM
Here he is being escorted out by police officers. As you can see, the two officers trailing behind are carrying the arsenal he brought with him in a large military duffel bag and a black-and-tan rucksack.

Chapter Fifty-Two

Autopsy

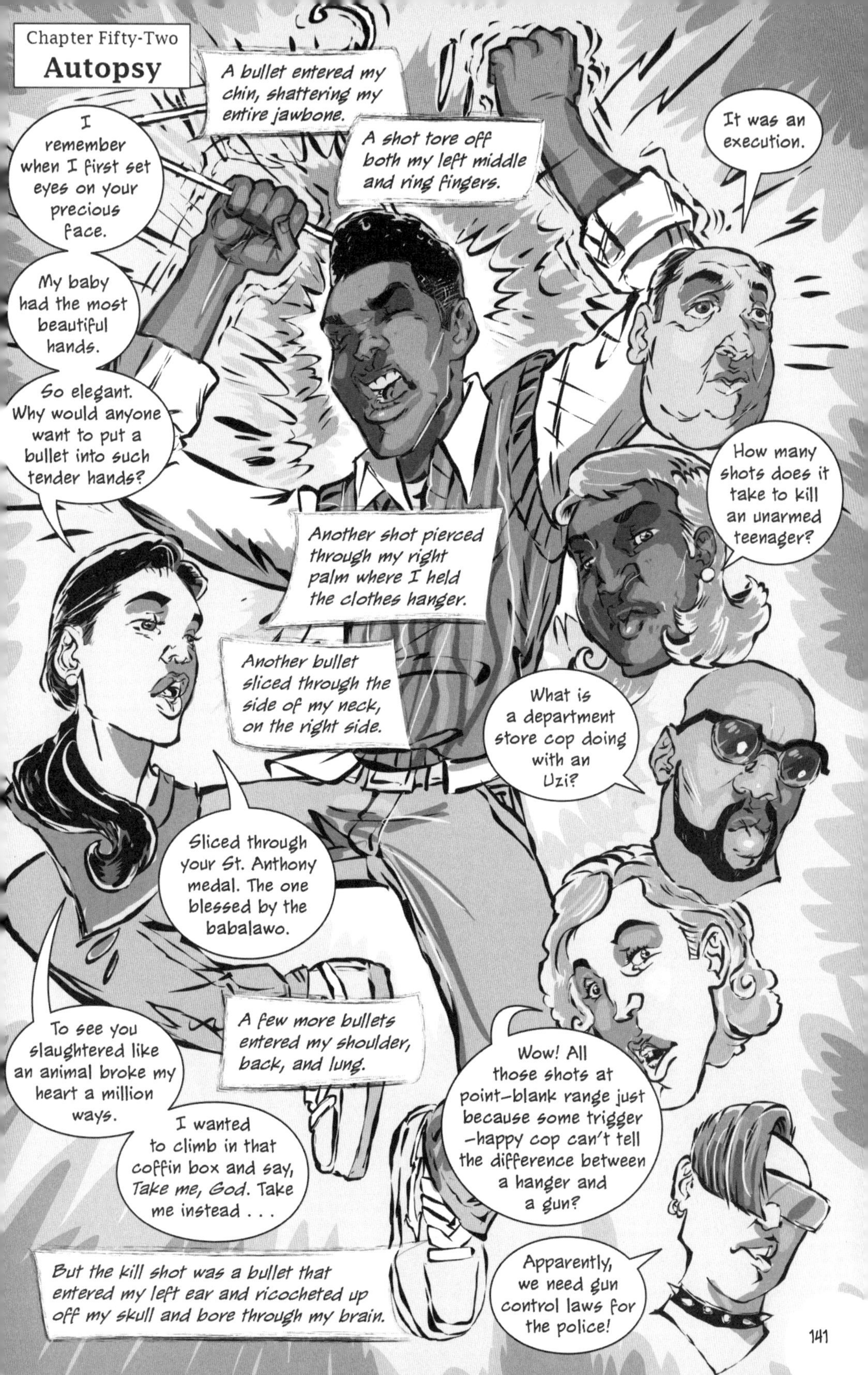
A bullet entered my chin, shattering my entire jawbone.
I remember when I first set eyes on your precious face.
A shot tore off both my left middle and ring fingers.
It was an execution.
My baby had the most beautiful hands.
So elegant. Why would anyone want to put a bullet into such tender hands?
How many shots does it take to kill an unarmed teenager?
Another shot pierced through my right palm where I held the clothes hanger.
Another bullet sliced through the side of my neck, on the right side.
What is a department store cop doing with an Uzi?
Sliced through your St. Anthony medal. The one blessed by the babalawo.
A few more bullets entered my shoulder, back, and lung.
To see you slaughtered like an animal broke my heart a million ways.
I wanted to climb in that coffin box and say, Take me, God. Take me instead . . .
Wow! All those shots at point-blank range just because some trigger-happy cop can't tell the difference between a hanger and a gun?
But the kill shot was a bullet that entered my left ear and ricocheted up off my skull and bore through my brain.
Apparently, we need gun control laws for the police!

Chapter Fifty-Three
No Charges

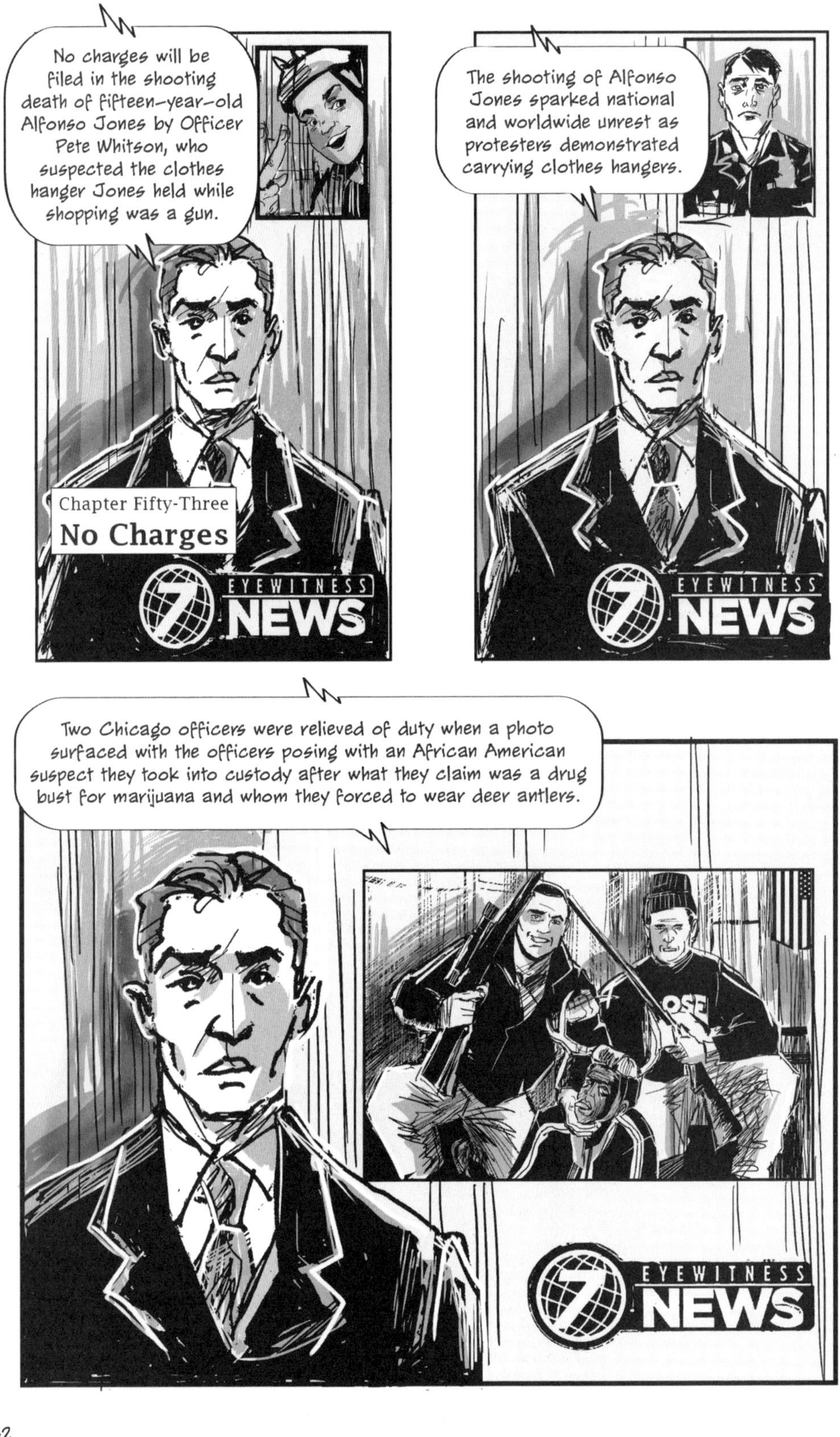
No charges will be filed in the shooting death of fifteen-year-old Alfonso Jones by Officer Pete Whitson, who suspected the clothes hanger Jones held while shopping was a gun.
7 EYEWITNESS NEWS
The shooting of Alfonso Jones sparked national and worldwide unrest as protesters demonstrated carrying clothes hangers.
7 EYEWITNESS NEWS
Two Chicago officers were relieved of duty when a photo surfaced with the officers posing with an African American suspect they took into custody after what they claim was a drug bust for marijuana and whom they forced to wear deer antlers.
7 EYEWITNESS NEWS

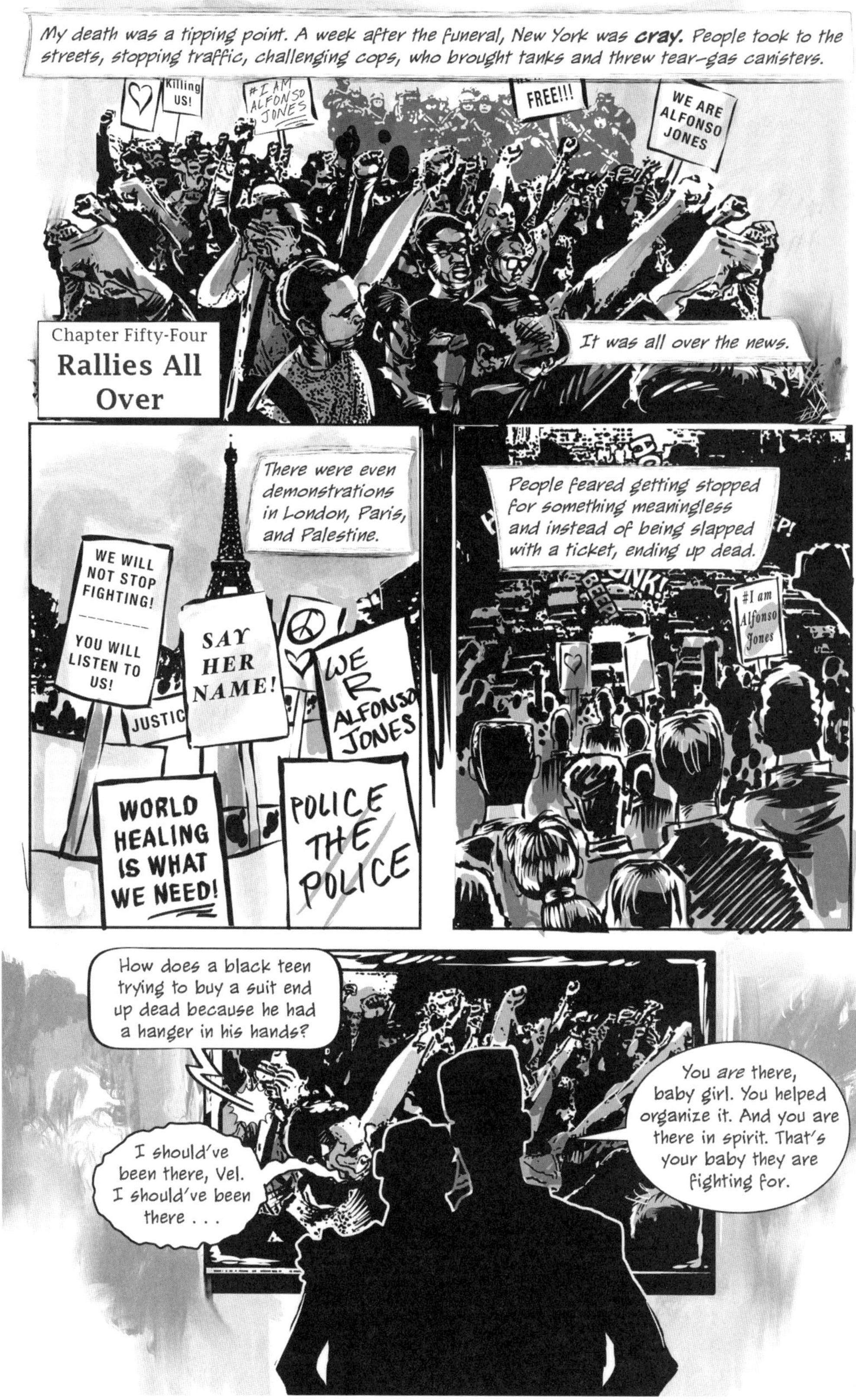
My death was a tipping point. A week after the funeral, New York was **cray.** People took to the streets, stopping traffic, challenging cops, who brought tanks and threw tear-gas canisters.
Killing US!
#I AM ALFONSO JONES
FREE!!!
WE ARE ALFONSO JONES
Chapter Fifty-Four
Rallies All Over
It was all over the news.
There were even demonstrations in London, Paris, and Palestine.
WE WILL NOT STOP FIGHTING! YOU WILL LISTEN TO US!
SAY HER NAME!
WE R ALFONSO JONES
JUSTIC
WORLD HEALING IS WHAT WE NEED!
POLICE THE POLICE
People feared getting stopped for something meaningless and instead of being slapped with a ticket, ending up dead.
#I am Alfonso Jones
How does a black teen trying to buy a suit end up dead because he had a hanger in his hands?
I should've been there, Vel. I should've been there . . .
You are there, baby girl. You helped organize it. And you are there in spirit. That's your baby they are fighting for.

Chapter Fifty-Five
Tanks and Tear Gas

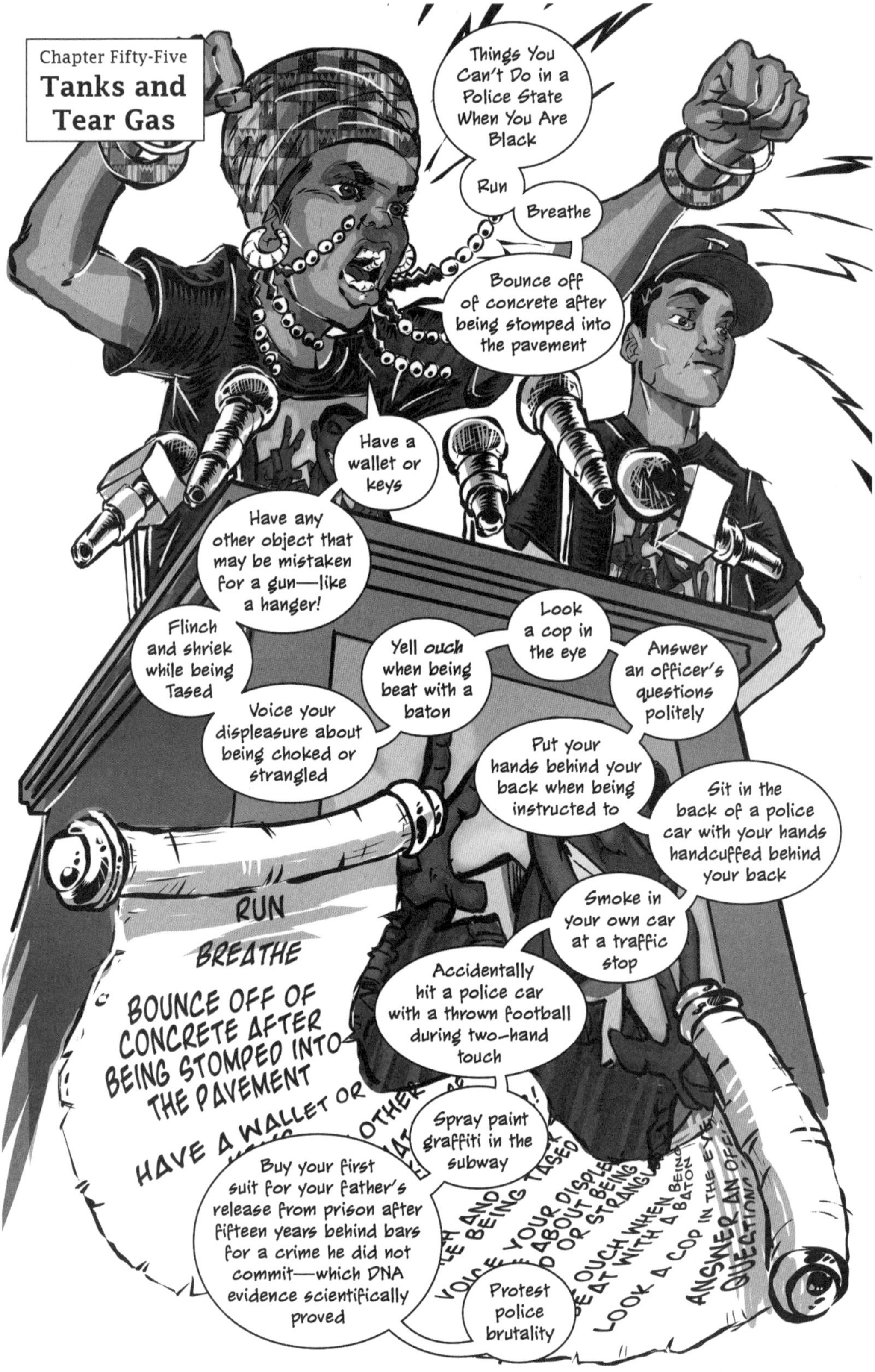
Things You Can't Do in a Police State When You Are Black
Run
Breathe
Bounce off of concrete after being stomped into the pavement
Have a wallet or keys
Have any other object that may be mistaken for a gun—like a hanger!
Flinch and shriek while being Tased
Voice your displeasure about being choked or strangled
Yell *ouch* when being beat with a baton
Look a cop in the eye
Answer an officer's questions politely
Put your hands behind your back when being instructed to
Sit in the back of a police car with your hands handcuffed behind your back
Smoke in your own car at a traffic stop
Accidentally hit a police car with a thrown football during two-hand touch
Spray paint graffiti in the subway
Buy your first suit for your father's release from prison after fifteen years behind bars for a crime he did not commit—which DNA evidence scientifically proved
Protest police brutality
RUN
BREATHE
BOUNCE OFF OF CONCRETE AFTER BEING STOMPED INTO THE PAVEMENT
HAVE A WALLET OR

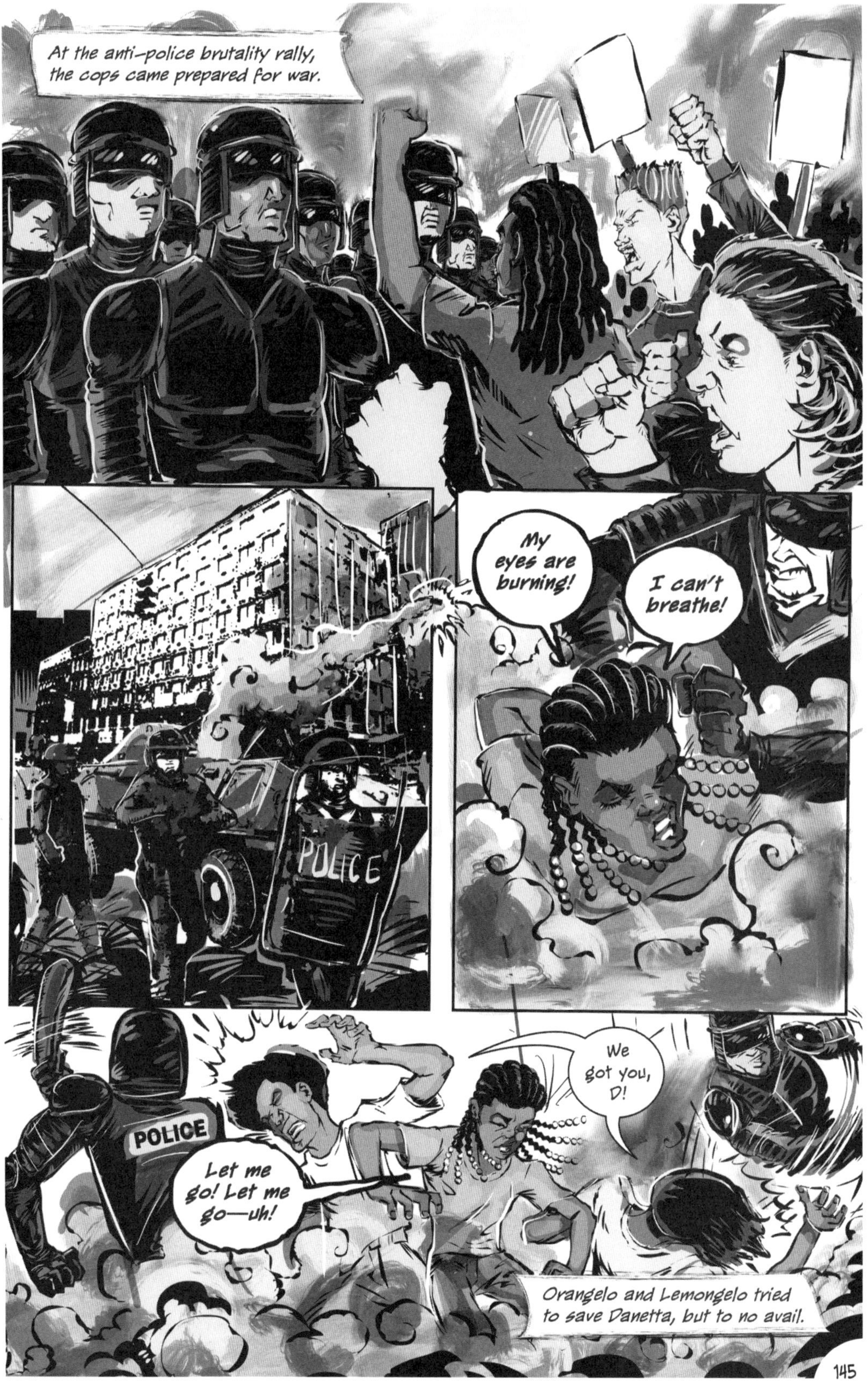
At the anti-police brutality rally, the cops came prepared for war.
POLICE
My eyes are burning!
I can't breathe!
POLICE
Let me go! Let me go—uh!
We got you, D!
Orangelo and Lemongelo tried to save Danetta, but to no avail.

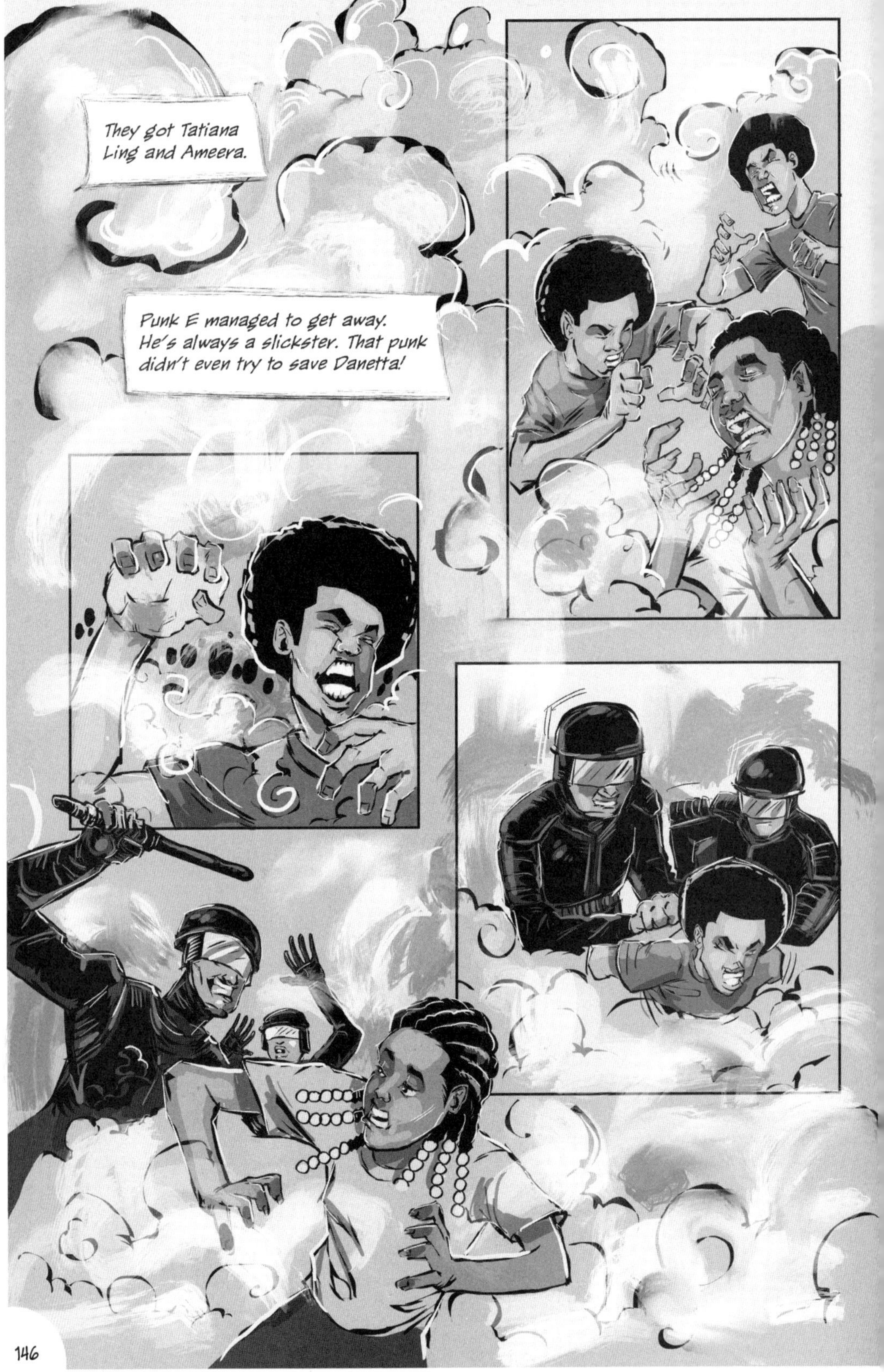
They got Tatiana Ling and Ameera.
Punk E managed to get away. He's always a slickster. That punk didn't even try to save Danetta!

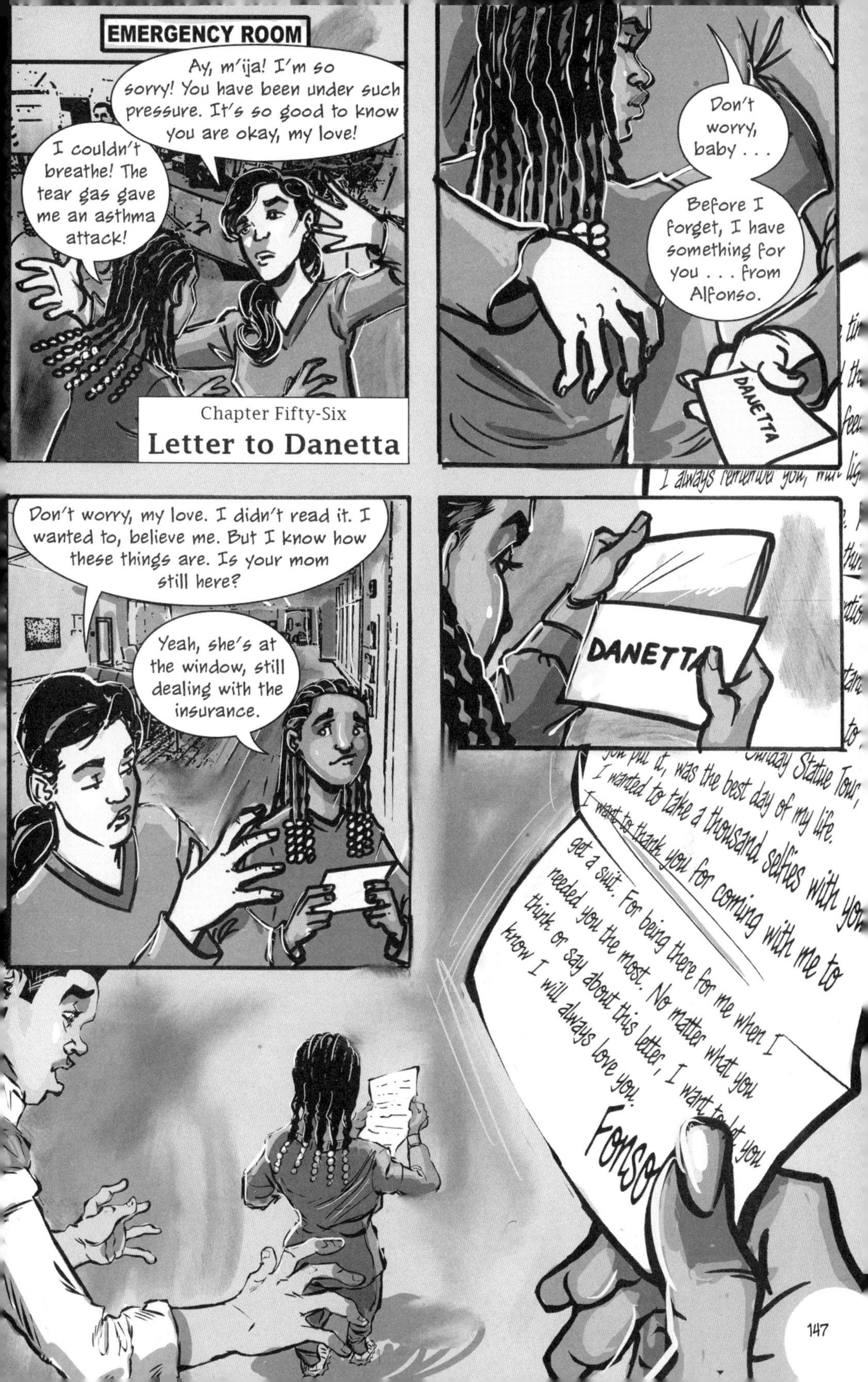
EMERGENCY ROOM
Ay, m'ija! I'm so sorry! You have been under such pressure. It's so good to know you are okay, my love!
I couldn't breathe! The tear gas gave me an asthma attack!
Chapter Fifty-Six
Letter to Danetta
Don't worry, baby . . .
Before I forget, I have something for you . . . from Alfonso.
DANETTA
Don't worry, my love. I didn't read it. I wanted to, believe me. But I know how these things are. Is your mom still here?
Yeah, she's at the window, still dealing with the insurance.
DANETTA
I always remember you,
Sunday Statue Tour,
you put it, was the best day of my life.
I wanted to take a thousand selfies with you
I want to thank you for coming with me to
get a suit. For being there for me when I
needed you the most. No matter what you
think or say about this letter, I want to let you
know I will always love you.
Fonso

Chapter Fifty-Seven
President

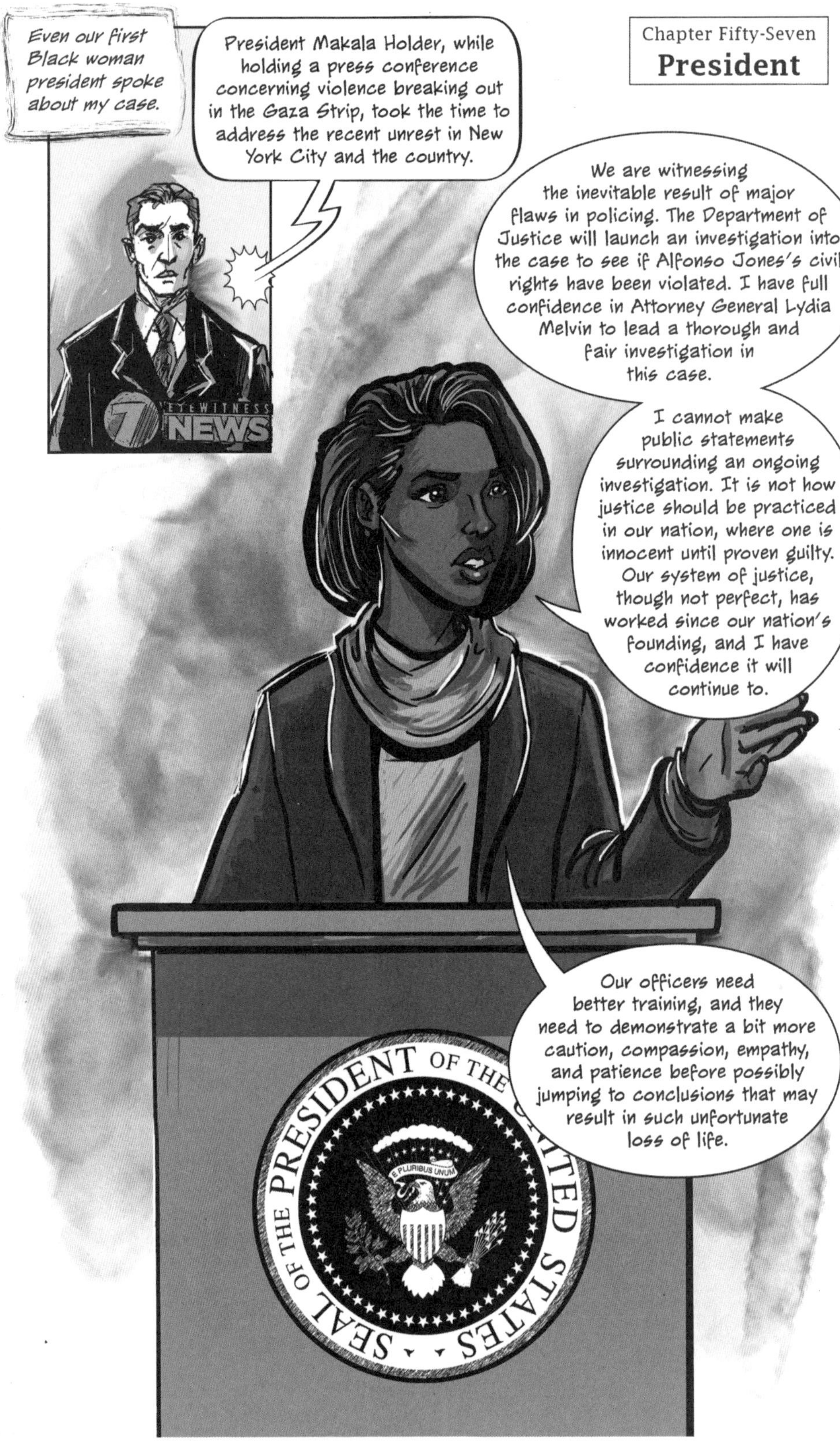

Chapter Fifty-Eight
Trial

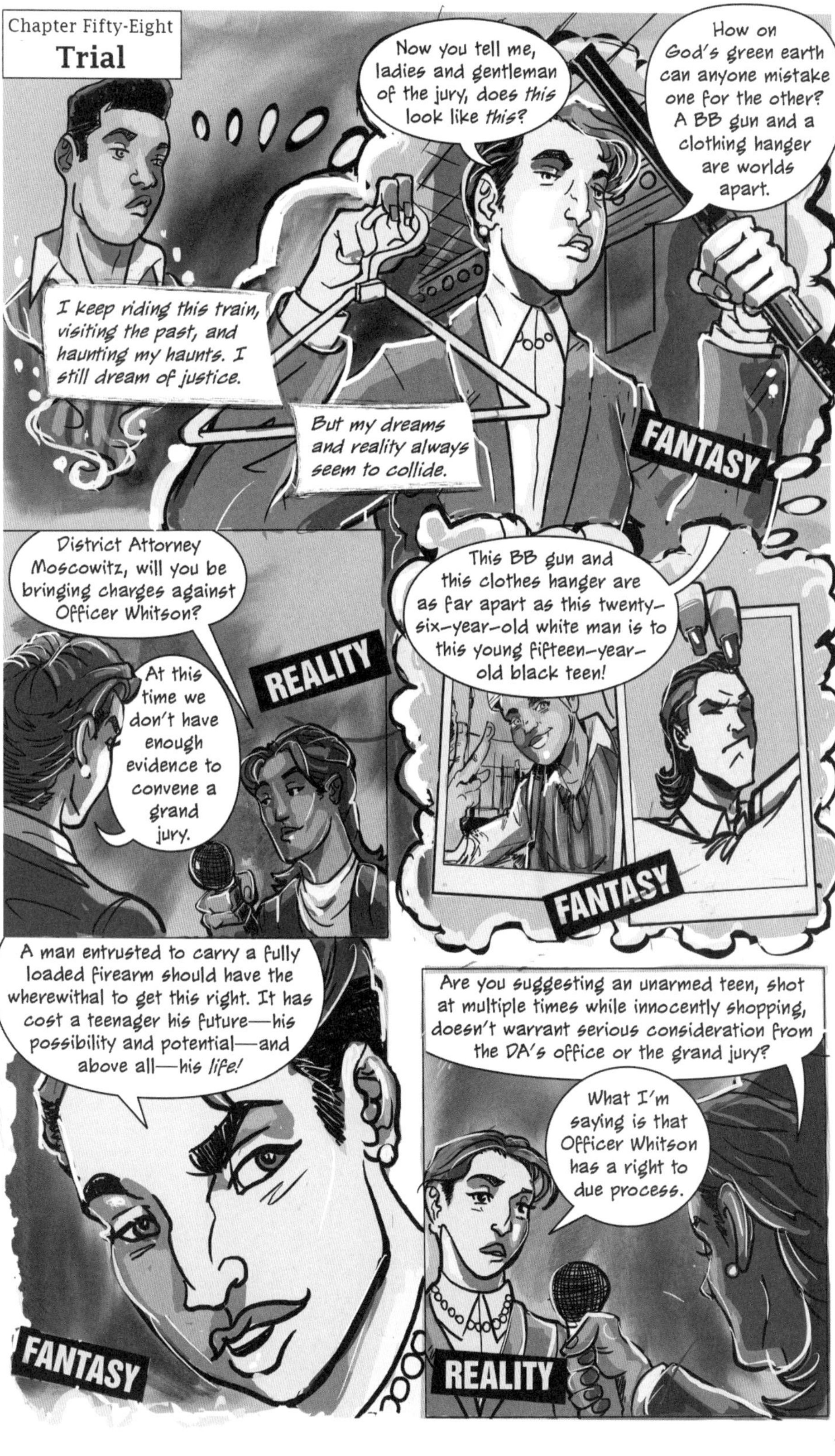

Now you tell me, ladies and gentleman of the jury, does *this* look like *this*?
How on God's green earth can anyone mistake one for the other? A BB gun and a clothing hanger are worlds apart.
I keep riding this train, visiting the past, and haunting my haunts. I still dream of justice.
But my dreams and reality always seem to collide.
FANTASY
District Attorney Moscowitz, will you be bringing charges against Officer Whitson?
REALITY
At this time we don't have enough evidence to convene a grand jury.
This BB gun and this clothes hanger are as far apart as this twenty-six-year-old white man is to this young fifteen-year-old black teen!
FANTASY
A man entrusted to carry a fully loaded firearm should have the wherewithal to get this right. It has cost a teenager his future—his possibility and potential—and above all—his *life!*
FANTASY
Are you suggesting an unarmed teen, shot at multiple times while innocently shopping, doesn't warrant serious consideration from the DA's office or the grand jury?
What I'm saying is that Officer Whitson has a right to due process.
REALITY

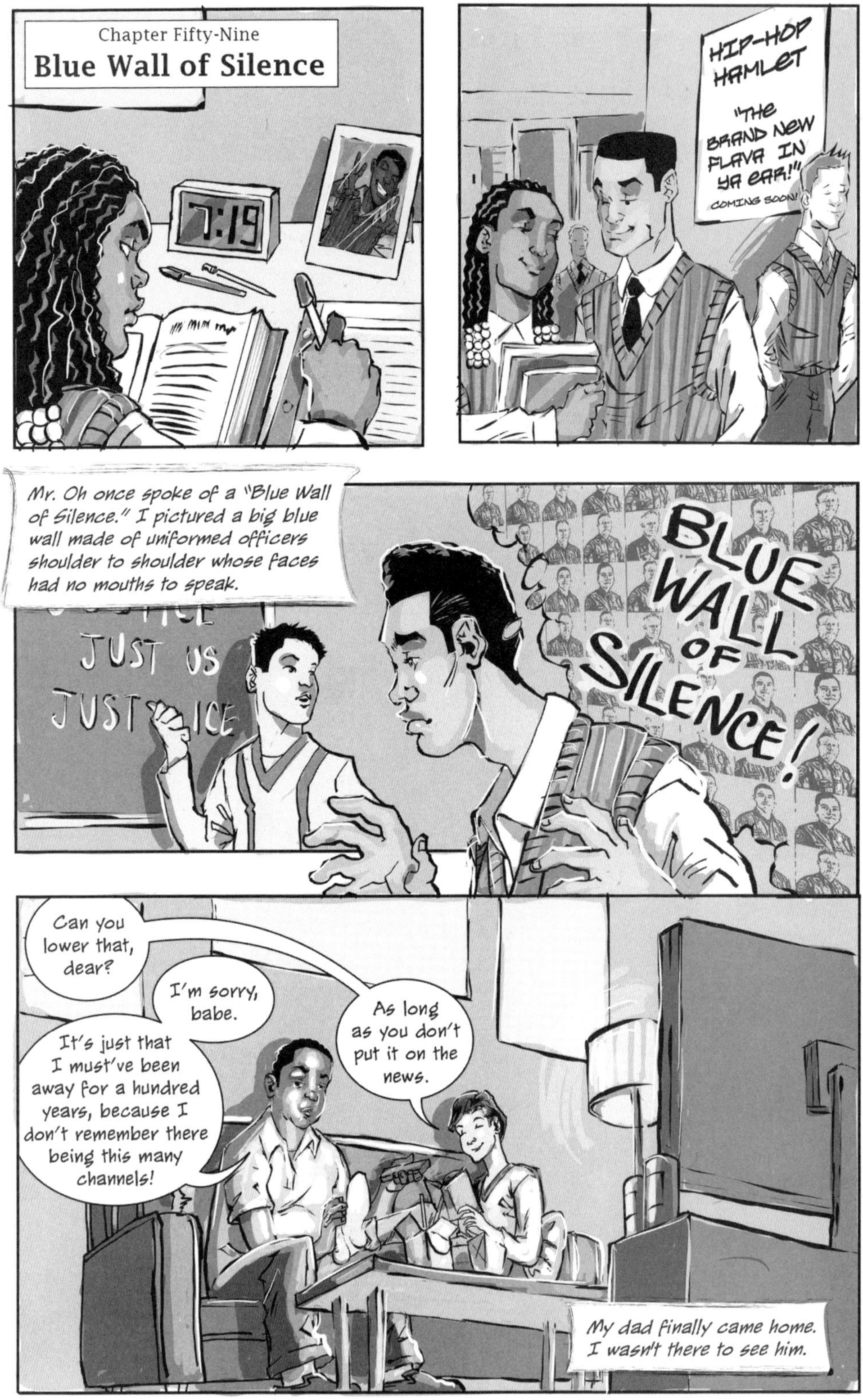
Chapter Fifty-Nine
Blue Wall of Silence
7:19
HIP-HOP HAMLET
"THE BRAND NEW FLAVA IN YA EAR!"
COMING SOON!
Mr. Oh once spoke of a "Blue Wall of Silence." I pictured a big blue wall made of uniformed officers shoulder to shoulder whose faces had no mouths to speak.
JUST US
JUST ICE
BLUE WALL OF SILENCE!
Can you lower that, dear?
I'm sorry, babe.
It's just that I must've been away for a hundred years, because I don't remember there being this many channels!
As long as you don't put it on the news.
My dad finally came home. I wasn't there to see him.

Chapter Sixty
135th Street

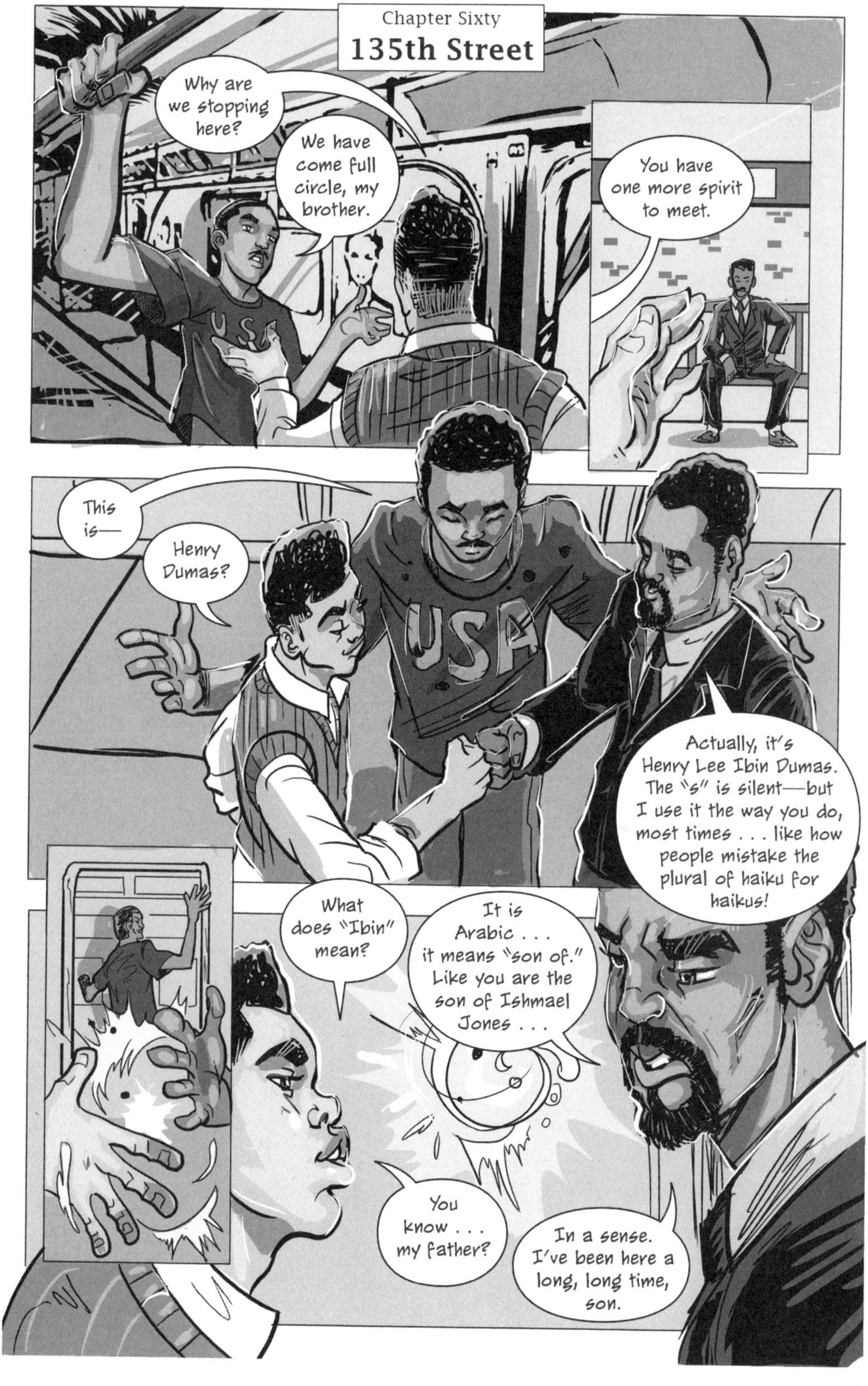

Why are we stopping here?
We have come full circle, my brother.
You have one more spirit to meet.
This is—
Henry Dumas?
Actually, it's Henry Lee Ibin Dumas. The "s" is silent—but I use it the way you do, most times . . . like how people mistake the plural of haiku for haikus!
What does "Ibin" mean?
It is Arabic . . . it means "son of." Like you are the son of Ishmael Jones . . .
You know . . . my father?
In a sense. I've been here a long, long time, son.

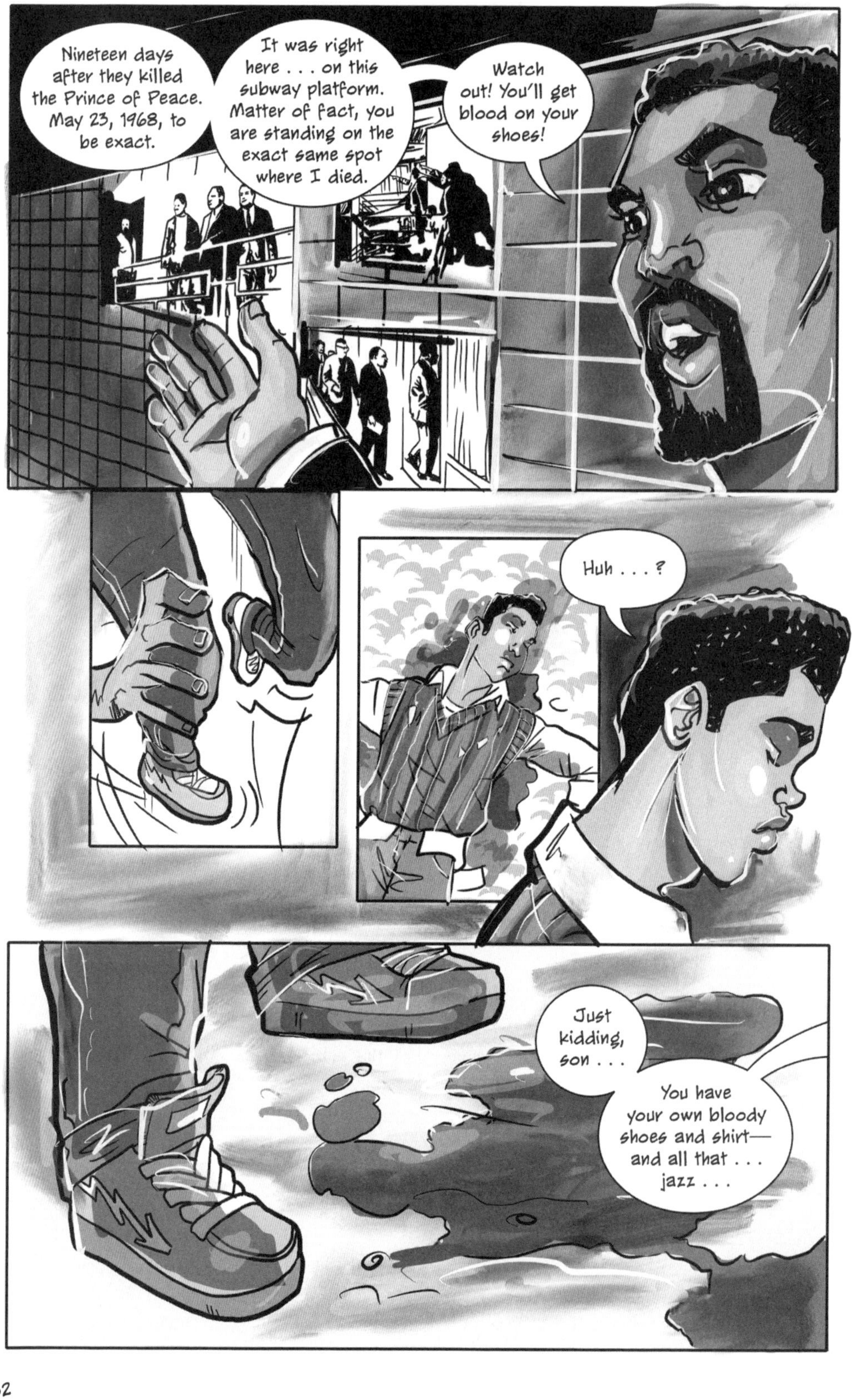
Nineteen days after they killed the Prince of Peace. May 23, 1968, to be exact.
It was right here . . . on this subway platform. Matter of fact, you are standing on the exact same spot where I died.
Watch out! You'll get blood on your shoes!
Huh . . . ?
Just kidding, son . . .
You have your own bloody shoes and shirt— and all that . . . jazz . . .

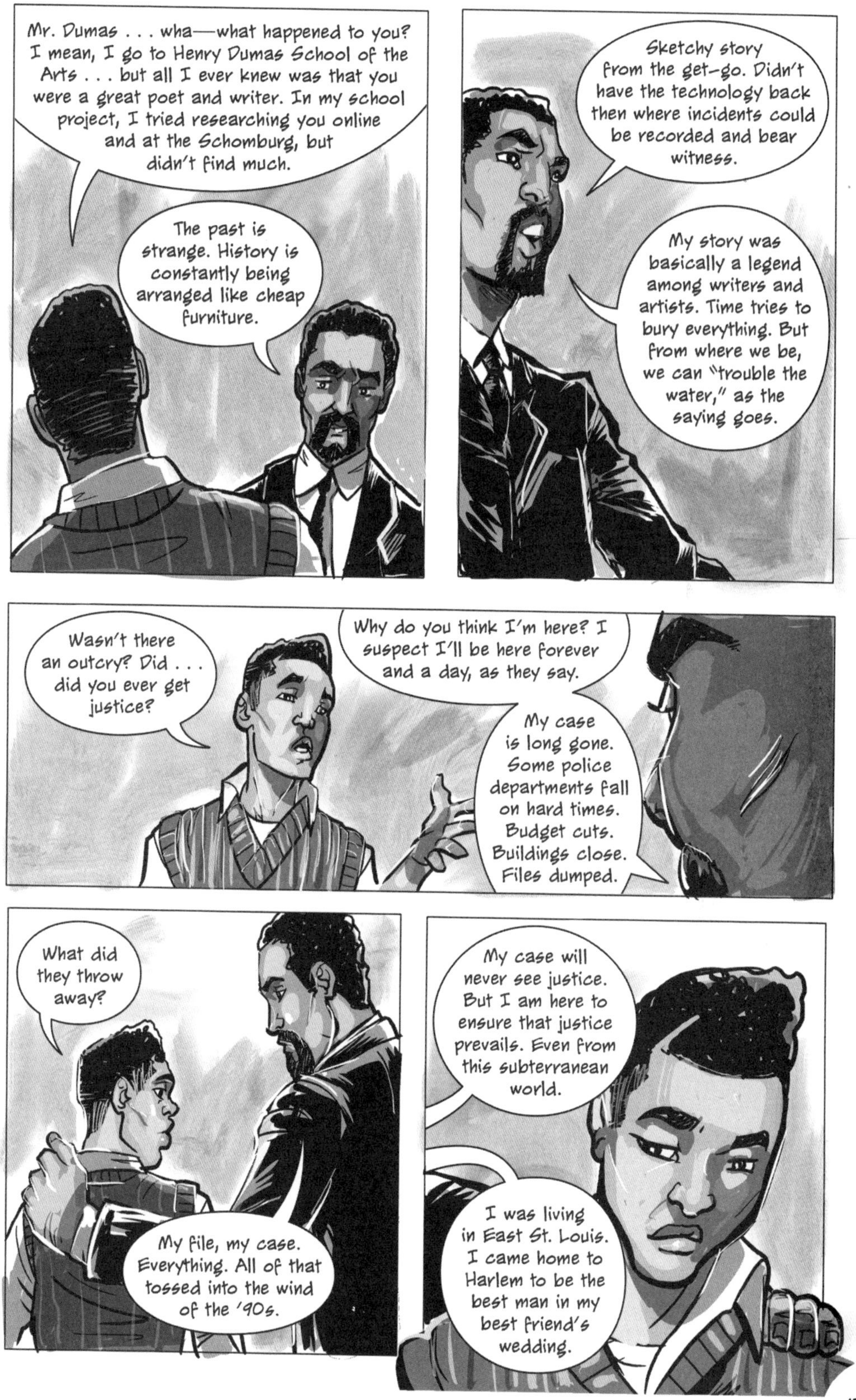
Mr. Dumas . . . wha—what happened to you? I mean, I go to Henry Dumas School of the Arts . . . but all I ever knew was that you were a great poet and writer. In my school project, I tried researching you online and at the Schomburg, but didn't find much.
The past is strange. History is constantly being arranged like cheap furniture.
Sketchy story from the get-go. Didn't have the technology back then where incidents could be recorded and bear witness.
My story was basically a legend among writers and artists. Time tries to bury everything. But from where we be, we can "trouble the water," as the saying goes.
Wasn't there an outcry? Did . . . did you ever get justice?
Why do you think I'm here? I suspect I'll be here forever and a day, as they say.
My case is long gone. Some police departments fall on hard times. Budget cuts. Buildings close. Files dumped.
What did they throw away?
My file, my case. Everything. All of that tossed into the wind of the '90s.
My case will never see justice. But I am here to ensure that justice prevails. Even from this subterranean world.
I was living in East St. Louis. I came home to Harlem to be the best man in my best friend's wedding.

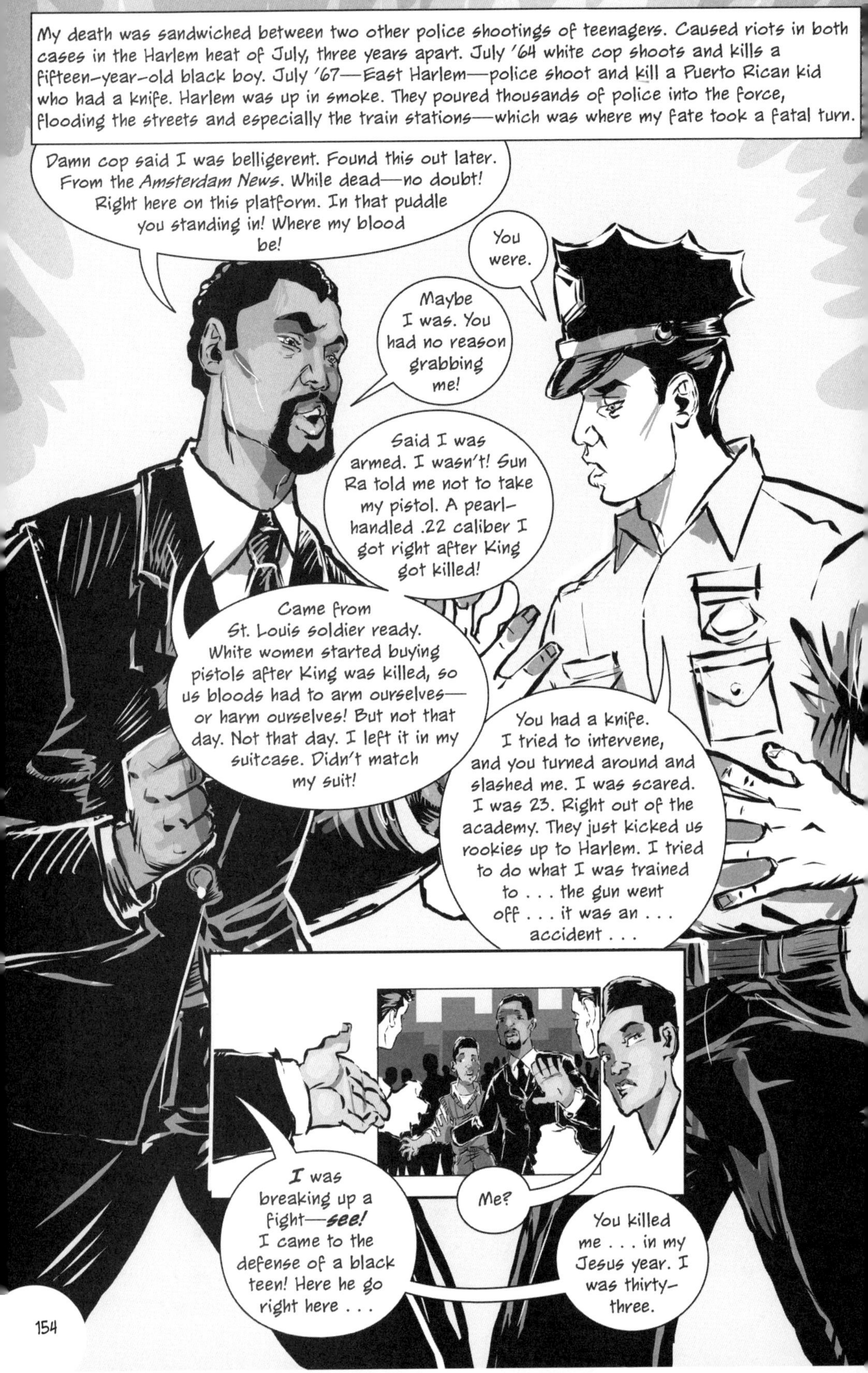

My death was sandwiched between two other police shootings of teenagers. Caused riots in both cases in the Harlem heat of July, three years apart. July '64 white cop shoots and kills a fifteen-year-old black boy. July '67—East Harlem—police shoot and kill a Puerto Rican kid who had a knife. Harlem was up in smoke. They poured thousands of police into the force, flooding the streets and especially the train stations—which was where my fate took a fatal turn.
Damn cop said I was belligerent. Found this out later. From the *Amsterdam News*. While dead—no doubt! Right here on this platform. In that puddle you standing in! Where my blood be!
You were.
Maybe I was. You had no reason grabbing me!
Said I was armed. I wasn't! Sun Ra told me not to take my pistol. A pearl-handled .22 caliber I got right after King got killed!
Came from St. Louis soldier ready. White women started buying pistols after King was killed, so us bloods had to arm ourselves—or harm ourselves! But not that day. Not that day. I left it in my suitcase. Didn't match my suit!
You had a knife. I tried to intervene, and you turned around and slashed me. I was scared. I was 23. Right out of the academy. They just kicked us rookies up to Harlem. I tried to do what I was trained to . . . the gun went off . . . it was an . . . accident . . .
I was breaking up a fight—***see!*** I came to the defense of a black teen! Here he go right here . . .
Me?
You killed me . . . in my Jesus year. I was thirty-three.

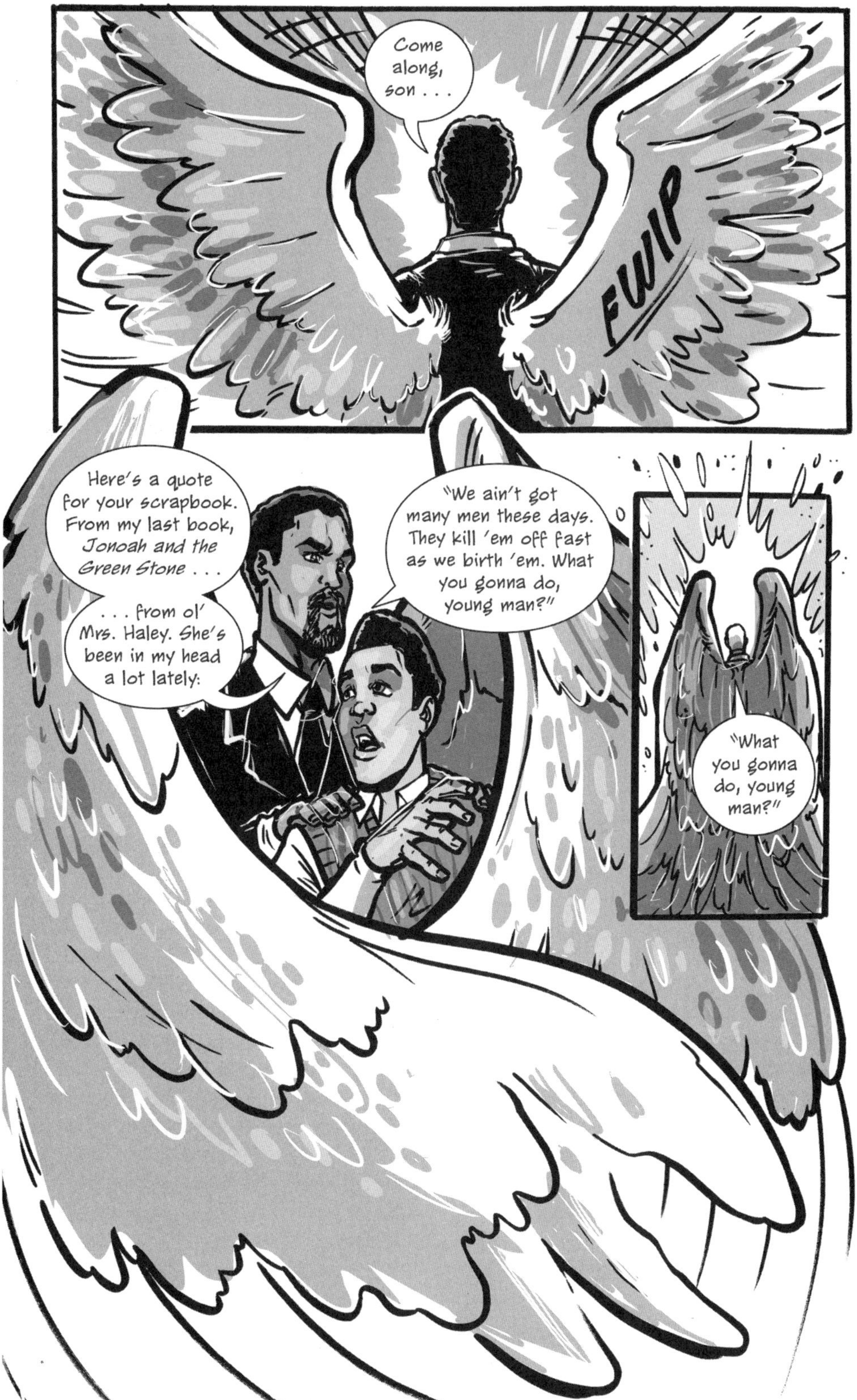
Come along, son . . .
FWIP
Here's a quote for your scrapbook. From my last book, Jonoah and the Green Stone . . .
. . . from ol' Mrs. Haley. She's been in my head a lot lately:
"We ain't got many men these days. They kill 'em off fast as we birth 'em. What you gonna do, young man?"
"What you gonna do, young man?"

Chapter Sixty-One
Shrine

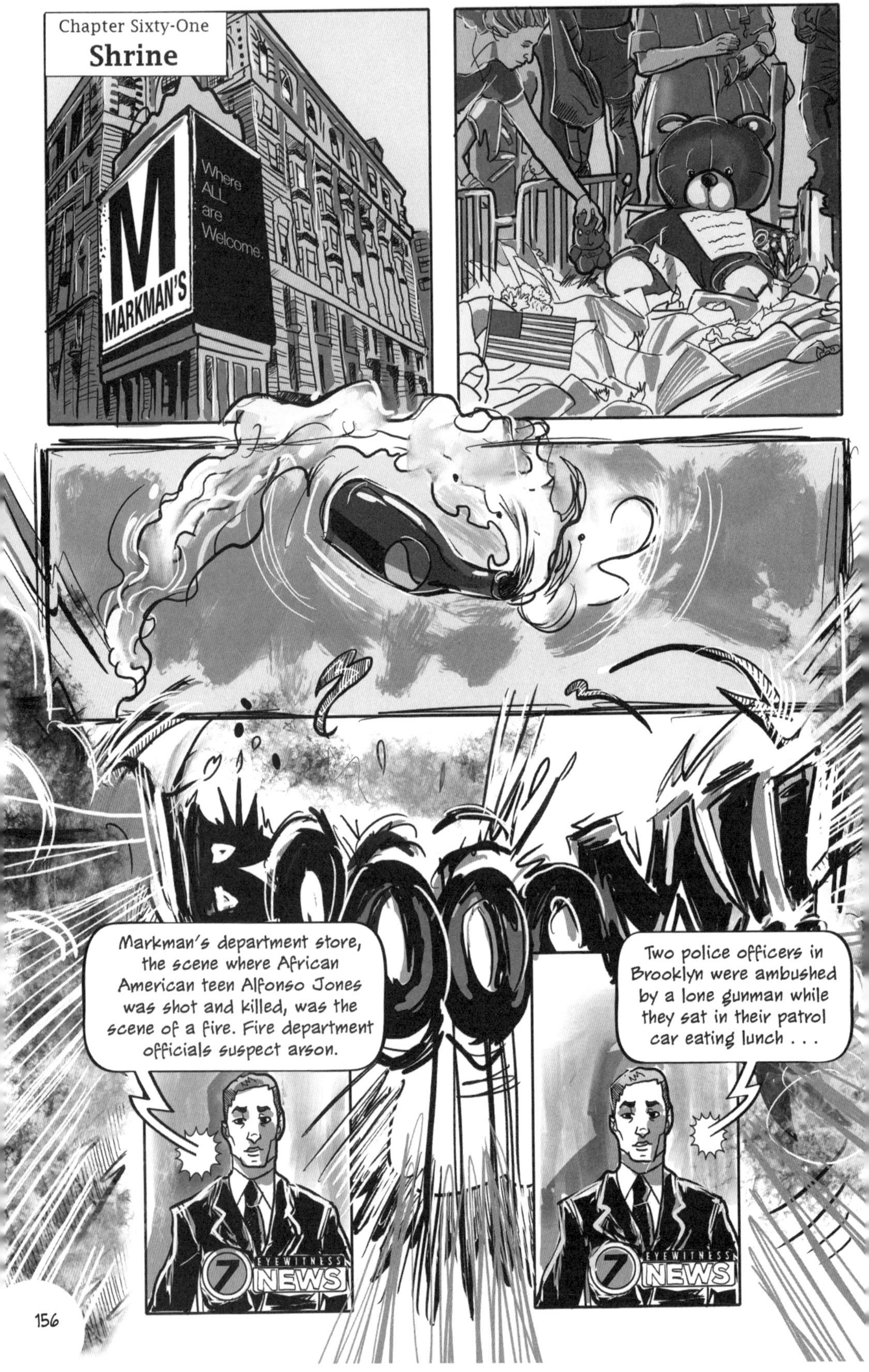
M
MARKMAN'S
Where ALL are Welcome.
BOOOOM!
Markman's department store, the scene where African American teen Alfonso Jones was shot and killed, was the scene of a fire. Fire department officials suspect arson.
Two police officers in Brooklyn were ambushed by a lone gunman while they sat in their patrol car eating lunch . . .
7 EYEWITNESS NEWS
7 EYEWITNESS NEWS

Chapter Sixty-Two

I Am Alfonso Jones

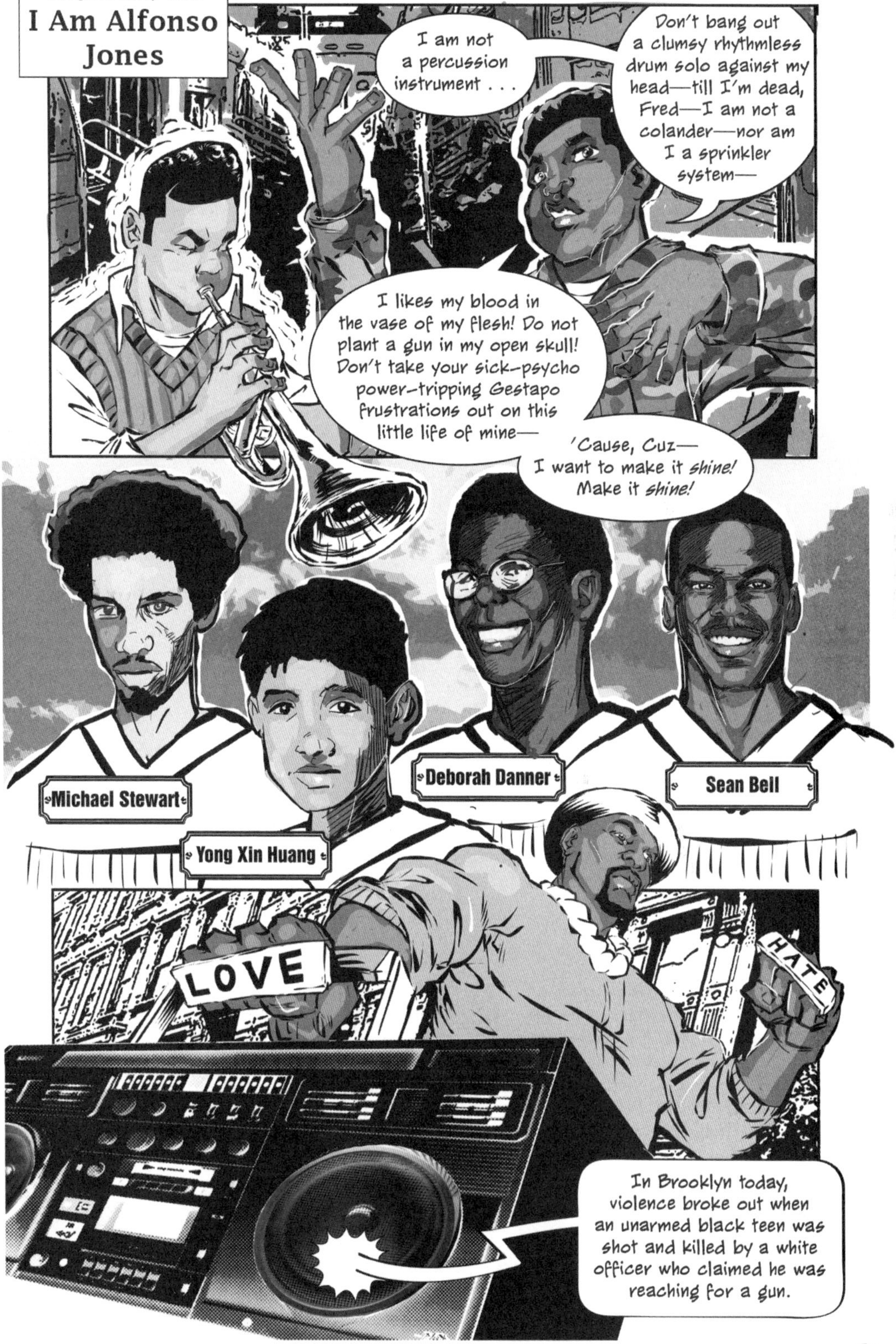

I am not a percussion instrument . . .
Don't bang out a clumsy rhythmless drum solo against my head—till I'm dead, Fred—I am not a colander—nor am I a sprinkler system—
I likes my blood in the vase of my flesh! Do not plant a gun in my open skull! Don't take your sick-psycho power-tripping Gestapo frustrations out on this little life of mine—
'Cause, Cuz— I want to make it *shine!* Make it *shine!*
Michael Stewart
Yong Xin Huang
Deborah Danner
Sean Bell
LOVE
HATE
In Brooklyn today, violence broke out when an unarmed black teen was shot and killed by a white officer who claimed he was reaching for a gun.

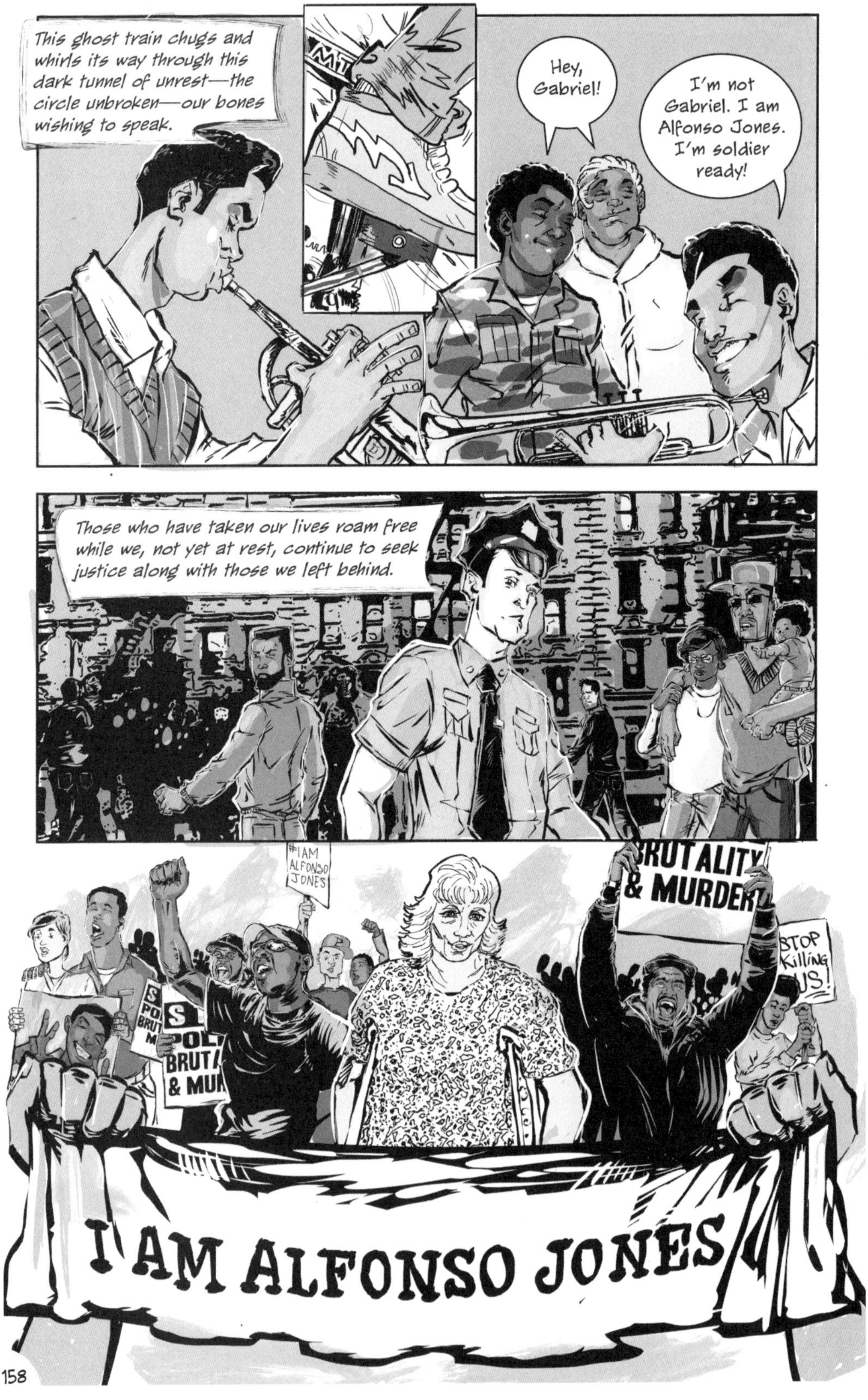
This ghost train chugs and whirls its way through this dark tunnel of unrest—the circle unbroken—our bones wishing to speak.
Hey, Gabriel!
I'm not Gabriel. I am Alfonso Jones. I'm soldier ready!
Those who have taken our lives roam free while we, not yet at rest, continue to seek justice along with those we left behind.
#IAM ALFONSO JONES
BRUTALITY & MURDER
STOP Killing US!
I AM ALFONSO JONES

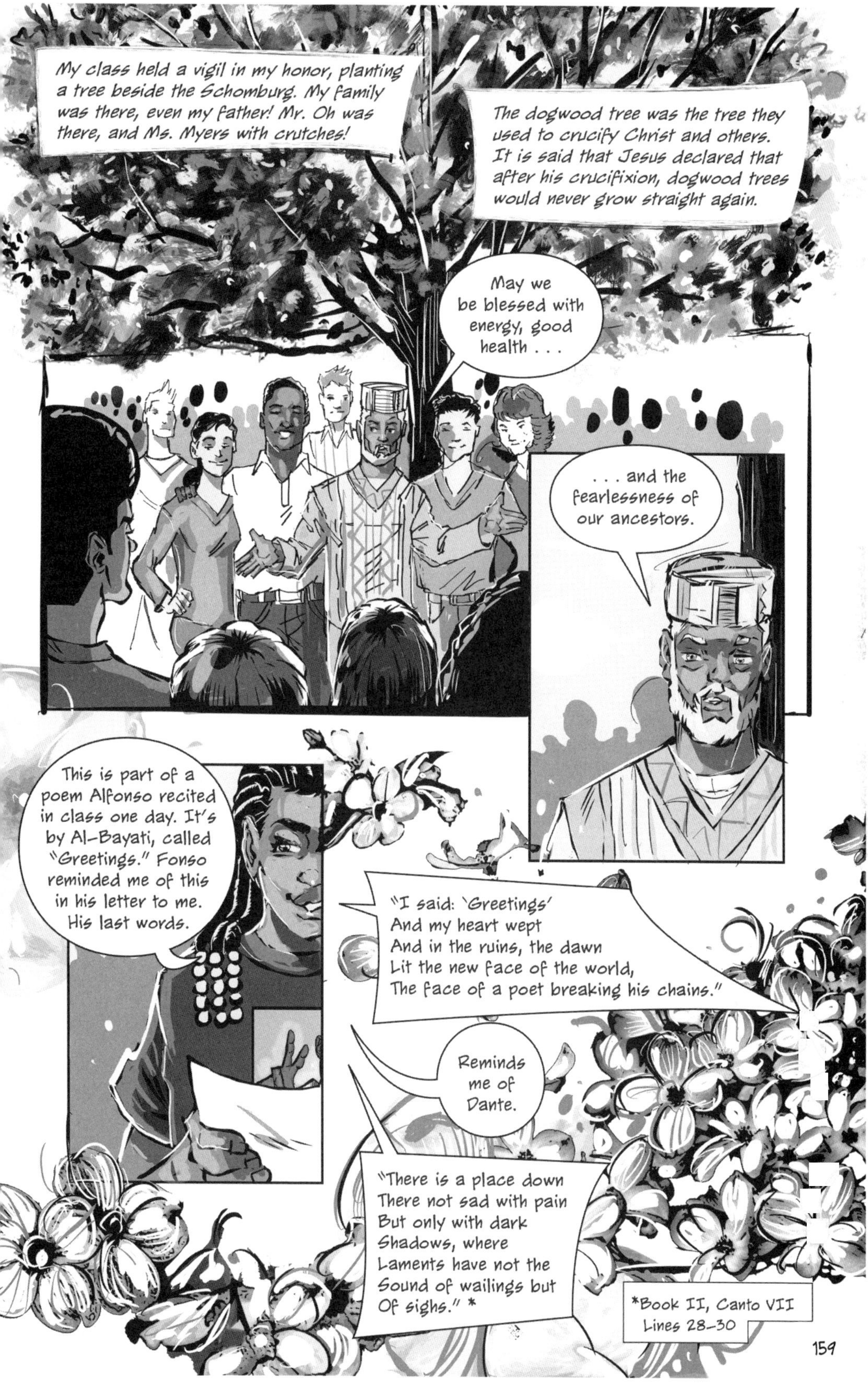
My class held a vigil in my honor, planting a tree beside the Schomburg. My family was there, even my father! Mr. Oh was there, and Ms. Myers with crutches!
The dogwood tree was the tree they used to crucify Christ and others. It is said that Jesus declared that after his crucifixion, dogwood trees would never grow straight again.
May we be blessed with energy, good health . . .
. . . and the fearlessness of our ancestors.
This is part of a poem Alfonso recited in class one day. It's by Al-Bayati, called "Greetings." Fonso reminded me of this in his letter to me. His last words.
"I said: 'Greetings'
And my heart wept
And in the ruins, the dawn
Lit the new face of the world,
The face of a poet breaking his chains."
Reminds me of Dante.
"There is a place down
There not sad with pain
But only with dark
Shadows, where
Laments have not the
Sound of wailings but
Of sighs." *
*Book II, Canto VII
Lines 28-30

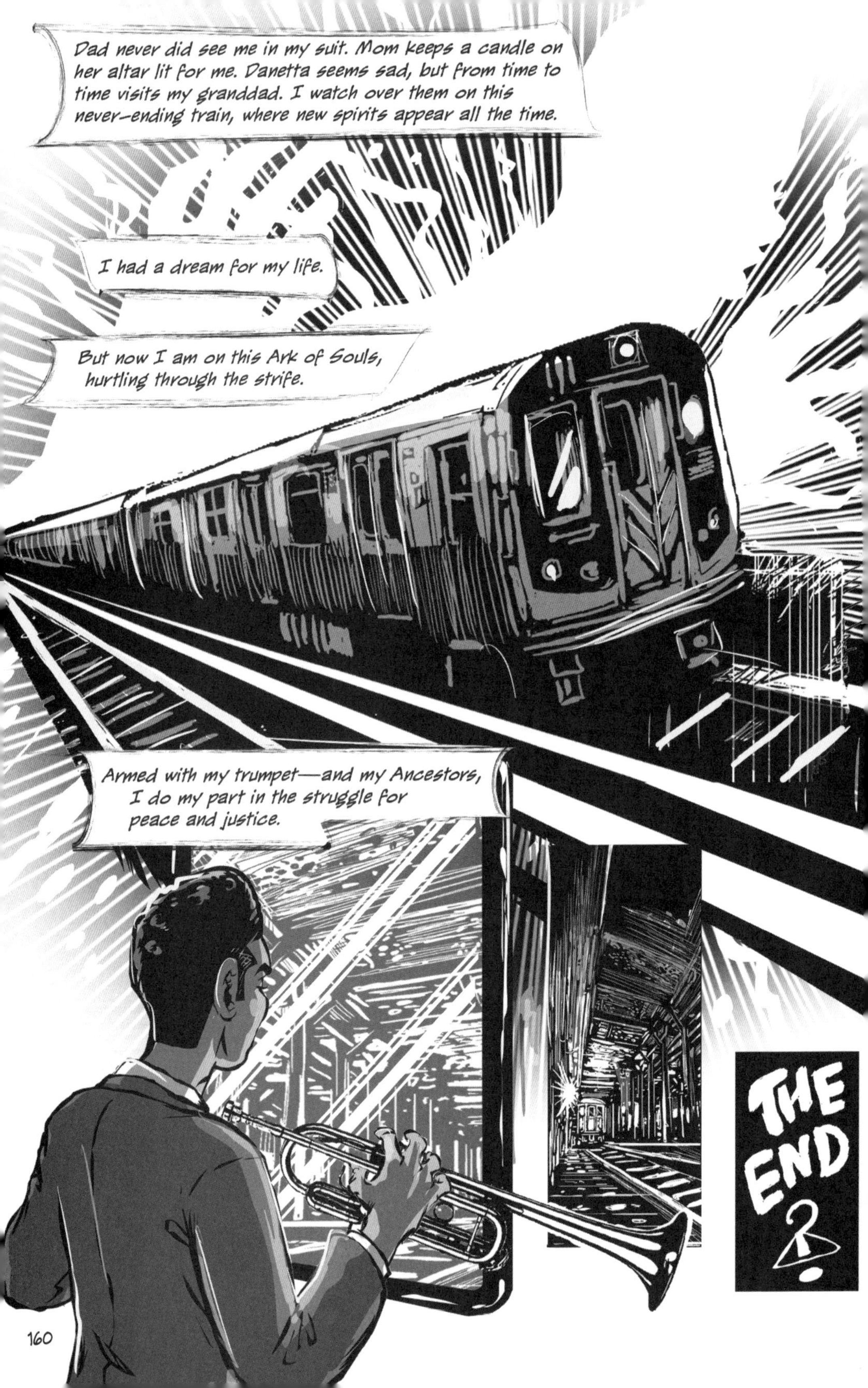
Dad never did see me in my suit. Mom keeps a candle on her altar lit for me. Danetta seems sad, but from time to time visits my granddad. I watch over them on this never-ending train, where new spirits appear all the time.
I had a dream for my life.
But now I am on this Ark of Souls, hurtling through the strife.
Armed with my trumpet—and my Ancestors, I do my part in the struggle for peace and justice.
THE END ?

Ancestors Wall

Henry Dumas
age 33; May 23, 1968
Harlem, New York

Clifford Glover
age 10; April 28, 1973
Queens, New York

Claude Reece, Jr.
age 14; September 15, 1974
Brooklyn, New York

Michael Stewart
age 25; September 15, 1983
New York City, New York

Eleanor Bumpers
age 66; October 29, 1984
Bronx, New York

Phillip Pannell
age 16; April 10, 1990
Teaneck, New Jersey

Nicholas Heyward, Jr.
age 13; September 27, 1994
Brooklyn, NY

Anthony Baez
age 29; December 22, 1994
Bronx, New York

Yong Xin Huang
age 16; March 24, 1995
Brooklyn, New York

Anthony Rosario
age 18; January 12, 1995
Bronx, New York

Hilton Vega
age 22; January 12, 1995
Bronx, New York

Amadou Diallo
age 23; February 4, 1999
Bronx, New York

Gidone Bush
age 31; August 30, 1999
Brooklyn, New York

Malcolm Ferguson
age 23; March 1, 2000
Bronx, New York

Patrick Dorismond
age 26; March 16, 2000
Manhattan, New York

Ousmane Zongo
age 43; May 22, 2003
Manhattan, New York

Timothy Stansbury, Jr.
age 19; January 24, 2004
Brooklyn, New York

Michael Bell, Jr.
age 21; November 9, 2004
Kenosha, Wisconsin

Sean Bell
age 23; November 25, 2006
Queens, New York

Oscar Grant III
age 22; January 1, 2009
Oakland, California

Trayvon Martin
age 17; February 26, 2012
Sanford, Florida

Tamon Robinson
age 27; April 12, 2012
Brooklyn, New York

Jonathan Ferrell
age 24; September 14, 2013
Charlotte, North Carolina

Andy Lopez
age 13; October 22, 2013
Santa Rosa, California

Kimani Gray
age 16; March 9, 2013
Brooklyn, New York

John Crawford III
age 22; August 5, 2014
Dayton, Ohio

Michael Brown
age 18; August 9, 2014
Ferguson, Missouri

Kajiem Powell
age 25; August 19, 2014
St. Louis, Missouri

Tanisha Anderson
age 37; November 13, 2014
Cleveland, Ohio

Tamir Rice
age 12; November 22, 2014
Cleveland, Ohio

Dontre Hamilton
age 31; April 30, 2014
Milwaukee, Wisconsin

Eric Garner
age 43; July 17, 2014
Staten Island, New York

Ezelle Ford
age 25; August 11, 2014
Florence, California

Dante Parker
age 36; August 12, 2014
Victorville, California

Akai Gurley
age 28; November 20, 2014
Brooklyn, New York

Rumain Brisbon
age 34; December 2, 2014
Phoenix, Arizona

Jerame Reid
age 36; December 30, 2014
Bridgeton, New Jersey

Janisha Fonville
age 20; February 18, 2015
Charlotte, North Carolina

Tony Robinson
age 19; March 6, 2015
Madison, Wisconsin

Phillip White
age 32; March 31, 2015
Vineland, New Jersey

Eric Harris
age 44; April 2, 2015
Tulsa, Oklahoma

Walter Scott
age 50; April 4, 2015
North Charleston, South Carolina

Sandra Bland
age 28; July 13, 2015
Hempstead, Texas

Rexdale Henry
age 53; July 14, 2015
Philadelphia, Mississippi

Freddie Gray
age 25; April 19, 2015
Baltimore, Maryland

Sarah Lee Circle Bear
age 24; July 6, 2015,
Aberdeen, South Dakota

Troy Goode
age 30; July 18, 2015
Southaven, Mississippi

Sam DuBose
age 43; July 19, 2015
Cincinnati, Ohio

Gilbert Flores
age 41; August 28, 2015
San Antonio, Texas

Alton Sterling
age 37; July 5, 2016
Baton Rouge, Louisiana

Philando Castile
age 32; July 6, 2016
Falcon Heights, Minnesota

Sylville K. Smith
age 23; August 13, 2016
Milwaukee, Wisconsin

Rodney James Hess
age 36; March 16, 2017
Alamo, Tennessee

Korryn Gaines
age 23; August 1, 2016
Randallstown, Maryland

Terence Crutcher
age 40; September 16, 2016
Tulsa, Oklahoma

Keith Lamont Scott
age 43; September 20, 2016
Charlotte, North Carolina

Alfred Olango
age 38; September 27, 2016
El Cajon, California

Willard Scott, Jr.
age 31; February 12, 2017
Durham, North Carolina

Giovonn Joseph-McDade
age 20; June 24, 2017
Kent, Washington

Jordan Edwards
age 15; April 29, 2017
Balch Springs, Texas

Tommy Le
age 20; June 13, 2017
Seattle, Washington

Charleena Lyles
age 30; June 18, 2017
Seattle, Washington

Officer Taylor Clark
age 32; June 27, 2017
Chicago, Illinois

Aaron Bailey
age 45; June 29, 2017
Indianapolis, Indiana

DeJuan Guillory
age 27; July 6, 2017
Mamou, Louisiana

Justine Damond
age 40; July 16, 2017
Minneapolis, Minnesota

Aries Clark,
age 16, July 25, 2017
Marion, Arkansas

Dwayne Jeune
age 32; July 31, 2017
Brooklyn, New York

Author's Note

Growing up in the Bronx, my life was not dissimilar to Alfonso's. I was fortunate to be surrounded by a loving family and community that nurtured my artistic interests and talents, but I, too, faced adversities. In our neighborhood in the Throgs Neck Housing Projects, we had a serious distrust of the police and, most times, saw them as an occupying force; but nonetheless we still managed to get along—or get by. As I've grown older it seems that more and more incidents of police brutality have emerged, not just in New York City, but also across the country.

As a literary artist, I realized I've been documenting—in poetry—police brutality cases since the late 1980s. From Eleanor Bumpurs (who reminded me of my own grandmother) to Charleena Lyles, a thirty-year-old pregnant African American woman shot to death by police in the doorway of her apartment, in front of her children, after calling the police for a possible burglary (possibly her estranged abusive boyfriend), I have amassed a full-length collection of poetry on such horrifying cases.

When Amadou Diallo was killed in 1999, I took to the streets in a major protest that began in mid-Manhattan and culminated in front of the courthouses in lower Manhattan. It was jam-packed, and when the protest ended and the massive crowd began to disperse, I recall being purposefully pummeled by a white cop who disguised his brutality against me with the excuse of moving the crowd along. The sneaky smirk on his face when he realized a friend and fellow poet, Suheir Hammad, witnessed the assault, yanking me away and saying, "Come on, Medina, we need you alive!" showed me all I needed know about how some people, hiding behind badges, abuse their authority and positions of power to get out their own anger and frustration. This is one of the reasons we need better policing and screening of those who serve in public positions where society entrusts them to carry a weapon and a badge.

What I wish *I Am Alfonso Jones* achieves is not solely to open up dialogues about issues of race and class and police brutality, among other topics the graphic novel addresses, but to also inspire and instigate activism in the form of fighting for better, more humane and responsible policing. I also want to put human faces and universal narratives to the lives of those destroyed by police violence and overaggression due to stereotypes, racism, anger, paranoia, and fear.

Ever since the Trayvon Martin killing and the subsequent trial of George Zimmerman, who was found not guilty in a jury decision that was confounding, to say the least, I have been posting incessantly on social media (and writing poems) about cases of police brutality and injustices against people of color as part of the Black Lives Matter resistance. As a professor, I also hold intense discussions among my students at Howard University in Washington, DC, and even have my students respond in writing and video, in which they speak out as poets and concerned citizens about their fear, confusion, and anger regarding the onslaught of cases of police brutality and the killing of innocent, unarmed people of color. I also published an anthology, *Resisting Arrest: Poems to Stretch the Sky* (Jacar Press, 2016) on police brutality and violence, featuring some of the most prominent poets in the country.

I Am Alfonso Jones is a culmination of my great concern for the inequality that rears its head in the justice system, the prison industry, and in the dangerous elements found in policing in America.

The inspiration for Alfonso's story was taken, in part, from the various national incidents broadcast on a seemingly twenty-four-hour news loop, traumatizing people over and over again. The young black activists in *I Am Alfonso Jones* are fictional depictions inspired by the real-life visionary activists Opal Tometi, Alicia Garza, and Patrice Cullors, who started the Black Lives Matter movement.

One particularly egregious incident took place in a major superstore where a young Black man was checking out a toy BB gun on sale when he was suddenly shot and killed by two armed police officers responding to another customer's 911 call.

That was also the major tipping point in Alfonso's story—the trauma of that reality where one could be in a secure environment shopping and suddenly destroyed for the color of one's skin, for the perceived threat in the imagination of a white officer armed with stereotypes and a loaded gun. How one could be yanked from one's life at a moment's notice, and how the bullets that destroy a young boy's brown flesh could do such irreparable damage to a family, a community, an entire nation.

That we hear from Alfonso in the afterlife of such ruin is a miracle of fiction. That Alfonso's death—though heartbreakingly senseless—is not in vain, but a symbol of resistance to police brutality and racism—is a miracle of faith.

—Tony Medina

The Real-Life Ancestors of This Book
(In Order of Appearance)

Eleanor Bumpurs was a sixty-six-year-old African American woman who was shot and killed by New York City police on October 29, 1984, as she faced eviction for being four months in arrears for a monthly rent of $98.65. Informed by the Housing Authority that Bumpurs was mentally ill and had threatened authorities with a knife and boiling lye, one of the police officers shot at Bumpurs with a 12-gauge shotgun, killing her for refusing to leave her apartment. Prior to her death, and suffering arthritis, mental illness, and other health problems, Bumpurs told her daughter Mary she was being threatened by someone in the building. Housing Authority officials reported other disturbing information on Bumpurs, and four days prior to evicting her, the city sent a psychiatrist to visit her. The psychiatrist assessed that Bumpurs should be hospitalized. Officers armed with plastic shields and a Y-shaped bar entered the apartment after knocking out the lock, only to discover a nude and knife-wielding Bumpurs. Officer Stephen Sullivan opened fire twice, blowing off Bumpurs' hand and hitting her in the chest. A grand jury charged Sullivan with second-degree manslaughter. The State Supreme Court dismissed the indictment for insufficient evidence. That ruling was overturned on appeal, and the indictment was reinstated. Sullivan was eventually acquitted, and the Bumpurs family filed a civil lawsuit against the city for ten million dollars in damages; the Bumpurs estate subsequently received two hundred thousand dollars. Social Services supervisors were demoted for failing to get Bumpurs proper psychiatric care and for not seeking an emergency rent grant for her.

Amadou Diallo, a twenty-three-year-old Guinean immigrant college student and street vendor, was shot and killed by four white plainclothes New York City police officers in the vestibule of his Bronx apartment building on February 4, 1999. The officers shot at the unarmed Diallo forty-one times at point-blank range, resulting in nineteen full metal jacket bullets entering his body. The officers claimed they thought Diallo's wallet was a gun. Although a police internal investigation ruled the officers' shooting was justified, the four officers, Edward McMellon, Sean Carroll, Kenneth Boss, and Richard Murphy, were indicted on second-degree murder and reckless endangerment. All were found not guilty. In investigating the circumstances leading to Diallo's death, it was concluded that Diallo was racially profiled; the officers claimed Diallo resembled the identification of a rapist they were searching for (or a lookout). Diallo, having come home from a meal forty minutes after midnight, was standing near his building when the four officers charged him; he then ran down into the vestibule, trying to get into his building. Diallo's parents, Kadijatou and Saikou Diallo, filed a sixty-one-million-dollar lawsuit against the city for gross negligence, wrongful death, racial profiling and other violations of Diallo's civil rights. They settled with the city for three million dollars, one of the largest settlements in city history for wrongful death. Diallo's death called into question issues of racial profiling and the role of racial stereotypes and bias in split-second decisions that may determine an individual's life or death. It also brought under investigation the use of full-metal bullets by New York City police officers.

Michael Stewart was a graffiti artist who was beaten to death by eleven police officers while in custody for spray painting a wall of the First Avenue subway station (the L train line) on September 15, 1983. Stewart, who weighed only 135 pounds, had facial bruises and wrist abrasions from the beating, and died of a heart attack that put him into a coma. A family physician present at the autopsy said Stewart's death was a result of strangulation. Police at the Union Square District 4 transit police headquarters claimed Stewart was arrested for resisting arrest, possession of marijuana, and drunkenness. Stewart's family disputed the police's characterization of their son, stating he was a calm, laid-back Pratt Institute art student. After arresting Stewart, police took him to Bellevue Hospital in handcuffs and leg irons while he was comatose. The medical examiner's final autopsy report contradicted his preliminary examination, claiming Stewart died of injury to his spinal cord in the upper neck. A grand jury indicted six police officers: three for criminally negligent homicide and three for perjury. An all-white jury acquitted all six officers.

Anthony Baez, a twenty-nine-year-old Bronx security guard, was killed on December 22, 1994, while playing football with his brother David during an altercation with police officers who placed Baez in an illegal chokehold. The incident occurred when Baez's football accidentally hit a patrol car. He and his brother continued playing in the opposite direction, but Officer Francis Livoti went to arrest David for disorderly conduct, and, as Baez protested his brother's arrest, he was arrested, leading to a scuffle with Livoti and three other cops. Baez, who was five foot six, 270 pounds, and asthmatic, lost consciousness and was taken to the hospital, where he was pronounced dead. The medical examiner stated Baez's death was due to the compression of his neck and chest, and was due to the actions of another person. Police accounts of the incident contradicted the Baez family's account. Police claimed Baez violently resisted arrest, while Baez's family stated he was limp when handcuffed and taken away. After an ambulance failed to arrive, officers took the unconscious Baez to the hospital in a patrol car. Livoti was first indicted on manslaughter charges; nine months later he was reindicted for criminally negligent homicide. He was eventually convicted in Federal Court of violating Baez's civil rights, and sentenced to seven and a half years. Livoti was released after serving six and a half years.

Henry Dumas, poet, fictionist, and Black Arts Movement pioneer, was born in 1934 in Sweet Home, Arkansas, where he lived for ten years before his family settled in New York City. On May 23, 1968, at the age of thirty-three, Dumas was traveling to a wedding when he was shot to death by a New York City Transit Police officer. For decades, it was believed that Dumas was killed at the 135th Street train station platform in Harlem in a case of mistaken identity. However, Dumas's biographer, Jeffrey Leak, observes that the rookie cop who shot and killed Dumas claimed he was threatening another man with a knife. No one knows for certain what the facts are, for the records of the shooting were destroyed in 1995 when the Transit Police Department merged with the New York City Police Department. Nevertheless, Dumas's killing, like his literary standing—particularly among the Black intelligentsia—remains legendary. The officer who killed Dumas retired from the police force and is currently a yoga instructor. Dumas, who had a difficult, frustrating experience getting published in his lifetime, has had his work resurrected, preserved, and published by his close friend, poet-archivist Dr. Eugene B. Redmond, and Nobel Prize Laureate Toni Morrison, who edited Dumas's books.

Acknowledgments

When making a book, there are a few clichés that are in order. You don't count your money, you count your blessings; and it takes a village to raise and nurture a book. Let me use this space to thank that village for taking *I Am Alfonso Jones* from my imagination to the beautiful book you hold in your hands. First and foremost, I must give thanks for the force of nature that is Stacy Whitman, my editor and publisher and the driving force behind the editing and artistic production of this first Tu Books graphic novel. To Jason Low of Lee & Low Books, visionary publisher whose mission it is to bring the wide-range of color and cultural expression to the palette of American children's and young adult literature. To the great artists I have been fortunate enough to work with, Stacey Robinson and John Jennings, two pioneers in the landscape that is comic books and graphic novels created by Black writers, artists, publishers, booksellers, collectors, and other Afrofuturists. I would also like to thank the multitalented Damian Duffy, who lettered (as well as created the logo for) *I Am Alfonso Jones*, helping this book to sing. Thanks to activist Bryan Stevenson for the powerful foreword. Much thanks to Makala Scurlock for being my first, second, and third reader, especially when I was too chicken to reread my own work! Thanks for everyone at Lee & Low Books and its imprint Tu Books who read the manuscript, and subsequently the PDF and ARC of the book, providing invaluable feedback, particularly Hannah Ehrlich, Cheryl Klein, Jalissa Corrie, Keilin Huang; and thanks to our literacy team, Jill Eisenberg and Veronica Schneider. I would also like to thank Katheryn Russell-Brown and Matt Dembicki, who offered early feedback on the manuscript. I would like to thank Wanda Zimba, our intrepid copyeditor, whose sharp eye and invaluable attention to detail proves why copyeditors are some of the most priceless people in the bookmaking industry. I also want to thank a team of inkers and colorists who helped bring this book to life on deadline (no pun or mixed metaphor intended): Anthony Moncada, Arie Monroe, Jeremy Marshall, Mike Harrington, and Nick Meccia.

I would be remiss if I did not mention folks who are an invaluable part of the Lee & Low Books family and whom I've known since my first Lee & Low book, *DeShawn Days*, in 2001: Tom Low, Craig Low, Louise May, Abe Barretto, and John Man.

To the Ancestors: A Village.

To the Youth: Stay WOKE!

—Tony Medina

Many thanks to my mom, Rainey Robinson-Graves, my aunt Gabriella Hoffman, and to Lucille "Chill" McCoy. Where would I be without the wondrous women who guided me? Shout-outs to my uncle Valiant, who introduced me to the love of comics. My graduate committee: Jasmina Tumbas, Gary Nickard, Reinhard Reitzenstein, and John Jennings, who wouldn't let me dodge Black trauma in the pursuit of illustrating Black joy. Your contribution to my education was far above and beyond what I imagined. I'm eternally grateful for the time you took to prepare me for my never-ending journey as artist, academic, and scholar. My TRIMEKKA Studiomates Jan and Charlie: we make comics, yo! Thank you, Ezra Jack Keats, your gifts filled me with a love to illustrate children's books. Thank you, Megan from Grindhaus Café, and Linda from the Champaign Public Library, as I spent most of the last year working in the peaceful community spaces you provided. Marissa, many thanks to you as we both encouraged each other during our intense work sessions this last year—we both have enjoyed watching each other grow. Finally, I'm grateful to our ancestors, who lived and died so that we can draw, fantasize, and love the world through imagery. I recognize my "great power and great responsibility" to leave the world in a better condition than I was received in.

—Stacey Robinson

Praise for *I Am Alfonso Jones*

"Medina, Robinson, and Jennings do for us what the ghosts do for Alfonso in their story. They help us to see. They help us to remember. They help us to understand. A must read."
　　　　　　　—**Gene Luen Yang**, National Ambassador for Young People's Literature
　　　　　　　and author of *American Born Chinese* and *Boxers and Saints*

"Tony Medina has written a powerful story that resonates with our current social climate. You must read this book!"　　　　—**Dan Santat**, Caldecott Award–winning author and illustrator
　　　　　　　of *The Adventures of Beekle: The Unimaginary Friend*

"Brimming with history and spirituality, *I Am Alfonso Jones* is a refreshing and necessary exploration into police brutality. With both word and art, Medina, Robinson, and Jennings have breathed new life into this longstanding movement."　　—**Ibi Zoboi**, author of *American Street*

"We are so fortunate that Tony Medina and his generation have taken on their shoulders the classic responsibilities of telling stories that embrace the hearts and souls of not only the individuals but the neighborhoods. A comic book is no longer something to laugh with but something to learn from. *I Am Alfonso Jones* is incredibly enlightening."
　　　　　　　—**Nikki Giovanni**, award-winning poet, author,
　　　　　　　and editor of *Hip Hop Speaks to Children*

"I can't say enough how important, beautiful, heartbreaking, and tremendous a book this is. Read it. Gift it to a young person in your life. Shout it from the rooftops. *I Am Alfonso Jones* is a crucial part of the conversation, and it demands to be heard."
　　　　　　　—**Daniel José Older**, author of *Shadowshaper* and *Shadowhouse Fall*

"A high-velocity, gut-wrenching story.... Packed with history, knowledge, and life, this is graphic storytelling at its best."　　—**Frederick Luis Aldama**, author of *Long Stories Cut Short: Fictions from the Borderlands* and *Latinx Superheroes in Mainstream Comics*

"*I Am Alfonso Jones* is a wonderful, sad, anger-inducing, slice-of-life-and-afterlife-with-a-helping-of-*Hamlet*-sprinkled-in-for-flavor of a graphic novel. It paints a searing portrait of the emotional heartbreak and pain at the origins of the Black Lives Matter movement."
　　　　　　　—**Randy DuBurke**, illustrator of *Yummy: The Last Days of a Southside Shorty*

"This story of love and rage is conveyed with a surreal cast of characters. Alfonso's story, and the stories of the others on the ghost subway, will both grieve and inform, allowing readers to access the language to talk about class and race discrimination, and the very real fact of the American propensity for violence by police against people of minority race and class. Despite the grim topic, there are sparks of light in Alfonso's family relationships, his classmates' clowning, and the love his community shows him, which will enable readers to consider parallels within their own lives. There is no solution to Alfonso's murder, no tidy wrap-up of his death in which the rest of his community lives happily ever after, but they do live, as we do—in love and defiance, never forgetting that justice has not been served."
　　　　　　　—**Tanita Davis**, author of *Peas and Carrots* and *Mare's War*